THE UNREQUITED

THE UNREQUITED

By Page Brown

[signature: Page Brown]

the Peppertree Press

ISBN: 978-1-934246-71-9
Library of Congress Number: 2007933045
Printed in the U.S.A.
Printed March, 2008
First Edition

To my family.

Those of us born at the end of the Second World War, the war that defined our parents, were in turn to find ourselves defined by our own war, one so divisive that it has taken decades to heal the wounds it inflicted on our society. Strangely, the war in Viet Nam is associated with the baby boom generation because we fought it, but it was in reality the policies and leadership of our parents that brought it upon us.

Like many other young men of the time, I found myself facing the war's issues on a college campus, then with more immediacy as an infantry officer during two tours in Viet Nam, first as a platoon leader and MACV adviser, then as a Vietnamese Ranger adviser. A young man's vague images of heroics in a just cause quickly gave way to harsh realities. Naiveté was replaced with a cynicism that remains to this day. Over the years the quest for answers that might bring peace of mind led me to study the history of the period. When GIs started going back to Viet Nam in 1995 and again in 2000, I returned to where I'd been stationed in order to find closure. But even after the trip, the answers were missing. I only discovered those answers when I reached further back into history to a period before any significant American involvement. Just as no man exists but for once being a child, so no nation exists but for its past.

In the archives of the French Indochina War, the tragic answers emerged. To convey them was another matter. Fiction allowed me to apply the very human experiences of my own involvement to the years of 1945 through 1955 when the Vietnamese engaged the French in a guerilla war and defeated them at Dien Bien Phu. It is tragic that we never learned the lessons that early period had to offer. Cloaked in our own righteousness we were to ignore those lessons to our detriment.

The stage on which the French played is the same stage Americans were to return to ten years after the French departed. The parallels are distressing. French attempts at "yellowing" their war became American "Vietnamization." Their Dien Bien Phu tactics were applied by Americans at Khe Sanh, and a similar disaster was avoided only because of superior air power. What had we learned from the failed French effort?

In *The Unrequited* the high ranking military officers and political leaders are real people. The principal characters on both sides are fictional. The major cities, villages, roads, and battles are also based on fact. Some scenes and buildings such as churches are fictional composites. For those who want to place the events in a greater historical context of Viet Nam, a chronology is included at the end of this book. A bibliography provides a place for further research. That said, this story is really about the human condition, love and lust, hate, lives destroyed, human sacrifice, and above all the human nobility that sometimes arises even in the worst of times.

-Page Brown

None here found their rest.

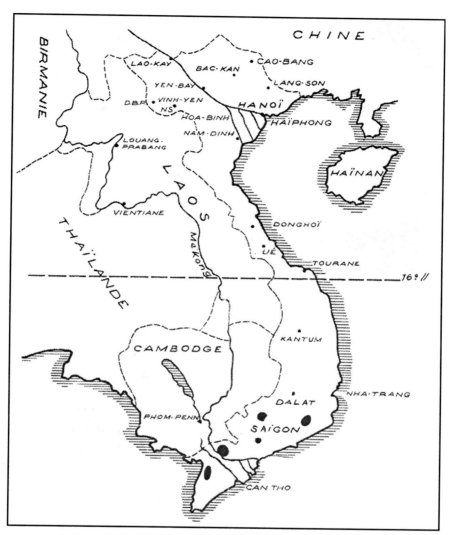

Map of Cochin China

INTRODUCTION

By the time the Japanese surrendered to General Douglas MacArthur on September 2, 1945, the struggle for Viet Nam was well underway. In a sense, the struggle had been going on since 111 BC when the Chinese conquered what was then called Nam Viet and incorporated it into their empire. Despite brief periods of revolt and freedom under the Trung sisters, the Vietnamese Joan of Arc named Trieu An, and the noble Ly Bon, the conquest lasted a thousand years until 931CE. The wars to maintain that independence from the Chinese were still ongoing when the first French missionaries arrived in 1615.

French conquest began with the seizure of Saigon in 1861. They established a colony in the south known as Cochin China and by 1883 had established a northern protectorate (Tonkin) and central protectorate (Annam). The Scholars Revolt, begun almost immediately after the conquest, was put down by the French in 1897. Plots against the occupiers continued, until in 1930 an uprising led by the Vietnamese Nationalist Party was crushed and its leaders imprisoned or executed. That same year the Vietnamese Communist Party was formed and renamed the Indochinese Communist Party with Nguyen Ai Quoc (Ho Chi Minh) as its leader.

When the government in France fell to Germany at the start of World War II, the Japanese occupied portions of Viet Nam. In May 1941 the Viet Nam Independence League (Viet Minh) joined with the nationalists to form a united front. The Vichy French negotiated a joint defense agreement with the Japanese that lasted until after the Vichy government was replaced by the French Republic. March 9, 1945, the Japanese, on the verge of defeat by the United States, seized control of all Viet Nam. August 15 the Japanese laid down their arms. August 17 Charles de Gaulle announced a French high commission to rule Indochina. August 19 the Viet Minh seized control of Ha Noi. Our story was already underway.

CHAPTER 1

Viet Nam, Quang Khe Village, August 5, 1945
Phan
Phan, a father

Her blood soaked clothing distracted Phan from the midwife's pungent smell and unkempt hair. She was whispering to the old men near the door, and something was wrong. Their inscrutable faces betrayed no answer until the midwife turned to him with a toothless smile.

"What will you name this first born son of yours?"

"Nguyen van Trang." Phan slumped to the dirt floor. He had a son to tell his tale of how a Nung orphan longing for freedom escaped the divine will of the great warlords of China and established his family in Viet Nam.

The elders bowed in turns, their chant in guttural tones, omm...ommm mani padma omm... reverberating from the ages. Phan knelt before a Buddha reposed between candles, its gold plate tarnished by the years, its gaze serene. The smell of dirt and mold mixed with the acid scent of incense. Grey smoke burned Phan's eyes and obscured the stern expressions of his parents' pictures along with those of ancestors

1

he knew from stories heard as a child, stories of the Chinese sons of Chinese sons, their names long forgotten. Their voices whispered: Go back to China where you were born and where you belong. Go back. Now he tried to make them understand he had come too far to return to China. Viet Nam offered him the hope of freedom.

The flames of the candles wavered in ghostly breaths caught up in the breezes of emptiness. He rebuffed them with silence but bowed again and again to express his gratitude. Then he carefully placed his crucifix in front of the family altar and prayed to the Catholic God he had come to fear more than all the Buddhas of all the realms. Father Custeau had given him the crucifix and raised him in his belief that any man who put another before God faced eternal damnation.

But what of his wife? The midwife had said nothing about her. He whirled toward the midwife, but she was gone. Defying the elders, he rushed to cross the village.

Cries from scavenging cats filled the air. Women chattered outside the midwife's mud hut, its palm-thatched roof glistening from a recent rain. Inside, blood-soaked rags smoldered in a fire, casting a faint light through the smoke. The midwife stood back to him, watching his wife, supine on a single wooden plank. Sheets covered his wife's still form. Her face was mottled, her hair sweat soaked and gray. Next to her, a baby wrapped in silk: chubby cheeks, black swirled hair pasted against his scalp, the child awake and calm as though the world already made sense to him. Panic and joy intermingled, choking Phan.

"Thi?" He whispered his wife's name. Her eyelids fluttered as she strained to smile.

"I gave you your son," she whispered.

The midwife whirled towards Phan, "You can't be in here."

"Yes, all right," he said. His smile broadened as he slowly retreated from the hut.

Later, when the elders left, he thought about the secret Viet Minh message he had received that morning, ordering him to return to the newspaper office in Ha Noi. The time for independence was at hand and they wanted him to become its voice. That was as he wished. Just not yet. His wife must have time to recover her strength before he left.

—◈—

In the days after the birth, hints of the nation's freedom reached the village, carried by the voices of peddlers and soldiers. The Japanese were defeated. Ho Chi Minh would soon enter Ha Noi in triumph and proclaim Viet Nam's independence. From their jungle hideouts Viet Minh soldiers cascaded towards the city like the torrents of spring, but still Phan hesitated to follow them. His wife hemorrhaged from her labor. His child was too newly born. And he didn't trust the French promise to form an independent federation. Before their complete humiliation by the Japanese, the French had ruled with arrogance. Before the war their soldiers had continued to extend their tyranny from the cities into the countryside. French tanks and airplanes had destroyed any village that resisted. The French beheaded the rebels they captured with a savagery that drove more peasants to join the Viet Minh. At the time Phan had witnessed the struggle and reported it, and his truthful words condemned him in the eyes of the French. He had lived as a fugitive. So now why expect a sudden French benevolence?

At night fitful sleep brought memories into his dreams: Ha Noi, cauldron of human flesh a million strong; conical hats mixed with comic European dress; French colonial buildings, their war-weary exteriors fading; ancient temples with images of Buddhas shrouded in the mists of burning incense; a Roman Catholic cathedral, behind it the austere compound for orphans where he had spent his childhood; Father Custeau with his stern and uncompromising expression.

In the beginning was the word, was the priest, Father Custeau, who alone spoke God's will. His was the power and the glory. His was the edict to serve God, to serve the church, to serve the French. Phan's lust for freedom beyond the church was a sin and when he had forgotten it he felt the snap of the priest's switch. Ask forgiveness. He heard the words until he

3

cried out. He was awake. His wife was holding him, her small hands running over his face, wiping the sweat. Her voice was deep with night, inviting and sensual. "It's all right."

"I was dreaming," he said, pulling her closer.

"We're safe here in the village," she said.

"I know," he said.

"You're going back to Ha Noi with the others?"

"I'm a journalist. This is my chance to be the voice of change."

"You have a price on your head."

"That was before the Japanese..."

"But the French are coming back."

"They've promised us independence. The newspaper is publishing again. They need me to write for them. They've sent a messenger." He had kept the courier's words from her until that moment. "You'll be safe here."

"You can't just pack up and leave us."

"I have a duty to my country."

In their uneasy silence, night's tranquility enveloped them. The previous day's heat seeped from the earth, warming their embrace. The jungle formed a wall around the two dozen huts of the village and the triple canopy protected them from the random French reconnaissance planes.

"I know you're going," Thi whispered in the silence. "We're coming with you."

On that night of terrible dreams it was decided. The rest was easy. They had little to pack. The ancestors came down off the wall. Phan caressed their faces clean, held the picture of his parents against his chest, remembering their last words, his tears hidden for fear his wife watched him from the shadows.

Phan carried a burlap sack lashed to a bamboo frame that rested against his hips and extended over his head. His wife carried the baby strapped against her breasts where the child suckled as they walked the long downhill path towards the highway to Ha Noi, a hundred kilometers away. They came from the dense jungle onto the Red River plain where the road crossed miles of emerald rice paddies that stretched horizon to horizon, flat and unbroken except by an occasional village, soiled huts crowded along the road. At night they slept in the open, surrounded by water and soaked by rain.

Refugees mingled with armies. Travelers repeated rumors of Chinese troops flooding over the borders from the north, French ships unloading troops in every port, Viet Minh across the countryside massacring Catholics in their churches and landlords on their farms, city dwellers thrown into prisons and tortured to confess to unspecified crimes, suspected communists beheaded by the French. Disease and famine spread. In the upheaval fear ruled reality. A general panic sent Catholics fleeing south, Chinese merchants north from Ha Noi into the countryside, tribes from the mountains into the cities.

Phan kept detailed notes: Tribes that previously fought among themselves for territory in the hills now traveled together as refugees along the roads; from the north, the Lolo Hoa, men with baggy pants embroidered along the hem, their women wearing multicolored vests, indigo trousers, leggings and a belt, their heads covered with turbans; Pu Peo women, their hair drawn forward and held by combs covered with scarves that fell to their shoulders; Bo Y, driven from their homeland in China by the Han centuries ago; Co Lao, recent migrants to Viet Nam from Guizhou Province in southern China; La Chi, who left their stilt houses; Giay, carrying their cotton gins; Lu with their black teeth filed to points to increase their beauty; Mang, Lahu, Coong, Sila once rumored to be extinct; Ha Nhi, Khang, Phu La, Thai, Lao, Kho Mu; La Ha men dressed like French priests without the clerics collar; Xing Mun, Zao, Pathen, Hmong, Tay, Nung, San Zu; and San Cha, watched over by genies only they could see; from the northern delta the Tho and O Du. All these tribes the Vietnamese called "Moi," their word for savages and the French called them "Montagnard," the word for highlanders.

Beside the road a dead horse bloated to twice its size. Vultures pecked it and crows darted between them to steal bits of flesh. A mother screamed for her child, refusing to leave its corpse beside the road. Orphaned children cast longing glances at her. Farmers trudged through the dust using their hoes for support. In the midst of the sick and the starving, men too weak to walk were carried by their wives and children. Dead babies were cradled in their mother's arms.

Phan stood out above the others on the road. The tribesmen followed him as if he were a shepherd who knew the way. He talked to them and learned why they had fought each other and then the French, and when the Viet Minh first arrived in the mountains, fought them as well. But the Viet Minh gave them weapons and paid for the food they ate instead of stealing it, lived with them, and promised them their freedom. They became allies. Now famine and disease forced the tribal men to seek work in Ha Noi to buy food and medicine and send it back to their villages.

Phan wrote what the tribesmen said in his notebook, but when he explained to them how his writing captured their words, the tribesmen refused to speak further, afraid their souls would be stolen from them in the written words.

In his journal Phan described the Chinese merchants fleeing north. They pushed heavily laden carts, small children riding atop their stacks of wares. The men wore the traditional pants and tunics of their class, their long hair braided in ropes hanging from beneath comic caps. The fast shuffle of their collective feet sounded like whispering. Their wives struggled to keep up on their tiny feet bound with silk. The sun turned their fair skin to a puffy red that might have been mistaken for inebriation were their exhaustion not obvious. The older children walked behind their parents. The smell of rice emanated from them all.

Thi pleaded to turn back.

Phan readjusted his pack so that it rode higher on his back. "We'll make it."

"Look at all these refugees." Thi gestured furtively. "It can't be safe in Ha Noi."

"As many are going toward the city, as are fleeing from it. The Moi aren't afraid."

"What do they know?"

"Where would we be safer?" Phan demanded.

"Back at the village. My family is there to help us. We have our own house. What more do we need?"

"Why didn't you say something before?"

"You weren't listening," Thi said. "And what about our child?"

"You don't understand what's going on. Nothing will be the same in Viet Nam. In Ha Noi I can make things better for our son."

—⚏—

Several days later they crossed the Doumer Bridge into Ha Noi, a city born from water. Below the bridge, peasant volunteers were shoring up dikes that held the Red River back. They entered a city built on land scooped from created lakes or carried from the surrounding hills. Merchant farmers pushed carts of vegetables towards tin-roofed markets. Women with baskets on their heads added to the crush of bikes, trishaws, and an occasional car.

Thi stumbled and then fainted. A trishaw behind them protected her from the oncoming traffic. Horns sounded.

"Get in," the trishaw driver said.

"We can't pay," Phan said.

"Just get in."

Phan bowed and lifted his wife from the street, at the same time holding their son's head against his chest to protect him. The trishaw driver lifted Thi's legs and placed her on the seat. Phan slid in beside her. The trishaw driver peddled into traffic. Phan turned to the driver behind him. "Why are you helping us?"

"You're Chinese."

"Yes, but how..."

"You're too tall for Vietnamese. Nung, I'd guess. Me, too. No one else will help us. The Chinese armies are massing on the border ready to find advantage in the chaos, so no one trusts us. Be careful. There are spies everywhere. Everyone's suspicious."

"I'm no spy."

"Get caught at the wrong place, it won't matter."

Phan directed the driver where to turn. The jolting brought moans from Thi, unconscious on the seat. They crossed the city over boulevards named after French conquerors, lined by buildings with Parisian designs. At every intersection they worked their way across and against the traffic, chaos in every direction, enshrouded by a sweet smell of those dead from famine laid beside the road.

A dozen old women in black pajamas squatted at a bus stop, arms over their knees, and drooling betel nut juices from between black teeth. Nearby a man repaired bicycles using tools from a wooden box that doubled as his seat. A shirtless boy with bare feet, his skin cracked like cheap leather, walked in traffic selling fruit from a basket. The trishaw driver ordered him away. A horn blared. Nothing moved. A hawker pressed a newspaper into Phan's hand and demanded payment. Phan threw it back. The hawker cursed and pulled a knife.

The driver waved a pistol. "Beat it."

The hawker cursed again and disappeared in the crowd.

"Put that thing away," Phan cautioned.

"We must protect ourselves. Since the Japanese surrendered no one's in charge."

"Soon we'll all be free." Phan said. He felt the first drops of the midday rain that relieved the oppressive heat that time of year. In a month it would be cool and pleasant, reason enough to celebrate the Chinese New Year. He tried to focus on the future, uncertain for the first time.

As it began to pour, the driver spread the trishaw's canvas roof to protect his passengers. Those walking in the street sought shelter against the buildings. Traffic flowed. The driver leaned forward, his face close to Phan's, trying to avoid the rain that pelted his body. "Are you sure this is right?"

"Just keep going," Phan said.

In moments they reached a quiet street lined with tamarind trees and French villas, the feudal fortresses that once dominated the land. Dark green shutters hid their occupants. In years past he had accompanied Father Custeau down these streets, calling on parishioners. He recalled the stately courtyards inside the thick stucco walls, the smell of flowers in full bloom, gardeners tending them as if they were children at play. He had listened to the French chatter of their homeland, their complaints of how their sacrifices went unrewarded. Father Custeau had reassured them that they'd be rewarded, if not in this world, then in the next for carrying out God's mission, the white man's burden. In the heat of the day they had sipped mint juleps, sitting in swings on patios and in lawn chairs under umbrellas. They had complained of their lazy oriental workers, as if Phan wasn't there to hear what they had to say. At the time he had suffered the loss of face in silence for the sake of the priest, his protecting father.

Now they turned into streets filled with Vietnamese, abandoned factories behind steel gates, barbed wire strung outside concrete walls. In the midst of the factories Phan found the warehouse where workers lived, each floor divided by bamboo partitions, each cubicle a family's home. The trishaw driver helped carry Thi to a cubicle on the second floor and then without a word he was gone.

———

For the next four days Phan didn't leave Thi's side. Each morning he sent a boy to buy fruit from the outdoor market and to fill a canteen with water. After Phan ate, he sucked on lemons to suppress his thirst, using the canteen water to wet Thi's lips and wipe her forehead to hold down the fever. He held their child to her breast to feed him. After the second day Thi's bleeding stopped, and on the third day she regained consciousness and spoke.

The following days they curled together like spoons, talking in whispers for hours. Each dawn, as through the night, Phan rose to wipe the sweat from Thi as she suckled their child. When Thi's fever was gone, he sent word to the newspaper that he was ready to return to work. They sent a boy around with Phan's first assignment and enough money to tide him over.

———

On September 2, 1945, Phan stood with his wife and newborn child in Ba Dinh Square. Great banners and red star flags flapped above the crowd of Buddhist monks, Vietnamese Catholic priests, peasants, merchants, and rebel soldiers. Ho Chi Minh, a frail man in his mid-fifties, dressed in khaki tunic, spoke to them from a wooden platform thrown together for the occasion. His hands shaking, Phan wrote it down word for word, "We hold the truth that all men are created equal... endowed by their Creator with certain unalienable rights...." Phan smiled. They were the same words he had memorized from Father Custeau's books. Ho trapped the West with their own words. How could they now refute those words?

To the crowd the man was Uncle Ho, a nationalist come to set Viet Nam free, an answer to their dreams. How many suspected what Phan knew from his early days as a reporter: that Ho Chi Minh was really Nguyen Sinh Cung, a communist who had spent most of his life wandering overseas, often pursued by the French, always plotting against them? And did that matter if Ho was a devoted nationalist?

Phan cheered with the crowd. His tears flowed with their tears. He turned away from his wife to hide the tears from her. Freedom so long sought had come quickly. After a thousand blows struck against tyranny's rock, this last blow had caused a sudden crack. Phan looked back over the crowd at the French villas filling the skyline of the city and then inexplicably felt himself shudder.

CHAPTER 2

Ha Noi, September 2, 1945
Thi
A patriotic frenzy

Thi scrutinized the men who lined the speakers' platform, stiff in Western suits, their white shirts soaked with perspiration, white jackets wrinkled in the heat. Only the one they called Ho Chi Minh wore Eastern garb. Nothing about these men mitigated her despair. She recognized stridency, too much pride, too much determination.

"The crowd is agitated," Thi said, but Phan didn't respond to her or her frightened touch. She studied her husband, now a stranger standing rigid beside her as he looked over those around him, his tears mingled in his sweat. When he turned from her, he was one of them, smelling of the excitement, a smell pungent and offensive, not the familiar smell of the village men at their work. She wanted to understand her husband and the peasants and soldiers surrounding him and their adulation of Ho Chi Minh, the emaciated coffin-ready man who addressed them. But too often beautiful words caused men to lose their reason, their common sense, and fear. What demons possessed them that wife, home, family were not enough? What dreams drew them from the comfort of their homes? What was the final consequence of those dreams? Talk of freedom was treason to the French, who already sent convoys of troops back into the city. Ho's speech would only provoke them.

Ho Chi Minh's rasping voice echoed over the crowd, and then fell silent. Those with rifles beat them against the ground; others stamped their feet. Their cheers crescendoed louder and louder. "Ho Chi Minh a thousand years, Ho Chi Minh a thousand years," repeated and repeated in one voice. The earth shook. Dust rose from the ground, and then trapped by the stifling heat on this windless day, settled back over the crowd. Thi's temple throbbed, the scene and sounds a terrifying dream.

Ho was led away, surrounded by soldiers, squeezed like a flower pressed between boards as the crowd swirled around him. Then she saw Ho Chi Minh lifted off his feet, carried along as if by a colony of ants. Thi glanced again at her husband and understood the significance. In Ho the crowd and her husband saw their dreams, their hope to escape the inevitable.

The masses enveloped the small black car that held Ho at its nucleus. The car sputtered to a start. The crowd pressed against it, energized by the strength of the man inside. The sounds continued long after the sight of the car winding through the narrow streets, the crowd trailing behind.

Phan, his face flushed and radiant, remained motionless, turned to the empty wooden platform as if that frail man was still on it speaking. Alone beside him, Thi waited for him to return to her, to release his dream to reality, to tell her it was all right. She shifted their son on her hip, and noticed his weight for the first time since the speech began. The child remained asleep, his tiny hands tightly gripping her silk shirt, his breaths warming her, reassuring her in a way she didn't understand, but felt just as if he was still within her.

Phan moved down the street without speaking. They returned home in silence, she walking beside her husband through the narrow streets. They ignored the curfew, adding to Thi's feeling of panic. They passed three armed French soldiers leading a string of Vietnamese men, naked except for cloth over their groins, their chains making a strange music. The French were quietly re-establishing their control. But had Phan even noticed?

Thi imagined her husband dragged from his newspaper office as he wrote, paraded through the streets into the square, there his head hacked off by repeated blows from a French axe or with a single blow from the guillotine that tumbled it into a basket. She'd be left without means. Her fate was now tied to her husband. No Vietnamese woman existed but through the means of a man. And for her son, their son, what fate? What right and profit left him by a father executed by the French, his head boiled and tarred, preserved and displayed on a pike, his body thrown into the lime pit meant for common paupers and thieves?

There would come a time for freedom, but not here, not now with the French in control of the country. The crowd's excitement had only increased her fears. Their senses had left them. They had cheered and chanted as a mob. Ho Chi Minh *muon nam*, for a thousand years. Those words still rang in her ears as they climbed to the second floor and wove their way through the giant maze of cubicles.

Once in their cubicle, Phan instantly fell asleep. Thi listened to his uneasy breathing. She remembered begging him to remain in the village. Her father and his father before him and the generations before them had provided for their families from that land. And when it didn't provide enough, they endured their fate. Thi had never wanted to venture down the trail beyond the gardens where she'd labored with her family, continuously cutting back the jungle walls, sowing, reaping, and waiting for the rains and after the rains planting the earth again.

—⁂—

Then the Viet Minh had come, choosing the village for its seclusion as if it had been there waiting just for them. The Viet Minh allowed the village chief to continue to collect taxes and pay tribute to the absentee French landlords in Ha Noi. The village chief never reported the Viet Minh presence and the French never came to reassert their control. But the village wasn't the same.

The Viet Minh soldiers had been polite, but crude, loud, and often drunk. Instead of working they cleaned their weapons and conducted drills. Her father warned her to avoid the soldiers, but the soldiers were everywhere. They loitered in small groups outside the huts and became so familiar she no longer saw them through her father's eyes. She admired their uniforms, their spirited camaraderie, and their pride. They marched erect, their backs not bent by years of stooping in the fields.

Then a tall and spindly soldier awkwardly cradling an old carbine rifle, appeared with the other soldiers in the nightly formation. He seemed strangely handsome. His eyes caught hers. She blushed and turned away, but as the soldiers marched off she caught his glance again. That night was the beginning, and afterward came days of waiting, glancing, their eyes tentatively meeting, not knowing if others noticed, caring, not caring, afraid the fragile relationship built on nothing but glances would shatter. Weaving clothes next to her mother, she dropped stitches, as she day dreamed she was married. In the fields her feet crushed the harvest as she weeded, not noticing until her father scolded her. At night she waited at the edge of the village for the soldiers' patrols to return, afraid he'd not come, afraid to be caught, and yet her eyes searched boldly. She took upon herself her father's obligation to find her a husband. Too many young village men had been taken as soldiers or their marriages already arranged. She didn't want a spinster's life, a burden on her family. She had seen too much pain in her father's eyes as the family sat together at dinner, one boy, six girls, too many dowries for a poor man. Although she had heard of the Western concept of romantic love, she was more practical. Love could be nurtured after her marriage.

She exchanged glances with her soldier, then gestures of recognition, a passing word of greeting. She learned his name was Phan. She sensed their relationship ripened. And then unexpectedly and unexplained he began to respond less to their chance meetings. He turned frail and lethargic, avoiding and avoided by the other soldiers. One day he disappeared. The villagers gossiped, but what could she believe? When she asked the soldiers, they laughed and told her he was living alone in the jungle. Something was the matter. What she had done next, she never understood: She sought him in the direction they pointed, the place he had entered the jungle.

Tangled vegetation choked off the light. The terrible silence and musty odor of rotting existence increased her fear. In this place of chaos her life might end without anyone hearing her last whimper. On her knees, she pushed aside vegetation and forced her way forward, stopping frequently, panting, no full breath of fresh air there for the taking. She lamented not having grabbed her father's machete to clear a path. Mosquitoes, ticks, flies, and red ants attacked her. Leeches clung to her. She fought them, swatting, brushing, itching her red and welted skin.

A spot of light drew her on. She found a trail, but it soon divided into three. She started down one only to realize it too divided again, that the jungle contained a vast network of such trails, a spider's web. She was lost but plunged further into the interior determined to find her Phan. Chance guided her, each trail the same as the next. She shouted Phan's name. Only the birds responded, flapping against the jungle as they flew away unseen. Then came a metallic jingling. She forced aside a tree limb to expose a tin can hanging from a string above the trail, an early warning.

"What are you doing here?" A form emerged. No longer clean-shaven, a long beard, hair unkempt, wild like an animal, his smell neither that of a man, nor something rotten, but the smell of ammonia which eventually replaced decaying life. A finger poked into his ribs would have pierced his spine. Only his eyes were still soft and serene. Pathetic, her father would later say, but she didn't see him that way.

"I'm here to see you," she whispered.

"Who sent you?"

Thi blushed, then in anger at his insolence said, "You're too harsh."

"Perhaps." He withdrew into the wall of vegetation from which he'd emerged, concealed by a rising fog drawn like poison from a wound. She was losing him again.

"I'm here on my own," she cried.

"Why?"

"To see you," she said, beginning to wonder herself why she'd come.

He hesitated. "I'm glad you're here. Just surprised."

"Why are you doing this?" she asked.

"What were you expecting?" Again the arrogant demand, his voice distant. "I must atone."

"What are you talking about?"

"You're not a Catholic. You can't understand."

"You've done nothing wrong."

"That's not enough." He pointed to a limb above his head, where a tree boa slowly wrapped and re-wrapped itself. Its eyes blinked and rolled back under a milk-colored membrane. "You see it? A sign."

"Of what?" she said.

"Temptation and sin." He wasn't making sense.

"It's just a snake, a tree boa." She laughed, trying to bring him back to her through conversation. What was he thinking? "I've heard the story of how the cobra protected the Buddha by coiling around him, its head flared over him as a shelter." Was that it or madness from staying in the jungle too long?

"It's here every day to remind me."

"They're harmless," she said, scoffing at his city idiocy. "I've seen them at the jungle's edge feeding on field mice and rats."

Her compassion grew to despair as she realized his condition. Others had made him mad. What they've created she'd have to repair. She reached toward him, took his hand as she would a child to lead him away. He didn't resist. Only he couldn't walk. No doubt he hadn't walked or eaten properly for weeks. She liked his depending on her, she his crutch.

His weight was greater than she'd expected, but not enough to deter her from carrying him down the trail. And as they walked, his steps measured like an old man's, the jungle fell silent, as if it to pay tribute to a vanquished comrade. She noted his passion for the dark, how he squinted and rushed as best he could across small clearings, as if he preferred the jungle without paths or light. He directed her at the forks, pressing her forward in a fragile way. She worried that if he fell he'd shatter, like a ceramic figurine.

—ɯ—

That was how she now remembered it as she rested next to her husband, listened to his disturbed breathing, understood the uneasiness which she shared with him. As he tossed, she stroked his forehead and wiped away his perspiration with her pajama sleeves. She harbored him within her arms, providing the security that his dreams stole from him. He was there next to her but still unreachable. Her gentleness met rebuke to the flailing arms that struck out against unseen enemies. As night crept past them, she waited, her own forsaken dreams murky remembrances lost in the unspoken consolation of him whom she'd chosen. And she realized her mistake in marrying a writer at a time when words were dangerous.

CHAPTER 3

Ha Noi, September 2, 1945
Hahn
The Rally

At the western edge of Ha Noi, the streets quickly filled with the crowds flowing toward Ba Dinh Square: men from alleys; shopkeepers from Hoan Kiem, their shops on Silk Street closed; shops emptied from Cotton Street and Paper Street; merchants from Dong Xuan market; students and Confucian scholars from the Temple of Literature; rice farmers from surrounding villages; beggars and pickpockets come to work the crowd.

Trishaws merged with bicycles and cars. Men on foot directed them, self-appointed marshals caught up in the spirit of humanities parade. In the square, men hammered at a make shift platform, quickly covering its exposed wood with bunting. Red starred flags flew everywhere. The sun climbed the sky like a theater spotlight hoisted overhead. Hahn had never seen anything like it before.

Although Hahn had been editor of the city paper for a

month, no one pointed him out as he stood in the shadows of a building. His diminutive stature drew no attention, except the occasional joke from passing French soldiers. The intensity in his eyes went unnoticed.

Hahn observed the knives, pistols, and brass knuckles the Vietnamese concealed up sleeves, there in case of trouble. A Surete staff car idled in an alley off the square. The driver split cigarette smoke rings with his tongue. Two Frenchmen in suits leaned against the car and wrote in their notebooks. Later they would tell it their way and never mind what happened. Their shadows stretched into the square and sliced across the path of the crowd.

You murdering bastards, Hahn thought, but smiled when they glared in his direction. One of them pointed. Suspicious or only making jokes? Hahn looked down, careful not to any longer meet their eyes. He side stepped against a wall.

Just two Surete, yet their presence caused the distancing predators caused in a herd. Hahn knew the way the French thought. They saw Vietnamese men as eunuchs, Viet women whores. They never cared how many were killed to keep it that way. All French were fanatics, like their priests, taught unquestioning loyalty to a mission they thought greater than themselves, their God its final justification. The black robed priests spoke with a single voice, blindly following the sacraments, sheep behind a single shepherd, but degrading and corrupt. The Surete had killed Hahn's father for some imagined wrong and let his mother starve in the streets. The French priests who then raised him tried to teach him what to think, but all the time he knew it was a lie. Their false God never owned him and never would.

Hahn tugged the handkerchief from his lapel pocket, and it unfolded as he wiped his face. He examined the sweat that stained it, then tucked it away. No bombs today, but soon, very soon. Naive to expect anything else worked against the bastards across the alley, but he'd listened to the arguments in his Communist Party cell and understood why this day had to remain peaceful. Publicly declaring independence cleared the air and let the country see that the Viet Minh had emerged in control of the movement. It signaled the French to pack their trunks and depart if they didn't want more loss of face than what the Japanese had already administered. Hahn was not deluded by this fantasy: a rapid resolution was unlikely given French arrogance and greed. Only that morning he'd helped prepare contingencies, rifles and grenades hidden throughout the city, maps to jungle camps, supplies stockpiled for a protracted revolution. Strike, then retreat, would soon be the order of the day, but for now the charade of peace would survive as if they expected the French to recognize Viet Minh legitimacy.

Until now beheadings were the only time the French had allowed crowds to gather, but today the crowd waited in the heat for Ho Chi Minh to confirm their dreams, like children under the spell of a storyteller. The masses intermingled and dreamed themselves soon free. Fools to think freedom so easily attained, yet useful fools to be recruited as soldiers and molded to the cause.

Thousands pressed toward the platform, while orchestrated whispers spread of Ho Chi Minh's approach, Nguyen the Patriot, a ghost emerging from the jungle. His guile so renowned, some doubted Ho existed or if so, that he was a single person. The Surete was once certain they had eliminated him and so they watched to see who would appear.

The crowd carried Hahn forward with it, away from the wall, their crush leaving him short of breath.

A row of short men with white shirts and ties lined up together across the platform. One of them waved. The crowd cheered. The microphone crackled. A man in front collapsed from the heat and was carried off. Sweat reeked the air. Someone yelled, and soon the whole crowd joined, shouting the phrase, "Freedom or death." Hahn tried to spot that first voice, but the man was hidden in the crowd.

"Is that him?" someone shouted.

"There's pretty Giap," another cried.

"Pretty as a cobra." The crowd laughed, drowning out Giap's first words.

"You know which one is Ho Chi Minh?" a man next to Hahn asked.

"He's not on the platform yet," Hahn said. The man's breath disgusted him. *Nuoc maum*, soured by beer. Hahn turned away. He stretched to see above the crowd of bobbing heads. Would he recognize Ho, a man he'd only glimpsed once at a jungle compound?

"Wish I'd see him," the man next to him said.

"He'll be here," Hahn said. The man was stinking worse, but there was nowhere to escape from him.

The men on the platform turned to watch behind them. Giap introduced a frail man in native dress, a colorless shirt with baggy pants and sandals. He walked to center stage. The crowd cheered, and Hahn realized he'd failed to recognize Uncle Ho. When the crowd fell silent, Ho began to speak, and his voice, high and shrill, carried through the crowd.

"All men are created equal. They are endowed by their creator with certain inalienable rights; among these are life, liberty, and the pursuit of happiness...."

"Beautiful words," the man next to Hahn whispered.

"They're not his words," Hahn said, straining to hear what followed. Others' words and literary skill. Ho's genius was practicality, the ability to control and manipulate, not originality.

Hahn, raised with the communist paradigm that he knew must someday bind all Vietnamese together, heard the words only as tools to recruit those the party needed to achieve victory. Let others be fooled by Ho's speech.

"What are you saying?" the man interrupted again.

"It's the American Declaration of Independence."

"Never heard of it," the man said. "Only Uncle Ho could write those words."

The man pushed into the crowd and disappeared.

"Viet Nam has the right to enjoy freedom and independence and in fact has become a free and independent country," Ho continued to the cheering crowd.

The crowd was stretching to its toes, their heads in continuous nods, lifted by the words. Then suddenly, too suddenly like all great moments, the speech ended. At first Hahn thought Ho had just paused. The crowd fell into an expectant silence. All eyes on him, the little man stepped from the podium. The crowd surged forward. And for an instant Hahn felt electricity through him. That little man, no better than any other (or was he?), with sheer strength of character could forge the Vietnamese people into a single will to freedom. That was what was needed. The communist state must come later. Now the crowd milled and rolled in waves. Ho Chi Minh was swallowed and could not be seen or heard.

Below the podium a familiar form...no...two...lingered beneath the banner proclaiming independence. The tall form was thin and unmistakable. Hahn checked the impulse to rush forward and embrace his friend. He must allow Phan to absorb the reality, to preserve the historic moment as only a writer of his talent could. The timing wasn't right for their reunion.

The crowd surged down a broad boulevard lined by government buildings three or more stories high, designed by the French, filled with French bureaucrats who peered from the windows. The crowd jeered at them in Vietnamese, then, "Ho Chi Minh, Ho Chi Minh." They raced to catch the black car that carried Ho Chi Minh away. Then someone began to chant "Liberté. Égalité. Fraternité." The crowd picked up the words which echoed off the walls. That was splendid, even if few in the crowd knew what it meant.

Hahn glanced back toward the abandoned podium. What held Phan back from following the crowd? Was that his wife beside him with their child in her arms? Why still in peasant dress, her, too? But her beauty shined through the dull garb. No matter, Phan would report to the newspaper soon enough, and then Hahn would give him a proper suit. He imagined the look of surprise on Phan's face at that moment. Time enough then to use their friendship for the cause.

CHAPTER 4

Ha Noi, September 3, 1945
Phan
Private moments, more or less

As they lay down together, so they woke: face to face, arms entwined. Phan kissed his wife's cheek, eased from under the stained and yellowed sheets, and pulled on the pants and shirt he wore each day. After buttoning the collarless black shirt tight around his neck, he bent to kiss his son. He slipped his feet into the made-from-tire sandals beside the sleeping mat and passed silently through the curtain that separated his family from the others.

Several men, huddled in the stairway, still played cards from the night before. They continued their game of *tam cuc*, too polite to acknowledge Phan and what they'd heard in the night. Phan straddled past the game, down the stairs, then into the street.

Somber grey shadows on bikes glided along the road. Letting the bikes sweep around him, Phan walked by rote, the back alleyways still familiar to him from long past days.

23

Dawn stretched first light down the streets in narrow fingers and massaged his face with the slightest warmth and light. Forms huddled against the walls. Men asleep and in this year of hunger, often dead. For a few cents a day crews with dump carts policed the streets, keeping whatever they found from the pockets of the dead. As the sun rose, those dead came alive with flies. Phan hurried to pass them. There was too much famine for a land with abundant rice fields. Too many wars, too much mismanagement and exploitation. And never a chance at self-government until now.

In the newsroom sweating men with ink-stained fingers, their shirt pockets stained from leaking pens, their pants grey where wiping hands left smears, rushed here and there with no pattern to their motion. A few restlessly rocked in old office chairs, looking helpless at their desks. Some ran their fingers through disheveled hair, while writing frantically to meet deadlines. In a nearby room the presses clanked and clattered, printing onto endless reams of paper that demanded words.

Phan stood in the doorway, waiting for a look of recognition, but these weren't the old men he'd left years ago, soft spoken Frenchmen devoted to their writing. Now young Vietnamese men stood in groups arguing politics, shouting and not listening to the others. Phan's stomach churned as he hesitated, no longer eager to step forward into the room.

"Get in there you fool." A laughing voice behind him, an arm around his shoulders, warm breathing near his ear.

"Hahn," Phan exclaimed as he embraced his childhood friend. "You survived."

"And why shouldn't I? The French never suspected me."

"And you, the most fanatic of us all." Phan laughed.

"But the most circumspect," Hahn added, pushing Phan into an empty room and closing the door. "I always make it a point of not getting noticed. Even here no one knows I'm the communist."

"And still a party member, I suppose?" Phan asked.

Hahn smiled. "Well, did you get a story at the rally

yesterday?"

"Of course. You must be thrilled Ho Chi Minh has declared our independence." Phan said.

"It's meaningless. The French will make a fool of him if he continues that way."

Phan hesitated before he spoke, "If the French are intent on regaining control, why haven't they imprisoned Ho?"

"They're not interested in making him a martyr."

"That's it?"

"Maybe they think he'll become their puppet," Hahn continued.

"Will he?"

"All he thinks about is independence. Because of it, he's not that good a communist."

"But I suppose you're still the inflexible communist." Phan forced a laugh.

"I'm that, and more," Hahn replied, never raising his voice. "Your friend, so I'm warning you to be careful what you say outside this room. I don't want you getting caught through your own carelessness. I'd be next."

"And I thought it was me you were worried about." Phan forced a laugh.

"I am. I am." Hahn threw his arm around Phan again. "You're here aren't you?"

"It was you sent for me?"

"Who else?"

"But the letter said the editor."

"That's me."

"You? It's hard to believe the French trusted a Vietnamese."

"They didn't. The Japanese threw the French reporters out of the office and brought us in to look legitimate. Now with the Japanese gone, we're left in charge, if only for the moment. The French are afraid to move too quickly after their humiliation."

As the two walked together through the room, Phan savored the smells of fresh paper and ink, smells that triggered his memories.

"This desk is yours." Hahn stopped to lean against a teakwood partners desk meant for two, face to face, working together. He tossed a bag from behind the desk. "Put them on."

"I can't accept these," Phan said after pulling out a suit, a shirt, and tie. He admired the fabric, the stitching, the feel and press of it. Not imported. Made in the shops of Ha Noi, a city full of tradesmen with much time and few customers, the best craftsmen from the villages of Viet Nam, competing to escape the labor of the fields.

"It's from the party," said Hahn. "Military uniforms aren't the only thing they supply those who serve them."

"Thanks, I guess. What do I have to do for them?"

"Just report the way you feel about our movement for independence. That's enough for now."

"When do I start?"

"Right now. I need you. There's no one working here but kids. We need good reporting of what's going on. They're all eyeing us: the French, Chinese, British. Even the Americans, though not for themselves. War can be averted, if they know we'll fight. Make that clear. Use the news to editorialize. I'll keep your articles on the front page."

And they embraced, children again for an instant, holding each other escaping the pain thrown upon them since birth. Then awkwardly they broke away. Hahn fled to his cubicle and closed the door.

Hahn's grin was a blend of perfectly even teeth with the one gold tooth in the center that reminded Phan of the orphanage and the French boy who'd constantly tormented Hahn and knocked out that tooth. Hahn, the smallest of them all, had been chosen by the French boy to receive derision about his size, and poking from behind, his ribs, his back, even his head a target.

When Hahn fought back, he was punched and kicked. That's how he'd lost his tooth. When Phan intervened, the French boy's mother, maid to the priest and some said his lover, pulled them apart. The priest punished Hahn and Phan with the strap, the French boy allowed to watch.

One day after that Hahn sneaked into the infirmary and stole a bottle of diuretic. Then each meal he supplemented small amounts from it in the French boy's milk. Only Phan shared the secret. Together the two watched the boy fall from health. He ran to the river to relieve himself. He vomited day after day. His mother grew sick with grief, the doctors she took him to were mystified as his weight dropped and he weakened. Then Hahn drew him into fights, and the other boys laughed at the big French bully who couldn't defend himself against the smallest of them all. The fighting ended with the French boy in the infirmary. They never saw him again. Rumor was his mother in desperation to save her son's life had taken him back to France where he died, or maybe he died on the way, or recovered and became wealthy. No one knew for certain.

Now it was Hahn and not the French who gave Phan what he'd always wanted. Yet something felt wrong about it without the Frenchmen in the offices to control and edit what he wrote. Where Phan now sat alone, two French reporters had sweated for years, glowering at each other across the partner's desk, forced to monitor what each said so that the Parisian aristocracy would approve, knowing that any mistakes would haunt them months later when the dispatches returned on ships from France. Phan wondered what his limits were to be.

Phan slipped off his worker's clothes, as he felt Hahn's eyes watching him. He pulled on suit pants that were too long and too large around the waist, fixed by tightening the belt and rolling up the cuffs. The shirt fit better and the tie held the collar together where the button was missing. In the suit jacket pockets he found a brown, bent photograph the size of a postcard: Frenchmen dressed in hunting vests and safari hats, rifles slung over their shoulders or cradled in their arms. They posed casually for the photographer's convenience, arranged by height and smiling towards the camera. At their feet were Vietnamese bodies stained with blood and next to them the severed heads. One of the Frenchmen grinned broadly and rested his boot on one of the dead.

Phan smashed his fist against the desk. Yet even now he hesitated to fully condemn the French. Their savior Jesus Christ taught him judge not. That word had rolled from Father Custeau's lungs, and filled his church, resonated off the walls and over all those Frenchmen who knelt before him and before God as they prayed and praised God with their songs. The great organ that filled the wall beside the altar resonated with the word of God. It had filled all the little orphans chosen to serve as altar boys, with that word and with awe and dread for the Almighty, and it still reverberated within Phan two decades later. Now, before the forgotten dead rose up and struck them down, he would give Father Custeau and those French disciples of God their chance as God must have meant them to have it.

CHAPTER 5

Ha Noi, September 4, 1945
Phan
Living with the past

The story on Ho Chi Minh's speech was completed the next day. Phan pushed back in his chair. A delicate smile crossed his face at the innocence of the words he'd selected to captivate newspaper readers. The final draft had written itself in the night, at times waking him with a burning fever. He'd had to assure his wife nothing was wrong. Night was the time of the truest insights. He'd been determined to remember and use his dreams in the morning.

Phan already plotted news stories and feature stories on Ho Chi Minh. He would write interviews and historic comparisons to build the image of a giant, repeating and repeating, until even the most skeptical accepted the greatness of Uncle Ho, the father of their nation. Create a legend and they will follow, a nation with a single voice. Hahn's faith in him and his abilities was well placed.

At that moment a familiar sadness descended over Phan. Nothing controlled it. Alone with his ghosts, they rose to greet him: A priest stood over him, shouting that he had betrayed the church. Accused and not forgiven, an orphan ungrateful for what the priests had provided him. Words from the past, spoken by those whose expectations could never be met by small boys. Hahn stood beside him, both of them naked, red welts across their bottoms, caned but unrepentant. In the cold damp cathedral, Christ loomed over them, their pain his as he hung on the cross, crucified for their sins.

Phan's face was wet with tears. He wiped them with his sleeve, stood and moved from the desk as if it were haunted. He strode towards Hahn's office, and with pretended indifference opened the door and threw the story on Hahn's desk. "Finished," was all he said.

Hahn glanced up over the metal rim of reading glasses. "That's quick," he said without any indication of real surprise.

"It's to the point," Phan said.

Hahn's eyes shifted rapidly over the pages in his hands. "This is good."

"I know." Phan was thinking about the priests and forgiveness, the possibility the church might still intervene to avoid a conflict. "You think the violence will resume?"

"It will," Hahn said.

"I'm going to see our old priest."

"I thought you might want that," Hahn said. "You'll be wasting your time."

"He's the only hope." Phan turned away. He walked across the office past the inquisitive faces on the young reporters wondering who this new writer might be who reported directly to the editor. Several followed him to the door and watched until he vanished into the crowded street.

—⁓—

At the end of Silver Street, distant from the markets, Phan entered a quiet, narrow lane. Lush green trees and grasses, tailored and trimmed with gardener's shears, improved on nature. An imposing cathedral overshadowed the trees along the avenue, its grandeur the work of generations.

Father Custeau had called it his Asian Notre Dame, but Phan had seen the real Notre Dame Cathedral in file photos at the newspaper and knew it was a poor metaphor.

At the cathedral's pinnacle and just below the cross above the entrance, masonry gargoyles glared down at Phan. As children venting their disdain for the French, he and the other orphans had called the figures frogs. Hanh had boasted that some day he'd climb those walls and topple the gargoyles from their perches. Phan never doubted him.

Now a solitary French soldier hidden in the shadows raised his rifle. Phan pressed his weight against the great cathedral door forcing it open. At the back of the nave, he touched holy water to his head, made the sign of the cross, and genuflected. As he rose, he beheld the epiphany of Christ hanging on a cross behind the altar. Christ's body was turgid, a golden color except for the blood from a spear's puncture in his side and from nails through hands and feet. The light that streamed into the cathedral through the stained glass windows high over the aisles to each side illuminated Christ. His head drooped but his eyes gazed towards those windows and beyond. As the sun rose towards noon and the moment of high mass, Christ's countenance changed and for an instant in the harsh light he appeared to ascend from his body.

Phan's childhood soul reawakened. He fell to his knees and prayed for God's forgiveness for any doubts he'd raised and for the sins he'd committed against the church. He sought this forgiveness directly from God, whose presence he sensed, free from any French intermediary.

He saw the hand of God in the figure of Christ and in the cathedral windows. There before him was God's manifestation. The French had failed to conceal God's will. The Vietnamese carver who had carried out the French wishes had created Christ with an occidental physique but all the passion in the mosaic emanated from oriental eyes. Cut in the lightest of colored glass highest in the windows, the tempestuous angels, the very instruments of God's will, fought the beasts of evil and sin that raged below them. Each angel had been given a famous Vietnamese face: the Trung Sisters who rose to oust the Chinese in 40 AD, Phan Dinh Phung and Phan Boi Chau who ages before struggled against the French in an attempt to maintain freedom.

Below the angelic forms who held them at bay were centaurs, chimeras, gryphons, manticores, primordial pagan forms whose evil faces resembled historic figures of the hated French: the cursed Napoleon III, who first approved French military intervention in Viet Nam; Admiral Louis-Adolphe Bonard, the French admiral who served as governor of Viet Nam; Paul Doumer, notorious French governor-general of Viet Nam at the turn of the century.

Phan realized the genius of it. A single artist had hidden the Vietnamese spirit of freedom in his work, and yet it was clearly there for all to see, defying the French juggernaut within its own soul. The artist had known that Christ died for the poor, the meek, and finally those most like him, including the common Vietnamese. Not for the Romans, the Pharisees, the French or any other rulers. But had the artist's guile gone unnoticed by all those generations of French priests, or had they feared to criticize what might have been inspired by God? Or was something more basic at work, the exploitation of cheap labor, the church afflicted with the same greed that brought the French merchants to a land they cursed as too hot, inhospitable, and malaria infested, but a place where they could steal the wealth and rule?

Was what Phan saw a trick of his senses? In his confusion he turned away from the altar, toward the secret room off the rectory, a room he'd discovered with Hahn years before. Phan entered the chamber where the greatest bishops of the cathedral were buried, their death masks protruding from the floor. Beyond it a dark corridor passed Father Custeau's offices, beyond them the rooms where priests had once stood at desks and translated the scriptures into Vietnamese. There was no sign of anyone. Phan proceeded rapidly to the secret panel, removed it and slid into the forbidden library.

The room had not changed, though the books were now heavy with dust. He touched them again, the very books which created his beliefs: Aristotle, Plato, Socrates, Rousseau,

Locke, the American Jefferson, and Defoe, some written in English, most in French. He strained to make out their titles in the light from a stained glass window near the ceiling. He ran his hands over the leather bindings as if to read braille. He stroked the yellowed pages with his finger tips. He sank into the soft leather chair in the corner, a childhood escape where he had curled with drawn up knees. Breathing with difficulty in the musty air, he let the years evaporate.

—✕✕—

The room had always been locked, but he and Hahn discovered a panel where nails were loose from rot. It opened without showing evidence. At first the room had given them privacy to hide and play. As they learned to read, they discovered books not taught or sanctioned by the church, books unlike any they read in class, filled with flights of imagination, dreams, and forbidden knowledge. Locke *On Property*, Marx the communist, Thomas Paine the pamphleteer who called for freedom even at the cost of his own blood. In this secret world they read and argued over what these Western men meant to them. At some point Phan had put non-fiction aside and lived through the writings of Dickens, Defoe, Shakespeare, and Twain, living in a world that still remained a fantasy to him. As he read, life had rushed past him in episodes.

In that room Hahn had sworn an oath of loyalty to the *Communist Manifesto* which promised to restore men to their natural equality and divide the product of their labors according to their needs. And he had sworn to avenge the French injustices. In the *Communist Manifesto* Hahn had discovered words that justified violently overturning the order of things. His mother had been expelled from their village by the French, to beg on abandoned streets with her only child whom a priest had later taken from the arms of her corpse. When Phan probed with a child's curiosity for more of Hahn's past, Hahn fell silent. What else did Hahn remember? What had he seen that still depressed him years later? Phan had known his friend well enough not to question him further. And that was when he first realized how little he understood his friend despite many hours together. Hahn's steel countenance still protected him from questioning.

Hahn was among the first to attend the Vietnamese Communists' secret meetings. Night meetings. He had left in the dark and returned in the dark, a shadow against the orphanage wall. While the other orphans prayed before breakfast, Hahn whispered strange tales of the conspiracies plotted the night before. Mines planted in streets. Men lying in ambush to kill and fade into the night. Assassinations. Phan never knew what to believe. He withheld his allegiance from the communists. After all, his nightmares were filled with Chinese soldiers, not the French.

Near the end of their days at the orphanage, Phan had rediscovered *The Light of Asia*, a book he'd earlier put aside, thinking it was just another story of Christ written by an Englishman. Instead it told the story of the Buddha, a man who found enlightenment on his own. And for the first time Phan understood why so many in Viet Nam followed the teachings of the Buddha. The Buddha spoke of man's suffering and preached that with compassion and generosity came wisdom and relief. Without the French God there was no one to judge and condemn. Actions brought their own consequences in a continuation of the wheel of life. Man became what he made himself. At the time, Phan embraced what the Buddha taught but kept it to himself, afraid of Hahn's ridicule and Father Custeau's retribution for following a forbidden religion.

—⚭—

Now Phan heard feet scuffing towards the door, a key turning the great lock. There was no time to escape.

"I thought it was you," Father Custeau said, his gentle smile unperturbed as he stared at Phan huddled in the chair. The priest looked much older, his thick head of hair turned white, his tall lean torso slumped and no longer over six feet.

"You're not a little surprised?" Phan said.

"In all these years only you and Hahn discovered the panel."

"You knew we came in here?"

"I knew."

"Why didn't you say something?"

"Would you have read these books if I'd ordered you to do so?"

"Perhaps not."

"I too read them when I first came here. It satisfied my curiosity about forbidden writings. They meant very little to me afterwards. I locked the room and followed the church's teachings. I thought you'd do the same. I thought you both would become priests."

"Are you disappointed, father?"

"Should I be?" Father Custeau threw the question back.

"I'm not without my sins."

"Nor are any of us, but do you seek absolution?" Father Custeau spoke in French. In fifty-five years the priest hadn't learned the language or the customs of the people he expected to guide in God's ways.

"Things have changed." Phan hesitated.

"They always do," the priest said.

"I'm back at the newspaper."

"I thought you might be."

"I'm married."

"To a Catholic girl?"

"She's not."

"Was the marriage sanctioned by the church?"

"The village where she lived was Buddhist. There were no Catholic priests."

"If you haven't consummated," The priest hesitated, clearly concerned.

"Father, I have..."

"Don't say more. You're to be married in the church. I'll see to it." The priest allowed no interruption, "You must return to God's flock. You must seek forgiveness." He paused, "Leave now. Come back tomorrow with the girl and we'll bring her into the faith. Go before you're discovered by others." Then, as if muttering to himself, "I should have burned the books."

"It wasn't the books, Father." Phan interrupted. "You taught us to think. Now we're not French sheep, and I've come here for your help." That was as far as Phan dared to go, deterred by his own conventions of courtesy, although he felt the rage within him grow.

"I'll pray for you, that you follow God's will and are forgiven the blasphemies you once imbibed in this room."

"Blasphemies, father? This room is where I found hope."

"You must find your divine guidance in the Bible."

"And what about you French? What guides you?"

"We're the missionaries of God."

"Even the Legionaries?"

"Carrying out God's will requires many different abilities."

"And doesn't God want all mankind to be free? Doesn't that include the Vietnamese?"

"God wants all mankind to be Christian."

"There's nothing to be said against the French? What about the Crusades, the Inquisition?"

"At the time the crusaders and the inquisitors were necessary to maintain the faith. The church had to be protected. And nothing's more important than to bring nonbelievers to the fold. Someday you'll understand."

"Father, stop the French generals before it's too late. They'll listen to the church."

"Its in God's hands," Father Custeau dismissed Phan with a wave. That was how it had always been with the priest, his world held together by what he accepted as God's will. That was what Phan had come to confirm, and now he knew he'd never return to the cathedral again.

"Damn your God," Phan shouted.

In the next instant priest grabbed Phan, sudden for an old man, and forced him across the room, past the bishops in the floor, all the time crossing himself as if demons inhabited the room instead of saints. Into the cathedral, where he pushed Phan to his knees before the altar and demanded he repent his blasphemy. Phan would never remember how he broke free, but he raced down the center aisle to the back of the nave. The door moaned and gave way. Warm air struck Phan's face. The door banged closed behind him. The French guard toyed with the trigger guard to his rifle. Phan bolted past him and across the road to a taxi.

In a German accent the driver demanded payment in advance. His knees near his chin, Phan settled back into the seat. He tried to exorcize the priest from his thoughts. He pulled out the tiny book he'd stolen from the secret room. *The Light of Asia*. In the cab's dim light, he felt as much as read the title imprint in the leather cover. By snatching the book he had hoped to retrieve his childhood from the priest who now rebuked him. Phan tried to find the words and passages that had given him peace of mind so long ago.

—⁂—

Memory cursed Phan. The priest had caught a boy named Binh touching himself in bed down where it was forbidden. "Mortal sin!" Father Custeau had thundered the next morning from behind the classroom desk. He locked Binh in a closet at the back and made the class pray for the forgiveness that never came in time. To escape his shame, Binh ran away. He fell into the Red River and drowned. Days later his little body was pulled from the water by a fisherman. On the table in an empty classroom, the priest laid the boy out, naked, for all to see. His body, bloated with shame, was still intact except for his missing shameful part. Father Custeau said that God in His wrath had torn it away as Binh floated in the river, that neither Binh nor any other orphan could ever escape God's wrath.

Phan's own lusts still tormented him, dividing his mind between right and wrong, heaven and hell, purity and sin. Nothing made sense. Even now Father Custeau's repeated warnings rose from memory like forgotten seeds spread over a barren field springing to life. Thinking all his feelings wrong, Phan tried to suppress them. For an instant the feelings stopped as when the wind drops out of a sail, but almost immediately he felt lost. The pain left inside him turned itself loose.

As the old Citroën rattled down the street, the driver cursed the Vietnamese every time he hit a pothole. The worse potholes tossed Phan off his seat. Slow down, he thought, but said nothing. Rain pelted the roof. The driver continued to curse. The windshield wipers banged at each stroke. Street lights flickered like broken candles. Faceless shadows walked along the streets, head down into the wind. The taxi threw sheets of water over them.

Then the windshield wipers scraped across drying glass. The storm had come suddenly and was suddenly gone. The driver cursed a trishaw operator who refused to pull to the side. The front bumper of the taxi struck the single rear wheel, tumbling the trishaw off the road and throwing the driver onto the pavement. The taxi driver laughed and shook his fist.

Then the rain renewed, pounding against the windshield in a way that continued until the taxi stopped.

"You getting out here?" The German voice was grating.

Phan raced to the front door of the newspaper, only then turning to glance back at the taxi. It was surrounded by the street kids who begged outside his office.

An old typewriter covered with grease and dust rested on the floor within the well of the desk. Phan lifted it to the desktop and used a handkerchief to wipe it clean. He rolled paper into the typewriter carriage. His fingers touched the typewriter's keys. Their cold metal sang through him. Ho Chi Minh, the liberator, rose from the pages, his frail body that of a saint and martyr. Phan had previously studied the man, but he'd left his notes behind when he had fled from the newspaper years ago. He didn't bother to search for them now, certain that the French reporters must have destroyed them or turned them over to French intelligence. He didn't need them to remember the man of many names: Nguyen Tat Thanh, Cung or Ba and Vuong, Chin, Line, Tran, and finally achieving fame as Nguyen Ai Quoc. The names only added to the legend and the mystery surrounding Ho Chi Minh and confused the French who hunted him as a common criminal. Ho's plight was the material from which he'd create his national hero, Ho's words of freedom a rallying cry. A George Washington? No, but perhaps Simon Bolivar, who freed his nation only to have it torn apart by differing visions. Most like Mao who would free his country to suppress it. No matter, the conflict of emotions that filled Phan gave him the energy he needed to write the story of the cry for independence, the story Hahn wanted him to write. Phan would inspire the Vietnamese to join together and force the French to recognize the Vietnamese God-given right to freedom. When the story was completed, he would find Father Custeau and convince him to support the movement. The church would maintain and protect the purity of the vision.

He bent over the typewriter, pulling at his hair, his sweat soaking through the fine shirt he wore. He typed out the dream, as if it could be lifted off the page and placed into reality. But for an instant he wondered was he fooling himself.

CHAPTER 6

Ha Noi, September 4, 1945
Father Custeau
Memory and Mass

The Latin mass tumbled from his lips, floated out over the congregation, touched them with devotion, humbled them into falling on their knees. His soliloquy rose into the rafters, but Father Custeau no longer heard the lofty words. Now he repeated the requiem as a habit, spoken without feeling. How many times had he said the mass? It was what his parishioners bartered for: their offerings in exchange for his prayers.

The front pews, reserved for the largest donors, were filled with the returning French men dressed in tropical white suits, their wives elegant in the latest styles from Paris, hats with peacock feathers, there for all to see. Their children wore the finest clothes, miniature preludes to their future. At Father Custeau's direction the congregation bowed their heads in prayer. Only then did he notice two Vietnamese sitting behind the French men. They were recent converts, humble in their poverty, their tattered work shirts scrubbed clean for the occasion. They, too, were God's children, but children needing the church's constant discipline and direction. Why had all the other Vietnamese parishioners abandoned their faith after all that he'd taught them over the years? Their numbers had steadily diminished since communism cloaked itself in the cause of Vietnamese freedom. Since the Viet Minh. Didn't they understand God had declared the church the instrument of his administration?

In his mind he heard Lord Jesus' final sermon, "Whatever you do for one of the least of these brothers and sisters of mine, you do for me." And at the Last Supper Christ washed his disciples' feet. Is that what God wanted from him? Why this challenge so late in his life? It was supposed to be a time for tranquility. Father Custeau raised his voice to drown out his thoughts.

After chanting the mass, Father Custeau fled to his rooms. He fell into the leather chair beside his desk. He prayed for God to show him the way. He hadn't beseeched God with such intensity since he was a boy. At that time Father Theophane had inspired him to devote his life to Viet Nam. A hundred years before Theophane had calmly walked in chains down the Avenue of the Great Buddha to the site of executions at the edge of the Red River. On that day the Vietnamese executioner was drunk. The executioner's sword first struck Theophane's cheek, then next cut his throat. A third blow lay the priest's head on his shoulder. The last bent the blade. Finally the executioner finished his work using the saber to saw off the head, raised it in triumph, then threw it to the ground. Or at least so the story went. The body was buried, but the head was displayed on a pike, then thrown in the river. A Christian fisherman recovered it after eleven days.

Father Custeau first heard the story at the Seminary for the Foreign Missions in Paris, where Theophane's headless body had been entombed. His head had been left at the Shrine of Martyrs in Tonkin. For reasons only God might ascertain, that story inspired Father Custeau to the life of a missionary. At the time he'd believed all men the same, language the only barrier separating them from the righteous path of God. Later he understood he'd been mistaken to think that over generations the missionaries had failed for so simple a reason.

Now as he silently prayed, footsteps in the hallway halted outside the library. Someone was prying at the secret passage. Had the pickpockets from the streets invaded his parish with their sacrilege? Was a petty thief the answer to his prayers?

Armed with the old bishop's staff he'd never claim, he seized the library key from its hook. The hallway was empty. The secret panel had been replaced. He turned the key in the library lock and forced his shoulder against the door.

"Oh God," Father Custeau struggled to control his voice. "Why have you returned?"

—∿—

The last sunlight of day reached the pinnacle of the stained glass windows where the angels danced near God as Father Custeau watched Phan flee the church, watched him, then ran after him to the door, almost crying out to him to return just before the door slammed shut. But what would he have said in response to such ingratitude?

My life's mission has ended in failure, he thought as he returned to his rooms. Fifty-five years a priest, and now they have all left me. The French parishioners had returned, but to a missionary they meant nothing. I might have stayed in France for all the good I've done. I have failed, I have failed, he repeated, and for an instant thinking of the pistol in his desk, there to protect him from the lawlessness in an ungodly, sinful world. He caught himself, the fleeting thought the worse of mortal sins. He imposed three days of fasting and flogging upon himself, but to what use?

When Judas betrayed Christ, Christ forgave him, just as Father Custeau now wanted to forgive Phan and all the Vietnamese whose souls were lost. In the nave Father Custeau paused before the altar. He prayed for his own death, one befitting a saint, that he might join with those buried in martyrdom beneath the cathedral floor.

When he reached his rooms, he knelt at the small altar

across from his desk and continued to pray for absolution for the poor souls of his Vietnamese, the fallen children of God. He felt the power of his prayer returning his strength. He prayed that the French army might quickly restore the Vietnamese to the church they'd forsaken. He felt God's will cast off his own doubts. When he rose from his prayers, as he braced his age-weakened knees by grasping the bureau, he felt a strange relief in the knowledge his faith had been tested. It was what he needed, a new struggle against something besides the losing battle against old age. He held to the certainty of God's will being done. He paused before the altar, crossed himself, then left the room.

In his bedroom he stretched out with his back on the board that had served as his bed for years. The board never straightened his body contours completely, but until the last few years it had delayed the curvature of his spine. Even in the middle of the day the interior room remained too dark for him to see with his failing eyesight more than the outline of his old sea trunk and a stool in the corner, all he owned or would ever own in accordance with his vow of poverty. His other acquisitions had always been for the church and for it alone. Greed for the Lord wasn't greed at all. He tried to remember when he first understood the distinction. As his eyes adjusted to the darkness, an altar boy rose from a stool on which he'd secretly been napping, "I'm sorry, father, I didn't hear you come in. Is there something I can do?"

"Leave me some privacy," Father Custeau snapped, then caught himself. "No, please stay."

The boy was handsome in a boyish way with his ambiguous origins mixed in the French and Vietnamese that was betrayed by his eyes. Father Custeau admired his skin texture, clear and golden from playing in the sun. He was beautiful in God's eyes, but would never be accepted by either the French or the Vietnamese communities in which he would have to live. At least there were others like him in the orphanage.

"Why aren't you in class?" Father Custeau demanded.

"I fell asleep." The boy's voice tightened.

"Come over here." Father Custeau touched the board

on which he rested. The boy complied, only pulling back for an instant when the priest put his arm around the boy's shoulder. "You've done this before. You must learn the self-discipline to break sinful habits, if you hope to ever escape Satan's grip."

"Yes, father." The boy fidgeted nervously, finger with finger.

Father Custeau rose and thrust his feet back into the sandals at the foot of his bed. "Now we'll take you back to class. And don't play with your fingers." He struck the boy's knuckles with a ruler that he kept concealed within the arm of his robe.

CHAPTER 7

Ha Noi, September 4, 1945
Mueller
Reenlistment

Mueller waited for a fare in the French quarter. Nightlife died early. He struck his foot against the gas pedal, catching the engine before it stalled and reviving it in a crescendo. The old Citroën spit a plume of smoke. "Damn frog cars," he muttered. He squeezed the steering wheel, and admired the strength of his gnarled hands. He smiled as he thought about the necks his hands had garroted. In the poor light he reexamined the small scaly red bumps that had covered his body for several weeks. He swallowed hard to clear his sore throat, then cursed. He was a soldier, not a cab driver. Not once sick in the field. Damn luck. Germany invaded France just when he received his sergeant's stripes in the foreign legion. All that time wasted.

"Chevron, you're the only one never deserted me." He stroked the wiry fur of the dog next to him. The mutt with German shepherd blood slept, his stomach rising and falling evenly against the seat's plastic covering. Then the dog's head twitched up and down and short breaths escaped between its teeth. Mueller snapped his finger against the dog's nose, and it went back into a deep sleep.

Mueller had been born in Germany during the Great War. His old man had never returned from that war. His mother said the old man had gone off and got himself killed, but with no pictures, no letters, Mueller suspected he'd just run off at the thought of the responsibility. Besides, Mueller's mother was a whore in her ways and never satisfied with just one man. When she died Mueller decided nothing tied him to a country that couldn't provide a decent job. The French foreign legion paid him well and sent him half way around the world to bully little heathens into Christian ways. Nothing to it, going into villages that somehow forgot the taxes they owed the French, marching the men off tied to each other, ropes around their necks, and leading them out of sight. Then the legionnaires hacked them to death with machetes or they sometimes choked them to avoid screams. They never shot the men, saving bullets for the villages that resisted, the same villages they burned afterwards as examples to the rest.

All the time he saved his pay, what he didn't spend on whores and liquor. When the Germans took on the French again, he was prepared. Thinking they'd throw him out of the legion, even though he hated Germany, he resigned his NCO commission. With his savings he bought the old Citroën. That was five years ago. He had got by driving the taxi, talking little to his passengers, afraid they'd hear his accent and cheat him out of the fare by using their French patriotism as an excuse. Later he learned the French had let the German soldiers remain in the legion.

When the Japanese took over Viet Nam, things improved for Mueller. His French passengers feared him during the Japanese occupation. But now the Japanese had lost the war, and it was hard again. Lately he'd taken Vietnamese riders, even though they couldn't afford the full fare.

Chevron started to whimper in his sleep. Mueller backhanded the dog. A French soldier on guard against looting marched back and forth under a street light in front of the ca-

thedral. Mueller knew the man was not a legionnaire because
his fear kept him in the shadows. The soldier glanced his way,
then swung around when the cathedral door squeaked open.
A thin man in a poorly fitting suit slid out. He was too tall for
Vietnamese, yet lacked the arrogant stride of a Frenchman.
Mueller glimpsed another man still inside. The soldier lifted
his rifle from his shoulder. The figure ran directly to Mueller's
Citroën and slid into the back seat. Chevron snarled, his head
over the back of the seat. Mueller grabbed his collar and at the
same time tightened his grip on the pistol in his lap.

"Payment in advance. And no funny business back
there or I'll sic the dog on you."

The fare leaned forward, offering a folded bill. Mueller
snapped it from his hand, examined it in the glimmer of the
street lights reflected inside the car. "Where to?"

"My newspaper office."

"Where's that?"

The fare explained.

Mueller tucked the money inside his shirt pocket. He
wedged the pistol between his legs and pulled away from the
curb. Chevron pressed his nose against the passenger side
window. Mueller reached across and cranked the window
down several inches. He kept an eye on the back seat fare
and a hand on the horn. He drove the narrow streets too fast
for funny business from the fare who he now had figured as
a Chinaman. Everybody had big ideas for Viet Nam, but why
was a Chinaman leaving a French church? Likely a spy, taking
French money. No matter, take a hundred yellows like him to
lick even the most inept squad of legionnaires if it ever came
to it. Watching the sneaky Chinaman, he almost missed the
turn for Hai Ba Trung Street. He cut into oncoming traffic,
the trishaws and bikes veering to avoid him. He pounded the
horn. Chevron barked at anyone who came close to the window.

"That keeps them on their toes," Mueller muttered,
laughing as the fare slid across the plastic covered seat, too late
grabbing for the strap inside the door. The fare's face turned
white. Nothing to those Chinaman, Mueller thought. Speed-

ing down unnamed alleys, he drove across the city, the Citroën's one working headlight splashing off blank walls. The air battered against the side of Mueller's face with a sound like the ocean and the faint taste of salt. Alive and free, no past to plague him, cause him pain.

"There's the building. That's the building," the fare shouted from the back seat.

Mueller felt the hand against his shoulder, shaking him. He struck the brakes, pumping his foot not to skid, felt the weight of his passenger thrown against the back of his seat. "Not bad time," Mueller said. Chevron started growling again.

The fare leaned against the door until it opened and almost fell as he stumbled from the car. He disappeared inside the newspaper office. A gang of kids from the shadows pressed against the car, several leaning through the open window, their weight too much for Mueller to crank it up. Chevron leaped across Mueller's lap. The kids drew back.

"*Di di mao, di di mao*," Mueller repeated the words he'd learned for get away. He held the dog back with the side of his arm. A youth jumped forward and tore Mueller's watch off his wrist. Mueller threw the door open and chased him. The dog barked and bounded forward. The boy fled down the middle of the street but never turned into an alley, no dark, dead-end trap. So it wasn't robbery. The thought flashed across Mueller's mind, if not to rob, than what?

Mueller whirled around in time to see the Citroën explode. Black smoke settled around the car. A crowd gathered and watched shop owners throw buckets of water on the fire. Mueller surveyed the crowd, his pistol concealed under his shirt. His recent fare emerged from a door and studied the car, peering inside the black remains. So that was it. Mueller whistled for his dog. He walked past the crowd towards the French army barracks. Chevron caught up with him at the end of the block.

"Good dog," Mueller said. "You get a piece of that kid?"

At the front desk Mueller asked to see the sergeant in

charge of enlistments. A guard watched him with the polite disdain legionaries felt for civilians. To Mueller these men in the rear weren't soldiers; they were clerks with uniforms who only used weapons once a year for a rifle proficiency test.

"You ready for me now?" Mueller spoke in his best French to a sergeant who sat at the desk.

"What you looking for, Fritz?" The French sergeant was immaculate, not a button out of place, just like they pictured the legionaries on recruitment posters.

"The little bastards blew up my car."

"Bad luck for you, Fritz," the desk sergeant said.

"I want my sergeant's rank back."

"A sergeant? You were a sergeant?" The sergeant stared across the desk. "No dogs in here, Fritz."

"The dog stays. That's the deal." Mueller reached across the desk, seized the sergeant by the throat and squeezed his high-buttoned collar at the Adam's apple, drawing him forward to keep him off balance. He stared into the bulging eyes and smiled, then threw the sergeant back into his chair.

Mueller received a cash bonus and at the end of the five-year enlistment he'd get a bonus, enough to retire on the economy if he survived. The desk sergeant wrote the figures on a paper for Mueller's signature. A paper Mueller couldn't read. Mueller never uttered a word, unwilling to let that little man gloat.

"Something the matter?" the desk sergeant said. "After this there aren't any more forms to fill out."

"Nothing the matter." Mueller signed with a mark, but the desk sergeant made no comment. He stood and stuck out his hand. Mueller felt the limp soft skin of a woman, but he shook it. "One more thing."

"What's that?"

"Tell the Surete the newspaper down the street is a nest for Viet Minh."

"That so?"

CHAPTER 8

Ha Noi, September 13, 1945
Phan
War news. Haunting memories.

The headlines from the south were never good:

Sai Gon, September 13,1945--BRITISH ENTER SAI GON, ACCEPT JAPANESE SURRENDER, BRITISH GENERAL GRACEY REFUSES TO MEET WITH VIET MINH;

Sai Gon, September 17, 1945--VIET MINH STRIKE IN SAI GON;

Sai Gon, September 21, 1945--GRACEY DECLARES MARTIAL LAW IN SOUTH VIET NAM;

Sai Gon, September 22, 1945--GRACEY ARMS FRENCH;

Sai Gon, September 23, 1945--FRENCH SEIZE CITY, ARREST VIET MINH GOVERNMENT OFFICIALS, MASSACRE VIETNAMESE;

Sai Gon, September 25, 1945--FRENCH MASSACRED

BY VIETNAMESE.

In the north the news was little better. Phan sat behind his desk reading the fragmented reports. The Chinese General Lu Han had crossed the border into Ton Kin to accept the Japanese surrender and was followed by Vietnamese nationalists allied to Chang Kai Shek. Only Ho's bribes held back the Chinese troops, who were little more than gangs of cutthroats.

—⁂—

Asleep at his desk, Phan dreamed he stood in a field at his home in China, his mother screaming and rushing toward him. As he admired the soldiers on horses approach their village, she swept him into her arms. When she lowered them into a well, he held tight to her neck, crying at her suddenness and seeing her fear. She stood in water to her waist and whispered for him not to cry. They'd be safe if they kept quiet. His feet hung in the cold water. It was too dark to see. The light above them was filled with screams and running horses. A bucket splashed next to him, and then was drawn up by unseen arms. Soldiers cursed the dirty water, threw the bucket back but never looked down.

It seemed they stood for days, first listening to the screams, then a dreadful silence. His mother was afraid to crawl up the five meters of wall. Then came a voice, his mother's cry of relief, and his father's face peering down at them. After his father pulled him on a rope, up over the muddy edge, Phan understood his mother's fear. The village still smoldered, each house a heap of charred wood. His aunt, an uncle, all his cousins, and the children he played with were piled outside the school. His father and another uncle had escaped because they'd been searching the jungle for a runaway ox.

So they rebuilt, but the warlords returned, mounted on steeds that, as Phan had grown older, seemed more like old mules than horses. This time his parents only had time to hide him before the soldiers broke down the door. From under the floor he watched pants and feet through the cracks. His parents' bodies twitched on the floor above him. Soldiers stepped into their wounds to make them scream. Not once did either of his parents glance in his direction. The soldiers searched their pockets, stripped off their clothes, and dragged their naked bodies into the street. Town dogs sniffed at them and licked their blood.

Later Phan was yanked from beneath the floor. He struggled to break free, but it was his uncle who rushed him past his parents' corpses and carried him across a rice paddy and into the jungle. The rifle fire still crackled from the village as they fled deeper into the jungle. Weeks later, nearly starved, they crossed into Viet Nam. His uncle left him with the first person willing to take him, a Catholic priest stationed near the border who processed orphans for the church.

Now Phan sobbed at his desk. He coughed and spit into a spittoon left behind by the French reporters. He rustled papers across the desk to conceal the sounds.

—∿—

Over the next few months a steady gale of news crossed Phan's desk. It seemed Ho embraced free elections. The January elections carried the Viet Minh to power in the National Assembly. Ho Chi Minh took office as president of the country, elected to head a Viet Minh that included communists, nationalists, Catholics and even some Mandarins who favored the emperor's return. Phan was elated despite new doubts about communist intentions. What danger could just ten communists in the legislature pose?

The Chinese and French reached mutually beneficial accords. The French would give up all claims to Chinese soil and in turn received assurances that Viet Nam belonged to them. Phan penned frantically: *The Chinese gave up what wasn't theirs to give.* The circulation of the paper increased. Independence whet the popular appetite for news. Phan collected the news and digested it for the Vietnamese, and he spoke with a clear message to the French: *Hands off.*

Phan left the office later each night, retreated down deserted streets, and fell onto the floor next to his wife. Asleep instantly, his body thrashed restlessly. Thi tried to coax him back to her, but neither her body nor her words worked. Finally, she slept on a separate mat.

In the morning Phan woke with a single thought: to gain freedom for his adopted homeland. His wife extended a steaming bowl of pho to him. He put it to his lips.

"Why can't you stay here today?" his wife asked.

Their son cried.

"Can't you keep him quiet?" Phan said.

"It's the only time you ever notice him."

"I'm expected at the paper."

"Stay and try your luck at cards," Thi said. "You're good at cards. The men always play in the stairway. We could use a little luck and a little extra money above what they pay you."

"No time."

"I know the French have reestablished military control." Thi said.

"Not completely. They still may give us our independence within a French federation." Phan shifted his eyes to the floor.

"We still have time."

"For what?" Phan snapped.

"To return to our village."

"The French must never again control us." Phan was on his feet.

"You must think of your family," Thi shouted, but Phan was already into the stairway.

CHAPTER 9

The Mediterranean Sea, February 3, 1946
Pasteur
Beyond a father's reach

The *Bearn's* reflection floated on the water under the sun's golden shield. As the ship's wake disturbed the Mediterranean where Tyrian warriors once sailed to foreign shores, Lieutenant Pasteur felt their spirit.... *Arma virumque cano, Troiae qui primus ab oris, Italiam, fato profugus, Laviniaque venit....* he recited from a tattered book he kept tucked inside his officer's tunic, a constant companion since his English school days.

Among the few to escape France with his family before the war, Lieutenant Pasteur's father had given Pasteur no alternative but to endure an English boarding school. At the time Pasteur overheard his mother arguing against sending him off. She wanted him taught at home, but her soft weeping only increased his father's determination and her reasons failed.

"The boy can learn a lot from the British," his father had said.

At boarding school Pasteur's middle-aged classics instructor always wore a black academic robe, for fear he took it off they'd send him to fight on the continent. The instructor's bow tie remained perfectly squared, his mustache trimmed, his English saturated with academic preen. He lectured on how Wellington won at Waterloo, how Henry the Eighth became a hero and was not really, as they said, a philanderer of note. The instructor claimed the kings of England descended from great Aeneas of Troy. But about Napoleon's conquests or English treachery against Joan of Arc, not a word.

The instructor repeatedly reprimanded Pasteur for his inattention: if the French had observed what happened to other nations and not collaborated with the Nazis, the war might have been shorter. It was a matter of flawed character. The other boys in the class had kept quiet, lowering their heads to hide their smirks.

Lieutenant Pasteur spit into the sea, straightened the gig line of his tunic, belt and pants, then crossed the converted aircraft carrier's deck. The press in his khaki trousers had vanished in the heat. His tunic was wrinkled and stained with sweat around the armpits. He gripped the steel stair rail to the bridge. A shiver ran through his neck and into his arms. With a touch to the brim of his kepi, he presented himself on the bridge. The commander chortled and clicked his heels. His paunch stretched his uniform at the waist. The tailings from meals stained his shirt.

"You look surprised," the commander said. Years of salt and wind had left his face the hue of teakwood.

"I expected my colonel to be here with you."

"The colonel is indisposed below deck. I don't think life at sea agrees with him." The commander smiled. After an awkward and lengthy pause, he pointed toward a thin bar of land on the horizon. "Son, do you know what that is?"

"No, sir."

"Where it all began, the seed of all great civilizations. The Holy Land of the great Crusades."

"Not much to look at," Lieutenant Pasteur said.

"Don't be too quick to judge. Great men walked across

those sands. Their teachings provided the spark for all our great civilizations."

"And still now, sir?"

"I should think so. The colonies still need Christian guidance, or they will lapse into barbaric ways." The commander secured the wheel with a loop of hemp.

"I'm ready to be posted, sir. I volunteered for Indochina and received specialized training to understand the jungles, rice paddies, and villages. My training ended months ago."

"You'll get there soon enough." The commander leaned forward in his chair. "It's a nasty place, Viet Nam, with an abhorrent climate and vile food. And don't expect those heathens to follow the rules of warfare. The Orientals are a godless race, and cunning fellows you can never trust. Turn your back, you'll pay a price. When you have a choice, avoid them altogether. Stick with your own kind."

"I'll manage, sir."

"I know you will, son." The commander's tone had changed. He checked the charts spread across a mahogany table behind the pilot's wheel, measuring distances and directions with a protractor. "Thought you might consider being my liaison to the army. That would keep you with my ship."

"Is that what you want, or is it what my father wants?"

"Wouldn't hurt your career."

"Or yours, I suppose, my father being who he is."

"Son, you should listen to advice."

"I do listen. I just don't always agree."

"We'll have to see whether they have a use for you ashore."

"I already have orders."

The full beard that hung like a walrus's tusk from the commander's protruded chin couldn't hide his dour expression. The lieutenant grasped the rail that marked the limits of the bridge.

"Your father's a fine diplomat, untainted by the Vichy thing. He made quite a name for himself in the resistance."

"He never left England."

"I was surprised General de Gaulle didn't call on him when he formed his government. Or did your father decline?"

"We don't talk about those things."

"Your loyalty to him is ... commendable."

"Sir, my father and I seldom speak."

"Just like my son." The commander clenched his fist. "But assure me you have more reason to refuse my offer than just a family quarrel."

"Sir, before my father, our family met its obligations to France by serving as active duty officers in the finest French regiments. My grandfather trained at Saint Cyr and like so many of his countrymen, died in the trenches near the Marne. I intend to carry on in that tradition."

"What you do in Viet Nam won't make any difference. Why not please your father by serving as my aid?"

"Because then I would betray the tradition of my forefathers."

"You never trained at Saint Cyr."

"There was a war prevented it. The English trained me well at their military schools."

"Nothing is the equal of Saint Cyr. I'm sure even now your father could see to your admission. Then you'd be properly prepared for Indochina."

"And maybe too late? I went through an English officer's training program."

"And got that scar across your cheek there? Not very promising."

"A prank, sir, as you know doubt know from my father. I got the idea from the ancient dueling societies. I used a razor. Put salt in the scar to keep it from healing too quickly."

"A proper job, I'd say. It botched your good looks. But this is more serious. You throw away your life." The commander flung his protractor across the chart table. "You're dismissed."

Lieutenant Pasteur rushed from the bridge, the rattle of the metal stairs following him below deck. He hit his head in a passageway, swearing as he emerged in the converted hanger where his men lounged and slept in hammocks strung three high. The stagnant air burned his nostrils. He tried to catch his breath. The only light came from the amber glow of small overhead lanterns.

When he entered the room, a guttural voice from a smog of cigar smoke called the soldiers to attention. Several soldiers sprang to their feet; others hid in their hammocks feigning sleep. Soldiers stood in their underwear at the foot of their hammocks, dragons, naked girls, the names of sweethearts long gone, tattooed in their farmer's tans. This menagerie of soldiers drew back their shoulders causing their chests to protrude, some hairless, some matted with black curls, one concave. Their faces perspired, the smell from their sweat mixed with the stench of burning diesel fuel.

"Carry on," Lieutenant Pasteur said, slipping down the row between the hammocks. He spoke to each in turn, concerned over each soldier's health, his mother or wife back home, a sweetheart not heard from in weeks. He ignored the smell of stale wine.

A soldier tipped another from his hammock. The unshaven man cursed and staggered to his feet. He snapped to attention. His arms and face were bruised from brawling. A scar zig-zagged across his groin. A nervous smile exposed decayed teeth. "Good morning, sir."

"Good morning, private." Lieutenant Pasteur was bad at names. He stepped away from the soldier.

"A word with you, sir." The soldier followed him.

"What is it?"

"About a mistake, sir. I was supposed to remain in France."

"You volunteered."

"Not for this. The magistrate promised no charges if I joined the army. No mention was ever made of the colonies."

"What charges were dropped?"

"Armed robbery."

"Consider yourself fortunate. You'll use the firearms you covet."

"What's that sir?"

"Just be satisfied you're not in prison."

The soldiers around the private chuckled.

"I don't think he understands what you're saying," one of the soldiers said.

"You explain it," Lieutenant Pasteur said. Looking back at him, the private's face had a terrible color of death to it. Later, thinking it over, the lieutenant decided it was the lantern's yellow light filtered through the smoke.

CHAPTER 10

Ha Noi, February 15, 1946
Lao
Life in the streets

The voices of Frenchmen carried across the market like syncopated drums. At toilet squatting in the alley, young Lao heard them and bounced to his feet, quickly tying the twine that held his shorts to his slight waist. Priests searched the streets for young boys to place in their orphanages. The priests had taken him four years ago, but he'd escaped with his only friend Khong. He grimaced as he anticipated the chase.

The priests served the dead on a cross, whose blood they drank, whose flesh they ate. They told terrifying stories from their book: people turned to pillars of salt, rivers parted to swallow armies, fire raining from the sky. They hung strange creatures from the corners of their buildings. They took money from the poor and built their temples for the man on the cross. They used French soldiers to jail or guillotine those who spoke against them. They called his ungodly innocence a sin. Lao figured they wanted to take away his freedom and steal his soul.

Lao crouched beside a sack of rice behind a crate of chickens in the street. Khong hid beside him. Lao heard the chickens snapping their beaks at insects on the ground and at each other as they crowded together in the corner of the cage farthest from him. His nose burned with their smell.

"Keep quiet or the priests will find us," Lao whispered to Khong, signaling him to crouch down. No one had taught Lao survival, but he had learned by watching the older orphans who skulked about in the city. He developed his own instincts and never befriended the other children, because he knew that when they gathered they drew attention to themselves. As long as no one noticed him, he would remain free. In his fantasies he used this ability to perform heroic acts, frequently slaying the dragons that appeared in his dreams, looking more like gigantic rats than the way he'd seen them portrayed on the walls of the church.

The priests swept across the road like gigantic bats in a flock, their robes swirling into wings. They rushed past the chickens, their sandals snapping against the bottoms of their feet. They turned over booths and interrogated women squatting behind baskets of produce.

"Get out of there, you runt." A merchant behind Lao raised a stick. "You urchins have got to learn. There'll be no stealing here."

"I'm not stealing sir," Lao whispered, pulling out the pockets to his shorts. The man started after him with the stick.

"Run, run now," Lao warned Khong. Darting deeper into the alley, he tripped and fell over a discarded box. He flung himself against a wall of shadows.

"Now we're safe," he said.

Lao squinted at the market to see if the priests reacted to the clamor. A priest had caught another little boy by his hair. The other priests continued the search in a sweep across the square. He heard their every word. "The Lord has called on us to save your children. Deliver the little lambs of God to us, and the Lord's mercy will be upon you."

A crowd of the poor and homeless gathered along the edge of the marketplace, their rage restrained to watching. A bald priest, gasping for breath in the heat, approached them. "God's children," he said. "Make peace with God and find salvation."

"Tell your god to be wary!" a voice from the crowd shouted, but no one moved against him or the other priests.

"Who called out against the Lord?" the priest demanded. The crowd remained silent. The other priests having completed their search ambled towards the crowd, turning over crates they might have missed and sampling an old woman's fruits. The crowd disbursed as the bald priest increased the pitch of his harangue. Lao edged toward the street, curious but staying in the shadows. "Keep behind me," he warned Khong.

A Vietnamese wearing a French uniform came out of the crowd and took the bald priest aside. Although Lao couldn't understand the foreign words, he felt his stomach tightening. He remained hidden and waited for the soldier to leave. He heard something behind him in the alley....other soldiers. As he ran between the booths, the soldiers caught him and held him for the priest. The priest picked Lao up by his shoulders. The priest's shaved head glistened with sweat. Sweat soaked his robes and stunk of aged perfume. Lao turned his head away from the smell. The priest shook Lao.

"You look familiar," the bald priest said.

"Let me go," Lao demanded. "You have no right."

"We have the Lord's right."

Up close the priest smelled like the cats in the alley, and it burned Lao's nose. Nothing about the gigantic priest was natural. His eyes bulged like saucers; his teeth protruded from stained lips like the tusks of a frenzied beast. Strong for a holy man, the priest had lifted Lao off the ground as if he inspected a chicken.

"You sure I don't know you?" the priest said.

Lao remembered the priest. He remembered how the priest forgave at the price of a whipping. Lao figured there had to be a worse punishment for escaping from the orphanage even if he'd only been held there a week. It had been long enough to realize that he preferred the freedom to live, sleep, and beg in the streets to their routine of work and prayer.

"What's on your legs?" The priest examined him, probing the red welts that ran up Lao's spindly legs.

"Your asshole soldiers with their cigarettes," Lao struggled to break loose.

"I'll teach you not to curse." The priest struck Lao across the buttocks. "You learn how to act and the soldiers will have no need to punish you."

"I want to stay here," Lao said. His beseeching black eyes were lost in sockets hollowed by hunger and lack of sleep.

"Living in the streets with the dogs? Look at you. You're half naked, filthy with fleas, and as ill mannered as any wild animal."

"I want to stay here," Lao repeated.

"You don't know any better."

"Never want to either."

The priest struck Lao across the buttocks repeatedly. "You're coming with us. A good bathing, clean clothes, then we'll get you into school."

"I'm too old."

"You can't be twelve. Still time for you to learn. Soon enough we'll make you into a God-fearing boy." The priest tightened his grip on Lao's arm.

Lao told himself not to listen to the priest's words, for he had seen their power. Converted men threw away the family altar and replaced it with an image of the man on the cross. Then like men with amnesia the converted forgot to care for their ancestors' graves. No matter that Lao had no family altar, he wasn't going to allow the priests to turn him against his kind.

Lao bit the priest's hand. He tasted salt and blood. The priest howled a curse as he tried to pull his hand away. Lao held firm. The priest shook like a buffalo in a water hole. He stepped back, tripped over his robe and fell, carrying Lao over with him. Lao landed on the huge priest as if tossed on a bed. His jaw snapped free of the priest, a piece of flesh between his teeth. He spat it like spoiled food. They remained entangled. The agony in the sweating priest's face frightened Lao. He struggled to his feet. He glanced towards the alley, but a crowd blocked his escape. Priests rushed toward him from all directions, their robes in surly billows. He darted toward the crowd, prepared to flay his arms and vanish in their midst. An old man waved to him and stepped aside. The crowd folded behind him and faced the priests as a wall. Lao grinned and shouted back, "You'll never take me to an orphanage," then turned and ran down the alley.

Lao had no plan. At the end of the alley, he turned down Hang Quat Street, coffins for sale along the street with beautiful gold leaf laid over black and red enamel. Somewhere his own parents lay in such boxes, or they'd protect him. He hurried past the coffins, then turned down Hang Thiec Street where tin-box makers pounded and cut the metal. Lao glanced back to make sure no one followed him. He'd formulate a plan and discuss it with Khong. He changed direction and headed for the road north to the village of Tong.

—⚭—

There were no priests at Tong's bars, where girls of pleasure plied their trade and money freely flowed to the tune of laughter and the pleasure of momentary forgetfulness. He thought of the opportunities: he'd run errands for the girls, who seldom ventured into the streets to face cat calls from the soldiers. Maybe he'd even pimp, shine boots for French soldiers, and steal their wallets if the chance arose, or beg for an imaginary family.

In the dim light of the first alley, a legless trash picker confronted him, waved a stick that he threw down, charging forward on a board with wheels, his arms working in coordinated sweeps. Lao hesitated, fascinated by the rhythmic movement of board and man, then darted past. Just out of reach, he asked what was the matter. The trash picker swore at him. Lao continued to the next street.

Scarlet letters hung as nightclub signs. Music throbbed from open doors. Call girls in the doorways chatted in twos and threes and winked at soldiers walking down the street. Sheltering themselves with fashionable umbrellas, they were women for men's dreams: High heels, short skirts, faces painted red with rouge and black with eyeliner that set them apart from the common peasant girls.

A girl caught Lao by the arm. Long legs exposed, hair bobbed, she floated ethereally, her body's fragrance the pollen of flowers. Her touch weakened his resolve.

"Leah, we better get back to the club," said another taller girl with smooth black skin.

"Come with us," the one called Leah said. Her supple fingers entwined his calloused hand. "I'm sure you could use some food."

"I'm no beggar," Lao said.

"You are a cute boy," Leah said, tousling his hair. "Just come along."

"Is it all right to go?" Lao said.

"Who are you speaking to?" Leah glanced down the empty street.

"My friend," Lao said.

Leah laughed. "What's your invisible friend's name?"

"His name is Khong." Lao said. "And he's not invisible.

"Bring him along."

"Little beggar looks like he could be your brother," the taller girl said to Leah.

Lao yanked away. "I'm not her brother,"

"Of course you're not," Leah said, stepping back. "Dawn knows how much I need a man to help me. Don't suppose you'd be that man?"

"Depends."

"Depends on what?"

"What you're going to pay."

"How about we feed you for a start, then see if we can come to terms."

"All right," Lao said. "But I'm not promising anything."

"A deal," Leah said.

Lao intended to watch everything they did, and hear what they really had in mind. He followed Leah from the street through the front door of the club. Music came from somewhere along the wall.

"Why did you bring that child in here? No place for a child. "

Lao moved from the doorway's shaft of light, his eyes adjusting to the dank room. The woman who bellowed was unlike anything Lao had seen before, even among the French. She sat in the corner on an armless chair, like an old frog squatting on a stump. Her legs spread, the fat of her thighs, encased in pale white skin, merged. She continually wiped her face with lace handkerchiefs clutched in puffy hands. Otherwise she was motionless, fanned by young girls quick to respond to her commands.

Leah pushed him forward. He pulled back.

"You be respectful to Mommyson," Leah said.

"Mommyson?" Lao's lip twisted, "That can't be her real name."

The fat shook as she bellowed. "That's right son, but it's all the name you need to know. You come over here, let me take a look at you."

Leah shoved his shoulders, and he stumbled forward across the room, through the pleasure girls and soldiers with unbuttoned tunics. Mommyson's ponderous arms wrapped around him. Her breath forced Lao to turn away.

"What are you afraid of?" the big woman laughed heartily, her jowls shaking the pendulous wattles on each side of her throat.

"Not afraid of anything," Lao said.

"I bet you aren't. That why you got them burns on your legs?" She lifted him, then set him back. "But you're still just a tad, all skin and bones."

"I can work hard."

"I bet you can. Just not here, if that's what you're looking for. Soldiers come here for diversion. I can't have them bothered by street urchins."

"What about the food she promised?" Lao pointed to Leah.

"That true?" Mommyson said.

Leah nodded.

"You can give him the food, then send him on his way."

"Yes, Mommyson," Leah said as she pulled Lao back. At the bar she lifted him onto a stool.

Lao stared into the mirror, curious to see his face, knowing it was his because it moved when he did.

The blackest fellow Lao had ever seen came up to them.

"What's yours today, Miss Leah?" the man said.

"Not me," she said. "The boy needs a bowl of hot pho."

"Guess we can manage it." The man stepped back, took himself a glass, then ice from a bucket, grabbed a bottle from lines of bottles along a shelf behind the bar. A fortune's worth of bottles. Standing with his back to Lao, he poured into a glass, his shaved head glistening in the sick yellow light of the kerosene lanterns. In the mirror, his black face contorted as he drank with no sign of lips, his reflected eyes piercing.

Lao slipped off the stool.

"Where you going boy?" the black man said into the mirror.

"Nature calls."

"Don't you go running off on us."

"I'm only going out back," Lao said.

"The pho be ready when you get back."

Lao headed towards a door that could only lead to the alley, all the time looking around like a tourist. Along the bar the girls leaned against French soldiers, touching them here and there. On the walls naked women lounged within the frames of smoke stained paintings. He walked between young women sitting around tables and waiting for more French soldiers to appear. They smiled and winked at him. He looked down to avoid their stares. Why were they laughing? Didn't they remember how it was before they found this place?

He stood just outside the door and peed against the wall among the dark stains from others. In the piles of trash he kicked away the nesting rats and gathered chewed cardboard and cans to construct a hut. "These will work to deflect the rain," he said, turning toward the wall where Khong stood. "If the boxes are not disturbed when we return, it will be safe. We'll stay here for now. Never mind about Mommyson. She won't find out about us out here."

"Gone a long time," the black man said. He pushed a bowl across the bar.

Lao put the bowl to his lips.

"I gave you a spoon," the black man said.

Lao put down the empty bowl. "Thanks."

The black man laughed. "Here, have another. Use the spoon."

Lao climbed up on a stool and brought the bowl in front of him. He held the spoon like a pencil and put it to his lips.

"You can slow down," the black man said. "You're safe in here."

CHAPTER 11

Ha Long Bay, Viet Nam; May 1, 1946
Pasteur
Military preparations

Lieutenant Pasteur had read that in spring the Red River surged from the north, flooded into the delta, and encircled Ha Noi. The river carried red sediment towards Hai Phong, leaving behind a residue of muddy water which nourished the rice fields. The river divided into other rivers, and other rivers joined into it. The intermingling rivers spread wider and wider, and year after year extended silt further into the sea.

Where the Gulf of Tonkin met the Cua Cam River, the salt water and silt intermingled into frothing foam. To the north and east, several thousand islands ruptured from the sea, great knees of limestone aged with rings worn by millennia of tidal surges; beyond them clear salt water reached to bottomless depths. At twilight the islands resembled Chinese dragons arching from the ocean to surround Ha Long Bay.

The *Bearn* had anchored with the French fleet. It was the largest ship among the flotilla of cruisers, destroyers, and other transport ships. Lieutenant Pasteur's soldiers were to disembark onto landing craft and travel upriver. Tides dictated the time. Meanwhile Pasteur used the deck as a harsh training site, a desert without sand. His platoon fixed bayonets and changed formations. He directed them in scrimmages against an imaginary enemy at the stern, forcing the platoon to fire and maneuver until it became second nature. A slight breeze from off shore provided little relief from their exhaustion.

A soldier fell from the ranks.

"Get him on his feet," Lieutenant Pasteur ordered.

"I think he has sun stroke, sir."

"Get him on his feet."

A sailor rose from the shade of the conning tower and dragged a fire hose across the deck. The first burst from the hose hissed as it struck the deck. The surge of water knocked several soldiers off their feet. Sailors on the bridge jeered. The soldier who had fainted rose to his feet. A weasel-faced soldier in the second rank raised his rifle towards the sailors.

"Steady there," Lieutenant Pasteur said, pressing the barrel of the rifle toward the deck.

"I wasn't going to shoot them," the soldier said. "Just fire off a round over their heads."

Something about the weasel-faced soldier made the lieutenant hesitate. He was new to the platoon, brought aboard with several others at Sai Gon. Experienced men, the colonel said as he assigned them to the platoons. Good additions. They understand the cunning of the Viets, he had added. Been in Asia through the war. Jap prisoners near the end. It explains their emaciation, but they'll be fit soon enough, just get them back on French rations.

"You fagots." The weasel-faced soldier shouted and made an obscene gesture at the sailors on the bridge.

"Leave them alone. We fight for the same thing. "

"No, lieutenant." The weasel-faced soldier glared at Pasteur and caressed his rifle. "Not any more."

"Maybe it's not immediately obvious," the lieutenant said.

"We're all in this for what we get," said the weasel-faced soldier. "There's plenty to speak for your kind. The rest of us just maintain your kind's wealth. It's not a new thing." The soldier walked toward the bridge.

"Stand at attention," Pasteur ordered. The weasel-faced soldier continued to walk away. Pasteur drew his pistol. "I said stand at attention."

The weasel-faced soldier glanced back and halted when he saw the pistol pointed at his face. Pasteur designated two men in the formation. "Take his rifle..... take him below. I'll deal with him later. The rest of you, that's all for now. Dismissed."

The platoon scurried toward the metal lining of the open door that led below deck. Pasteur climbed to the bridge. A local pilot had come aboard during the night and now he directed the ship to its anchorage. Pasteur had met him at breakfast in the officers' wardroom, and the two had talked. Pasteur was eager to learn what the pilot had found behind the Oriental mystique. The pilot was curious what was happening back in France. The pilot had not seen his Paris home since before the war and had heard nothing for the last two years. His family likely thought him dead. His wife had always had eyes for other men, and he doubted she'd waited for him. No matter. The Vietnamese *congais* pleased him and expected very little.

The pilot said that before the war there had never been much of a French navy in Indochina: Two cruisers, less then a dozen gunboats, some flying boats. The British had blockaded the French fleet when the Germans occupied France. One of the cruisers, the *Suffren*, sailed from port and never returned. The other cruiser and some of the gunboats defeated most of the Thai fleet, but without re-supply from France, the ships eventually became casualties of mines, accidents, and lack of parts. The Japanese received control of Indochina from the Vichy government and relegated the French military to administrative duties. In March 1945 the pilot had been imprisoned with the rest of the French military and only recently freed.

Now the pilot signaled Pasteur to join him.

"Was there trouble down there?" the pilot said.

"Nothing I can't handle."

The pilot smiled. "We've all got our hands full."

The pilot said Viet Nam was never going to be the same again for the French. Ho Chi Minh had declared Viet Nam an independent country and his militias still controlled most of the countryside and occupied the major cities of Hai Phong and Ha Noi. The pilot said he was afraid of the greeting awaiting the troops when they disembarked.

The two men sat in deck chairs and drank tea served to them by a coolie the pilot had brought with him. Pasteur asked about the interior. The pilot said he was not familiar with the interior in the north, but he believed it a place to avoid. Years before he had served as an officer with the French Brown River Navy that patrolled the rivers in the southern Mekong Delta. The officers of those gun boats began wearing camouflaged fatigues instead of the white uniforms of the fleet. Then they disappeared from the functions held for French society, preferring the drinking bars that their enlisted men frequented.

The pilot said, "I can see you're a gentleman of good breeding. Let me use my connections to arrange a transfer to the general staff."

Pasteur tried to explain that what he did was by choice, that comfort and safety lacked importance to him and that since childhood he had dreamed of testing his courage. The requirements of duty and patriotism were to be met.

"Let's go below and have lunch in the officers' mess," the pilot said.

Pasteur felt trapped. At the table the pilot ladled a bowl of soup and placed it in front of Pasteur.

"You should try this. Broth and noodles and a little meat. The Vietnamese call it *pho*. They are very proud of it. It is safe since they boil it. If you still insist on going ashore, you must be careful what you eat. They will offer you some very nauseating foods. It isn't pleasant to crawl on your knees vomiting, although it will amuse the Vietnamese."

"I'll be all right."

"You should listen to me. As you see, there are very few of us. The Viet Minh target French officers."

"Why are you so insistent?"

The pilot hesitated, his fork half way to his face, then dropped the fork into the middle of his own tray. He pushed the tray to one side and leaned forward. "The jungle is unforgiving and it gives you very little time to learn. That much knowledge I have gained. I too came here eager to see the world and prove myself. The commander of my first river boat had served in the navy for twenty years, coming up through the ranks. He had little use for academy officers like me. He was a man with nothing to his name, and his family had no title back in France. At the time we were still subduing the interior, expanding French territories from Sai Gon into the Mekong Delta beyond My Tho.

"On our first operation the army led the way. We followed them along the river in our naval gun boats. Every night we linked up. Our boats protected the army from attack over the water. They in turn protected our boats from a land based attack. Every night the infantry and naval officers ate dinner together before returning to their units. We'd listen to the infantry officers bragging of their exploits. Their trucks were loaded with what they called contraband which they openly discussed dividing among themselves, just as armies have done for centuries. One night the talk of contraband included a Rolls Royce.

"My lieutenant was not a clever or original-thinking fellow. He had spent his life taking orders and doing it faithfully without any gain to himself, but those infantrymen gave him an idea. The morning after the Rolls Royce appeared, he ordered us from anchor before the infantry broke camp. We moved down river rapidly until a village came into sight. He ordered the machine guns to fire on it. While it burned, we went ashore, and he selected what was to be loaded on the boats.

"At night we rejoined the infantry and they were decidedly less cordial. We were on to their little game and played it well. We kept this up for weeks, until the boats were loaded to capacity. For another week the lieutenant selected and upgraded what we carried, dumping the second rate into the river. If any of the villagers resisted, the lieutenant ordered their execution. Finally his greed was satiated, or so I thought. We passed several poor villages, leaving them for the infantry.

"At the provincial capital, which was little more than a very small town, the lieutenant ordered the local Vietnamese officials to meet with him. When they arrived, they were greeted with friendly gestures from the lieutenant. He pointed out a stack of French watches which previously, without explanation, he had collected from the crew, including my own fine Swiss that I treasured as a gift from my father. The lieutenant pointed to the booty-laden gun boats. "We've come to trade," he said and waited for the interpreter to translate. None of the village officials spoke. Several rose from where they squatted on the ground. Responding to the lieutenant's gestures, they inspected several watches, including mine. We watched them make their way to the ships and examine the booty, at first from the dock and then at the lieutenant's urging, aboard the ships where they rummaged through stacks of furniture, clothes, images from family altars, oil lamps, a few books. When they returned their demeanor had changed. There was a fervor within their eyes. 'They want to know what you want in exchange,' the interpreter said. 'Money? Silver or gold?'

"The lieutenant spoke with a wry smile, 'Gold or silver. Everything's a bargain. We can't take anything back to Sai Gon.'

"'Even the watches?' the interpreter said, caught up in the excitement.

"'Even the watches.'

"The lieutenant understood the fever of greed. The officials left, and when they returned they carried bags filled with gold and silver, French francs, and the local currency, piasters. Some had brought their wives, others friends with their own hordes of currencies. To this point our raids had never discovered the caches of wealth we suspected were hidden in the villages. Now they openly brought them to us.

"The lieutenant nodded approval. That's the moment I understood what he had planned.

"Treachery," he shouted. "Traitors to France." He raised his pistol and fired into the Vietnamese. The sailors spontaneously fired from the perimeter they'd formed. There was no possibility of escape for those men and women.

"I, too, participated, although I hadn't meant too. I don't know if the lieutenant had informed the sailors what he intended. Certainly I didn't know before the shooting started. He must have figured I'd protest the scheme. When the shooting began, there was a frantic effort by the Vietnamese to escape. I suppose I feared some might be armed. Several men ran toward me. I had drawn my pistol as a reflex. I fired at them before they could reach me. Instinctual, the way we're trained. They fell. Later I saw they were unarmed. It was over in an instant, although now it replays in my mind very slowly.

"The lieutenant returned our watches to us. We kept the booty and the money. The lieutenant divided it between us before entering Sai Gon. I think he gave me more than my share to insure my silence. That was when I recognized the face of France in the lieutenant. We had become little more then pirates. I requested transfer and received it with the lieutenant's blessing. I never said a word about what happened. Only now I'm telling you. Still there isn't a day those images don't haunt me. Now you understand the evil we're doing here?"

The rest of the officers had come in to eat and left. The two remained alone at the table. As the sailors cleared around them, Lieutenant Pasteur grabbed several pieces of chicken from a plate.

"Why did you tell me?" Pasteur quietly demanded.

"If you won't transfer to save your life, perhaps you'll do it for your soul."

Pasteur rose to leave, "I won't miss my chance."

"Where are you going?"

"On deck."

"Be careful, the heat will make you crazy."

Pasteur walked to the bow of the carrier where he observed the bay and mainland coast. A single hawk appeared, soared briefly over the ship as if inspecting it, and then disappeared among the rocks on an island. Otherwise the bay was lifeless. The fishing boats from the morning had drifted away. There was no breeze, and the harbor itself seemed a single silver sheet on which the motionless French fleet rested. The haze obscured the coastal villages wavering within waves of heat, which began at the ships and continued as far as he could see. An unnatural world with no sound, earth bleached of color with no shadows or darkness for squinting eyes to rest and find relief. The sun burned his back and neck, raising blisters. The sun bled the sweat from him until his fatigues resembled dried papyrus. When he rubbed the back of his hand across his cracked and blood-caked lips, his skin tasted of salt. And he understood why men went mad in the sun.

Pasteur wanted to stand there and be alone and think about the things he had heard. There was very little privacy on the *Bearn* since the quarters were cramped and because he imposed continuous training on his men. Now alone and greatly affected by the heat, his thoughts wandered to what he had read about the distant past, a time when the great Vietnamese dynasties of Trinh and Nguyen clashed and the first Portuguese and Dutch traders came ashore with missionaries, who wandered the land converting peasants to Catholicism. They had found the emperors dressed in the armor of knights and armies that fought with lances, swords, and great pikes capable of killing the war elephants that thundered across the delta's open plains trampling those who stood against them. The Europeans had cleverly allied themselves, bringing muskets and cannon to the battlefield in exchange for trading privileges and tolerance of their Catholic religion. Later only French priests like Alexandre de Rhodes remained, their visions longer, determined to stay and convert Indochina into a Christian colony. Those ancient clerics, mere footnotes in history, had a determination that foreshadowed centuries of conflict, and ultimately the realization of their dreams.

Pasteur admired the courage of those men crossing the world in small sailing ships, struggling against disease and primitive conditions, traveling among hostile natives, and often martyred. And what followed was the French military, adventurous and brave against the odds, fighting the savage hordes, who attacked in wave after wave. The French had defeated those Oriental armies with little more than force of will.

As he stood staring toward the shores, Pasteur felt as one with those brave men as they strode ashore, laden with packs and bandoleers of ammunition, soaked with silt from the sea and sweat, raising their rifles high. What had they thought as they faced the vast and hostile land stretched before them? What had driven those men that now drove him? More than mere survival. Forces within them, beyond their control. And what world had they created for him?

That night the colonel alerted Pasteur that the troops were to disembark early the next morning.

CHAPTER 12

Ha Long Bay, March 1, 1946
Haussmann
God's chosen men

The platoon snapped to attention. Their rifles reverberated on the ship's deck. Then the command to port arms. Palms slapped wooden stocks. The platoon pivoted towards the foredeck, Haussmann again part of the whole. He felt the collective consciousness of the men around him and attuned himself to their murderous natures. He felt synchronized to a common cause, emboldened by the righteousness religion taught. His mind rushed ahead to the day they would forge ashore into the darkest jungles, to hunt the unfaithful. A harsh wind carried the stench from that land, reawakening his long-held loathing of the recalcitrant heathens. He trained with God's chosen men who prepared to bring the Vietnamese to account.

As the platoon reeled to face an imaginary enemy, memories caused Haussmann to shudder. In prison the Japanese had isolated him from his platoon and kept him from his Bible. Although he had heard gunfire while in the cell, he'd never believed the stories of Vietnamese resistance against his Japanese wardens. Instead he suspected a conspiracy among the yellow-skinned brothers, a wink and a nod between them.

When the British had freed his unit, many had chosen to return to France. Not Haussmann. In France it would be too difficult for a German, even with the French citizenship the foreign legion would have awarded him. He joined the newly arrived Ninth Infantry aboard the *Bearn* in Sai Gon Harbor on its way to Ha Noi. Once in Ha Noi he figured to transfer back to his old unit.

Confined below deck during the night, Haussmann fell victim to the stagnant air and rolling seas. Around him, even the few men too proud to cry out under Japanese torture crawled about on their hands and knees, moaning and gagging in the stench. In the morning they all found relief on deck. French, German, African all gasped for a whiff of fresh air.

Haussmann caught the line of soldiers in his peripheral vision, his head straight ahead. A sergeant barked commands. The formation snapped to attention. Lieutenant Pasteur paraded at their front, French arrogance forged in his high forehead, aquiline nose, and extended chin. His wire-rimmed glasses imparted the look of an academic, not a soldier in the infantry.

Behind the lieutenant great islands humpbacked from the sea. Sailors waved sampans away from the ship. As the lieutenant growled a new series of orders, his voice at first cracking and awkward, then growing confident, Haussmann obeyed with indifference. It was too much a charade to be taken seriously. Combat had altered Haussmann's perceptions. The lieutenant paused and smiled. Haussmann could see that the lieutenant tolerated sloppiness. Was it an accommodation for the heat or uncertainty over his authority? Finally the lieutenant declared a period of rest.

The soldiers fell in heaps, their faces contorted and red, none speaking as they guzzled from canteens. Haussmann remained on his feet, thumbing the pages of his Bible. Lieutenant Pasteur approached and offered his canteen.

"No thank you, sir," Haussmann said.

"What's that you're reading?"

Haussmann smiled, as a man with a secret might. "The Bible, sir."

"That why they call you the preacher?"

"I'm not sure why they call me the preacher." Haussmann held out the little black book to the lieutenant's extended hand. Gold leaf embossed the German words Holy Bible on black. "Just now I'm reading the story of Jonah. It's comforting."

"You should leave that reading to the priests."

"We're not all Catholics, sir."

Haussmann studied the officer, one of the many, smug, ordained by French church and state to restore the colonial pride their fathers had lost in Europe. The French were trapped in endless cycles of masses, confessions, consecrations, dispensations, their lives regimented by rites and rituals, communions, christenings, pilgrimages. Papists still believed they lacked the individual freedom to speak directly to God, a right that Martin Luther had long ago proclaimed. Haussmann pressed the Bible against his chest.

Haussmann noticed Lieutenant Pasteur sweated more than most, and his heavily starched khakis clung to his spindly legs. The lieutenant sniffled and squinted, then wiped his nose and eyes with a bandana tied around his neck. He chewed on his dried and caked lips as he stretched to replace his canteen in a pouch in the small of his back. He wiped his nose and eyes again before he spoke. "That smell burns my nostrils. What is it?"

"*Nuoc maum*, sir. Its made in factories on shore." Haussmann slipped the Bible under his shirt. He shifted his rifle from shoulder to hip.

"You've been here before?"

"I have."

"What's it like ashore?"

"Ha Noi has its French charm."

"I hear it has a university for training Confucian scholars."

"I wouldn't know about that, sir." Haussmann rested his rifle against his hip. "The city is the only worthwhile place in the Red River Delta, so we'll fight to get it back."

"I think the Vietnamese will negotiate after our show of strength." The lieutenant struck at an insect on his unshaved cheek.

"Don't presume with the Vietnamese, sir. They're not like us."

The lieutenant smiled in a condescending way. "You can carry on now."

The dismissal stung like a slap in frost air.

CHAPTER 13

Ha Long Bay, March 5, 1946
Pasteur
Childhood memories

At night Pasteur dreamed of his mother's second pregnancy. A child at the time, he'd begged his mother to take him riding, begged until she did, riding side-saddle, the custom with aristocratic women. Her horse had reared and thrown her, ending the pregnancy. No more children, the doctor said.

His father condemned Pasteur for it and sent him to boarding school, to a room alone where he couldn't harm her or others. There boys repeated dreams of vampires and witches and creatures they never identified. His dreams were different. In them he saw terrible things that happened and other things not yet happened.

In his dreams nothing from the past was lost, just misplaced to emerge in dark moments beyond the grasp of his waking censor. And even now in this place so apart from his old world there was no escape from his father's judgment. The dream festered and boiled like a typhoon rupturing his memory. Of what dangers did his unconscious try to warn him by surfacing in his dreams? His mind sorted through the images, his mother's breath, and her perfumed bodice as she leaned over him and whispered.

The sea lifted the massive carrier, swaying the hammocks in which the soldiers slept. Pasteur surveyed his men in those black cocoons outlined against the white-washed metal walls. A door near the engine room opened. The sailor outlined in it carried a lantern and pursed his lips to pipe a piercing sound. The whistle sent the infantrymen dropping to the floor, swearing about what time it was and asking what was the matter that the sailor had to raise the dead. "You grunts is going to be humping those filthy packs of yours 'fore this day is finished," the sailor said. "Don't keep your colonel waiting up on deck."

Someone threw a boot in the sailor's direction. Amidst continued profanities, the hammocks fell and were rolled and tied on top of packs, ammunition secured, boxes from the mess emptied into pockets. Rifles heavily greased to protect them from the salt of the ocean were broken from their stacks, slung over shoulders stooped from the weight of packs. Pasteur inspected the soldiers as they passed. He climbed the metal stairs behind them, glanced back at the empty room, then turned and walked away.

In grey clouds and grey sea the early light touched the peaks of the islands and continued past the shoreline to the mountains. At first the strong wind made a pleasant atmosphere despite the humidity. Somewhere below in the hold bells sounded. The sailors lowered ropes along the port side to the waiting landing craft. Since the previous day, the swells and chop built significantly and now threatened the operation.

Pasteur advanced to the port side where sailors paused to smoke after tying off the ropes. He peered over the side. The landing craft appeared insignificant beside the carrier. Waves broke over the decks of the craft obscuring its crew. After sailors dropped webbed netting over the side, a sailor from the landing craft scampered up as natural as a monkey.

"You waiting for us to drown down there, sir?" the sailor said.

Pasteur's colonel staggered toward the lieutenant.
"Get your troops over the side," the colonel said, averting his glance from where the landing craft bobbed alongside the carrier as if it made him ill. Haussmann led the platoon down the hemp webbing. As troops dropped into the hold, a sea surge threw them off their feet. Ink smoke from the idling engines engulfed the soldiers. Though the bilge pumps continually regurgitated, a foot of water sloshed within the hull, fouled with vomit from the first arrivals. A soldier slipped from the webbing, his fall broken by those on the landing craft.

"Cast off," the coxswain shouted. Pasteur landed awkwardly in the middle of his men, but three soldiers still hung in the nets. He imagined the landing craft cast off, the men swallowed into the sea. He struggled to free his pack and stretched to reach the net. A sailor held him back, "What are you doing sir? No returning now."

"You wait. We got to help them, you damn fool," the lieutenant shouted, breaking free. Rain pelted his skin, making his face a running river. An endless wall of fog rose from the ocean to besiege the fleet. Pasteur clinched the tangled snarl of ropes. Fear tied the first soldier, who refused to release a single fist or legs from the webbing. The net swayed with the wind and sea. Pasteur concentrated on each reach and pull, not to be thrown from where he hung.

"What's your name?" the lieutenant yelled.

"Fisk, sir." The soldier's expression loosened.

"Well, Fisk, you know what you must do."

"Yes, sir, but I don't think I can."

"You'll make it. You're more than half way down."

The soldier descended toward the upturned faces waiting like a clutch of nestlings. Lieutenant Pasteur continued to climb.

The weasel-faced soldier who came aboard at Sai Gon dangled upside down, held by a single leg as if caught in a trap. His pack hung like the sandbag weight on a hanged man. The stock of his rifle wedged into the netting. He looked resigned. Pasteur loosened the shoulder straps. The pack fell to the deck below. He cut the rope, disentangling the rifle. The weasel-faced soldier righted himself with the strength of an acrobat, and slithered down into the arms of his companions.

The final soldier clung to Pasteur like a drowning man. Feeling his own strength failing, Pasteur broke the man's grip and ordered him to proceed. Pain and an increasing numbness, forced Pasteur to grasp each braid with a concentrated effort. At the last instant he fell, knocking over those who attempted to catch him. As he lay on the hull, the vibration of the engines resonated through him. Helpless to move, he couldn't command his soldiers, the men he was expected to protect. His voice trembled with a strange laughter.

"What's the joke?" asked the weaseled-faced soldier who was collapsed beside him.

"Our insignificance."

The sailors cast free of the carrier. The coxswain turned the landing craft toward the river. All this Pasteur ascertained from where he rested without actually seeing it. The river flowed against them as the engines churned and the bow, pointed upstream, deflected undertow. At midday the birds that usually followed fishing junks joined them from their roosts on shore. Lying on his back, his pack supporting his head, Pasteur watched the birds circling and floating overhead. He heard their cries for food as they followed off the stern.

Haussmann turned to Pasteur. "What do you think, lieutenant? Will we be as lucky as the first Frenchmen to come to this place?"

"They were priests," Pasteur said.

"I hear the women had never seen such large men with so much hair over their bodies. At night they sneaked to where the priests were sleeping to satisfy their curiosity."

"What did the priests do?"

"They kept something between themselves and the women all night."

"A sword, I suppose," Pasteur said.

"No, lieutenant, the priests did not carry swords," Haussmann grabbed himself at his crotch. The others laughed. Pasteur laughed.

The weasel-faced soldier had fallen asleep against Pasteur. When he woke, he quickly straightened his pack and moved away. "Excuse me, sir."

"Are you all right?" Pasteur said.

"Yes, lieutenant."

"You don't look well," Pasteur said.

"I grew up looking this way. I had pox as a child and almost died."

"You were lucky."

"No. I should have died."

"You got a cynical attitude."

"We all got attitudes, lieutenant."

"What's mine?" Pasteur challenged.

"One that gets the rest of us killed."

The weasel-faced soldier's stare made Pasteur uncomfortable.

"You don't like what we're doing here?" Pasteur said.

"I have no beef with these people." The weasel-faced soldier closed his eyes.

"You think I do?" Pasteur said.

"I think you got a cause. I've always been afraid of men with causes."

"Causes give us noble purposes."

"And for each cause, there's someone got the opposite cause. Otherwise there would be nothing to fight over. Who's to say the better cause? And the causes that start out being right maybe change or get corrupted. Maybe somebody tries to make something out of the causes for themselves." The weasel-faced soldier lighted a cigarette, "There's a world of good intentions out there, but the right words aren't enough. Men carrying causes conceal their real intent. They're judged by appearance. Some like me are disfigured, and so their intentions are given a negative meaning. Some with physical beauty fool you. The same is true of the causes themselves. They bathe in words of beauty: compassion, charity, the true good will of God, but those are merely words and many conceal evil. In the end, each man must choose."

A corpsman crouched beside the weasel-faced. "I'll check you."

"I'm just fine," the weasel-faced soldier said. "Check him."

"Let me see those hands, sir." The corpsman turned to Pasteur's hands as if reading palms.

"Guess I wasn't strong enough," Pasteur said.

"Everyone saw what you did."

"Are you finished?"

"Ugly wounds," the corpsman said, studying the hands. "See the bone here?"

He poked.

"Damn," Pasteur said, pulling back his hands.

"Sorry. I'll be more careful, but I must disinfect and cover them."

The corpsman opened a small pack that he carried on a strap over his shoulder. He swabbed the wounds, cleaning off the blood that had caked fingers, hands, and forearms up almost to Pasteur's elbows. He covered the fingers with gauze individually and wrapped them together. When he finished, the hands resembled white mittens. The lieutenant relaxed against his pack.

When Pasteur fell asleep, dragons rose from a raging sea to face the boats of the fleet. The dragons had human faces and spoke of their anger, saying there was a place for everything and that their place was in the sea and man had been given the land. An admiral on the carrier responded, telling them that man was without limitations, except as his abilities might temporarily restrict him. Man had conquered many lands and many seas, and even the air no longer limited him. With time the heavens would fall under his dominion, and God, if He existed, must prepare for an assault from his creation. The nature of man was to consume, and that required him to conquer all within his capabilities. Pasteur added that the dragons should listen carefully to what the Admiral said. Since man often attacked his own, he would not hesitate to slaughter the dragons. If they wanted their species to survive, they should present no front against the ships. The dragons withdrew to consider what they had heard.

—⁓—

Pasteur woke and was relieved that his childhood nightmares had ended and that now his dreams had no applicability. He tried to reorient himself, to figure the ship's location and the time of day. The landing craft neither heeled nor rolled and seemed becalmed except for the constant vibration of the hull as it traveled up river. The engine clanked. Pasteur imagined this landing craft on the beach of Normandy. Impossible, but he inspected it for some sign, some marking of combat.

Inside the hull, it was impossible to ascertain their position. He could only see four steel walls, one that would become a ramp. He picked his way to the stern between sleeping soldiers intermingled with equipment. He painfully climbed the ladder to the open wheelhouse. Three seamen in camouflage fatigues leaned along the rail. No insignia, no way to ascertain their rank or who was in charge. They didn't speak.

Other landing craft surrounded them, moving in concert like a family of young waterfowl, sometimes one drawing away a distance, but immediately returning to the safety of the group, shifting position within the group yet never exceeding the protective circumference. Only a machine gun covered with a dark green tarp distinguished the vessel from a civilian barge. Ahead a gun ship cruised, another to the rear.

Pasteur looked across the muddy waters toward the shore. A wilderness of vines, lotus, and other vegetation that belonged neither entirely to the land nor to the water, intertwined in disarray, concealed the banks. He studied the edge of the river. The pilot had said there were things to be learned not found in any military manual. Along the river any fisherman or farmer with a rifle might consider himself a patriot and shoot at a French convoy. Where the Viet Minh was organized, they set up ambushes along the shore, usually around a bend, but always from the safety of the thickest vegetation where pursuit by foot or water was impossible. Those areas were best approached with reconnaissance by fire. That meant now and then a fisherman or farmer was accidentally killed. The pilot had said that was to be accepted as necessary.

The pilot had said he knew very little about what it was like for the infantry, only what he had seen from a distance and overheard in the bars. He thought it was probably much worse for infantry than being on the water because the land provided the enemy places to set mines and booby traps everywhere there was a path or road. The villagers dug pits and placed stakes along the bottom of the pits that they covered with defecation to insure infection. The pilot suggested Pasteur travel behind civilians. Even if they hadn't placed the traps, they likely knew their location. To catch guerillas was impossible. There were thousands of acres in which to hide and very few French soldiers. The guerillas often dressed like civilians and easily passed through checkpoints undetected. In the villages of the far territories where ambushes were frequent, it was necessary to round up everyone, select those who looked most likely to carry out the ambushes and shoot them. It was dirty work and without honor.

Now the little armada was coming around a bend, and Pasteur saw what the pilot had been talking about. His heart started thumping. The boats in front of him continued. His boat followed them. The gun boat which he'd almost forgotten kept between them and the shore. The engine continued to clank, and the Lieutenant worried it might fail altogether. A few miles past the jungle, he spotted a pattern of unnatural clouds. He figured it came from the coal furnaces of Hai Phong. The boat continued clanking towards the city, now passing open fields, rice plantings in deepest greens, richer than the imagination's richest colors, moist and lush and in the open where everything was visible. Closer, oxen submerged at the river's edge, their reptilian horns and heads, their unblinking grey eyes just above the surface, nostrils snorting, observing all that passed without reacting further, then emerging to tear vegetation from the bank, ruminating, then re-submerging. A single bull rose from the water, the river weeds slipping from his back leaving a wet shadowing trail as he jostled down a paddy dike parallel to the river. He sniffed the air to catch the Frenchmen's scent.

A single rifle shot, then others ringed the convoy like skipping stones on the water, their retort partially masked by the engine's noises. The gunboats responded, their chattering guns emitting a stream of scarlet tracers that wavered over the fields and disappeared in the grey vapors that drifted from the distant city. The herd of water buffalo brayed as if fatally struck, then surged together in a prehistoric stampede, lumbering toward a distant village.

A sailor held binoculars to his face and followed the horizon.

"Chinamen," he concluded.

"Chinamen?"

"Look for yourself."

Pasteur focused the binoculars on a distant outcropping of mud and wooden huts used as a military outpost. A battery of artillery was being readied. The soldiers wore the long-sleeved sky blue jackets and puttees of the Chinese regiments that had crossed the border to secure the north country for the allies. The artillery guns had American manufacturer's markings, so too the wooden cases of shells being kicked apart. A soldier locked a round into the breech of an artillery piece. The other soldiers adjusted the height and direction of the barrel.

Pasteur understood their intentions. A radio behind him crackled. The sailor who had handed him the binoculars tried to break into that conversation. Agitated, he pounded the handset. When Pasteur watched the Chinese again, several soldiers retreated across the open rice fields toward the artillery. The gunboats fired inaccurately at them. The gunboats turned around. The other landing craft followed and waved for Pasteur's boat to follow. The sailor threw down the handset and turned hard on the steering wheel. A shell from the Chinese artillery landed where the boat had been the previous moment.

"Close enough," said the sailor.

Another explosion. A sheet of water fell on the boat, and Pasteur grabbed the rail. The pilot steered close to shore and around the bend in the river. The engine overheated and spewed oil over the water. They drifted down the river and along the shore. When they halted, the anchor wouldn't hold and they drifted again, coming against the jungle bank, where the seamen tied the boat to branches that reached out over the water. The other boats did the same. The seaman listened with the radio to his ear and several times he spoke into it.

"What the hell is going on?" Pasteur said.

"The Chinamen didn't get the word to let us pass."

"Hell, that's obvious."

"The commander of the Triumphant asked to meet with a Chinese representative."

All that day as Pasteur waited with the crew, his men removed their shirts, constructed shelters from the sun with the bedrolls and ponchos they carried, and slept in the hull. Some played cards. All complained. Occasionally a soldier climbed to the side deck and relieved himself. Otherwise the boat remained motionless. Pasteur imagined the things the river carried told a story, but he only saw the chaos. The river was time in another form. There was no ability to change it. The river treated everything with equanimity. The harm was in the way men related to it. Everything had its purpose, but it wasn't always related to the purposes men chose.

As the sun fell and disappeared, the radio came to life. The sailor listening was somber and when he'd finished with it muttered something under his breath.

"What is it?" Pasteur said.

"We stay here tonight."

"Put your squad ashore as an observation post," Pasteur pointed at the weasel-faced soldier. "The other squads remain on board. I'm coming as an observer."

The sailor forced the bow into the jungle vines. The squad disembarked from the bow, fell, and were swallowed in the mire with their rifles barely held above the waterline, their packs set like packages on their heads as they struggled to climb the bank.

The squad positioned itself in a rice paddy beyond the jungle aiming the machine gun down a dike toward a distant village with nothing in between to conceal anyone approaching. The narrow dike prevented forming a perimeter, so the squad lay along it in a line with Pasteur in their midst. The weasel-faced soldier assigned the order of the watch, and then took his place.

Pasteur rested on his back. The sky was black. The stillness added disorientation. Only occasional rustling created reality. Water soaked Pasteur's uniform and cooled his skin. The ground on which he slept was invasive, agitating. His mind gathered the few webs on which all reality subliminally rested. His ghosts floated down river, ferrying him toward the underworld. Small points of light bobbled across the horizon.

"Lanterns," the weasel-faced soldier whispered in his ear.

"Are you sure?"

"A platoon, at most a company, judging the distance between the lanterns," the weasel-faced soldier said. The lanterns that stretched across the horizon turned and came in a line straight toward the squad, then turned again as they continued along the invisible dikes that guided them as if on rails. They walked in the squad's direction.

"What are your orders, sir?" The weasel-faced soldier sounded anxious.

Pasteur hesitated. What if they were villagers with some legitimate purpose? He had brought a radio, but any sound would carry across the open. His soldiers slithered off the dike and aligned themselves in the paddy waters.

"Orders, sir?" the weasel-faced soldier repeated.

"Fire."

The machine gun burst the quiet night, tracers perforating the darkness, tracking and overshooting the disappearing lantern light. The squad fired their rifles at random and in disorderly fashion. Then mortar shells from the gun ships burst randomly in the fields beyond them, followed by silence. No movement, no return fire. Blackness. Pasteur ordered his men back to their positions. They waited, rotating the watches. Pasteur tossed restlessly. At dawn he ordered the squad to corroborate what had occurred. They crossed the dikes to where they imagined the lanterns had been and found nothing. The rice paddies were without sign of disturbance.

"We did see them here," Pasteur said, almost as a question.

The weasel-faced soldier did not answer him. The following night Pasteur remained on board, but sent a squad as before. They went and returned without sighting the enemy. At noon the boats were radioed instructions.

"We're cleared to land on Haly," the sailor on the radio said.

"Haly?" questioned Pasteur.

"The Vietnamese call it 'Island of the Dead.'"

"Sounds appealing."

"Better than hanging onto the side of this river. Anyway, from there I think you'll go to Ha Noi. Now that's a place to see."

CHAPTER 14

Ha Noi, November 23, 1946
Phan
The inferno

Windows rattled, the floor quaked. Phan rushed to the front of the office. A column of trucks rolled past, artillery in tow, their Japanese insignias painted over, the French insignias restored, canvas drawn down like a shroud to conceal the troops.

Hahn burst from his office. "It's happened?"

"Some kind of alert," Phan said. "Nothing to be concerned about."

Hahn turned back towards his office. "Follow them and report the story."

At last there was activity. Recently Phan had found himself rooting for some terrible act, a demonstration of French cruelty to put into headlines. For months he had recorded the words of diplomacy, story after story, diplomatic riddle within riddle, a web of complex negotiations between the French and Vietnamese buried in banalities: Saintery, sent from France to negotiate, recognized Viet Nam as a free state, but left French troops to patrol the streets of Ha Noi. By April the French had given the Vietnamese self control, but retained authority over them. Ho Chi Minh scurried off to Paris to complain. Photographs sent from France showed French diplomats in black tuxedos hovering over him. When Ho returned to Viet Nam, he had been greeted as a hero, but everyone knew he'd lost the negotiations. The French informed the Vietnamese they must learn to live within the French domain. On November 9 Ho Chi Minh appeared before the National Assembly, admitted failure, and offered to resign. The Assembly, with nowhere else to turn, asked him to remain as their president.

Now Phan pushed through the reporters who blocked the front door and dashed into the street. He ran beside the trucks, choking on their diesel fumes. Shortness of breath, too many cigarettes, fatigue.... His thoughts fragmented in the heat.... Where are the taxis? The convoy consumed the road in a show of force. Phan felt joy, dread, and the tug of a chase. The trucks disappeared. There was no short cut to catch them. He asked those he passed the direction the convoy had taken.

An old bus traveled towards him, the sign HAI PHONG over the windshield. The bus rocked from side to side, too many passengers hanging from the doors in the front and back, the roof stacked with baskets of fruits, vegetables, laundry, the ancient engine coughing unburned fuel. Phan leaped and his feet caught on the running board. Outstretched hands pulled him in among the compacted riders.

At the next stop the bus discharged, then ingested a sea of flesh. Phan allowed himself to be crushed further inside, down the aisle, no longer in danger of falling from the side. The bus surged forward, threw him against a young girl. Her breasts pressed against him causing an instant of desire. Something real. She avoided his eyes as his apology hung awkwardly in the air. An old woman squatting at his feet, chewed betel nut in a world of legs. He stared down at her sagging breasts. Her black-stained teeth unmanned his desire.

Glancing over heads through dust covered windows, he watched the city turn to countryside. Endless rice fields replaced crowded markets, shops, and tenements. The bus limped, slowed, lurched, and hit potholes, pitching him against the seats. At each stop Phan asked the entering passengers if the French trucks with artillery had passed them as they waited. Each time they answered a simple yes with fear and suspicion in each face.

Outside Hai Dong he overheard whispers that the artillery was to be used on Vietnamese civilians, retribution for resistance to French customs officials in Hai Phong. More passengers left the bus at each stop. None got on. The city of Hai Dong greeted the bus with silence, its streets deserted. There the bus emptied. The driver walked to a window where tickets were sold and had an animated discussion with the cashier. Phan waited patiently for him to return. Ahead of schedule, he assumed. Waiting for more passengers. But why the empty money bag taken from the cashier?

When the driver returned to the bus, he glared at Phan, then fell into his seat and emptied the coins from a wooden box into the bag.

"You must get off," the driver said. His mustache twitched, animating an otherwise expressionless face.

"The sign says Hai Phong."

"No Hai Phong today."

"Is something wrong?"

"The French have given two hours to evacuate Hai Phong before they shell it. The time is almost gone."

"I must get there." Phan felt his prize story slipping from his grasp. Writing was his life, the thing he did so well. At the orphanage even the priests had admired his abilities and asked him to compose the letters they sent to their families back in France. He had heard the priests confide among themselves that he knew how to turn a phrase. The other orphans had asked him to write their pleas: to be released from the orphanage to distant or imaginary relatives; to commute their punishments; to consider training them as priests; all to gain them advantage with the priests.

As a writer he had felt himself without equal, but it never satisfied his ambitions. He needed this cause. For years during his youth he had lacked direction, read desperately, his mind wandering aimlessly over printed pages. Until the day the fiery words of Thomas Paine resonated with his spirit. Freedom: his cause in a single word. What pride he had experienced at the moment of discovery, alone with Hahn in the forbidden room. And now the fight for freedom lay just twenty miles down the road.

Could he bribe the driver to take him to Hai Phong? Phan tried to judge the man's poverty. He made a grand gesture by displaying a money clip and counting most of it off bill by bill. He held it out and waited for the awkwardness that rose with greed and meant a deal. The driver hesitated, giving him hope.

"Take it," Phan demanded. "Just get me to Hai Phong."

"It's not possible with this bus." The driver was shaking his head. Phan watched the power of money at work. Then, "Wait here. I have a friend with a car. Perhaps I can borrow it."

The driver disappeared into the night. Phan sank against a lamp post in the light that provided security for the cashier. Heard thunder. No, it was the artillery. Time was being lost. He jumped to his feet, paced across the parking lot, empty except for the bus. Where was the driver? Abandoned him for a fool? Not likely. Not without the money.

A motor bike approached, its tiny engine annoying like a fly buzzing at his ear. It wobbled, its puny headlight fluttering in the dark. The bus driver grinned at him. Anticipating payment, his disposition had changed.

"Couldn't you find a car?" Phan yelled over the humming motor. The bus driver's grin vanished. He stopped, straddled the bike and waited, not suspecting Phan's apprehension to riding behind him. At the orphanage they'd always walked or taken public transportation. According to the priests, motor bikes were dangerous and only for hooligans.

"Best I can do," the bus driver said. "Everyone knows

they're shelling Hai Phong. No one wants to lose a car."

What mattered was getting to Hai Phong. Phan awkwardly threw his leg over the seat. The bus driver peddled desperately, muttering for Phan to push. Long legged Phan thrust with his feet as if he meant to leapfrog off the seat. The engine gained strength and took over the effort, speeding them through the town and into the countryside. Sheltering himself from the wind, Phan rested his face against the driver's back and watched the road ahead.

Almost immediately they rode headlong into a human stream from Hai Phong. Carrying packs and bags, they were plunderers of war or refugees with their few possessions. Some bore the wounded and dying.

The bus driver never slowed the bike, but maneuvered around people. Phan held tight against the man's back, relieved every time they avoided a pothole, cursing when thrown into the air. The speed increased his exhilaration, his feeling of freedom.

As the number of refugees increased, maneuvering through them became more difficult, finally forcing them to dismount. Then Phan spotted the French trucks just off the road, the artillery pieces unhooked and pulled into line across a field facing to the east. The smell of gunpowder choked the air, but at the moment the guns lay silent. He heard the guns from French ships in the harbor.

The French artillerymen wrestled wooden cases of shells off trucks and stacked them behind the guns. Vietnamese coolies policed ejected brass casings, and threw them into a pile, the casings ringing with the dissonance of cracked bells. Then an officer gave the order to resume the barrage.

At first the artillery fired in an orderly way, seriatim. On command, the lanyard pulled, each gun exploded with a blaze of flame from the muzzle, the gun thrown back on its heel. Later the battery fired at random, each retort lighting the night.

Refugees scurried past French infantry lined along the road and in the open fields, ready to defend the artillery from a guerilla attack. As Phan and the driver proceeded, a French soldier stepped forward. "You cannot go in this direction."

"But we must," Phan answered in his perfect French and continued without breaking his stride. He made no explanation. The bold move carried the moment.

At the edge of Hai Phong a short round had exploded on the road. Those who survived dragged themselves away, their cries of pain a cacophony. Some of the wounded were tended by relatives. Most were ignored by the terror stricken refugees, who stepped over or trampled the wounded in the stampede to escape. A woman wailed. She had no legs and would die within minutes.

The bus driver grabbed Phan's arm. "We can go no further."

"We'll cut across the rice fields."

"I can't damage my friend's motor bike."

Phan suspected the bus driver owned the bike. The man clearly had no stomach to proceed. Phan gestured toward the road with a dismissive wave, "Just leave."

"I have five children and another on the way."

Phan understood and handed the driver a fist of wadded bills. The man half bowed and disappeared in the flow of refugees.

Night's chill turned the air. Ground fog hung over the rice fields, the stars little more than pin holes through a black panel. The ground dropped into blackness. Distant fires outlined Hai Phong. A fireball plumed over the city.

Phan lost his footing, slipped off the road, sliding down the bank, striking rocks. Disoriented and on his backside, his eyes failed to perceive his surroundings. He rolled over and groped for something familiar to orient himself. His hands sunk into things cold and wet with a putrid smell. He felt as he crawled and recognized fingers, sticky hair and faces from bodies thrown over the bank. He tried to control his panic with short gasps for breath. Death in the abstract had never terrified him. These dismemberments were another matter. He scrambled up the bank, hands working in the dirt like rakes, pulling him up and at the same time removing the blood.

Along the road the flow of refugees had increased. Phan

rushed to retreat with them to Ha Noi. He'd report what he'd seen, not mention he never reached Hai Phong. He was close enough to make the claim. Now he was safe except for the danger of a short round and that had already happened and unlikely again. Then something told him not to go back. Not yet. On an impulse he slid back down the bank, over the bodies and into the rice field. Holding his sandals, he ran blindly into the black and limitless expanse. Quick steps kept his feet from sinking into the mud. He grew confident on the level field. Then he stumbled against a dike, fell, and crawled over it on his hands and knees, lost his sandals, barefoot resumed running with a feeling of liberation that overwhelmed all fear. He gasped for breath with an odd exhilaration.

Most of the shelling came from the French ships. They targeted the Vietnamese section of Hai Phong. Ahead of him wood buildings were collapsed. What the shelling began, fire completed. Flames filled the sky. In the flame's light Phan easily covered the remaining distance and entered the city. Fire jumped the road. Tin roofs curled like paper, broke loose and caught up in drafts, blew over the buildings. The heat drove away the curious, spontaneously consuming those too close. Phan watched the fire leap to a building next to him. Tenants raced in and out its doors, piling their belongings in the street until the heat forced them away. Two women appeared in a third floor window. They crawled onto the window ledge. One paused, and then jumped, crashing onto the ground, motionless. The other turned back into the room where the flames consumed her. The fire roared as the building fell. Driven from their secret places, rats filled the streets. Street dogs, confused by the number of rats, attacked them, chasing through the streets, biting in all directions, biting refugees. Frantic and distraught mothers screamed for their lost children. Those who hesitated to mourn their loss were themselves consumed.

Phan retreated into the rice paddies, standing in the water, then on a dike. A man in flames raced from the inferno. Phan chased him, knocked him down in the water, tried to beat out the flames. Skin mixed with clothing came off in his hands. The man fought him, struggling in the water until all his flesh was consumed. Only the man's expressionless eyes remained un-charred as he lay in mud and water breathing in gasps. Phan watched until the man ceased breathing.

Phan stumbled onto a dike, stretched out along it, and fell into a restless sleep. He didn't dream. He woke in a dark void, almost a relief, except he knew that was how insanity began. But what was wrong with that? He'd chosen that reality as an escape. He slept again.

He woke with the sun streaming down on him.The surrounding water glistened like an endless field of diamond crystals, the dead man from the night before just an island. From the city rose what might have been a huge tornado, a funnel of black smoke from the embers of the Vietnamese quarter. Particles of ash fluttered to the ground like so many black and gray butterflies. The ash covered the refugees who rested along the sides of the road. It covered the water. It covered Phan as he walked in the direction of Ha Noi. He was slinking past the refugees, wary like an animal, afraid they might rise to attack him. Little separated the living from those who'd died in the night. The horror had left them all catatonic, yet it wasn't their madness, but the madness of the French which filled Phan's thoughts. Why had the French attacked? Surely not just as an object lesson. He had to write the story, but was any of the creative impulse left in him?

CHAPTER 15

Ha Noi, November 24, 1946
Hahn
Escape and betrayal

Hahn left the new reporter waiting outside his office door. The reporter wore a hand-tailored suit, a perfect fit. The file from his private school revealed a record of youthful rebellion, but nothing to seed the hatred needed to sustain a Communist party member. Hahn studied the file, and then glanced up at the pacing figure with the handsome face, the delicate features, the hands that looked manicured. Like a porcelain doll. Hahn laughed at the thought. Out there a look of agitation. Let him wait for at least two hours. Test him with life's petty annoyances.

At noon Hahn invited him into his office. The young reporter stood in front of the desk while Hahn shuffled through the drawers hunting for a pack of cigarettes, then lit one as if he were alone and going on with his work.

The reporter cleared his throat, "Excuse me sir."

"Be patient," Hahn replied without looking up from the new galley he reviewed. Hahn followed his instructions for testing new recruits to the letter, everything scripted, all the alternatives of behavior foreseen. So he began, subtly taking away personal control, manipulating a new reporter's mind. The recruit must be quickly trained and programmed or eliminated. Hahn reported to the Communist party committee in exact detail what happened at these meetings. Following instructions was as important as the result. It started the process of evaluation. No doubt other members of the party watched the new reporter at the same time. Everyone was responsible. No one above suspicion. The slightest difference or omission in a report raised inquiries, an interrogation to verify commitment. That was how the party operated, keeping a record on everyone and frequently reviewing performances, not tolerating actions that deviated from the party line. At the same time the party raised class consciousness to prepare for the bitter struggle. Everyone had his place in the dialectical union of people formed through self-criticism, punishment, retraining, and even execution if it called for that extreme. Only with party discipline would they prevail against the French imperialists and the reactionary bourgeoisie within their country.

Communism demanded Hahn's complete attention. Beneath it all lay his pleasure in the intrigue. The party had found him in the streets outside the orphanage and first showed him how to poison the French boy who tormented him. Then the party took him as their child and raised him. Father and mother, he worshiped them, the men in black who met in shadows and plotted bombings and assassinations. Their bombs exploded daily in cafes, in markets, at the theater, killing the French and their sympathizers, spreading terror through the country. The party taught him how: smile at his enemy in the street; beg from him so his ego would let you nearer to him, accepting your pretended innocence, after all you were only a child. But it was his enemy made him cruel by taking away his family, his country, a normal life. And he would slip a bomb in beside that enemy, set the timer, and walk away.

The priests who judged Hahn lazy never suspected he lacked sleep because he lived a double life. Only Phan had known the truth and kept the secret.

"It was you sent for me," the young reporter interrupted, agitated, childish, pouting. He shifted his weight from foot to foot and at the same time rocked from heel to toe.

This young reporter would never do, but Hahn shuffled the papers in front of him as if interested and looking for a certain page. There was nothing there to review; only the briefest of facts with none of the personal detail to which he might react. No matter.

"Says here you lived in Hai Phong with your family. Your father is a wealthy industrialist. Were you unhappy with them? Is that why you left?"

"I don't see how that matters." The youth compounded his mistakes, failed to understand that nothing remained private from the party, and yet he still continued, "Aren't you interested in seeing how I write?"

"I'll conduct the interview. Just answer." The shortfalls of the new reporter multiplied in Hahn's mind. Impatient. Combative. Too resistant to authority. That was enough. In all the years with the party, Hahn had made only one exception to the guidelines: Phan, the only one outside the party who stood by him, never questioned him.

The noise of shouting distracted Hahn. A small boy wearing the remnant of beggar's shorts darted down the aisles past the desks towards the cubicle, avoiding the grasping arms that tried to stop him. For an instant Hahn saw himself in his younger days. Anguish forced the thought away.

"Here, Mister," the boy tried to catch his breath, at the same time holding out an envelope. Hahn hesitated. He glanced at the boy's feet, filthy and covered with sores. Like hands, feet told a lot.

"Where'd you get the envelope?" Hahn demanded.

"Some man in the street," said the boy. "Paid me with this and said you'd match it."

The boy pulled a coin from his pocket. Hahn examined it, saw the hole drilled through the French figure. He took the envelope.

"Get yourself settled," Hahn said to the boy, motioning to a chair. He turned to the new reporter and walked him to the door, showing him out, sending him to a desk after tucking a new baggy suit under his arm, "A reporter's suit," he said. "We'll try you out." The suit had a picture stuffed in the pocket. Hahn closed his door. The boy sat quietly waiting. Hahn tore open the envelope, unfolded a single piece of paper, and decoded the message sent from party headquarters. French soldiers on the way to the newspaper office. Proceed with plan. He removed his suit jacket from the back of the chair, then shredded the note and burned it in the ash tray.

"Thanks, kid. Now come with me." Hahn wrapped his arm over the child's bare shoulder as the signal and left his cubicle taking his time, noticing the circular rings on the child's back left from heated cups which, according to practitioners of Chinese medicine, sucked poison from the patient. He calmly walked to the door past the reporters at their desks, nodding to some, smiling at others. Several reporters, likely secret Communist party members, perhaps sent to watch him, grasped the significance of what he did and stood up to leave. The rest remained, but Hahn took no steps to warn them. They were the patriots with no political understanding, now left for the French to conveniently eliminate.

In the street he slipped the child money and sent him off, distancing the child, but not the memories.

Hahn's first week at the orphanage the priests gave up trying to remember his Vietnamese name and called him Shorty. The name stuck. When he learned to read, he found a French thesaurus and looked up the synonyms for short: deficient, inadequate, insufficient, lacking, meager, runty, scant, skimpy, slight, and wanting. That provoked him into becoming ambitious, arrogant, authoritative, and aggressive, and always coiled like a snake, ready to strike. After he'd poisoned the French boy, the Vietnamese orphans admired Hahn but feared what he might become. He became a communist. The communists wanted those willing to do anything required to defeat the French and he was willing. He smiled thinking about it.

He moved down the street and into the shadows of

an alley. Though he had already been warned, Hahn sensed trouble on his own, sensed it like others sensed the coming of rain. There were no Frenchmen in the streets. Their cars were gone from the open garages, taken into villas set up as defensive compounds. From a distance came the familiar shuffle of troops in formation. Coming toward him from the same direction and unaware of the danger, Phan approached alone.

"Quick. Get over here." Hahn spoke in a forced whisper. He reached out and his arm was momentarily caught in the light of the street.

"Who is it?" Phan strained to pierce the shadows. "What's the matter?"

"Get over here," Hahn repeated, stepping out of concealment. Phan ducked into the shadows just as a French patrol rounded the corner.

Hahn put a finger to his lips.

"We should get inside," Phan said.

"That's where the French are going," Hahn answered.

"We must warn the others."

"It's not necessary."

"Are they already out?"

"Some."

"And the others?"

"Expendable." Hahn started to whistle, low and out of tune, as a child when he first learns. The French were entering the building.

Screams pierced the windows and the walls. They heard the death screams. The killing had to be completed. The troops must leave no survivors to recount the incident, only rumors of a massacre, easily denied. After all who would believe stories of unprovoked slaughter?

The French soldiers exited drunk with violence, staggering, their expressions wild, their uniforms disheveled, rifles slung, carrying furnishings from the office as souvenirs. They disappeared down the street.

Phan rushed from the hiding place ahead of Hahn, headlong into the building, not breathing until he shrieked. Hardly a sound came from the place itself. The dead spread over the floor mingled with the broken chairs and desks. Papers thrown from drawers were soaked in blood.

His handsome looks hadn't saved the new reporter. On his side, he was a porcelain doll with a center tooth chipped, but turned over the back of his skull was covered in blood and oatmeal, that could only be his brains.

"Why?" Phan moaned. "And why did you escape?"

"I received a tip," Hahn responded with a sly grin.

Phan bent over the young reporter. He reached inside the boy's pocket, drew out the picture: the French, the bodies, the heads. "It's the same picture you gave to me," he shouted, throwing it to Hahn. "You knew that this would happen."

"Did I?" Hahn replied.

"Why weren't they all warned?"

"I did what the party ordered."

"That's not a good enough explanation."

"Today the French made martyrs of these men. They will serve the cause well."

"And how will we replace them?"

"Those in the party escaped. The men who died were simple patriots. They never mattered. Now they do. They will gain a reputation of courage and honor. Be heroes."

"Why did you save me?"

Hahn watched the vein throbbing along Phan's neck, the anger shaking his body.

"You write too well," Hahn said.

"That is it, isn't it?" Phan settled onto the floor beside the dead reporter. "Did you know about Hai Phong, too?"

"The intelligence wasn't confirmed."

"And now I can confirm it. The French shelled the Vietnamese sector. It's destroyed. Hundreds of casualties. There's no hope for peace. Are you satisfied? Is that what you wanted to hear?"

Naiveté, Hahn thought. Phan had always been a dreamer, as if things that mattered had a good ending, but no one freely surrendered their control freely. All masters built a system of beliefs to justify their rule and they described the victims of their tyranny as children needing guidance, lazy, naturally inferior, backward, a burden to the race. Only rebellion taught the masters differently, and when it happened, the masters resisted for exploitation gave them ease of life. "We must leave, before the French return looking for anyone they missed."

"What about the newspaper?" Phan said, as he struggled to his feet.

"Finished for now. The French will soon control the city. We'll have to start again in the jungle. General Giap has already established camps along the Chinese border. Go back to your wife and child, and I'll get word to you. Don't come back here. The French police will be watching the building."

CHAPTER 16

Ha Noi, December 2, 1946
Phan
The executions

Phan's wife begged him not to go. The newspaper office had been abandoned for more than a week.

"There's no danger." Phan reassured her that what he was determined to do was safe. French presence on the streets had increased, but their attack had brought no other changes. Without newspapers, the shelling of Hai Phong was merely a back alley rumor, a footnote in history, and it had been Phan's duty to change it. And still no word from Hahn.

Each day Phan's shame grew that a single attack had silenced the press, so easily frightened, so completely repressed. The cry for freedom should have meant more. What if even a single printing press had survived the destruction at the newspaper? Then to publish the story of Hai Phong Phan needed just one typewriter. Just one. Besides, the handwritten notes and stories in his desk invited discovery and even greater danger.

Finally the shame in neglecting his duty drove Phan back to the newspaper. He cautiously walked past the abandoned site, then doubled back and peered into shadows, searching for any sign of danger. The windows were boarded, the front door intact. He tested the doorknob. It was locked. He worked his key in the latch. It opened.

Inside the room scattered furniture and the smell of mildew. Someone had removed the dead reporters. The only light squinted through cracks in the wooden slats nailed over the windows.

"Hello?" No response.

He worked his way toward his desk, stumbling several times in the semidarkness. The front door slammed shut. "Someone here? Who is it?"

No one answered.

No one was there to set the type. No one was there to run the presses. He'd just gather his papers and leave. His hands fumbled through his desk. Empty. On the floor pencils and blank paper, but not his hand written notes. A shadow moved in the faint light, a man in a suit outlined against an open window. At least it wasn't a soldier.

"Stand where you are," the man said, waving something from the shadows. A badge caught the light for an instant. "Is that your desk?"

Phan didn't answer.

The man emerged from the shadows.

"Surete," he said. "Do you work here? What's your name?"

The policeman spoke perfect Vietnamese. There would be no deceiving him.

"Nguyen van Phan."

"Oh, yes, I've heard your name," the policeman said. "You write seditious articles."

"I think you're mistaken," Phan replied.

"I'm not mistaken. You consider yourself a patriot?"

"Yes, I do."

"You have done yourself a disfavor. Come with me." The policeman strode toward him but did not touch him and kept walking past. Phan followed him into the street.

The policeman signaled to soldiers smoking beside a

military truck. The soldiers escorted Phan to the truck, then tied his arms behind him and bound his legs together. Phan looked toward the policeman for relief, but the policeman had climbed into a sedan. When the soldiers blindfolded Phan, he protested. A soldier struck him in the face with a rifle, tearing the blindfold over one eye. In a single motion the soldiers heaved him over the tailgate, dumping him on other prisoners who groaned as he landed in their midst. His head struck a stomach. The man recoiled and hit him with a knee, cursing unintelligibly.

"Sorry," Phan mumbled.

"Be careful how you move."

Wedged between the other prisoners, Phan tried to pull himself upright. All he could see was the blue sky. The metal truck bed bruised him when the truck hit potholes. He couldn't judge time or distance.

—⧛—

Through the tear in his blindfold Phan recognized the entrance to Hoa Lo prison when they passed beneath its arch. Ha Noi's prison for martyrs. The guard who had struck him dragged him from the flatbed. As other prisoners fell on top of him, he curled to protect his face and braced against their weight. Two French soldiers lifted him to his feet. He asked them to remove the blindfold and untie his hands. They beat him, then carried him to a cell, locked his legs in a wooden yoke, and removed the blindfold and ropes. His cell lacked bed and toilet bucket. Knives, wire, and several pliers were displayed on the wall outside the cell. Left alone for hours, Phan had envisioned the worst by the time two men entered the room.

"Hello again, Phan," The policemen who spoke perfect Vietnamese addressed him with the same familiarity as before.

"What do you want from me?"

"I think you know," the other Frenchman said.

"I have no idea." Phan concentrated on the cross that dangled from the policeman's neck, swinging like a metronome. God's will be done. He counted with the rhythm; one, two, one, two.

The second Frenchman struck Phan from behind, knocking him back against the wooden bench. "We're not fools. We've read your articles. We know your feelings. You were seen returning from Hai Phong. Why were you there?"

"I'm a reporter."

"Terrible what the Viet Minh did in Hai Phong. Their arrogance attacking our customs men. We gave them quite a lesson. Now don't make us treat you the same." The Frenchman stepped back, as a signal for his gentler companion to resume the questioning.

"You are a member of the Vietnamese Communist Party?"

"No."

"You work with a communist named Hahn."

"I work for Hahn my editor, as a reporter."

"Who are the other members of your cell?" the soft spoken French policeman asked as if they were sharing confidences.

"I am not a communist," Phan answered.
The gentle interrogator stepped aside. The other struck Phan in the face. Phan choked in his own blood. The Frenchman kicked and punched him, raining blows until Phan fainted. They threw water into his face and when he became conscious beat him until the Frenchman had to pause to catch his breath. Blood filled Phan's mouth, caked on his teeth and blocked his nose. He could feel the blood running down his legs. Was this how he was to die? His own death had never been so real to him.

"I can't stop him, if you don't cooperate," said the gentle interrogator sitting across the room. "You must be honest with us or he will kill you."

"Sir, I admit that I am a patriot, but I am not a communist." The two interrogators exchanged glances. They're enjoying this, Phan thought. The beating resumed. The fury of the punches no longer caused him to suffer, each punch more like pressure crushing him. Were they using the pliers?

He couldn't see. He tried to think of Thi and their child, but dying was too solitary and personal.

He clung to consciousness, as if it meant his life. His consciousness floated free within a body that refused to respond, telling him to just give in, let sleep carry him away. Helpless but no longer afraid, he floated in meaningless time. Voices surfaced.... Throw water on him... Lift his feet. Drop his head... Don't let him faint.... You went too far.... What use is he if he doesn't confess? ....Get the soldiers to take him away. Let him die in their cells.... They'll know what to do.

Later he was lifted off the bench. A tight grip around his arms convinced him that he wasn't dreaming. Again the pressure, but no pain. He tried to find some connection to his body, to the room, to the voices he heard. Nothing responded, yet he wasn't dead. Then why was there no feeling? Was he being moved? Where? Did they think he was dead? He thought he cried out, but there was no sound, no way to tell them he was still alive. Or was he?

He felt the hard wooden bench, tried to see it. Morgue slab or prison bed? Or had he been returned to the Surete? His eye lids were caked shut, like the pinkeye in his childhood. He picked at the blood. He opened his eyes to see a dark room with high, narrow windows that let in only the slightest ray of light. Chains around his ankles held him to the wooden bench. There were other benches along the walls, each with a prisoner in chains, over twenty men chained along the walls.

Sitting up, head between his knees, he coughed up blood, and then vomited.

"Use this," the prisoner on the bench next to him slid a pail towards him. The man's hair grew in all directions. A beard and mustache made it clear he hadn't shaved in months. "Bad enough in here without you're adding to it."

"Sorry," Phan apologized.

"Don't worry."

"How long have I been here?" Phan said.

"They brought you in here yesterday, late in the day. You've been lying there groaning ever since. We didn't know if you'd make it." The shadow spoke with a border region accent.

"Why are all these other men here?" Phan's voice sounded strange to him.

"Don't know exactly, comrade. We never talk about our lives in case torture loosens our tongues. Or one of us may not be what he seems and report what's said to the Surete. Not that it matters."

"What do you mean?"

"This is a kind of death row. There are only two sentences from here: Death by guillotine or life in Poulo Condore prison. I'm not sure which is worse."

"For what crimes?" Phan whispered, praying to himself that the men were convicted murderers or rapists and that his being there was a mistake.

"Political."

Phan felt faint. He turned away so the other prisoner wouldn't see the tears in his eyes.

He remembered. In February 1930 there had been a revolt. The French had quickly captured those who participated. Father Custeau had escorted the orphans to the court house to see the administration of French justice under the banner of "Liberty, Equality, and Fraternity." They packed into the crush of spectators. Phan was eight, too short to see more than the tribunal of magistrates seated high above the prisoners, prosecutors, defenders, and the French police and soldiers, but he heard it all. The defendants were accused of belonging to the Vietnamese Nationalist Party and making bombs. Their defenses were denial, claims of coercion and deception by the Surete in extracting confessions, and patriotic duty, the last certain to incite those who judged them. Guilty, guilty, guilty, the gavel echoed in the courtroom. The crowd demurred. The gavel beat against them like a drum. Into the silence poured the court's pronouncement. At the end the two sentences, death or life in prison. Soldiers dragged the prisoners past the boys. Phan remembered their faces, now understood the marks they wore, the yellowing and the blackening, the deep blue impregnated beneath the skin. Now he faced the same fate. The past lived again.

He waited for days for the Surete. He knew the interrogations continued until each prisoner confessed. Others were taken and returned, fresh blood covering their faces. He languished on the bench, fed intermittently with broth and stale bread, otherwise ignored.

Early one morning soldiers crossed the prison courtyard. The reverberation of their boots marching in step echoed off the prison walls. The metal gate opened and the lights came on. The prison warden advanced down the center of the room pointing out inmates and announcing their sentence to the guillotine. The soldiers cuffed them, chained them, and took them away. Phan wept when they locked the iron door behind them. Then a sense of ecstasy overcame him. He felt reborn, spared for at least another day.

CHAPTER 17

Ha Noi, December 2, 1946
Thi
A prisoner's wife

Long before Phan's imprisonment, boredom had destroyed Thi's appreciation for city comforts. She longed to return to Quang Khe, where working in the fields gave a sense of self sufficiency. In the city everyone depended on others for their jobs and their daily needs. Now war shortages meant mass starvation and plagues. All day Thi had cared for her son while her husband worked. He spent little time with them, convinced his writing contributed to the struggle for independence. His writing was his world, a man's world that excluded her. What difference would there be for women once Viet Nam was free of the French? Of all the men only her father had seen her abilities, treated her as an equal, and taught her to read and write and think independently.

Poverty trapped her in the tenement of cloth walls in the enormous room where they stayed. Their only privacy was the turmoil that made single conversations difficult to separate from the constant noise. She longed for the quiet of her village.

Recently she had found an escape, putting her son in a pack each day and exploring in a different direction. On one of her walks she stopped in Hoan Kiem Park. Along the street near the entrance, women gathered to sell flowers. Their broad brimmed hats sheltered them from a fierce sun. In the sun the brilliant multicolors vibrated in bouquets humming with bees. She asked the price for a single flower. It was too expensive and too impractical, dead within a day. Still, the natural beauty tempted her.

French women with parasols strolled along the lanes with nannies pushing baby carriages. Some lay on blankets in the grass, laughing together, French wine served to them by Vietnamese chauffeurs and maids in uniforms. Armed soldiers lingered discreetly among the trees. Willows and flame trees, burning red with beauty, lined the lake shore in the park's center. In the middle of the lake the Turtle Pagoda, Pagoda of the Returned Sword, three stories high and pleasant to view, reflected in the water. Thi listened with delight to an old man tell the story of Le Loi, the hero who had come to the lake at the time of the Chinese invasions. At the time a turtle rose from the lake and handed Le Loi a magical sword with which he drove out the Chinese invaders. After his success he returned to the lake and threw the sword back into the water where the turtle recovered it. There the turtle waited with the sword for the next time it was needed. But that was centuries ago and just a children's tale. It did not explain to Thi the growing national obsession with freedom.

Thi had seen all the sights two or three times, explored in all directions. If she had money to spend, she might have continued venturing into the city center to visit museums, operas, theater.

Now she squatted on the mat, her son playing around her, secure and preoccupied with the few simple toys they had bought him. She thought frequently about his future. Phan's writing wasn't dependable employment, not in a society struggling and impoverished.

The cloth curtain wavered. She glanced at the shadow cast through the translucent light.

"Thi?" The apparition at the cloth hesitated. She recognized the voice. Hahn thrust the curtain back and stood motionless before her.

What about this man inspired Phan's loyalty to him? Hahn was short and sweaty, his coal black hair unkempt, swept back with the frequent strokes of spread fingers. His intense eyes attacked her. Not her body; other men did that and she accepted it. His eyes raped her soul.

"Your husband returned to the newspaper. I had warned him the Surete were watching the building. They've arrested him. He's been taken to Hoa Lo Prison."

Thi swept her son off the floor, rushed into the street headed for the prison. She started to hail a trishaw, realized she had left her money under the mat and ran along the street. Her son, sensing her alarm, cried. At times lost in the city, she came suddenly upon the prison, stark among the innocent buildings busy with commerce. Rust from barbed wire strung across the top stained the faceless stucco walls. Blind to the outside world, it had only a few window slits covered with bars.

Desperately searching for an entrance, she raced along that wall. She heard cries from the widows high above her. She tried to think what to do as she ran. She found the entrance blocked by a solid iron door with guards checking papers, turning most away. She joined a small line to enter. She tried to imagine what to say, but images of the recently resumed public executions crowded out her rational thoughts.

From within a wooden booth a French officer directed Vietnamese guards in French uniforms.

"Papers." A guard held out his hand to her when she reached the front of the line.

"I haven't any. My husband has just been taken inside. I must see him."

"You must have papers," the guard said.

"Papers for what?" she screamed. "You have taken him without a reason."

The French officer looked over from the booth, "Is there a problem?"

Thi hesitated, trying to compose herself. Her son's crying never ceased. "Sir, they've taken away my husband and
brought him here. I must see him."

"There are procedures."

"That's no answer," she insisted. The Vietnamese
guard pulled her from the line.

"Please, you must leave. You will only make matters
worse," the guard pleaded, lowering his voice. "They punish
the prisoners for any trouble from their relatives."

"I didn't know," she said. Defeated, she retreated down
the wall. Hahn moved toward her. She wanted to ignore him,
but she ran toward him, seeking help, needing reassurance
that soon everything would be all right. Her husband was
in prison which might mean he faced the guillotine. She felt
Hahn's embrace, his arms like blocks, stiff and wooden, un-
flinching. His breath smelled of rice wine and bad teeth. She
struggled to break loose. "You did this," she sobbed.

"There was nothing I could do." No anger, no apology.

"You can save him now," she demanded.

'We don't have the strength to attack French strongholds."

"You mean you won't do it."

"I mean we can't," Hahn replied.

Everything was spinning. She remembered hearing
Phan repeating a priest's name in his sleep.

"I'll find help on my own," she said, leaving Hahn
standing in the street. She wept as she ran, telling herself
she must remain calm. Her only chance was to convince the
French priest to use the power of the church to secure Phan's
release. What would move him? She'd say anything, but she
knew nothing about the Catholics. She wished she'd listened
when Phan rambled on about the orphanage, the priests, and
their God. She wished she'd learned about confirmation and
the necessity of marriage in the church, the terms they'd re-
jected despite the priest's request. She remembered hearing
it said the French God sought retribution more often than
forgave. And that he alone was to be recognized. She would

pretend Phan had wanted all three of them to join the church, three for the price of one, to get that one out of jail before he was separated from his head.

As she hurried toward the cathedral, the soldiers in the streets ignored her, a desperate young woman with a child on her back, likely a servant late to do the bidding of a French family. Poverty drew little attention to itself.

The great cathedral rose above the French villas, above the trees. The French God dominated everything and everyone within his reach. He demanded recognition of his omnipotence. She read it in the spire of the church, the great door, the stained glass images that faced the street, the image on the cross. But what God took pride in the agony of his son? In her confusion she banged at the cathedral door. Her cries went unanswered. Her disembodied plea floated freely in a world in which she feared there was no God to answer. The cathedral bells drowned her cries yet gave her hope. Eventually the bell ringer would come out. She waited.

Hearing voices inside, she again banged her fists against the door. The voices ceased. She waited, afraid they'd left the room. Her ear pressed against the cold metal latch, she strained to hear them. Then she heard chanting unlike any from the Buddhist temples, that of young men, their high pitch achieving impossible notes. She began to believe in their meaningless words. When a pause came, she pursed her lips over the latch key hole and shouted. Through the latch hole, she watched one of the smallest boys leave the choir, walk down the central aisle past the pews to the back vestibule, and finally reach the door. He turned the latch and pulled, but the door didn't open. A single push and she was inside. The door slammed shut by its own weight. Candles flickered beside the altar.

She saw a grand organ with pipes to the ceiling, the altar, an empty bench beneath it, and the choir bunched together, twelve boys, not a boy over twelve, and no adults. Her eyes searched the shadows.

"Over here, child." The deep voice of a man contrasted with the choir. "What do you want?"

"He was bringing me here, but now they have taken him."

"Slow down, my child. What are you talking about?" Concealed in a black robe, a stooped priest limped from the dark and endless rows of pews.

"Are you Father Custeau?" The name escaped her lips.

"If I am, you have the better of me."

"My husband is Nguyen van Phan. They have him in Hoa Lo Prison." When Thi spoke, her child began to cry. He was too old for nursing but when he pulled at her blouse, she allowed it to assure his quiet. Had the old priest heard her? "My husband is Nguyen van Phan. They have him in Hoa Lo prison."

"There is nothing I can do for you."

"They will execute him." She felt her voice tightening, her eyes filling with tears. "He's done nothing wrong."

"It's a matter for secular authorities." The priest appeared unmoved. "You must take your plea to them."

His words carried the staccato intonation of a sermon. The choir of boys waited and listened, their eyes filled with loss. The priest waved a dismissive hand toward them, sending them fleeing like pigeons startled from the rafters. "They're too young to understand. Foolish children, lost without God in their hearts."

Thi fell against the tile floor. She tried to raise herself, her crying son, from the floor. The priest helped her to a pew, clucked to calm the boy. "There my child," he said. The priest's hands trembled. For a fleeting instant it occurred to her that he was the one who put Phan's name on the list of enemies of France.

CHAPTER 18

Ha Noi, December 2, 1946
Father Custeau
A visitor

When Father Custeau dismissed the choir boys, they dashed from the cathedral to play beyond God's direction. Father Custeau had been the same before he was shipped to a monastery as his family's gift to God. In his mind, his father sternly repeated the importance of sacrifice. But was a son's life his father's to give?

After years cloistered in the church, Father Custeau still searched for meaning. Charity, humility, chastity, poverty remained just words. The holy vows he'd taken before he had any worldly experience kept him imprisoned. Weak will and physical lust had plagued him into old age. Too late now. Were the good only passive souls who'd lost their lusts when they lost their potency?

He sought peace in old age, unable to forsake or to fulfill the holiest of the catechism that Christ set forth to his apostles: "Go therefore and make disciples of all nations, baptizing them in the name of the Father and of the Son and of the Holy Ghost, teaching them to observe all that I have commanded you; and lo I am with you always, to the close of the age." His duty remained to redeem the lost for God.

When Phan's wife fainted, he had lifted her from the floor and taken her child, a child soon without a father unless he intervened. Still harboring anger at Phan for deserting the church, he momentarily thought the child might be better off. The Surete had acted on his warning, but now he understood his responsibility.

"Because of your husband, you and your child are lost to the kingdom of God, unless you take the sacraments," he said. He wanted Phan's wife to understand that even in an hour of need God watched and judged.

"All is lost without Phan." The young wife wept.

"After baptism your husband committed the gravest of sins, separating from God. Now God's will must be done."

"You can save him."

"Only God saves us." The girl and her child must receive the sacraments. "Only through God can you save your husband."

"What must I do?"

"Promise you'll make him confess his sins and repent. You and your child must be baptized and follow the teachings of the Holy Mother Church."

"Anything, father." Thi grasped his hand, kissing it desperately, a ritual Phan must have told her. There was hope. Father Custeau believed her to be sincere, believed she'd do as she promised, if not from faith, then from the obligation of the promise.

"Charlemagne," Father Custeau summoned his servant. So seldom did that happen that Charlemagne fell as he was rushing to his side, full of good intentions but incompetent. His portly belly stretched his oversized frock. Charlemagne was the perfect servant and had been since brought from France to serve the previous and last French bishop. He'd wanted to be servant to the famous, whirling through life in a society far above his station. And he might have made it if Father Custeau had become a bishop, but the church drew its new bishops from the Vietnamese priests.

"Take the woman and her child to my quarters and see that they are fed. Then report to my office. I'll join you there after prayer."

Father Custeau knelt at the altar and thanked God for delivering them to him.

—∿—

Father Custeau sent a letter to secure Phan's release. Several days later the prison warden replied with due formality that Nguyen van Phan awaited trial for treason. Thi's tears convinced Father Custeau he must travel to the prison. He ordered his car brought to the front of the rectory.

The car rolled down the drive and along the tree-lined avenue. The day was too hot, the smells too strong for Father Custeau. He turned his face from the window and buried his head within his once powerful hands. He only raised his eyes when the car was at the prison gates. Here he knew evil men faced their final judgment before God took his turn with retribution. Here murderers, rapists, robbers, and thieves waited with the anarchists set on destroying the colony and infidels who preached against the church. And now here Phan, raised in righteousness but lost in his own misdirected quest for freedom, awaited his fate.

A guard stiffened when Father Custeau rolled down his window. "Father, what are you doing here?"

"I've come to see the warden."

"Is he expecting you?"

"I expect not."

"I'm sorry, father, but I'll have to check." The French soldier stepped back into the guard booth. The muffled voices could be overheard. No, he's here now... that meddlesome old priest. Send him away... I think he'll insist....then I'll see him.

"The warden will see you now."

The car eased through the archway. The gates of hell. With all the rumors, Father Custeau expected screams. Before the state, the church had been master of the craft of torture. Graphic drawings and descriptions in monastic diaries from medieval times preserved the details. Father Custeau had studied the illustrations as a young seminarian in France and never questioned that they represented God's intentions. Even now the church sanctioned such methods if it led to the salvation of lost souls.

In the prison yard cell doors faced Father Custeau from all sides. Charlemagne set the brake, and they waited as the warden strutted toward them. He wore a uniform that was his own creation, and on his chest it was covered with ribbons and medals that likely dated from the Napoleonic Wars when France was at its greatest. "Father, this is a long way from the cathedral. What brings you here?"

"You have a prisoner named Nguyen van Phan?"

"You know we do. The Surete picked him up at his newspaper. He writes subversive articles praising Ho Chi Minh. You came all this way to ask me that?"

"Did the Surete tell you he had been seen leaving my cathedral?"

"They did inform me." The warden answered abruptly, the subtle inflections of his disdain barely concealed.

Charlemagne opened the car door with a flourish, leaving Father Custeau staring at the warden's highly polished black shoe. Father Custeau lifted himself from the car. "You realize he is here on information we supplied to the Surete. For reasons I cannot now explain, the church must again lay claim to him. You won't object to my taking him with me?"

"That's not possible, father. We have our own complaints."

"Then perhaps we should make this is an official visit, an investigation into why a church representative has been detained by the authorities, an inspection of conditions under which he is being held with a full report to the church in France."

The warden blushed, "And if the man leaves with you?"

"The matter is closed, a simple mistake."

The warden rocked on his boots. "Do you assume responsibility for him?"

"I will take responsibility."

The warden summoned two men with shaved heads wearing prison uniforms. Tattoos covered their muscular forearms. They carried black lacquered clubs on their hips.

"Here, father, you may want this." The warden handed Father Custeau a starched and neatly folded handkerchief, which Father Custeau put to his nose. Inside the cell block Father Custeau's eyes adjusted to the meager light from a single window near the ceiling. Father Custeau felt light headed. Charlemagne steadied the priest. A guard worked the key to a century old iron lock, then counted down the row of prisoners. He struck a match to see the number scratched on a bench, and then lifted a prisoner. The man covered his face.

"This is your prisoner," the guard said.

"Phan?" Father Custeau failed to recognize him.

The prisoner lowered his arms, "Father Custeau?"

"Your wife will be glad to see you're safe," Father Custeau said.

"She came to you?" Phan struggled to speak.

"She's the only reason I'm here."

"Thank God you did, father."

"Father?" A single prisoner responded. Then others began crying, "Father ...Father ... Father... Father."

"Silence," the guard shouted. The cries ceased. The guard carried Phan to the door. "You carry him from here."

Charlemagne held Phan from falling. As they crossed the common to the car, tears eroded the blood caked on Phan's lips.

"It's a wonder you're alive," Father Custeau said.

"My wife mustn't see me like this."

"Don't worry, she won't."

CHAPTER 19

Ha Noi, December 5, 1946
Phan
A jungle life

Inside the cathedral Thi was slumped beside their child on a wooden pew. At the sound of the door she dashed down the aisle. Phan limped toward her. She supported him and covered his face with kisses, "What have they done to you?"

"It was my fault." Phan tried to pull himself erect but fell onto her.

She struggled to hold him up. "What have they done to you?"

"Everything's fine now," he said, running his hand through her black silky hair. She eased him onto the pew beside their child whose eyes sparkled with recognition.

"Why?"

"They thought I was a communist."

"Because of Hahn," she said bitterly. "I told you to stay away from him."

"I don't think that was it."

"Then your writing. We must leave Ha Noi."

"She's right. I may not be able to save you the next

time," Father Custeau spoke from behind them.

"This is our city," Phan said.

"Don't yell at him," Thi cried. "He saved your life."

"And what was in it for him?"

Thi glanced away.

"There was something, wasn't there?" Phan shouted.

"They were baptized." Father Custeau said. "Their souls are saved."

"Damn you." Phan struggled to stand. "Don't you understand we don't want you here?"

"May God have mercy on your soul. May he forgive your blasphemy." Father Custeau made the sign of the cross. Phan felt himself falling off the pew. He tried to catch himself.

—⁓—

Phan woke stretched out like a corpse. How long had he been unconscious? They had taken him home. He watched Thi asleep beside him on the mat, his son sleeping at her breast. Her steady breath reassured him. Phan moved to touch her, but pain in his arms and neck prevented him. Motionless, he watched Thi, and relished her tranquility, remembered how it had been when he had first seen her.

She had glanced at him standing in formation, blushed and turned away. After that his eyes had looked for her wherever he went in the village or the fields. She was perfection. He discreetly asked her name from members of his squad. No one knew. He inquired about her parents. No one cared. At night in dreams, her beauty's temptations intermingled with the old priest's lectures on the virtues of chastity, and his admonitions to join the priesthood.

Phan had wanted more than the fantasies that filled his hours. Nights he tossed violently, keeping his squad awake. His thoughts frightened him. He lusted for the girl, the sight of her smooth flesh enough to set his mind racing.

His squad complained to the platoon leader that Phan, his mind always elsewhere, constantly stumbled on patrol and could get them killed. He overheard the squad talking: dangerous intellectual; Catholic; Chinaman; spy. He didn't belong in the Viet Minh. Better he didn't go on patrol. Remove him from the squad. They never suspected Thi's role.

After the platoon leader spoke to him about the complaints, Phan ate alone. The squad was initially satisfied, but within a week their criticisms renewed. He slept outside. That gave him another week. The platoon leader told him enemy activity was down so he wasn't needed on the patrols. Phan kept to himself. At the nightly political meetings no one approached him. When he stopped attending the meetings, no one said a thing. He stopped bathing. He smelled. His hair grew long with a pathetic beard, thin and wiry. Nothing felt right about the beard when he pulled his fingers through it, but he kept it to be defiant.

The Buddha's words mingled in his thoughts. Sorrow and the end of sorrow. Recalling his parents, he wept over the harsh life of an orphan, the thrashings from the priests, the threats of eternal damnation, the demand for the submission he refused to give.

When the villagers joined in whispering against him, he fled into the jungle to escape all reproach and free himself from the village gossip, which he knew would reach Thi's ears.

The rains were torrential from the moment he was on the trail. The rain dissolved the film of dust that covered his face, and took all shape from his clothes, weighting them with a chill that permeated his body and caused him to shake. He stripped his clothes off and stood naked, the rain pelting his skin. He ran under a double canopy where only mist reached him on the jungle floor. He crouched and kneaded the water from his clothes. When he dressed his clothes were cold, but soon warmed with his body heat. He felt clean, almost comfortable, and free. But was freedom to mean loneliness and despair?

After the storm the jungle smelled clean. He matted braided vines into a shelter. Just enough light filtered through the canopy for him to gather nettles and edible leaves. His attention turned to tastes and smells. He wandered like a village dog, nose to the ground. When he was saturated with the flavors and odors of the jungle, he studied its colors. The jungle was seasoned with greens. Overhead he caught glimpses of blue and occasional magenta where the silhouettes of king vultures circled on currents of air. Time lost meaning. Memory recycled the past, his parents gone and yet not gone, living within him, their presence real and troubling. Old frog sunning on a stump. Where had he heard that? When the emptiness of the silence left him nothing to grasp, he talked with himself. He paced between the trees until he wore a trail.

For weeks he fasted to demonstrate his mental strength, as priests did during Lent. When he ate again, the roots he dug failed to satisfy him. He craved the food of the village, especially the meat. The welts from insect bites hardened until his skin resisted all but the most vicious insects. Mosquitoes went unnoticed A line of red army ants still brought a flurry of oaths.

Separated from inhabited places, he separated from time. During the day he dreamed about Thi. Or he put Thi's name on an apparition of white flesh. Then memories of the orphanage crushed his dreams. The priest caught him with the others swimming in the river. And what are these, the priest screamed holding up their clothes. A whipping followed. One day the orphans, strung like pearls on a string, hand in hand passed through the red light district to spend a day in the local park. Music erupted from the open doors, and the boys caught glimpses of girls' bare legs undulating like snakes around the soldiers they entertained. Look straight ahead, the priest demanded. He dragged them past the doors. Such a quick walk. The little legs raced to keep up and sometimes fell, scraping knees, but never releasing their tiny hands from each other. Abomination against God, the priest shouted. And whose fault, Phan thought, sinking back on the jungle mat.

When Thi found him what a sight he must have been with his unkempt hair, his face pocked from insect bites and hardened into a crust of reddened flesh. She had treated him with respect and reasoned with him. She told him what he did was unnecessary and alarming, and asked why he did it.

She wouldn't understand. He still wasn't certain himself. She didn't press him further, content to repeat her entreaty that he accompany her back to the village.

His desire for her had reawakened as soon as she spoke. He never asked why she'd come searching for him. He'd followed her from the jungle and was soon drawn into the daily routine of village life. He'd worked with Thi's family in the rice fields and never returned to the Viet Minh. He married Thi in a simple ceremony conducted by the local Buddhist priest.

—⁓—

A child cried with increasing intensity. Phan struggled to escape it in his mind, then realized the cry came from beside him. His wife cradled their son and fed him until he fell asleep again.

"Are you feeling any better?" Thi sponged Phan's forehead with a wet cloth. "You've been delirious all night."

He placed his hand on her cheek. Thi withdrew his hand, held it in her own, examining it. His fingernails had been torn off during his interrogation. She soaked his hand in a small dish of warm water, stroking his fingers until the caked blood dissolved. A seizure started as a tremor in his fingers. His shadow from the light of a single candle, danced on the curtain. Thi gripped his wrists, fighting to hold him.

"You must see a French doctor."

"It's the French did this to me."

"Father Custeau can arrange it."

"And must I confess my sins to him?"

"At least take his advice to flee the city."

"When Hahn orders it."

"Hahn?" Thi cried out. "After this you'd still listen to him?"

CHAPTER 20

Ha Noi, December 7, 1946
Doctor Astray
Birthday party

N urses and orderlies, concealed along the wall behind the door, jumped out and shouted best wishes to Doctor Astray. As the candles burned, he tried to act surprised. Candle wax dripped onto soft white frosting. Doctor Astray stooped over the cake.

"Don't think about the candles, Doc," his young nurse said. "Just blow them out."

Doctor Astray, stomach exposed between the bottom buttons of his tropical shirt, pants slipped below his hips, tried to act composed in old age. He hadn't liked himself for years. He stared at his nurse, taking in her white skin's purity, her breasts pressed against the starched uniform, her slender legs. Her youthful indifference to him increased his desire. He smiled. She was a last chance. He felt like an eighteen year old, afraid to act upon what he felt, afraid of the rejection it would most certainly bring on him. He looked into her blue eyes and blocked out the thought of her as the daughter he never had.

"The old man needs time to catch his breath." A male orderly, youthful lifter of stretchers, broke the spell. Everyone in the room laughed.

Doctor Astray lifted his pants to their proper height. He leaned forward to where he felt the heat from the candles and blew.

As the candles smoldered, Doctor Astray savored the lingering odor. For the first time in days he smelled the antiseptic meant to smother traces of decay. He had stopped noticing odors through the years of drudgery, a life of humoring colonial wives about their imagined symptoms, listening to endless chatter meant to break the monotony of tropical days, his silent raging against the frustration of feeling trapped. The diseases of those truly sick stuck him in a monotonous routine: malaria and dysentery with accompanying fevers, vomiting, and diarrhea. An occasional case of elephantiasis sparked his interest.

Doctor Astray served the middle-class French colonials, who were thrilled to find a Paris-educated doctor willing to devote his life to such an inhospitable place. Enough French patients meant he never had to treat the native Vietnamese. Since his return from Paris in 1933, the Sofetel Metropole Hotel had provided him elegant accommodations at the heart of French social life. When the local ladies had urged him to take an apartment, the hotel manager had lowered his room rate. Socialites and celebrities in Ha Noi for a visit sought him out or at least crossed his path at the bar. Together with free bar privileges, that convinced him to stay. What he did was a living, not a great living but certainly better than the living he once made in France. At a time of life when he should have been retiring to the countryside in France, he was only starting to save for it.

Like him afraid to admit defeat, Western society petrified in the heat and humidity of a hostile country. In the '30s there had been sparks of rebellion from the natives, but the army easily maintained control through a series of public executions. His living continued even when the Japanese forced concessions from the Vichy government cowering back in France. He knew the concessions were a sign of weakness in a country where only strength established respect. The Japanese, who boasted of themselves as a master race, maintained order. He'd treated their officers and their concubines and carried on with his regular practice. Now, with the war ended, the Vietnamese revolt resurfaced. Something felt different, the Vietnamese more a threat with the bombings, the assassinations and in the last week, open fighting between Vietnamese and French for control of Ha Noi. But a shortage of military doctors guaranteed him interesting work. The once great surgeon in him reemerged.

"How old are you, Doc?" The orderly interrupted his thoughts.

Doctor Astray frowned, "Old enough."

"You already know his age," his young nurse said.

"Come on Doc, how old are you?" the orderly said.

"Cut the cake," his nurse said.

"Someone get a knife from the operating room," the orderly said.

"You get it," Doctor Astray said.

"Whatever you say, Doc." The orderly put up his hands in mock surrender.

"And how long are we going to wait?" Doctor Astray said.

"My back hurts. Too many casualties to lift today," the orderly said, moving slowly.

"This is only the start," Doctor Astray said.

"There are too many for one man to carry."

"You volunteered."

"To shut my old man up. He wanted me in the Infantry. Crazy as it was, I couldn't duck what he wanted altogether."

"Live with your decision, hurt back and all. You'll find it different during a war."

"What do you know about wars, Doc?"

"I was in the First War."

"You are an old man."

"Most days I agree with you," Doctor Astray said. The

young nurse handed him a scalpel. He pierced the frosting as if it were skin. "Who's first?"

"How long will this fighting go on?" his young nurse said, as he placed the slice in her mouth.

"Long after you're safely in France."

"I don't think I could leave these boys."

"That will change. It gets gruesome."

A champagne cork popped, ricocheting off the ceiling. Laughter.

"I won't change," his young nurse said.

"You get a sense of hopelessness." Doctor Astray gazed absently from her to the operating table covered with plates of meat and cheese.

"You still try to save them," the young nurse said.

"I patch them best I can," Doctor Astray said.

"You waste a lot of supplies," the orderly said.

"Are you amused?" Doctor Astray cut another piece of cake.

"You two quit bickering and eat some cake," his young nurse said.

Doctor Astray frowned in her direction, not caring to be compared with the smart tongued orderly. "Damn flies," he swatted around his head.

"Cake's drawing them," his young nurse said.

"Take what's left to the patients." Doctor Astray settled into a chair in the corner and tried to appreciate the party. The frivolity increased as the nurses drank champagne directly from bottles. After several minutes Doctor Astray slipped from the room. He walked to the critical care unit where a soldier's wail reverberated from the walls.

The night nurse bounced from her chair. "He's been like that all night, doctor. Nothing seems to help." She nodded towards a corner bed under a mosquito net, a giant cobweb shifting imperceptibly in the slight currents of air. In the moonlight the night nurse's face glowed with an unearthly radiance.

Doctor Astray walked to the corner bed and reviewed the chart that described what soldiers in the field called a gut wound, unlikely to make it to the hospital. This one had made it that far. Astray spoke to the night nurse, "Go for a walk and get some fresh air. I'll look after him for awhile."

After the night nurse left, Doctor Astray opened the mosquito netting and leaned forward. He grasped the soldier's wrist to get a pulse. The wail diminished to a sob. Bulging eyes that pierced the darkness observed every movement.

For years Doctor Astray had known when a patient's time came. He'd gained the knowledge from an old French madam brought to the hospital from a rubber plantation. He diagnosed her with heartburn and a stomach ulcer. The old madam never contradicted him, but she sent for her lawyer, then her relatives, and calmly explained what she wanted done when she died. Her relatives protested, so too her lawyer, and Doctor Astray supported them. Alone with him, she asked for a fatal dose of medication. He refused, telling her she had a long life ahead.

"You have been a doctor too long not to see death's hand written on me," she chided him. "Look closely and remember it. Don't let other patients suffer when their time comes."

The old madam died two weeks later without ever having left the hospital. Doctor Astray performed an autopsy expecting to find she had willed herself to death. Her body was loaded with cancerous tumors. He wondered how she had concealed the pain. He vowed to follow her advice.

Now he stepped to the drug and surgical supply closet and removed a bottle and tablespoon. He poured a liquid that reminded him of dark molasses into the spoon, leveled the spoon in the moonlight, and held it to the soldier's cracked lips. The soldier instinctively sucked, his mouth settling into a smile. The frail body twisted toward Doctor Astray and a hand purple from needle punctures rose from the sheets.

A tremor in his own hands caused Doctor Astray to pause. An accursed symptom for a surgeon, signaling loss of dexterity, or even worse, a loss of confidence. Father Custeau called the tremor a penalty for playing God, as if modern medicine affronted God's will. Such foolishness. Doctor Astray was just getting old. Father Custeau would never approve of the judgment he now made, but compassion demanded it. God's will wasn't enough. He returned the medicine to the cabinet.

"You gave him a sedative?" the night nurse said.

How long had she been standing in the doorway? "He'll rest quietly for the night," Doctor Astray said as he walked past her.

"They're looking for you at the front desk."

His young nurse stood in the hallway, drunkenly defiant. She gulped directly from a bottle of champagne.

"Where'd you come from," Doctor Astray blurted, like a small child caught.

"So much frightens me," she said. Her eyes fastened on him. "Yet at times I feel detached."

"That's not so bad."

"We all know what you do, Doctor, and none of us blames you."

"I don't know what you mean." Doctor Astray brushed past her. He felt her watching him, imagined her eyes dropping to his bowed legs as he limped, slightly stooped, along the corridor. Perhaps some of his baldness showed from the back. He imagined his nurse's pity for him, and it stung him at every step. He recalled how as a youth he'd pitied others who at the time would have been half his present age. Somehow overnight he'd become old. Sciatica shot pain down his left leg and kept him from making a faster escape from his nurse. The pain was continuous. At night it prevented his sleeping more than an hour at a time. The pain kept him in constant motion. Others called him restless.

—◊—

When Father Custeau summoned him to treat a student of his, Doctor Astray didn't hesitate to climb into the black limousine that waited for him in front of the hospital. Charlemagne sat beside the driver, leaving Doctor Astray the entire back seat. They drove through streets where walls wore fresh pock marks from random gunfire. Scattered patrols of

French soldiers nervously glanced their way but let them pass unquestioned. Then they crossed into a Vietnamese section through a barricade which a French sentry drew back, then half saluted as they rumbled onto the unpaved street. Here shattered furniture lay stacked against vacant shops, a burned out jeep tipped against a lightless lamp post. Faces appeared in doorways and disappeared. A dog sniffed at their tires as they stopped before turning into an alley. The headlights caught the jaded eyes of a boy pressed against the wall, a rock partially concealed in his clenched hand, lowered to his side. The car crushed boxes along the way, then emerged between warehouses where men squatted in doorways playing cards by candle light. The driver parked, front wheels over the curb.

Charlemagne opened the car door and lifted the medical bag from the seat. Doctor Astray followed him inside, up stairs, and through rows of cubicles partitioned by sheets. Charlemagne pulled back curtains as he went, speaking a single name. Finally a young woman directed him, her pancake breasts swinging where she pointed.

Doctor Astray heard the coughing first. Charlemagne held the curtain until Doctor Astray knelt beside the young man. A small child played nearby.

"What do you want?" the young man on the mat demanded.

"You're Phan?" Doctor Astray said.

"I didn't send for you."

"If you had, I wouldn't have come." Doctor Astray continued to open his bag. "I'm here as a favor to Father Custeau. Now stay quiet so I can examine you."

Doctor Astray held Phan down with one hand and listened to his chest with a stethoscope. He examined lacerations on the scalp. On the other side of the curtain he heard the whispers of Vietnamese. A young woman pushed open the curtain.

"You can't be in here," Doctor Astray said.

"I'm his wife."

"Your husband received quite a beating," said Doctor Astray. "Must be a communist to get picked up by the Surete."

"He's a great reporter," Thi said.

"Seems the Surete weren't impressed," Dr. Astray said. "I'll do what I can. He's hardy. It's up to you to get him to rest."

The doctor wrapped Phan's chest. He sutured the deepest cuts, after cleaning the open wounds. "He has two broken ribs and scalp lacerations. Keep him at home and out of the affairs in the streets. He can't survive another beating."

"It's not up to her," Phan said.

"Maybe you should listen to your wife. No point asking you to listen to me. Your mind is made up on westerners. I can see it in the way you look at me."

"Maybe if you left us alone, we'd feel different."

"We?" Doctor Astray said. "You people aren't ready. You get rid of us you'll end up ruled by communists. It'll take a lot longer to free yourself from them."

"That's the way you see it."

"Not a lot of other ways to see it. Civilization isn't something you can take up over night. You develop it in every citizen's mind over the years. Takes generations. You're just not ready. You'd end up destroying everything we've built up here, and then you'd be back in mud huts, fighting each other for what little was left. We won't let that happen." Doctor Astray threw his medical instruments back in his bag. "You should be working with us instead of building barricades."

The young woman reached out her hand in gratitude. She left him with several coins. He fumbled with them.

"I know this isn't enough," she whispered as she withdrew her hand. "We'll get you more as soon as we can."

Doctor Astray floundered to return the coins, then pushed back the curtain and retreated. The rancid smell of nuoc maum laded the sweltering air. He tore open his collar and lowered his head to recover from a sudden dizziness. Vietnamese surrounded him, the children in front, staring and giggling, parents further back, also failing to mask their own curiosity. Europeans still remained a novelty. All those slit eyes riveted on him, conditioned over decades to placid observation and passive acceptance of imposed realities. As he struggled to catch his breath, their inexorable eyes followed him, taunting him like the dead in the morgue. Charlemagne supported him with an iron tight grip around his arm.

CHAPTER 21

Tong, December 17, 1946
Lao
Lao's alley

Lao walked backward, the way he'd seen soldiers on patrol. When he was sure no one followed, he turned down the alley. Outside the back door he had completed his cardboard fort and stockpiled it with stones to peg at the rats. Hitting them wasn't hard. He stopped to admire the fort and make sure no one had tampered with it. The alley was choked with garbage bags, beer bottles, old liquor bottles, enough stuff to pick through to survive. Lao stepped cautiously. Another time he might have searched the trash, but Leah and her friends provided him enough to eat. He folded back the cardboard that acted like a door, reached in and arranged the rags, ready for a nap before nightfall when most French soldiers visited the club. That was the time he ran errands for the girls. He squeezed down into the box and closed the door behind him. It was hot, but at least it wasn't raining. He hated the rain. The roof of flattened tin always leaked somewhere and dripped onto his bedding. He felt around the floor and found the tobacco jar where he kept dried beef. He chewed until he fell asleep.

He woke with the walls of his fort shaking.

"You going to help tonight, or you want me to find someone else?" Dawn said.

At first he thought to ignore her, but then he remembered how much better things were getting for him.

"I'm sorry," he said, pushing open the door as he started to cry. "I fell asleep and had a bad dream."

Crying always worked He turned it on and off. Women had this instinct about crying they couldn't overcome, even when their common sense told them something else. They had a lot of street savvy, but he knew how to get around them. Even Mommyson. She knew he lived in the alley, but she looked the other way. The men were different. The bartender enjoyed kidding around, but he'd throw anybody into the street for no reason at all.

Dawn reached over and hugged him. Her skin was smooth and warm. He didn't take his eyes off her. She was as dark skinned as the bartender and at times he wondered about her relationship with him. She worked her fingers through his hair, caught a louse and popped it between her fingernails.

"Why do you do it?" Lao asked politely.

"We can't have you bringing lice into the club."

"I mean with the men." Lao twisted to face her. He didn't understand the soldiers and the girls touching them constantly, the girls always coaxing money out of the soldiers. Going to the rooms, groping like animals. Thinking about it sickened him.

"I make my living from the men," Dawn said.

"You don't need them. Khong and I can take care of you."

"It isn't enough."

"It is enough."

"We need the French soldiers' money."

"I hate them," Lao said.

"Someday you'll be just like them."

"I'll never be like them," Lao said.

"We'll see when you have a little more manhood and

money in your pockets." She laughed and tossed his hair.

Lao pushed her away. Inside the bar the music ended. Loud voices, then a woman's scream. The bartender's voice. Silence. Music again.

"I'll come inside tonight," Lao said.

"Leah and I have visitors," Dawn said. She rested her hand on Lao's neck and her thumb worked across his cheek where he'd cried.

When Dawn closed the door, the music sounded far away. Lao settled into the rags, leaving the cardboard door open. He studied the outlines in the alley. Rats scampered over the boxes. He picked up a stone.

Gunfire, then Lao heard shouting. Something moved at the end of the alley. The shadow advanced. He felt his heart start thumping. He gripped another rock. The shadow advanced. He pitched the rock.

"Damn kid, I'm hurt enough."

"What are you doing here?" Lao whispered. A Viet soldier in black pajamas supported himself with a rifle.

"Why are you out here?" the soldier demanded.

"I live here."

"Alone?"

"With my friend Khong. He'll be back any minute now."

"Is this the ...club?"

"Yes," Lao said, "but you can't stay here."

"Why not?" The rifle pointed at Lao.

"French soldiers inside."

"I'll stay with you." The soldier fell into the rags next to Lao.

"Mister?" said Lao.

"You got to hide me, kid."

"You stink something bad. Are you all right?"

"They gut shot me," the soldier said. "Can't feel it anymore."

The soldier lay motionless.

Lao tried to think what to do. He reached down and touched where the soldier clutched his side. The clothing was soaked and had started to grow sticky.

"Mister, you got to leave."

The soldier didn't answer. Lao started thinking faster. The soldier had ruined his fort, blood stinking up the rags. When the French Surete found the soldier, they'd turn him over to the priests, of that much he felt certain. He had no place to hide the soldier. If Mommyson found out, she'd have the bartender throw them both out, just because she didn't want trouble for the club. The soldier needed a doctor. Lao didn't even know a doctor. What a rotten piece of luck. No matter how he thought about it, the soldier spoiled everything for him.

The sound of shooting in the streets resumed, coming from all directions. The door to the club opened, and Dawn stuck her head out, "Get in here quick."

"Can't," Lao said.

"Get in here."

"Something you ought to see," Lao said.

"Not now."

"Someone's hurt real bad."

"What are you talking about?" Dawn stepped out and closed the door behind her.

"He's in here," Lao said.

Dawn stumbled in the dark and almost fell on top of him.

"What's he doing there?"

"He's been shot."

She examined the soldier. "Help bring him inside."

"What about the French soldiers?"

"They ran from the club when the shooting started. They won't be back right away."

They lifted up the soldier. He bled on them. Several times they had to stop to get a better grip.

"Where you going to put him?" Lao tried not to sound excited.

"There's a place behind one of the closets."

"You can hide a man in there?"

"Don't ask questions." Dawn studied his face. "That's

the way it works. Somebody gets caught, they don't know about the rest of us."

"Even Mommyson?"

"No questions."

Dawn kicked a hidden door behind umbrellas in the hall closet. Inside the secret room a bed and a very small oil lantern, just like in spy stories. They dragged the soldier into the room and dropped him on the bed.

Dawn crouched over the soldier. "This is the one gets information from Mommyson." Other girls crowded into the room. They stripped the soldier and cleaned his wounds. The only remaining blood surrounded two little holes where the bullet had gone in and come out. Lao was glad the soldier remained unconscious, the cleaning being so humiliating. He compared the soldier's body to his own. He saw no reason to think he couldn't be a soldier too. He watched the girls tear sheets into bandages. When they finished with the soldier, he looked like a mummy.

Mommyson came into the room, inspected the soldier's bandages, then stared at Lao. "Take off your pants."

Lao looked at her like she was crazy.

"Take off the pants. The Surete will question that blood."

"Nothing under them," Lao said lamely.

"You won't show me anything I haven't seen before."

Lao unbuttoned the shorts and bent down, kicking them off with one leg and turning away as he handed them to Mommyson. Dawn tossed him a sheet, which he tied around himself like a toga.

"If you just wash my shorts, I can wear them wet," Lao said.

"That's what I figured," Mommyson said. She was laughing when she left the room.

Lao crawled into a corner with the sheets covering all but his face. They left him with the wounded soldier. He listened to the umbrella being put back against the closet wall and the hangers put up on the rod. The room reeked from all the perfume. He started to feel claustrophobic. It was creepy, just him and the mummy. To keep from crying, he pretended he was behind the enemy lines in Germany where everyone wore a swastika. He was the hero, of course, and all the others tried to get him out of the country because of what he knew being so valuable. That was the way he remembered it from a movie he'd watched the only time he'd sneaked into the back of a French theater in Ha Noi.

"What you staring at?" he shouted at Khong. "I'm not scared."

He curled up in the corner for an hour, still imagining he hid out in Germany. Leah was right about his needing a real family and not just Khong. The two of them talked about it a lot. She had the same problem, not knowing who her dad was. Her mom had told her he was a French soldier. That was hard to deny given Leah's big round eyes. In a way that made her worse off. The way Lao figured at least being a complete orphan, his parents left him looking Vietnamese. Important people didn't like half-breeds. Too hard to tell where their loyalties lay. Once Lao heard a legionnaire tell Leah the apple never fell far from the tree. The legionnaire laughed when he said it, but Leah didn't like it. Being a half breed whore was worse than just being a whore. Maybe nothing was worse. No, being alive without arms and legs and getting up in the morning and being set out beside the street to beg was worse. If you looked around, you could always find someone worse off than you.

The mummy started to moan. Lao tried to see him, but they hadn't left a lantern or even matches. The only light inched from under the secret door. Lao crawled over and tried to tell what was the matter by reaching toward the noise, feeling his way like reading braille. He was careful not to poke out the fellow's eyes. When he touched the lips, he felt something wet. No way to tell for sure whether it was drool or the soldier was bleeding. He decided it wasn't sticky enough for blood. Anyway there wasn't anything he could do about it. He only had the cloth wrapped around him. Why not stuff it in the fellow's mouth to keep him quiet? That was in the movie too. He remembered everything in the movie, maybe because it was the only movie he had ever seen. Anyway, in the movie the guy died. Suffocated, rather than betray where he and the hero were hiding. That was all right for the hero, but the fellow was sure stupid for himself. The fellow was a Jew, whatever that meant.

"Don't you have anything to say?" he said to Khong. "Sometimes I wonder why I keep talking to you. You're never any help. Well, maybe sometimes."

Lao crawled toward the door to listen. No point killing the fellow with a rag if French soldiers weren't out in the hall. Maybe if heroes thought that way instead of trying to be heroes, more of the common folks would live. That would make a dumb movie, but he didn't care. Who was he kidding? He wasn't a hero, and anyway if something happened to him no one would notice or care. His leg had fallen asleep where he sat on it, so he pretended he was wounded as he dragged himself over to the door. He got his ear down against the crack of light and listened. They played music in the bar as if nothing was wrong. Good thing too, because the wounded fellow was beginning to moan. Lao felt annoyed, but then when no one came he started to relax. The Viet Minh must have really scared the French, but Lao understood how the French operated. They ran off and pulled themselves together. Then they'd come back with a lot more soldiers and start shooting any one around just to prove they hadn't been scared. Course they'd been scared. Everything turned out to be a lie with them. Except the killing was real.

Someone walked up to the closet and started taking down the hangers. Lao couldn't tell who it was because of all the moaning by the wounded soldier. Nothing like in the movie. Maybe it was his fault because he hadn't stuffed a rag down the fellow's throat. The door opened. Someone was there in the room with Lao, but the sudden light blinded him so it was just an outline. It was the kind of thing he hated the worse, people coming up on you without letting on who they were or what they wanted. He thought he'd scream, only the someone already started to, maybe not a scream, more like a gasp or maybe a sigh, something that let him know something was very wrong. The form darted to the wounded man as if Lao wasn't there.

"Leah?" Lao heard himself speak.

"Why didn't you call for help?" It was Leah.

What kind of a thing was that for her to say? He was trying to save the fellow from the French soldiers, maybe even the Surete. Didn't she know what the French did to their prisoners? He watched her sopping up the blood.

"I didn't know what to do. You left me in the dark with no way to even see him." Lao started to explain. He wanted to ask her why she didn't know not to leave him alone, and that leaving him with a dying man was pretty much the same thing as leaving him alone. Instead he started crying. This time it didn't seem to be working. Leah never even glanced over at him and other girls crowded around the mummy, ignoring Lao. They brought in fresh bandages and a bucket of water. Lao glared at them. They all started to sob. It took a lot to make whores sob so he figured the wounded soldier was dead. Then one by one the girls slipped past him without a word. He watched Leah bathing the fellow's face.

"I'm not to blame," Lao screamed.

"To blame?" Leah looked up. "For what?"

"His death."

"You silly boy. He'll be fine." Leah smiled. "You thought he was dead?"

"Don't laugh."

"I'm not laughing at you."

"Whore," he said what popped into his head.

Leah glared at him. "Where did you hear that word?"

"Everywhere. Everyone uses it."

"It's a terrible thing to say."

"I don't care."

"But you do care." She crouched beside him. "What is this really about?"

The rain of tears resumed. He tasted the endless sea of tears on his lips.

Leah touched her forefinger to his lips, "I understand you, my little brother."

"You won't tell about this?" Lao said.

"I won't tell."

Lao snuggled against her, tucked in her arms.

"We won't let anything happen to you," Leah said, her hand upon his blazing cheek.

CHAPTER 22

Ha Noi, December 19, 1946
Pasteur
City in chaos

In the streets of Ha Noi, Lieutenant Pasteur sensed the uneasiness caused by Ho Chi Minh's agreement allowing French troops back into the north. The lieutenant and all officers were under orders to avoid the Viet Minh militia and at the same time to reassert control over buildings once controlled by the French. An earlier generation of soldiers had established the Indochina colony. Now it was time for his generation to restore it.

In early morning light the administrative buildings of the French military command glistened like new construction, their ochre faces coated with fresh paint, the black iron fence recently re-lacquered. Once again guards marched back and forth. Nothing Oriental about these structures, they resembled the government buildings in southern France, imparting a sense of relief in Lieutenant Pasteur as he entered. Leaping the stairs two by two to his new office on the second floor, he passed a Viet woman with a whisk broom slowly sweeping her way down. She smiled and bowed.

Inside the orderly room Lieutenant Pasteur scanned the faces of those waiting for him: the usual deserters under guard, soldiers refused leave or administrative transfer there to complain, squad leaders waiting for the morning briefing, the German named Haussmann, who had joined them at Sai Gon... he a welcome addition for his experience fighting the Viet Minh while in the legion. Lieutenant Pasteur remembered Haussmann's still-unopened orders of transfer on his desk. He wanted time to figure how to dissuade Haussmann from leaving, but the enlisted soldiers' backwater chain of communications must have worked too quickly. "Morning," he snapped perfunctorily as he entered his office.

Straight up in his chair, Lieutenant Pasteur summoned Haussmann from the orderly room. "I have your orders."

"Very good, sir." Haussmann dropped his salute and reached for the papers.

"You can stay with us."

"I'd never make much of a Frenchman," Haussmann said.

"You don't know that. You've already spent five years in the legion. You're entitled to citizenship. Why don't you try it? From what I know of the legion, you don't belong with them."

"I don't fit into the city, sir."

"This is only temporary. Once Ha Noi is pacified, we'll take to the field."

"My outfit in the legion is at Tong. I came north to re-join them."

"Well then, Haussmann, I guess its adieu," Lieutenant Pasteur said. He shook the stout man's hand.

"Adieu, lieutenant."

—∿—

At the morning briefing for company officers, the captain told them what they already knew. Two days before a company of infantry had cleared the streets of Viet Minh partisans in Ha Noi's Hang Bun section, killing as many as a

151

hundred Vietnamese. Yesterday French troops had successfully occupied the Viet Ministries of Finance and Communications.

"Today," the captain continued, "we are receiving
reports the Viet Minh are setting up barricades and making
holes in the walls between houses to resist our imposition of
order. The colonel has ordered them to cease these activities
and disarm. You must be prepared to deploy your platoons if
they fail to comply."

"What's the likelihood?" one of the lieutenants asked.

"Damn unlikely they'll comply," the captain said.
"The communists got the Vietnamese believing they're ready
to rule themselves. Mess of it they'd make, but we can't tell
them a thing right now."

Since leaving France, Lieutenant Pasteur had continually imagined himself leading a platoon through dense jungles or withstanding an attack at a remote outpost in the wilderness. It never occurred to him that Ha Noi was more than
a brief stopover.

At noon time as the soldiers started toward the mess
hall sporadic gunfire could be heard from the center of the
city. Lieutenant Pasteur was standing at the window for the
breeze when the first mortar rounds landed between the barracks. Counter batteries fired at random into the buildings
surrounding the compound. Lieutenant Pasteur turned out
his platoon as ordered. They climbed into two trucks with the
overhead canvas removed, and he led them in a jeep through
the streets. Almost immediately they came to a barricade of
overturned carts and furniture. Instead of the din of battle that
he expected, silence greeted them, then a snap that sounded
like a twig underfoot, and then another. His platoon tumbled
off the trucks, several soldiers falling lifeless in the street.
Then another snap; the windshield to his jeep shattered. In a
single motion he leaped and fell beneath the vehicle, where
he lay beside his driver. Bullets bounced around them and
off the jeep like in a penny arcade. He shouted to the squads
to deploy to either side and return the fire. But to where? He
searched for some sign of movement from a sniper's rifle bar-

rel pointed in their direction. He waited, anticipated, then felt a blush of shame. What heroic figure ever huddled like this? He'd never pictured himself cowering. He had pictured himself proudly charging at an enemy bunker under a hail of bullets. Now although there wasn't an enemy in sight, he couldn't move. He had been betrayed, sent into an ambush where his courage faltered, when no enemy assaulted him face to face. To skirmish among rows of houses and blocks of buildings was like battling blindly through a maze. His men crowded against the walls, afraid to move, or did they wait for him to lead? He tried to imagine himself leading a heroic salvation.

A roaring armored vehicle rounded the corner behind them. Its machine guns rotated from building to building, directed by an invisible crew. It drove straight past them, pushing aside the barricade and continued down the street and out of sight as if to mock Pasteur's dilemma. Had the captain who betrayed him suspected how he'd react and sent this monstrosity? Still concealed behind the jeep, Lieutenant Pasteur ordered the dead soldiers loaded into the trucks. He didn't want to know their names or care about them again. His platoon rose when he ordered and filed along the street. Leaving the vehicles, they traveled on foot, smaller targets for an ambush.

Lieutenant Pasteur sensed the platoons scorn for him. They didn't understand. The enemy had hit and run, but what he'd done was reasonable: the Viet Minh might have left someone behind to shoot a soldier foolish enough to step out into the street, but now there was no point trying to make the platoon understand. Next time. Then all before would be forgotten.

A machinegun chattered in the distance, the armored vehicle under attack, exposed by the reckless courage of its crew. A man in black pajamas wandered to the center of the street in front of the platoon. A coordinated trap?

"Hands up," Lieutenant Pasteur said, signaling the gesture as well. "Mao linh."

The man held his hands out with palms together, bow-ing repeatedly and chattering in Vietnamese.

"What the hell does he want?" Lieutenant Pasteur barked.

"I think he's saying he's no Viet Minh," a soldier replied.

"Or thinks the lieutenant's a priest." The others laughed.

"Look, he's wet himself."

"Maybe he's a drunk."

The weasel-faced soldier broke from the ranks and started to drag the man off, "I'll take care of this."

"What are you doing?" Lieutenant Pasteur asked.

"I'll shoot him, of course," the weasel-faced soldier said.

"Can't have you doing that."

"You want him behind you?"

"Bring him along," Lieutenant Pasteur said.

The weasel-faced soldier struck the man in the stomach with his rifle butt and kicked him on his way down.

"What are you doing? Lieutenant Pasteur demanded.

"Checking him for weapons." The weasel-faced soldier lifted the man onto his feet. "What if he has a grenade?"

The man held his face against his sleeve, soaking up blood from his nose. Others from the platoon tied the man's arms behind him, and dragged him forward.

The shops that lined the street, had their doors boarded or gated. Cautiously creeping forward, the platoon scrutinized the rooftops and alleyways. Someone thought to push the prisoner ahead of them into each open alleyway. A soldier behind Lieutenant Pasteur fired his Thompson machine-gun into a solid wooden fence of what once must have been a courtyard, now overgrown with vegetation. A cat slipped from beneath and sprinted down the street in front of the platoon. Several soldiers fired, but the cat disappeared into safety. Whatever recourse the Viet Minh had taken against the armored vehicle had ended, leaving the streets silent. This only increased Lieutenant Pasteur's anxiety. He again cursed those who sent him into the city.

CHAPTER 23

Tong, December 22, 1946
Mueller
A chance encounter

"LEGIO PATRIA NOSTRA," "The Legion Is our Fatherland" proclaimed the sign over the entrance at Tong where Mueller trained. The recruiter had promised him his old rank, and the shortage of replacements ensured it. He stood beneath the arcade veranda of the barracks, one of two facing each other across the drill field, and adjusted his kepi. He was careful not to fingerprint the bill of the hat as he adjusted it to fit squarely on his head. Chevron pressed against his pants. When he stepped out onto the parade field, the sun burned his face and when he turned toward the front gate, it burned the back of his neck, his kepi a verification of French style over practicality. He clutched his first pass to town since rejoining the legion. He swaggered past the guards at the gate, Chevron at his heal. The guards grinned. "Go get 'em, sarge."

Instead of civilians shouting for his taxi, he was greeted with, yes sir, excuse me sir, as people moved aside to let him pass. Beggars and whores waved with invitations to the bars outside the gate. Each honky-tonk sported wooden signs that flashed in the sun like cheap Christmas ornaments. Their words of welcome promised more sex, more drinks than the others. Barkers at the doors screamed: "What you want? Maybe a girl, maybe something more, maybe something special?"

He didn't listen to the words. He'd heard them all before. He went to a bar he remembered, a place where Germans felt welcome, even with its walls covered with cheap forgeries of Monet, Rubens, Cezanne, all hoaxes, pictures of a France he'd never seen and never wanted to see.

Sitting beside other German soldiers but avoiding their conversations, he drank French Beer Laroi and when the Laroi ran out Vietnamese Ba Mui Ba, both tasting weak and artificial, not like the stout German ale. And yet how would he know? He had tasted only a few swallows before the French ran him out of his own country, bankrupting it, in peace destroying what they couldn't on the battlefield, stealing German morale. Yet the French gladly used Germans to fight in their wars to do those things for which they had no stomach.

The bar girls pleaded for drinks of tea and tried to coax him to a room upstairs. They were different girls than he remembered, but it had been years since he'd been able to afford this bar. Different yet the same. Their methods hadn't changed: they set their lure as women always did, manipulating men for their own purposes. He understood why his father had run away from his mother. She was like the others. Beatings had failed to change her. He imagined his father was too proud a man to be manipulated by a woman. After he ran off his mother brought in other men, making Mueller leave the single bed where they slept together and wait hidden in the hall, all the time hearing the men, the laughter, the cries, the arguing over money. He would return when she called him and hold her as she wept, until finally she'd fall asleep in his arms.

As he'd grown, he'd fought the men. At first they held him away as he flayed at them until he was exhausted. Their laughter reached him even now as he remembered the one he'd knifed and the look of dread on his mother's face. She, whom he protected, screamed at him, holding the stabbed man in her arms. She cheated him, her only child, the only man who had truly loved her.

Mueller took his time sipping beer, eyeing the whores. He ordered ribs that tasted more like water buffalo than steer. He had money to spend, but wasn't in a hurry. He dismissed the first whore with a wave of his hand. Make them wait for the moment when he was finally ready. Soon enough they would find him more than they bargained for. When he drank enough, they'd discover the more challenging forms of a man's limitless appetites.

Chevron sniffed at Mueller's pant leg. Its tail beat against the floor as it studied him with saucer eyes. Mueller bent and poured beer on the floor.

"Hey, sarge, you're a welcome sight." A soldier slapped Mueller on the back. Mueller turned and the soldier recoiled as Mueller's dagger slashed the air between them. "Wait. Remember me? Haussmann."

"I remember you." Mueller stabbed the dagger deep into the bar. "But that doesn't mean you can sneak up behind me."

"You haven't changed, sarge. You're still the same old cobra," Haussmann said, attempting a laugh. Mueller wasn't athletic, but that didn't matter. He was rugged and determined, ruthless when it mattered.

"I'd keep it in mind, I was you."

"Seen you watching the whores," Haussmann gestured toward the girls. "No need paying for what you'll be getting free."

"Not likely. Things haven't changed that much."

"Not in here. Village girls." Haussmann laughed.

"Frenchies want retribution for the massacre. Quite a surprise to them when the Viet Minh struck back in Ha Noi. They figured after they shelled Hai Phong, no more problems. Other day Sainteny was injured by a mine that exploded under his car. Whole thing coordinated. Beats all, but them little slant eyes was always sneaky. Too near Christmas. We'll loose our holiday passes."

"How do you know?"

"Heard rumors." Haussmann spoke with pride.

"Rumors don't make it so."

"They do when you overheard them from French officers."

"Then you'd better keep your mouth shut. Too many stinking spies around here." Mueller glanced around the bar but saw no one near enough to make his point. The bar girls had backed away when he'd pulled the knife.

"Sure, sarge." Haussmann answered.

"Our squads aren't ready." The beer was warming Mueller into conversation.

"You think so?" Haussmann said.

"Too young, too innocent." Mueller pointed with his eyes to three legionaries with girls giggling on their laps.

"Those young soldiers are as good as any," Haussmann ventured.

"Doubt it," said Mueller.

"Hitler started them," Haussmann said. "Young boys were easier to train while they still obeyed their mothers. Never gave them a chance to think for themselves."

"Hitler had it wrong."

"Tell that to the Frenchies," Haussmann said. "Our German boys sat in Paris cafes just weeks into the war. It'll be just as easy for them here."

"That why so many came here?"

"Their SS tattoos have more to do with it. They're hunted men now the war's over. Lucky for them the legion doesn't ask questions."

"That so?" Mueller was indifferent. Germany wasn't his concern, hadn't been in years.

"You were gone from the legion a long time," Haussmann said.

"A few years."

"Heard you drove a taxi."

"Maybe."

"They took you back anyway?"

"I took them back." Mueller pulled his dagger from the wooden bar. "Heard anything else about me?"

"Just talk."

"Talk gets dangerous." Mueller waved his knife back and forth in front of his face, following it with his eyes.

"I see that." Haussmann reached down to pat Chevron, but pulled back when he growled. "Ugly mutt."

"Leave the dog be." Mueller turned back to the bar and started to think about what Haussmann had said about going into the field. Barracks rumors never turned out exactly as what was spread, but there was always something to them. He was ready for the field even if his men needed more training. His Germans were dependable. The other men in the unit might work out except for the Viets. Crazy idea yellowing the war with natives.

A bar girl rubbed against him, trying to sit on his lap. "Buy Leah a drink."

"Not now," he said, staring at her. As she rose up on his knee, her short skirt rose exposing black-laced panties. Her blouse was low, padded, and propped with stays, her hair cropped like the flappers of the Roaring Twenties. That must have been a fine time in France, but he had only seen it in magazines the legion sent to the field. The girl's Franco-Asian face said it all, a child of the brothel, trapped there unless she married a soldier.

"Why do you send girls away? Maybe you don't like girls?"

"Maybe the girls in this dump are lousy company." He pushed her away.

"You think I'm afraid of you." She came back at him, grabbed him by the ears, kissed him hard and deep, and then touched him gently, straddling his knees.

"Sit over here." He gestured to the stool next to him. "Buy yourself a drink. I'll pay for just one."

"Just one? Maybe you cheap, Charlie."

"You're too young."

"Twenty-three."

"Never happen."

"For sure, sergeant. You ask anyone."

Mueller leaned back and stared at the girl. "You go tell Mommyson I'll take you overnight."

"You need to pay for a room, too."

"No room, I'll take you with me to the barracks."

"They don't allow."

"They do for me."

The price was agreed, and they left together. She gripped his arm, but he shook her off. He carried a bottle from the bar and drank it as they walked. The dog followed them.

"You crazy, sergeant. Why do you let that dog follow us?" the girl said, all the time laughing, reaching for his arm. He waved down a passing legionnaire jeep. He lifted the dog into the back seat.

At the gate the guard waved Mueller past as if Leah wasn't with him. Now she was very quiet. In the barracks he walked her to his bed, separated from other beds by wall lockers. The empty bottle bounced across the olive blanket, fell onto the floor and rolled against the wall.

"This is it, sergeant? This no room," she said.

"This is it. Clean sheets, polished floor." He sat down and unlaced his boots.

"You'll be nice, sergeant?" She quickly undressed.

"You be gentle, sergeant," she said laughing nervously.

He laughed. "You little fool, get on the bed."

Later, Mueller came from the shower and stood with a towel around his waist. Chevron slept under the bed. Soldiers returning from town gathered around his bed. "What you got there, sarge?"

Mueller reached down and threw the sheet back. "What do you think of that?"

Leah curled in the bed, protected by her arms. Her face was bruised, her skin red and welted.

"Jees," the soldiers muttered.

"My new whore," Mueller announced.

"What happened to her?" Mueller ignored the question.

"How did you get her in here?" a soldier said, admiration in his tone.

"The guard used to be in my old platoon."

"You get caught, they'll bust you."

"That's nothing new. "

"You got to get her out." Who spoke? It didn't matter. No one disputed Mueller further.

"Guards don't change until midnight." Then, "She's good, I'll give her that. Think I'll get a place in town. Adopt her as my wife." He laughed, pulled on his trousers, settled on the bed, and stepped into his boots. She laced them, staring nervously at him.

"Time to go," he said casually, reaching down, slapping Leah on her backside, "Get dressed."

Leah reacted immediately, drew her blouse over her head, slipped on her skirt, and then her panties.

"You got spunk," Mueller said. "How much Mommyson gonna want for you to come live with me?"

"You want a Vietnamese wife?" Leah said.

"Yeah something like that."

"No problem, I think."

—⟋⟍—

No problem cost almost a months' pay, but when Mueller told Mommyson she didn't want to see his ugly side, after she'd seen what happened to Leah, the price dropped in half. Mueller had to wait a week to get another pass to look for a house outside the base but Haussmann was wrong about no passes. Mueller spent half a day hunting for the office the top sergeant said was good for locating rentals. The office building was in the middle of a block of connected tube houses with shops and restaurants. Each tube house ran from street to street with living quarters in the center, kitchen in the rear, and open to the alley. A neighborhood impossible to effectively search, Mueller recalled. When he finally found the office the accordion gate that went wall to wall was pulled down and padlocked. He cursed and leaned against the wall to wait, closely watching those who went past, feeling their hostility. His instincts told him to move on, stay a moving target, but he'd spent too long searching for the place. A Vietnamese child approached, his tiny hand outstretched begging for money.

"Di di mao," Mueller said, reaching for his pistol. Chevron growled. The child turned and ran. Mueller moved down the street, away from the building, watching every movement in the street.

At the corner the child turned and looked back, then ran again.

A fat man in a tropical suit arrived outside the building. He removed the padlock and lifted the steel mesh gate. Then he disappeared inside, open for business, if a little late. By the time Mueller walked to the office, the fat man was established behind a desk.

"What can I do for you?" the fat man said, using a handkerchief to wipe the sweat from his forehead.

Mueller glanced around, making sure there was no one else in the room, "You got a place to rent?"

"Sir, you came at a good time. More than enough places are available to rent, not just flats but houses, even a villa or two. What happened in Hai Phong and Ha Noi scared everyone. A lot of those who lived here through the war just up and took their families back to France."

Although the fat man failed to stand, his manner was obsequious. Mueller noticed his hands were stained with ink. Out of habit he kept wiping them on his pants. Fewer French must have meant his promotion from being a printer.

"Enlisted soldiers don't earn much pay." Mueller said gruffly. "Price has to be good."

"That your dog?" The fat man said, pointing to Chevron.

"Would seem so."

"What about a new three-bedroom house with a beautiful yard of sandalwood trees?" The fat man grinned, and showed him a picture. "Forty-five piasters for an entire year. If I might suggest sir, trade your francs on the black market before you pay, and you will have more than enough money to cover it."

"Too much." Mueller pressed his fists against the San-
ford leather holster belted to his hip.

"Too much, sir? You jest." The fat man laughed nervously.

"Too much. Keep the beautiful trees."

"Impossible, sir. You are being unreasonable with
me."

"Then I'm afraid you and I cannot do business." Mueller turned to leave.

"Wait, sir. What do you consider reasonable?"

"Thirty-six piasters a year, paid at three piasters a
month. No more."

"You are a very difficult man to please sir, but I accept
your offer." The fat man reached across the desk, offering his
clammy hand. Mueller squeezed it until the fat man leaned
forward in his seat, laughing nervously.

"I expect everything about the house will prove satisfactory or my money will be returned." Mueller released the
fat man's hand.

"You will be pleased, sir. You have my personal guarantee."

CHAPTER 24

Tong, January 1, 1947
Leah
A home

The house the sergeant leased for them had peach stucco walls and inside the rooms were painted white. European tile floors vibrated in reds and green pastel florals. Room after room, Leah wandered for hours, laughing, touching everything in sight, over and over to assure herself it was real. A separate kitchen. Their bedroom, one of three, furnished with a canopy bed covered by a silk spread, on each side beside it matching dressers, his and hers, large enough to hold a dozen families' clothes. A private commode, a room with a door at the rear, porcelain sink, toilet and tub, all adorned with magnificent gold fixtures. In the living room a teak floor and a silk rug with beige field and red border, a Chinese dragon at its center. Beside it something called a settee and couches with cushions. On the walls tapestries, oil paintings with scenes she took for France, serene country with castles in the distance and placid cows grazing in green fields. Everything about it a fairy tale dream. What had possessed the previous French owners to move away and leave behind such beautiful furnishings? Their loss was her lucky fortune.

Now after weeks with her sergeant gone each day, she quickly slipped into her routine and it was better than with him there. She wound the gramophone, lay down on the carpet, and was carried away by the aria it played. She floated with dreams of the paradise she'd found, a place of pleasure and ease where all her needs were met.

Though the sergeant had promised it all to her, she'd heard promises from other soldiers many times before. It was something they needed to say. For whatever reason, for men the cash payment for a woman's personal services was not enough. After the first time, when she had waited for a young soldier who never returned, it no longer mattered. Other girls told her it had happened to them, would happen again, and it did. Beau co butterfly they called the French soldiers who fluttered from bar to bar, girl to girl, seeking nectar, spreading seed, always looking for something they never found. Their fears and desires drove them with a sudden desperation, those strange hairy giants, so vulgar, smelly and unkempt.

Stretched out on her back in the living room, she laughed and laughed, staring at the pure white ceiling as if it were heaven's sky. Beneath it, reflections of the trees in the yard danced lightly on the walls. Only sixteen, Leah was already mistress of her own house, the man she called her husband a successful soldier, a German like her father, whom she'd never known.

Leah now believed in Mueller, the only man who'd ever given her all he'd promised. She accepted his terrible rages and his hatred toward women, for she was certain they would fade, certain her lighthearted spirit would prove infectious. She was determined to have only one man in her life, permanently escaping the brothel. Not that she condemned her life as a prostitute. What was so terrible? The attempt to survive and escape poverty? Were other Vietnamese women so much better off as chattels whose fathers selected their husbands, husbands who took other wives and concubines? No one questioned the men. What made men so much better than those they fraternized? She felt a single tear slide along her face.

"This what you want?" Lao startled her. She had left him in the kitchen shining Mueller's many pairs of boots, and now Lao held a pair over her, toes pointed down toward her face.

"The boots are wonderful." She recovered quickly. "How did you do it?"

She sat up and turned the boots, inspecting them as if she cherished them. Lao grinned. The week before he'd been living in a cardboard box in the alley behind the brothel. Leah convinced the sergeant that he needed the boy to care for his uniforms, to deliver food, to bargain with the local merchants. The boy will more than pay for himself, just you wait and see, she'd told him.

Lao claimed he was sixteen, Leah's age. She figured like most street kids, he probably had no idea of his true age. He was certainly younger than sixteen, an age he must have chosen to please her. Leah knew Mueller would never question it for he was like the French and viewed all Vietnamese as children.

In just a week Lao had become more active, running through the house playing with imaginary friends, calling them by name, pleading with Leah to play hide and seek, something she'd never imagined doing. When he called to her from hiding, his voice betrayed his location, but she pretended not to be able to find him. He finally tired and jumped out from a closet, laughing uncontrollably. She messed his hair and pretended to scold him, telling him he was too clever for her.

Now she watched him dance away with the boots swinging freely by their laces. His body lacked a man or woman's shape, his sex concealed by a pair of shorts, the only clothes she'd ever seen him wear. His skin which at his age should have been smooth and white was dark and scarred.

"Leah...Leah." She heard the sergeant's demanding voice calling and jumped to her feet. Was it so late? The day had disappeared in an instant of her dream.

"There you are." The sergeant stood in the doorway,

a featureless shadow outlined in the light. "I thought you'd run off."

"I'd never do that," Leah answered.

"Yes, you're right. I'd never let you."

She felt a dark foreboding as he came toward her, cold and detached. He grasped her around the waist, lifted her to his height, and kissed her hard. His rough skin irritated her face. It had already caused a rash that she concealed with makeup.

"I'm not early. Why are you surprised?" He inspected the room, his eyes filled with suspicion. "Is something wrong?"

"Nothing wrong," she said softly, afraid she'd alarm him, wake the angry ghosts that haunted him, and afraid to let him know how wonderful she felt. He wouldn't believe he was part of it, at least not yet. She felt herself going naked in his stare. She wanted to cry out, stop it, stop that wanton look of lust and avarice when you greet me, but he was what she needed, and that was that, take it as it comes. If she pulled away, he'd strike.

"I suppose there's nothing ready for me to eat," Mueller grumbled.

"Eat now, sir. I'm sure the cook has something ready."

"Cook? What damn cook is that?"

"You said do something about the way the food was prepared. I found you a fine cook, experienced with a French family. Now the food not taste like Vietnamese." She paused, moved in the direction of the bedroom before he could protest, "You should dress for dinner now. Your clothes are all laid out on the bed."

In the bedroom the sergeant dropped his uniform on the floor, and she picked it up as he expected. She folded it along the creases to keep its military appearance.

"There is blood on here," she said.

"Not your concern. Blood's not mine," Mueller said. Standing in just a pair of olive drab underpants, he grabbed for her and missed. Then he lunged, caught her hand, and tossed her on the bed.

CHAPTER 25

Bac Can, February 3, 1947
Hahn
Training camp

Tran Quoc Tuan Military Academy was too pretentious a name for the series of clearings under the jungle canopy a short distance from Bac Can. Although the tallest of the trees were left untouched to conceal the bamboo huts from scouting aircraft, the jungle floor had been cleared for training future Viet Minh officers in close order drill, use of rifles captured or stolen from the French, hand to hand combat, and use of the bayonet. Under shelters with palm leaf roofs, a hundred soldiers could huddle listening to the lectures on tactics, on conducting a guerilla war, and the indoctrination necessary for officers to endure the years of hardship that might lie ahead.

On his first day in command, Colonel Hahn inspected it all. Later the guards accompanying him groaned to their comrades that it was well there were no white gloves available or he would have inspected the jams above the doors and the corners of the floors for the slightest dust. Hahn reprimanded a soldier too slow to his feet when he entered the barracks. He caught another soldier huddled over a fire roasting manioc and trying to steal a minute's warmth. With a sweep of his arm, Hahn cleared the disordered platform beds that slept six under a single blanket, scattering random bamboo helmets, bamboo canteens, and bamboo knapsacks. He cursed the cadets as a ragtag mob, undisciplined, and unfit to be even common soldiers and certainly not ready to lead a nation.

The green recruits from the cities and villages selected to become the future officer corps of the Viet Minh soon started the barracks' legends of the steel colonel sent to command them. It was just as Hahn planned it. He intended to prepare them employing methods used by military men since the earliest armies. He'd gleaned the ways from a random assortment of Chinese, Japanese and French manuals purloined from Father Custeau's secret room.

Hahn pushed back from the desk in his office and gloated over his assignment as commandant of the officers training camp. At last a soldier's career. No more slinking down the streets of Ha Noi at night to meet with conspirators. No more crouching in the back alleys like a common thief plotting assassinations and bombings.

The first sergeant in the adjoining room directed the drill instructors on the methods Hahn had taught him. "Take away their parents, brothers, sisters, take away their past. Make them understand we are their family now. Their loyalty must be to us and to their squad, their platoon, their company, above all to the communist cause. We will live with them, share their hardships, and draw them in as our comrades. Treat them as adopted children in need of discipline. Make them confess their faults in barracks meetings, humiliate the worst of them, praise and promote the most devoted. Watch for leaders. Those who question the party's authority must be quickly reeducated or expelled."

Hahn knew conditions would also test the mettle of the recruits. For each meal they would get a single bowl of rice and some watery soup, at night a blanket per squad, and a single quilted jacket for the sentry. No uniforms. The recruits wore the clothes they arrived with, some without shoes, and all unprepared for the harsh climate. Their doctors were boys with no training, chosen at random from volunteers. It didn't matter. There was little medicine, little sanitation, no mosquito netting to prevent malaria, and little quinine to treat it once it started. This was no sunshine warriors' cause.

"Arma virumque cano, Troiae qui primus ab oris, laviniaque venit"-- "I am singing of the arms and of the man," The Aeneid echoed in his memory. What would the old priest at the orphanage think if he knew the martial spirit, first learned in his Latin class, now flourished in a communist revolutionary's heart.

Although Hahn had been disappointed when he received the assignment as commandant, now he realized how important it was to be teaching the future leaders of the movement. They would carry his lessons across the nation, and marvel at his genius. And Bac Can was close enough to the high command that his camp might be visited by General Giap or even Ho Chi Minh himself, giving him further recognition.

"Sir." A soldier broke the spell and waited standing at attention.

"Is it necessary?" Hahn demanded.

"You seemed troubled, uttering words in a strange tongue. I thought something might be wrong."

The soldier himself spoke strangely, with insubordination instead of gratitude. Hahn determined to remember him for future discipline. He noted the man's tribal face, darker and full, his eyes popping from his head. He'd probably been recruited from a nearby village to be useful as a guide.

"Anything else?" Hahn demanded.

"This came through channels." The soldier handed him an envelope privately addressed without his rank and post correct. The writing was in Phan's bold strokes.

"You're dismissed. Wait outside." Hahn paused while the soldier left, then carefully pealed back the seal noting that someone had previously opened the envelope.

I hope this correspondence finds you safe and well. As you know I was incarcerated at Hoa Lo prison after I was arrested. As usual you were right about the danger. They thought I was Viet

Minh and interrogated me about you. I never said a word to involve you, but from their questions I am certain they are already convinced you are a communist. Imagine my relief when I found out that you disappeared from the city after you saw Thi and learned of my arrest. I am sure it was none too soon.

Anyway, my wife remembered Father Custeau and prevailed on him to secure my release. It has taken weeks for me to recover from the Surete's friendly persuasion, but now I am able to get around without a cane. Things are difficult in Ha Noi. The French constantly patrol, and there is a curfew. When Father Custeau secured my release, he said next time he wouldn't be able to help me. Since that time my wife has kept after me to leave Ha Noi and return to her family home. There is no work for me here, and so I have agreed. We leave shortly. I wanted you to know that if I can be of help you can reach me in the village. I have spoken with a mutual friend and he has indicated he thinks he can get this letter to you. For obvious reasons I will not say more except to wish you well. Your friend, Phan.

At the first reading nothing of harm, but now Hahn rested the letter on his desk and using a ruler, went down it line by line trying to imagine what the political office at headquarters might have read into it. Was there any pattern on which to imagine a code? Mention of Father Custeau was at the least indiscrete, but Phan was naive. Hahn knew he must report the letter and turn it over to the intelligence officer. It had only been a day since he had been instructed to summons Phan to the headquarters. There was no coincidence in that. The soldier he had already dispatched to Ha Noi to find Phan and inform him must be recalled, another sent to Thi's village. That might be enough to allay any suspicion the party held toward him. Hahn quickly wrote to the Ha Noi headquarters.

Later the sound of leaves rustling high in the canopy drew him toward the window, but he was mistaken. The sound came from scuffling feet and the murmurings of the new recruits as they were turned out from the barracks by the drill instructors. The recruits milled about with anxiety ingrained on their pimpled faces. Still strangers to each other, they didn't speak, waiting for the instructors' directions. The instructors took their positions, spread out across the drill field like shepherds. Each in turn gave the order to his recruits to form ranks in front of him. The recruits struggled to determine their correct positions. The late afternoon sun broke through the canopy and splashed its lustrous colors over them. The sergeants barked orders. The recruits settled into wavering ranks. To Hahn it looked like a schoolyard at recess.

A dog was slinking through the ranks, his nose to the ground searching for the scent of scraps dropped from the pockets of careless recruits. The dog's eyes filled with fear. He continually darted to avoid the random kicks. His mange and exposed ribs saved him from the cook's kettle. Just buying him time, Hahn reflected, knowing what a shortage of supplies and the effects of hunger did to otherwise rational men.

Hahn glanced at his watch. In front of the window and just feet away the first sergeant reviewed the troops, quietly waiting to assume control. His hands were clasped behind his back, fingers ridged, his heels together at attention, the pleat in his trousers unbroken. Finally the ranks settled into order.

"You are pathetic," the sergeant bellowed from the porch like Othello on stage at the Ha Noi opera. "You call yourselves soldiers? I call you rabble. We should send you back to suckle from your mothers, but we will yet make you into soldiers."

Hahn stepped back from the window, resumed his place behind the desk, content just to listen to the well-rehearsed tirade, knowing for the rest of the day and in the days to come the sergeants would harangue and harass the recruits until their minds were emptied of any thoughts except to please the whims of their commanders. The recruits went into close order drill, crossing and re-crossing the field, their feet scuffling in a rough cadence, raising clouds of dust that drifted through the window.

The odors of the camp enveloped Hahn: sweating soldiers, the evening's soup in preparation, the open latrines. A leaf floated through the window and settled on the desk next to him. A lizard dashed across the floor rocking like an overloaded wagon, and climbed straight up the bamboo wall to disappear in the rafters. Comrade, keep away or the recruits will have you for a meal, Hahn joked to the well-concealed lizard. The harsh bark of orders continued. The recruits were marching off the field, turning towards the pits where they'd learn hand to hand combat. "Your other left," he heard a sergeant shout, and then the blow. The cadence quickened.

There was little time to train. The French were heavily armed and expanding their control from Ha Noi and Hai Phong out into the countryside dangerously close to the camp. Hahn had heard rumors the paratroops of the French foreign legion were being prepared for some kind of operation. Only the highest generals had been briefed, but that did not prevent the word leaking that the recruits might receive abbreviated training and be rushed into combat units earlier than scheduled.

A fog rolled in from the direction of the mountains, consuming the falling sun. Beyond the fog in the trees voices shouted as if ghosts haunted the edge of the camp. Hahn imagined in the future the sorrowful wailing of mothers as sons they'd brought forth onto the earth were returned to them as corpses for burial. As an orphan, he understood the loneliness they would feel, the emptiness left in their existence. Yet there was never a special word for their status; the mothers who've lost children remained nameless. Was it because their grief was so much greater? And what about the fathers who were expected to contain their grief with somber expressions of resignation? And to dig their children up in three years and scrape their bones clean, interring them once again in new graves as was the custom. There was nothing prophetic in his vision, only the probabilities as he reasoned them.

And what about Phan's dream of freedom? Hahn was not clinging to illusions: the Viet Minh used the cause to rally the country, but their ways left no room for freedom. Democracy would be a casualty of its allegiance with the west. Besides, in Viet Nam there was no tradition of democracy, no experience of what it meant.

CHAPTER 26

Tong, February 3, 1947
Lao
At last a home

Leah hovered in the doorway to the child's bedroom. A miniature railroad car cradled in his hands, Lao scrutinized her from where he squatted on the floor. In return for her kindness, he forgave the belittling smile on her face. Why had she chosen him from all the street children to live in this paradise? He could not fathom what she saw in him.

"I don't think the sergeant is coming home today," Leah said. "Come into the kitchen. We can eat together."

"Go ahead. I'll be right there," Lao said. He straddled the track and aligned the wheels of the railroad car between engine and caboose. "Choo...choo...choo...choo." He created the noise as the train rolled from his grip. He glanced up after several minutes. Leah remained in the doorway.

"I'm coming," Lao said.

"Bring the train," Leah said.

Lao clutched engine car and the caboose under his arm and followed her through their palace. The palace was of Lao's dreams. The inside walls were white as eggshells, delicate and clean, with even whiter high ceilings. There were separate rooms to eat and sleep, separate beds, blankets to fold back at night, real ready-to-slip-between sheets. It had a Frenchmen's water closet, in a corner room with sinks and bowls and water that ran on command to carry away the waste.

French clothes still filled the closets, and Leah had discovered a closet of toys that fulfilled Lao's dreams. He had laid out train track in the children's room and placed a black iron engine and red caboose on the rails. He stationed brightly painted metal soldiers at the intersections. Then he dug through the other games in the closet, first removing carved wooden block houses, then figures and figurines to populate the city as he built it around the tracks. The toy city filled his day. Khong had stayed away.

The kitchen spoke of mayhem. Chairs shoved against the wall. Headless chickens strung across the room on a clothes line while their heads garnished a bowl of greens. Onion peels, potato eyes, and the shavings of fruits covered a table, the counter covered with piles of discarded spoons, each coated with a distinctive sauce, jelly-smeared knives, bloody meat scraps. Eggshells filled the sink. Overturned spice jars splayed their contents in abstract patterns over the cutting block. The smell of coriander and turmeric filled the air.

"Why do we need that cook?" Lao nodded toward the corner where a floury apparition whirled among the pots and pans.

"I can't cook," Leah said. "He was the chef for Madame ... until she fled to France."

"Maybe she fled to escape his cooking," Lao said.

"He is a fine chef. He comes from Ha Noi."

"Maybe the sergeant will kill you when he finds out you gave him a job," Lao said.

"I already told him, the sergeant hates my Vietnamese cooking. This man can cook anything."

"But he looks very expensive," Lao whispered.

The cook ignored them as they ate, constantly touching each other to confirm it was real. Lao figured he loved her.

In the morning she sponged Lao in the bath. The soapy

water stung the scratches and the scabs that never healed, but then the warmth relaxed him until he almost fell asleep. Leah cradled his head in her arms. She wouldn't let him sink. She fed him three times that day and started teaching him to read and to speak more French words than those he used to beg for food. She was his mother, father, brother, sisters, grandfathers, grandmothers, aunts, and uncles.

In the streets Lao laughed with every step, skipping to keep pace with Leah. The same stories he had heard on the streets about the French villas, he now repeated with firsthand knowledge to anyone he met. He returned to the markets to shop with Leah, to carry the things she bought that only the French could afford. Armfuls, lifetimes worth of things.

She entered a tailor's shop. "We'll turn you into a proper French gentleman."

"I can't have you spending money on me," Lao said. "It's wrong what he makes you do for it."

"I want to share with you," Leah said. "You're my family now."

"I like the shorts I'm wearing," Lao said, stubbornly.

"Keep them too," she said, "but now you are old enough to own a school boy's uniform. The sergeant has influence. I can enroll you in a French school."

For an instant Lao forgot the streets and thought about the school. "I don't think he wants me go to school."

"You're wrong," Leah said. "You'll see."

"The sergeant doesn't want me around." Lao said.

CHAPTER 27

Tong, February 3, 1947
Mueller
A mission

"This will be your platoon's final test. I guess you could call it a live fire exercise," the camp commander said as Mueller stood at attention before the officer's desk. The commander handed over a topographical map that was covered with glossy acetate to protect it from the permeating dampness. Nothing on the map indicated the heat and humidity, or the leaches and mosquitoes that infested the impenetrable jungle over layed by the co-ordinates of the locations.

"A bit irregular," Mueller quipped. The young lieutenant seemed to take no notice of his remark.

"Here's your objective. Don't worry; a tank with mounted flame thrower has been assigned to accompany you. It's a day's operation, no more. You know what is expected of you," the lieutenant said.

Black crayon circled Quang Khe, a village twenty kilometers from the French camp and marked beneath it, HOSTILES. Mueller saluted.

"No one to complain about their treatment afterward,

sergeant?"

"No, sir." Mueller wheeled and returned to the barracks. He ordered the platoon to prepare combat gear, full battle dress, a full week's rations just in case, live ammunition, and grenades. "This is what you've been waiting for, men. We turn out in formation tomorrow morning at 0500 hours."

In the flurry of activity he forgot his new home, forgot Leah and the annoying boy, his mind saturated with the beauty of war, anticipating the ecstasy that came when life was taken at whim, free from the suffocating restrictions imposed by society.

At dawn the men stumbled into formation. Mueller's platoon was what the brass politely called multi-ethnic. Helmets mixed with bush hats and turbans; two squads of Germans who had survived Hitler's campaigns through Europe stood next to Moroccans recruited and trained in Tunisia; the fourth squad was Vietnamese, locally recruited because of the shortage of men sent by France.

Mueller inspected his men. This morning even the disciplined Germans were unshaved and ill equipped. They tried to avoid carrying everything they considered unnecessary, gambling that in the excitement their lax preparation went unnoticed. Mueller reminded them they were all legionnaires with a tradition to maintain. He sent them back to the barracks to collect the unopened boxes of ammunition, a heavy machine gun, and anything else they'd abandoned. He shouted at the retreating soldiers, "Discipline maintains the legion's superiority!"

The flame-throwing tank soon emerged from behind the barracks and edged toward the formation, a brute cast of iron that belched diesel fumes. The turret resembled an overturned pot with a gun barrel for a handle. Peepholes for the crew were hidden in camouflage nets that hung over heavy armor plates. Its tracks chewed up the ground it crossed.

A young soldier shouted, "Look at her. She'll give us a taste for Vietnamese barbecue."

"The world never smells the same after your first whiff

of flesh," an old soldier retorted.

The tank halted. A hatch popped open, and two young men appeared simultaneously.

"Look, we're surrounded by them monkeys," said one of them, feigning terror.

"You get hit in that tin can because we're not watching out for you, you'll wish you spoke better of us," Mueller retorted.

"Sorry, sergeant," the tanker who had spoken said. "Where do you want us?"

"In the middle of the column just behind me. I'll give orders when and where to use that thing."

Beyond the gate the platoon divided into two files and marched along the road, the men slumped under their equipment's weight. Mueller did a communications check with headquarters. The radio operator clipped the headset next to his ear, setting its constant static loud enough to hear above the tank.

Soon the fortifications became a hyphen on the expanse of emerald green rice fields. To the north ahead of them the jungle darkened the horizon, void of detail until the morning light reached the tree line, revealing the snarl of symbiotic growth. The dust from the marching formation encased the soldiers in its vermilion cocoon.

A lambretta over-filled with workers approached the column. It announced itself with the sputter of its motor as it swerved off the road to avoid the column and tipped over into a muddy field. The point man deployed to search the distraught workers, who struggled to upright their vehicle.

"You are Viet Minh?... Viet Minh?" The point man's question brought protests of innocence. He ordered the workers to remove their clothes and stand with hands on heads, lined up along the road. The search for weapons proceeded. The soldiers went through the clothes and the lambretta, then finding nothing, backed away.

"Keep your rifles ready and keep moving," Mueller ordered.

The point man was an old Moroccan chosen for his

stamina in the heat. The Moroccans were a filthy lot, never bathing and often unshaven, a habit they brought with them from their country where water was always scarce. A turban hid the Moroccan's unkempt and receding hair. Years before, his unit, after initially resisting a Japanese attack, had surrendered. The unit was massacred for what the Japanese considered an act of cowardice. Mueller never questioned how the Moroccan survived. Now the Moroccan viewed Orientals as a menace to be exterminated whenever the opportunity arose.

The Moroccan set a slow pace for the column. The lambretta and its workers receded on the horizon. In the heat and monotony, the column stretched into an unacceptable length and Mueller ordered it to halt until the last of the soldiers caught up. He gave five minutes to rest. Noticing a bundle of rags floating in the watery field, he sent the Moroccan to check it out. The Moroccan left his pack and slid into the muddy water.

"There's a body in this mess," the Moroccan shouted.

"Don't touch it," Mueller said. He stepped to the tank. "You got some rope with you?"

They dragged the body up on the roadway. Mueller recognized the man as the police chief from the village just outside their post, a decent man who came into the compound to co-ordinate local operations and the third police chief appointed by the French in the last four weeks. He had insisted on living in his village. He had been stabbed multiple times and a rope tied around his neck like a noose with a hand painted sign that read, THIS FATE AWAITS ALL LACKEYS OF THE FRENCH COLONIAL DOGS.

The extent of rigor mortis led Mueller to think the man had been murdered in the village, put on display, and then thrown into the rice field.

"That's what the lambretta was doing out here," the Moroccan said, as he walked away.

"Don't worry, we'll get our chance," Mueller reassured him.

Those were the last words before the explosion. Mueller leaped into the ditch. The Moroccan crumbled at the edge of the road partially inside a crater created by the explosion. His right leg was turned backward, and still attached by several tendons. Shrapnel from the land mine had frayed his uniform.

The medic reached the Moroccan before the others. He quickly removed the Moroccan's belt and tied it as a tourniquet above where the leg was severed.

"Form a perimeter," Mueller said, ready for a ground attack.

The Moroccan was dying, but Mueller figured he might live for days in a comatose state. Headquarters would send a patrol to return the soldier and that would require the platoon to wait and be exposed to a potential enemy attack.

"Take a break. I'll relieve you." Mueller said, waving the medic away.

The medic returned to the perimeter and rested with the other soldiers.

Mueller bent closer to the Moroccan. "You know what I must do."

The soldier tried to smile. Mueller slipped his bayonet from his belt and placed the blade beneath the collar of the soldier's uniform and then with a swift stab severed the aorta, being careful to conceal the slice once the blood no longer flowed. He returned the bayonet to its scabbard and rejoined the other soldiers. "He didn't make it. We'll bury him here and dig him up on our return. Make sure the grave is well hidden. No point giving the Viet Minh something else to booby trap. Bring the boots to me and divide the ammunition among the squads. Anything else is yours."

The medic, a frail and pathetic looking German who refused to carry a weapon, whispered the sacraments with a cross pressed to his lips. Mueller ordered the Viets into the lead.

It wasn't far to the trail that turned toward the village, where the jungle offered relief from the broiling heat. Mueller ordered the tank to widen the trail by pushing over trees. Fire ants cascaded from the falling branches, forcing the column to walk further and further behind. The soldiers rolled down their sleeves, turned up their collars and covered their faces with towels. To avoid the ants Mueller ordered the column to precede the tank despite the danger of mines and an ambush. Every time a jungle sound alarmed him, he brought the tank forward and used the flame-thrower to clear the way.

The tank engine's rumble carried through the jungle, so Mueller expected to find an empty village, but as the platoon entered, children ran into thatched huts. The soldiers ordered the villagers from their homes and Mueller ordered those slow to obey shot. Methodically working their way through the village, the legionnaires set the huts on fire. As villagers ran from their burning homes, many were shot by the Moroccans to avenge their comrade. Some villagers chose to burn inside their homes. Those who survived were herded beneath a banyan tree and huddled in the shade. A guard stood over them. One of the Moroccans circled the group, surveying them until a young girl caught his attention. He signaled for her, and when she refused to comply he seized her by the arm, dragging her into one of the few remaining huts. When the Moroccan returned alone Mueller ordered the hut burned.

"I'll take care of the rest of this," Mueller said to the guard, stepping toward the group of villagers. "Where are all the men?" he asked through one of his Vietnamese soldiers. He reached out and grabbed a child at the edge.

"Where are all the men?" he repeated, wrapping a thin wire around the child's neck. He lifted the child off his feet. The child let out a little bark as he struggled to pull free. A woman threw herself toward him. The guard bayoneted her.

Mueller remembered the words from the colonel's speech delivered before the assembled troops on the parade field at Tong early in their training: We are here to put out the fire of insurrection.

"Finish them," Mueller ordered, and the Moroccan squad fired into the villagers. The Viet Minh would not recruit anyone in this village.

The legionnaires dragged those they'd shot into piles and threw gasoline on them. The flames and heat sent them back.

CHAPTER 28

Tong, February 4, 1947
Leah
With friends

Leah zigzagged down the alley, skipping between the puddles. Her nostrils burned from a combination of the daily rains and urine sprayed against the walls by drunken soldiers stumbling home at night. The rapid clink clack of her high heels syncopated the silence and sent the rats into hidden spaces beneath boxes, bloodied sheets, and the day's cans and broken bottles. A dozen beady little eyes stared at Leah. A single rat remained to defend a chicken carcass, a meager harp of bones. Leah edged along the wall to avoid its fetid bite. She slipped into the back of the bordello, past the bedrooms along the unlighted corridor to the room where Mommyson conducted business from an old rocker covered in red velour. Some said it was an antique imported from America, brought to her years before by an admiral of the U.S. Navy infatuated with her beauty and wit.

"Look at you, child. You look an undertaker's nightmare." Mommyson touched Leah's makeup in its thickest place, her finger carefully chipping at it. "What happened here?"

Leah remained silent.

"You don't have to stay with him," Mommyson said, softly spreading the remaining makeup to hide the bruise.

"I guess it's part of the deal," Leah said. She allowed Mommyson to hold her. "He loves me or he wouldn't spend so much money on our home."

"It's all right dear, there's always a home for you here."

"He'll change," Leah said, not looking Mommyson in the eye.

"I'm afraid they never do." Mommyson's **words** sent a shudder through Leah. Mommyson continued **to hold** her, squeeze her, her arms surrounding, her fingers **probing** flesh. "You seem a little bloated. You must be gaining **weight**. I suspect it's time you see our doctor."

"No." Leah broke away. "A child is what Mueller and I need. We need a family."

"Of course, my dear."

"I want to see the girls."

"Go ahead, they're in the bar."

Leah floated down the corridor among the familiar smells that lingered; French perfume, a touch of jasmine, a man's stale sweat, a touch of scent from a woman's time of month, tobacco from an imported cigar. Even the antiseptic cleaner didn't expel those smells.

Midday was a lazy time. The motor of the ceiling fan moaned and rotated the four great blades shaped like palm leaves. The shades were pulled, the front door closed to a crack, just enough to allow the barker to sit inside on a chair and still monitor the empty street, ready to call out if a soldier happened past. The girls were stretched out on bar stools, their blouses unbuttoned, their short skirts hiked up over their thighs. The bartender glanced through French adventure magazines stacked beside the rows of gin and whiskey bottles behind the teakwood bar. Leah noticed the familiar Renoir's painting of a nude archer. Someday she'd move to Paris with Mueller and then she'd locate the original painting and sit by it for hours, free of the taint and smell of sweating men, contemplating that silken white beauty and the soft and ample flesh, the breasts and loins charged with the energy of life, yet still maintaining innocence. She'd try to understand why the slain deer at the woman's feet added to the beauty of the painting.

"Back again, Leah?" The girl who spoke had dark eyes sunk into her head, leaving the appearance they were crossed. Cosmetics partially concealed a rash and lesions, the vestiges from venereal disease.

"You don't forget your family when good luck comes your way." Leah said.

"Enjoy it while it lasts." The girl went back to manicuring her nails.

Leah searched the room for Dawn. The two girls had made a pact to earn enough to escape from Viet Nam together. Toward that end they worked hard to give their men pleasure The other girls said they possessed the insatiable sexual appetites of soldiers. Nymphomaniacs, the soldiers said. Mommyson had warned them of the danger in their excesses but they had carried on with an enthusiasm that anticipated the riches that ensured their freedom.

Even with her back to Leah, Dawn was unmistakable with her perfect black hair cascading over her shoulders like a satin mane. Perched on a piano stool in the corner she pecked out "Chopsticks" with one finger. No one listened to her as she enthusiastically bounced from key to key.

"Where'd you get the lousy piano player?" Leah teased from across the room. "I hope she doesn't play her men as poorly."

Dawn turned and leaped to her feet. She dashed across the room, embraced Leah, and kissed her long and deeply. Then she stood back and studied her. "You look ghastly. Sit down and tell me what happened..."

Leah explained about Mueller and her pregnancy, but spared other details.

Dawn touched the front of Leah's skirt. "And what about this?"

"Something I've always secretly wanted," Leah whispered to avoid being overheard by the other girls. "We've got a wonderful home to raise a family."

"Does your sergeant know you're pregnant?"

"Not yet."

"When you tell him, you'll be out on the street. It'll be too late to do something about it."

"That's not true."

"Get it taken care of now."

"Can't you see I'm happy?" Leah let her disappointment show. Dawn still believed they could earn their way out of prostitution. Leah had figured out they'd never earn enough money for their dreams. Here was her chance to escape to France.

"And what about the way he treats you?"

The bartender poured himself a drink, pretending he wasn't listening.

"Let me have some of that," Leah said, pointing to the gin.

"Didn't know you drank the stuff," the bartender responded. He grabbed a gin bottle, shook it to get the sediment on the bottom swirling, and then poured it into a tumbler. Leah pressed the tumbler tight against her lips and threw her head back. It burned down her throat. She spun around on the bar stool to confront the room.

"None of you will ruin this," she shouted. She fled the bar, almost knocking the barker at the front door off his chair. She ran down the street, but the heat quickly took her breath. She leaned against a building and watched the sun fall like a hot spark consuming itself.

CHAPTER 29

February 4, 1947
Quang Khe
Mueller
Mission accomplished

Quang Khe village smoldered far behind them, but its smell soaked Mueller's clothes, permeated his skin, and congested his nostrils as he led his platoon back over trees crushed beneath the tank, past the sections of incinerated jungle. The smell stayed with him even when they reached the gravel road where breezes carried fresh air from over open water. His shadow was an outline in the water punctured with rice stalks that wavered with him and his gypsy band as they carried away those few things with value snatched from the village. The old break in his arm, his father's last remembrance gift to him, ached with a new intensity.

He traveled with the pack. The rhythm of the pack dictated what happened. At the village, catching the scent of weakness, the pack had attacked and destroyed the enemies of French control. With no individual responsibility or will, the pack had avenged their denigration and discomfort, the accumulation of frustration and hate for a place they must endure.

When the platoon passed where the mine had exploded, the medic called out, "What about the Moroccan?"

"We have enough to carry. We'll leave him here. It's as good a place as any." Mueller waited for protest, but the Moroccan squad remained silent, their heads down marching toward the post. Easier than he'd thought. Maybe they'd expected it, understood he never meant to carry a corpse back just to throw it into a different grave. Fatigue played a part, but it all came down to their survival. They needed his deadly ability to keep the greatest number of them alive. His efficiency in the village drew their admiration, let them know he would eliminate all resistance and protect them from the avoidable, be it ambush or attack. The rest was left to fate.

Within an hour they reached their post. The soldiers threw off their uniforms, dropped their gear in heaps, and bartered over the few worthless souvenirs looted from the village. Then their attention turned to dust-caked feet and blisters. The men snapped towels against other's buttocks, raised red welts, and howled, feigning animosity as friendly push and shove carried them into the showers.

Mueller crossed the parade field to the headquarters. Without a word he bestowed an ivory Buddha from the village on the lieutenant and reported the single Moroccan casualty and what had happened afterward.

"You killed more than fifty?" the lieutenant asked casually.

"More than fifty."

"Darn good show," the lieutenant said. That was how the top brass rated his effectiveness. The lieutenant wanted the number of enemy killed spread through the post, repeated in other headquarters where orderlies and NCOs were always ready to gossip. The enlisted men would carry what they overheard back to the barracks and into the town and bars.

Mueller understood the lieutenant's wanting to get his share of the glory. If favorable stories made their way back to France, the general staff would send word that their generals were expected to recognize the units and the officers.

"What was the resistance like?" the lieutenant cautiously continued, sliding back in his chair behind the desk. A smoldering cigar encased his head in smoke.

"They set off a mine outside the village. That was where we lost the Moroccan. The Viets tried to conceal themselves in the huts. We had to flush them out of hiding."

"Necessary, I suppose."

"Yes, sir. And afterward we burned the bodies of those killed in the fighting. Best thing to do with so little time to bury them."

"Nothing left of them, no remains?"

"Nothing."

"Always best, that way no questions raised." The lieutenant paused, watching a puff of smoke from his cigar rise to the ceiling. "I'll be putting you and your men in for commendations."

"Thank you, sir. Is there anything else?"

"No, sergeant. Take some time and spend it in town with your new wife." The lieutenant smiled mischievously. So he knew about Leah. Mueller didn't worry after what he'd just heard. He saluted sharply.

He marched across the drill field, past the guards. He felt their stares of admiration. In town the Viets gave ground to him in the street, afraid of confrontation. Yet there was no way they could know what happened to the village, not yet, and then it would be rumors and never anything more.

The putrid smells of Vietnamese food, half cooked and inedible, annoyed Mueller as soon as he approached his front door. The little boy standing there distressed him even more. Just before he left he had told Leah to get rid of the boy. Yellow race's obstinacy, ignoring what was said when it didn't coincide with their wishes. If Leah was testing him, she had made a big mistake. Pushing the boy aside, he crossed the white tile floor toward the master bedroom, leaving a pattern of mud from his cleats. He entered the bedroom like a looter, but Leah wasn't there.

Chevron leaped off the bed, and greeted him with

wagging tail.

"Good boy," he said, shaking the dog's head. Then he kicked off his boots.

"Leah!" he shouted. He heard her respond from somewhere in the house. Almost immediately she appeared, crossing the room, throwing her arms around him. He stood coldly glaring down on her satin hair.

"I didn't hear you come in," she said.

"What's that boy doing here?" he demanded.

"I need someone to help me."

"You don't need him. You got all day to yourself with nothing to do. I told you to get rid of him."

Leah stared down at her feet.

"Is there something else?" Mueller demanded.

"I needed someone to help because I'm in a family way." She paused, catching her breath. "I sent for my mother to help me, but she only arrived today."

"What are you telling me?" He coldly inspected her.

"Is that all you can say?" She started crying. "You're going to be a father."

"Get rid of it," Mueller clenched his fists, "or I will."

"I'm too far along," she said.

"How long have you known?"

"I thought you'd be pleased." Leah tried to hold his hand. He pulled away.

"Pleased?"

"You'll have a family. Something you must have always wanted."

"Are you crazy? I'll take you to the French doctor at the post. Let him deal with this. And send your mother home."

Mueller went straight to the living room. Leah's mother rested on the couch. Once pretty, no doubt. She looked up and he stared into the piercing black eyes. My God, he thought, my whore from years ago. Was it enough time for her to age this much? Fifteen, sixteen years. Then she'd dressed in the short skirts and blouses of the brothel. Now she hid her hair beneath a traditional black turban and wore peasant's clothes.

Her expression changed when she recognized him.

Quick to recover, she stood up and was scratching at his face, trying to put out his eyes. He pushed her away, threw her down, and choked her. Leah tried to pull him off. "What are you doing?"

He reached back and struck her, then drew his knife and slashed at the woman's throat. She went limp. Then he turned on Leah. She backed away.

"You've killed her," Leah screamed

"You said you were twenty-six. You lied." He spoke calmly. "Now tell me the truth."

"Sixteen!" she blurted out as if the word would stop him. "I'm sorry. I thought you wanted someone older. It really didn't seem to matter."

"You little whore. You planned this together all along." He cornered her in the room.

"Think of our child," Leah screamed.

"Our child? You witch, your mother was my whore."

"What are you saying?"

"You bitch, I won't let you do this to me."

Mueller swung the knife around, arcing it as a scythe, slashing her neck within its sweep. She struggled to speak as she fell onto the floor. Her lips moved with words lacking the breath to feed them.

Mueller dragged Leah's body beside her mother, tied them together with his belt, and rolled them in the rug so only their feet protruded. He opened the rug and tied their legs against their chests, and rolled the rug again. He searched the house for the boy without finding him. He showered and dressed in a clean uniform. He walked to the post, found the orderly at headquarters, and told him the lieutenant wanted him to take a jeep. The orderly handed him the keys.

After dark Mueller loaded the rug into the jeep and drove to the river. He waited for a break in traffic and then pushed the bundle off the bridge. The guards on the bridge abutments below him whispered nervously, their voices carrying over the water. Then a grenade exploded, sending a shower of water into the air next to Mueller.

CHAPTER 30

Highway Four, February 4, 1947
Phan
Retreat from Ha Noi

Phan shifted the pack higher on his back and cradled it in his hands to lift the weight from his shoulders. The straps no longer tore his skin. He smiled at his son perched on Thi's shoulders. The child giggled back. Thi glanced in his direction, her warm smile reassuring him they were doing the right thing returning to the village and her family.

Phan recalled that same glance in the excitement of their first married nights, their desires mutual and insatiable, filled with an intensity impossible to maintain. He remembered his initial tentative caresses, natural and accepted, her body responding, her back arching into him. Passion. Purity. Tenderness. Wordless thoughts exchanged. They had drifted with their desires, sometimes whispering their hopes and dreams, lips to ear. Sometimes they slept arms and legs entwined. Day after day with unbroken affection, happiness streamed into his soul and transformed his harshest edges. He had felt himself a part of her and that feeling still lingered, but everything else had changed.

At a roadside café they stopped to sip tea and listened to the waitress gossip. Route Four closed. Heavily armed French convoys caught in Viet Minh ambushes. At night French outposts besieged, their defenders trapped inside.

"They're digging trenches across the road at night." The waitress nodded toward three mud covered men hunched over a table.

"Why?" Phan said.

"Keeps the French from moving their tanks."

"Slows down our vehicles, too." Phan said.

"That's not important."

"You know who they are?" Phan said.

"When you leave, pay the old woman in the corner." The waitress hurried to take away the emptied tea pot.

Traveling north across the plains, Phan and his wife and child passed the remains of French trucks destroyed by mines. The flow of refugees traveling south increased. Phan maintained his outward composure for the sake of his wife. They reached where the trail to Quang Khe met the dirt road, the narrow path now obstructed by crushed and broken trees. Boot prints filled the deepest ruts.

On the trail they crossed sections of jungle where trees smoldered and embers burst into flames. Smoke hung in a fog among the trees. They soaked rags with water and placed them over their faces to breath. Every half hour they rested, wiped away the sweat and sometimes swaddled their child.

"Listen," Phan whispered.

"What is it?"

A sound like the grinding of teeth came from the trail ahead. Branches snapped with the murmur of voices. Phan placed a finger to his lips. They hid in the thick vegetation, crouched together, swatting the red ants that attacked them.

French soldiers appeared on the trail ahead of a tank, shouting over the engine's noise, sweating heavily, laughing, and swearing. They carried rifles, machine guns, belts of ammunition wrapped across their chests, canteens clanking against grenades. The smell of burned diesel filled the air. The tank rose and fell over the fallen trees.

The baby let out a cry. Phan clamped his hand over his son's mouth, holding him firmly, whispering that it was all right.

The French stopped. A soldier pointed. The tank turret swiveled, the barrel aimed in their direction. Liquid squirted from it in a steady stream that exploded in flame. A plume of fire consumed nearby trees.

Phan embraced his wife and child behind a meter-thick tree that sheltered them from the heat. A flock of jungle parrots flew from nearby trees. A French soldier pointed at the parrots and laughed. The column of soldiers moved forward, the tank turret twisting from side to side.

"What was that?" Thi's voice was trembling.

"A flame-thrower." Phan squeezed the body of a red ant that clung to his son's cheek and popped it between his fingers.

"They came from the village," Thi said. "What's happened to my family?"

"They're all right." He gave the reassurance he didn't feel. He knew all the villages withheld French taxes, an easy order for the Viet Minh to give with no cost to them. In fact, when the French took their retribution, it increased recruits to the communist cause. Now Phan rushed to catch up with Thi who was practically running. Phan understood what the village meant to her, her sacrifice leaving it, the instinct that drew her back, and he loved her for her loyalty. Ahead of him, Thi climbed over a tree trunk across the path. Phan tripped on a sapling, but caught himself. Thi turned around and glanced at him, then continued rushing along the trail.

At dusk they entered Quang Khe village in ember light. The walls of houses were baked into rock monuments and fossilized in place. The surrounding jungle was haunted by the skeletons of blackened trees, their withered leaves limp on branches. Fragments of bodies lay in the ash. Vultures and crows grazed over the village, devouring any flesh that remained.

Thi stood motionless, unable to acknowledge what her eyes told her. Phan wanted to hold her and run his hand across her cheek, but she was rigid, a glass figurine ready to shatter at a touch. Not knowing what to say, he said nothing.

Nearby two king vultures jousted over a carcass. Their naked heads and wattled necks thrashed awkwardly with threatening gestures and terrible rasps to frighten off the others. The smaller of the giant birds backed away, waiting an opportunity to dash forward and rob a piece of flesh. The larger king vulture held the carcass down with vise grip feet and tore at the flesh, its horned beak bright red with blood.

A kettle of vultures, white-backed and long-billed, together with another king or two, floated in circles above, effortless in flight, carried by wind in currents and drafts, some mere black specks in a darkening sky. Three white-backed vultures approached the village, riding down drafts, their wings extended fully two meters as they glided to the ground. The king vulture charged them, but then retreated, taking a scrap of flesh. The three birds fought among themselves for the remains. Thi charged at the giant birds, throwing stones. The vultures hopped into flight. A sudden wind battered the village. The late day rains swept in, extinguishing the embers, and clearing the smoke that lingered in the clearing.

In the morning Phan remembered his reporter's assignment for the first time in days and took out his note pad and wrote:

Why didn't the villagers run away, take to the jungle at the first sound of the tank? Because of their faith, their disbelief, an unwillingness to acknowledge the sinister nature of man? Or was it an abiding loyalty to place, a determination not to be driven from their homes? Or simple stupidity. Better to run off and find out later you were wrong. There was no question of their standing and fighting with nothing more than machetes and axes and a few shotguns used to hunt game for special holidays. And so they had perished like those who failed to flee a storm, destroyed by the laws of war. And already the wind carries seed from the surrounding jungle, planting it in the ash from which plants will soon emerge. The rain restores the earth to its innocence.

The weak perish... That was all it taught.

CHAPTER 31

Quang Khe, February 5, 1947
Thi
Past and future

At dawn Thi rose from the matted leaves. She wandered down familiar trails into the family fields, where rice stalks broke the water surface, a million wavering green blades. A foot-powered waterwheel with paddles to lift water from canals to fields stood in silhouette. A wind whispered through it in her father's voice, thanking the fields for his family's living. She saw him as he paddled water. She saw him bent in the fields, inching along in the water, stroking the rice as he weeded it. As he stood to stretch, his hands pressed against the arch in his back, and he smiled. She reached to kiss his cheek gently so he wouldn't disappear.

He spoke to her: The fields are yours now. She bent and pulled the weeds, worked her way between the stalks of young rice, careful not to step on them, to stay between the tender rows. She followed him down the rows, plain to see if you'd planted rice before. The sun danced on the foliage in the tops of distant trees, and as it rose, it reached down to warm and set the rice to growing. The sun caressed her and she accepted what time carried, no matter her own wishes.

At dusk Phan came for her. He waited in silence at the edge of the field with their child cradled in his arms. Earlier in the day she'd felt him watching her, standing at the jungle edge. She imagined that as he stood there he daydreamed like all the men who spent their lives reflecting on their own need for independence at the same time they denied it from their wives, their daughters, and even the sons they cherished and expected to carry on their names. Phan must understand that for her freedom existed when neither French nor Viet Minh controlled the village. Left alone, the village of her childhood was a place of independence and joy. She had been fortunate to have two mothers. Her natural mother was the younger, married by common law to her father when his first wife, who loved Thi as her own child, grew too ill to care for their home and work in the fields. Her half brother and half sisters were much older. Since she was the youngest, they pampered her, treating her as if she were their child, taking on the responsibility with delightful playfulness. They confided in her as they grew up so she always knew what to expect in herself as she grew older. It gave her a maturity that delighted her father. When he became a village elder, he sat her at his side where she listened and learned the wisdom passed down through the generations.

Later the French arrived to extract taxes. They'd promised the village a school, but nothing came of it. The villagers complained to the elders that they had less to live on, and it was true. And what can you do about it, they demanded of the elders. The elders hesitated for nothing was the answer. But nothing wasn't a solution. More hesitation. Then they ordered a new field cut from the jungle, one maintained by everyone, to pay the taxes so each farmer kept all he grew. It didn't take much. The rice paddies were terraced on the side of a hill and hard to build, but the rice was sticky rice and brought a premium price at the market. The French might have raised their taxes for the new field, but the village concealed its existence, each farmer reporting only what he owned. And that was how it was settled and their sense of freedom restored.

Though her father had never learned to read or write, he was wise. His plot of land wasn't the largest, nor did it yield the most, but that was to be expected when he spent so much time on the affairs of the village. Everyone turned to him, and in the council of elders his voice carried the day. He convinced the villagers to bring a teacher into the village on their own so the children could learn to read and write and speak in French. He saw it as necessary in the modern world.

Thi tried to imagine his advice now. Traditionally the land descended to the eldest living son but where beyond that? Certainly as the only surviving child her claim had legitimacy. If she limited herself to only the land her father had owned, who could complain? There was still the problem of convincing Phan they should remain in the village.

That night Phan cooked a stew. They ate in silence. Thi whispered, "Can we stay?"

"I've never farmed before."

"I can teach you."

"And when the French return?"

"They can't burn the earth. We just start over again as many time as its necessary."

"We must secure our country's freedom." An uneasy silence fell between the two.

A cacophony of sounds erupted from the jungle, as birds of the canopy anticipated the passing of day. The sky darkened. The jungle fell into silence, turned cold. Nothing moved. The huts continued to smolder. When the wind picked up, the embers glowed, then turned into a small flame. Thi and Phan camped at the jungle edge where they could stretch their hammocks between the trees. Thi rocked in her hammock and stared at the hypnotic flames as they consumed the last of the village in a dozen separate fires where the homes once stood. Now she felt comfort in sleeping alone. It was better to avoid Phan's attentions and another child until they built a home. Phan slept in a nearby hammock, their child where they'd hear him if he cried. In their travels they had accustomed themselves to living in the open. For now the crops demanded all their efforts. After the rice was planted and nurtured to a harvest, and the grain safely stored, there would be time for building a home.

Now there were no more nightmares, just confusion about the past. The village had accommodated both sides. When the French came, the village paid their taxes. They even added the Christian cross to their altars beside their ancestors and the image of Buddha. When the Viet Minh came, the village took down the crosses and invited the soldiers into their houses, fed them, and let them use their fields and trails for maneuvers, even attended the nightly lectures on Marxism without complaint, never questioning the communist lack of religion. They made all the necessary accommodations to each side and yet something had gone very wrong.

Thi tried to understand what had provoked the French to violence. Were the ancestors angry at those accommodations the villagers made? Surely they wouldn't bring such a scourge on their own descendants for so little reason. Thi wanted to speak to her ancestors, but fire had destroyed the shrines and ancient photographs. Her memory couldn't recreate their images, and even if it could, she had no artistic skill to preserve them. She had no access to the ancestors to regain their support. The balance with nature was broken, the harmony lost. She felt helpless and alone.

The embers outlined the chicken pen they'd built during the day. Thi smiled now as she recalled the moment when the three chickens wandered from the jungle, the only survivors of the French massacre. Phan had wanted to wring their necks and enjoy several good meals. Keep them alive, Thi suggested, they will provide eggs for years. And if the French return? Release the chickens and they'll flee into the jungle. And if they wander off again? Rebuilt the pen.

Phan had accepted her argument, acknowledging that when it came to surviving in the countryside her judgment bettered his. They cut bamboo stakes a meter tall and drove them into the ground side by side. For a few moments the chickens searched for a way out. Then Thi threw rice into the cage, and the chickens immediately forgot their desire to escape, content to pick the soil for the rice and ruffle their feathers in the dust. Just like us, she thought.

There was enough rice to feed the chickens for months. The French soldiers had stacked the rice at the edge of the village and soaked it in gas, setting it to burn, but they left without stirring it. Thi and Phan raked what remained, sorted it in piles, the charred rice for the chickens, the untouched rice for themselves.

The next morning Phan found an ox- plow, threw it over his back, careful not to let its sharp metal hook catch his skin. Thi carried the yoke and rope, their child upon her back. When they reached an old section of the field, drained and fallow and full with weeds, Phan put the yoke to his neck and dragged the plow. Thi walked behind, balancing the wooden handles like it was a wheelbarrow, steering a straight course the length of the field to turn and return as it forced open the earth.

When Phan fell from exhaustion, Thi lifted the yoke to her shoulders. She did everything from memory: plow and harrow the field, transplant the seedlings she had seen and weeded the day before, pray to Ong Linh Than Tho Vo, the spirit of the soil, for the rains needed to soften the soil. Sweat mingled in her tears as she pressed against the wooden bar. The unyielding plow behind her gradually gave way to her will. The fragrances of fresh earth stirred by wind, drove her forward. Her feet submerged in the mire below the broken crust of cracked and hardened earth, cooled there, a relief from the intolerable heat if only for her toes. She sensed Phan's steady grasp on the handles of the plow behind her. The earth appeared to roll in waves where Phan had plowed before her. She wanted to rush to finish, but the dragging weight prevented haste. Here nature taught her to live at its pace. What more was there to learn than what it taught? She felt her soul being nurtured by Mother Earth, and she was pleased.

CHAPTER 32

Tong, February 5, 1947
Lao
Flight

"Can't you help out?" he demanded of Khong, as he reassembled the boxes to his old home. Then without a word from Khong, a terrible realization came to him: because he was witness to a double murder, even in the alley he wasn't safe. The sergeant would realize the danger as long as Lao was alive and keep seeking him.

"We got to get out of here," Lao muttered, knowing Khong would follow. He ran from the familiar alley. He crossed through the marketplace into the shadows inhabited by the insane and the orphaned and the limbless crippled by the war. He understood the rules of the primitive struggle to survive that raged around him. He avoided the cardboard boxes and the wooden boards with wheels on which legless men pushed themselves around, the starving dogs that roamed in the garbage and bit the unwary randomly.

Lao felt safe. The place quickly resettled into his bones, the smell of it, the filth, the familiarity with sudden death, especially on cold nights when some who slept in the streets never moved again and were swept away with the refuse the next day. Everyone was hard yet fragile, just a little away from death. In this section of the city the war didn't matter. There was nothing to loose. No one would notice him while he waited an opportunity to escape into the countryside.

The wary merchants' glances followed him. Words trailed him. Get lost. Go away. And worse. He maneuvered like a lizard, never hesitating when he rushed across the open space between vendors. He hid among the booths crowded under the great palm roofs of the marketplace. He slipped under a table, slipped from outstretched hands, darted toward the next blockade. His slight build allowed him to escape his pursuers, eating what he snatched as he went, laughing at awkward attempts to corral him. And if they caught him they'd beat him, and likely nothing more.

The sun stood over the marketplace roof, raising perspiration on old men hunched over cards. He paused to watch them, waited to see who won, then followed that old man back to his booth.

"You got a lot of luck," he said to the old merchant.

"You followed me?" the old merchant demanded, as he paid and dismissed an old woman there as guard and carried on inspecting his fruit as he talked. He rearranged what he approved, leaving the best of it in a row across the front of his table. Several times he dropped spoiled fruit into a basket at the edge of the table. His black pajamas shined from wear. His nose dropped sharply, pressed into his face, like a pug fighter.

"Maybe you could use some help."

"I got no need for a street kid's help."

"How do you know if you don't try me, mister? You'll see." Lao watched the old merchant's reaction. "You just give me a blade."

"What are you talking about?" The old merchant's somber face took on a sterner look.

"I need a knife. I'll protect you, but I gotta have a blade. Something happens I gotta use it, you just say some street kid did it and ran off and you get your protection."

"That's what you're offering me?" the old merchant paused. "I don't need protection."

"Every night I can stay here under your table. The next day you got the same spot, people know what to expect, where to find you. Good for your business. I've done it before. No need paying me, except some fruit and vegetables, enough for me to live on. Not the good stuff, just what you'd throw away at the end of the day 'cause it's bruised or wilted."

"I take it back and slop the pigs."

The way the old merchant said it, Lao figured the deal was all but made. "Good spot like this, you'll sell your fruit quicker, ample reward for the little I eat."

Lao grinned like he was speaking to a grandfather.

"Nights you got to sleep," the old merchant said, "what happens then?"

"I got a friend."

"Oh yeah, what's his name?"

"Khong."

"Where is he?" the old merchant asked. "I want to meet him."

"He'll be back tonight." Lao could see the old merchant wanted to believe him.

"I'll give you a shot. Just keep in mind you or your friend steal from me, you're finished."

"Don't worry, mister, I'd never steal from someone hires me."

"You stay under the table. I can't have it looking like street kids are hanging around." The old merchant gestured.

Lao slid easily beneath the table, crouched and peered back out. He quickly named it "the world beneath" and began telling Khong imagined tales of the passers-by. A rice farmer with feet too long submerged in the rice paddies, covered with calluses and deep scars from careless swinging hoes became his noble prince, often wounded in battle. Women wearing sandals made from rubber tires, their legs tanned despite the long black silk pajamas, twice a day trudging through the market for fresh fruit and vegetables, ice a luxury beyond their means, were all maidens in waiting. A woman with sandals covering all but her polished toes with that film of red dust that covered everyone regardless of status, was a lady in distress. A Eurasian woman with a short skirt, large and solid, unafraid, was a terrible witch. Beggars reached out to her, clinging to her arms that hung too far below her tight belt. French soldiers' boots quickly joined her, the evil dragons. The beggars fled.

At the table a woman quibbled over tomatoes, too costly, too ripe, and no longer fresh. Her cackling voice drew Lao's attention. His merchant at first didn't respond, then acknowledged her price and countered. A bargain struck, she disappeared in the crowd with her woven reed basket filled.

"Please let me have the vegetables she complained about," Lao piped, reaching out a hand next to where the old merchant stood. A single tomato dropped into his hand, skin broken, oozing juices in his palm. Quickly eaten, almost inhaled, his hunger now ignited by the new security he felt, hidden and protected beneath the table, the old merchant standing guard.

Lao heard the prices falling as the market crowd thinned, the old merchant afraid he'd misjudged demand and would leave at the end of the day with too much produce still not sold. Anxiety crept into the old merchant's voice, making it harder to bargain. The women who approached the table pushed their advantage. For an instant Lao allowed the old merchant his sympathy, seeing how age lowered his resistance, made him sell for less than fair worth. The witches were taking advantage of him.

"You get back under there," the old merchant barked. Lao caught himself clinging to the old man's leg, trying not to cry. His feelings for the old man vanished in the bark of those words. He scurried into the recesses of the table, feeling cornered and exposed.

"You can't trust any of them," he warned Khong.

Just before dark the old merchant bent over and muttered to him under the table, "You take good care of my place. You better be here in the morning when I come back or no deal." The old merchant dropped a pile of vegetables and a peeling knife next to Lao and walked away. Lao said nothing, hating him, thinking he'd seen him for the last time. He ate from the pile, most of it still good, food the old merchant could have used for his family. The old man confused him. He settled into the recess where the table touched the outside wall of the old market building, crouched so that his knees and arms were pulled together, and clasped the peeling knife against his chest to wait.

Those left in the market hurried now, gathering their wares and fruit into baskets that they lifted onto their heads or tied on bicycles or strung on poles balanced over their shoulders. Those who had tables folded them and leaned them against the wall and Lao realized that his table stood alone and doubted he could defend it. Realizing there was no longer safety in their numbers, those left worked quickly, tying the last bundles and then disappearing in the growing shadows.

Boys began digging in the waste, dogs sniffing for some scrap of meat. Old women dragged bags into which they stuffed what they judged worth trying to sell the next day. The first of the gangs appeared. Someone among them called to Lao, "What you got in there?"

"Nothing you want between your ribs," Lao shouted back.

"Get out here, show me," the older boy replied.

Lao crouched up on his knees so that he could swing the knife, keeping his back against the wall so that the gang's numbers wouldn't help them. Only later he realized they might have pulled away the table. The biggest youth stuck his head under the table, staying back out of reach as he looked around and backed away. "The kid's got nothing."

—⁂—

Later, when Lao was slipping into sleep, they grabbed him and pulled him from under the table. He never had a chance. One gripped him by a leg and dragged him, yelping like a pup. Afraid and half asleep, he squinted to see who'd seized him. They wore the casual uniforms of the Viet Minh. "Nothing is going to happen to you. Just come with us. "

"Let me go," Lao cried out. "Or you'll be dealing with my friend Khong."

"Where's he at?" one of the soldiers asked.

"He'll come looking for me."

"That so." The soldiers lifted him to his feet.

Lao watched for a chance to escape. They kept too close for him to run away even after the one with the vise grip released him and let him walk on his own. Ahead of him shadows grouped around a small fire. An older man was already speaking when they reached the fire. "We're aiming to drive the French out, and you boys can play a part if you want."

Lao recognized the speaker as the wounded soldier Leah had taken in at the club, but the man didn't seem to recognize him.

"What do we get for it?" a youth shouted.

"You get your pride."

"Can't eat my pride," the boy responded.

"We can't promise anything better right away. When the French are driven from our country, we'll make sure everyone gets taken care of equally like they should. Freedom comes first."

What kind of freedom? Lao figured what adults promised never amounted to much. Most times they ran him off when something good came around. He wasn't interested if that was what they meant.

"So what you want us to do?" asked the boy who had earlier stuck his head under Lao's table.

"For now just watch the French and anyone dealing with them. We'll be meeting here every night, and you report what you've seen."

"That's all? We're doing that anyway, waiting for a chance to snatch some wallets." The boy howled derisively. Those around him laughed.

"That's all," the older man said coldly. "Except I'll be telling you boys some stories every night and beginning to-

206

night I'll tell you how the Viet people came to exist. It is the story of a dragon and a fairy."

There was a ripple of laughter.

"Fairy tales, mister?"

"Legends of our past," the older man said quietly. "Traditions passed down from generation to generation."

"I guess we could listen a little." The older boy acted as spokesman. The others crouched around the older man, who began with the story of a magic king and a dragon maiden whom he married. From them came Lac Long Quin, Dragon King of the Lake.

As the older man spoke, Lao felt the power of words with a beauty and rhythm that pulsed in his head. The Dragon King endlessly fought off dragons, monsters, and invaders with the same gallantry Lao often dreamed himself. He could imagine this older man standing before his students in the day telling them the story. Lao had seen students in freshly pressed uniforms as they walked to school, and now he imagined himself lying in bed at night after school, Leah lulling him to sleep by repeating the stories. He sat transfixed, the teacher and his "mother" as much wonderful dreams as the king and dragons. Just as his feelings cascaded through a world of wonder unconnected to any place he'd ever been, the older man stopped.

"You boys think on Lac Long Quin and what it meant for him to be free. I'll be telling you more about him tomorrow night," he said. "And don't forget, keep watching the French for me."

"Yes sir," several said, and they were speaking for the rest. The outlines melted away, first the Viet Minh, then the boys, many of them retelling parts of the story they had just heard.

Lao remembered the table and darted away in the dark, hoping he'd find it still in place, and knowing the merchant would throw him back into the street if he failed to protect it. He edged along the shadowy market wall until the table blocked his way. He paused. Underneath a dog dug at the earth, eating the grease mixed into it. A well aimed rock drove the dog away.

Lao's hands searched the darkness for the knife. He felt the smooth blade buried by the careless rooting of the cur. Lao wiped it against the ragged clothing over his waist and replaced the disturbed earth.

The ink black sky already carried the faintest hues of dawn. The sound of the night dogs was replaced by the chatter of the returning merchants as they spread produce from their baskets around them. Wafts of smoke filled the air from newly lit fires. The smells of sticky rice, pho, fish, pork, chicken, vegetables, in stews or cooked separately, intermingled. The smells ignited Lao's hunger as he waited. The old merchant was not among the first, and Lao found himself defending the table.

The market filled as if the merchants magically rose from the earth, but Lao knew they had walked for hours from the outlying villages. At that early hour when there were no housewives to buy their produce, the merchants purchased from each other and sold to women who carried the food in their baskets and walked toward the other sections of the city to sell it on the streets and door to door.

The strange warm familiarity to that opening scene came with a sorrow for Lao realized now he must abandon his dreams for the daily struggle to survive. Already he anticipated the next night and the further adventures of the king Lac Long Quin.

The old merchant arrived with his baskets of vegetables, panting and unsteady on his feet. Lao questioned his choice of the old merchant, but smiled politely, glad to hear there would be plenty to eat, because the basket fell on the way, damaging much of the fruit. The old merchant quickly resorted the fruit and spread it on the table and, indeed, that unsuitable for sale created a large accumulation upon the ground. Accustomed to immediately devouring anything he found, Lao quickly made himself sick and retreated out of sight.

The first French soldiers of the day rode to the edge of the market in jeeps. Even the shortest of them had to stoop not to bump the tarp roofs of the market. Lao counted one lieutenant and two sergeants, six enlisted with them, but they bought enough food for ten times that number, or that number for ten days. They paid in French francs, not bargaining but paying what they thought appropriate and more than the merchants would have expected. The sergeants tried to speak with the merchants but finally gave it up and took what they wanted. The lieutenant hung back. He was younger and fair skinned except for the red from the burn of the sun.

Lao spoke to the lieutenant in the French he'd learned from Leah and Sergeant Mueller, and in the end the lieutenant paid the merchant an exorbitant price. By the time the French left, their trailers were heavily loaded with food. The lieutenant said the next time they came to the market they'd use Lao to negotiate with the other merchants and it might turn out better for them all. When he was gone Lao started to think there must still be a way to deal with the Frenchmen peacefully and that the storyteller was wrong. He figured the storyteller was trying to get information, but more importantly, recruit all of them for the Viet Minh. Otherwise those stories about freedom didn't have a point and he didn't see the man wasting his time.

The tarps strung over the marketplace, flapped like laundry caught in a strong wind, driving the smoke from the cooking fires into Lao's face. The frantic cries of a dog tied to a pole added to his dismay. A man beat the dog to prepare it for cooking, in accordance with an ancient belief that the slow process tenderized the meat. After less than an hour the man tired and cut the dog's throat. He quartered the dog before dropping it into a large kettle of boiling water. Chickens impaled on sticks roasted beside the kettle. A young girl twisted them slowly, circling the fire, her face black from the floating ash. When she stopped to play, the man kicked at her, and she hurried back to rotating the chickens. As the man strained pieces of the dog from the boiling water, he threw them into a crate of live chickens which fought over the scraps.

The old merchant ladled a bowl of soup from a bowl next to the table. He spoke deferentially to Lao, "You might want to try some of this."

Lao first just stared, but then reached out and accepted the bowl filled with steaming vegetables and small pieces of meat. The old man handed him chop sticks and dished himself a bowl. Lao waited for the old merchant to speak what was on his mind.

"If we supplied the French, there would be no need coming to the market. You could live with my family in the countryside," the old merchant said. "That young soldier liked you. It seemed like he was in charge."

"He was their officer. Doesn't mean he has the say on where he gets the supplies."

"Maybe next time you can speak to him about it."

Lao paused, pretended to think about it, having observed that adults who acted that way were often taken more seriously. Then he said, "I'll see what I can do."

The old merchant winked at him, the first warm facial gesture since they'd met.

CHAPTER 33

Tong, February 6, 1947
Mueller
A Problem

The problem of Lao remained. At Leah's brothel Mueller explained to those who listened that Leah had returned home with her mother. No, he didn't remember the village name. They all sounded the same. Had they seen Lao?

"Saw him in the alley, but then he disappeared," Dawn said.

"Probably went with Leah," Jimmy the bartender said.

"Lao seemed to be afraid," Mommyson told him. Mueller lingered to keep an eye on them. What did they really know and what did they suspect? He drank casually from a frosted beer mug and listened. Dawn glanced in his direction, pulled her knees to her chest, and stretched her arms around her legs as she balanced on a bar stool. Her chin rested on her knees. Trying to tease him and to size up what kind of money he had left. Maybe she wondered about Leah. What had Leah confided to her? He tried to squelch her speculation with his stare. She was stunning, but it was too soon after

Leah's death to approach her. Not that whores had principles, but they wanted you to think they did. He paid the bartender for his drink. "Take the rest for yourself."

"Thank you, sir." The bartender pocketed the money. Dawn still watched him. He walked over to her.

"Next time maybe we can do something together," Mueller said as he left.

The heat off the road struck him like an open flame. He glanced up and down the street, warily scrutinizing the rows of houses where ocher buildings appeared white in the bleaching sun. Years before the French had abandoned these houses for newer villas further from the city. Now the Vietnamese converted them for their businesses. Mueller watched for suspicious movements, anything that signaled danger, even a sullen face lurking in the shadows as he hurried towards the Old French Quarter and his home.

Old French Quarter, he laughed at the French claim on antiquity in this ancient nation. The streets and buildings in the quarter sprang from mud during the building boom in the twenties. Colonialism had taken hold and only the start of the World War had prevented the French from exploiting the entire country. Their sense of cultural superiority blinded them to the reality that what they wanted wasn't the same as belonging to the land. Mueller understood French arrogance. The Germans also thought they were a superior race and even tried to purify their nation. Not a good thing for the son of a prostitute.

Remembering his mother brought back the anger. She treated him as a hindrance, screaming, crying, and cursing him from his earliest memories. Her hatred filled him like a serum and was what had protected him from Leah until her lies made him kill her. Now he must find Lao and bring the problem to an end.

Mueller searched the local markets. He tried to think where a street kid might run, and how he'd try to hide. The woman held out vegetables and fruits for him to buy: grapes and something like oranges and papayas in baskets and further down the row bananas and the ugly dragon fruit. Although he hadn't eaten since the morning, the effort required to negotiate a purchase kept him from shopping. A constant surge of Vietnamese whirled past him, bumping into him and continuing as if they didn't notice. He felt questioning eyes squinting at him from the shadows, windows, and doorways. His gait quickened, as he moved with the caution of a predator that senses danger to itself. Through the business-lined streets, through a park and around a lake, he continued at an unrelenting pace.

The noises of the city fell away as he entered into the suburbs where Vietnamese were routinely stopped. The stares from behind cast iron security fences suspected all strangers. At each corner policemen in white uniforms reassured the French residents by their presence. Now proceeding at his leisure, Mueller tried to collect his thoughts. Lao had gone to Mommyson's as he anticipated, but something or someone had frightened him off. Mueller tried to recall his childhood and how he'd reacted and where he'd run those many times. A predator had to think like its prey. His memory clouded with the subsequent years of running and the hatred and fear that followed.

He reached the familiar streets near his home, but a block away grew cautious and approached it from an alley. A string of empty military jeeps had parked in front of his house. The white jeep of the Surete stood out. One of the military jeeps pulled a trailer filled with debris. Seeing no soldiers, Mueller approached it, all the time watching the door to his home out of the corner of his eye. He inspected the contents of the trailer: a net, the fish extracted from it and stacked in one corner; a grappling hook tied to rope; a chair petrified from years under water, its mother of pearl inlay still shining in cracked black lacquered wood dulled with age; and the rug from his living room. Though it was too stained to distinguish by the beige red border, he recognized the center design of dragons.

Mueller quickly retreated back across the street and waited where he could see but not be easily seen. He heard hammering inside the house. The Surete emerged with several blood stained tiles from the bathroom floor. They led his dog, tied and restrained with a muzzle, still struggling to pull away. His lieutenant followed the Surete from the house and assigned a soldier to remain at the front door. Mueller counted the soldiers and realized there was no way to slip past them and recover his belongings and certainly not the cash he kept taped inside the toilet. He turned and jogged down the street.

In two minutes he stopped dead in his tracks. A soldier on guard outside a French administration building was watching him suspiciously. Why run, Mueller thought, you know better. He smiled as he walked past the guard, "Good day for a jog."

When the road was abandoned for the curfew, he came upon a legion of men tapping bricks. These men were prisoners suspected of petty crimes forced to labor improving streets. Ahead of them prisoners dug away the mud and replaced it with a thin layer of sand in which to set the bricks. Several prisoners had shovels with broken handles, but most used their hands. These prisoners wore only small cloths tied around their waist and it was easy to see their protruding ribs. French guards loitered among them, smoking cigarettes and sipping tea.

On the hour exactly, a guard blew a whistle, and the prisoners were brought to the center of the street and counted by an officer, who then with a single command ordered them back to working. A bucket of water passed between them, to each a single sip.

Great swarms of mosquitoes surrounded the torches used to light the place, their numbers never diminishing despite the fact that large sallies of them, coming too close to the flames, spontaneously ignited like sparklers.

Mueller moved into the light.

"Aren't you out a little late?" a young lieutenant from among the guards demanded.

"Sorry, sir. Won't let it happen again." Mueller saluted and moved rapidly past him.

"Hey, I know you. Aren't you Sergeant Mueller?" one

of the guards said, coming up beside the lieutenant.

"You must be mistaken," Mueller said, not slowing his pace.

"No, I'm certain. The Surete is looking for you." The guard stepped toward Mueller.

Mueller ran, staying up against the walls of the buildings, trying to keep in the shadows. As they shot at him, he heard ricochets off the roadway and the walls and the breaking glass in second story windows. Their excitement and inexperience kept them firing high. At the first alley he turned, then followed it out onto the next street. He felt his heart thumping against his chest, felt the pain in old wounds in his legs, the lead against the taut muscle, tearing flesh. He climbed a fence, ran through a yard, dogs barking from inside a house, and veered into the rice paddies and along a dike. He settled into running at a steady pace, his feet barely rising off the ground. He fell into a rhythm. At first there was pain, later fatigue, but then a peaceful feeling, and he traveled without the thoughts that usually plagued him, as if he were outside himself.

The moonless night and a dark blanket of fog concealed him. Guiding himself by sounds, he crossed the open fields, distancing himself from Tong. At times his mind drifted to a place of hope, secure at home in a little cottage in the German countryside.

In the dark he passed a French outpost near the road. A sentry fired a single shot that struck close to him. It was an old carbine from the Vietnamese militia by the sound of it. In the morning he would face a daisy chain of such French fortresses along the road and challenges from the patrols that cleared mines placed during the night. He decided it was worth the risk to let himself be captured by the Viet Minh. There were others who had done it, and volunteered to serve as their advisers. In fact, it was whispered that a German deserter who served Ho Chi Minh had taken the name Ho Chi Long. The problem was how to stay alive long enough to explain his value to the Viet Minh. It was a war with few prisoners.

At the next village he rested at a roadside café, a shack with dirt floor and stools and a single table. In the morning light, he watched from behind a bench as a man entered, lit a fire, and filled a kettle. Then he moved to the middle of the room. The proprietor was the kind of fellow whose eyes, when looking at someone, never seemed to focus.

"Coffee, sura," Mueller said, trying to order coffee with sugar. The fellow nodded nervously, looking around for someone else. He brought the coffee with the familiar thick, sweet taste like cough medicine.

"I'm Viet Minh," Mueller said. "Toi Viet Minh."

"No. No Viet Minh here." The proprietor shook his head desperately.

"You speak French?"

"No." The proprietor paused. "But maybe a little."

"I want to serve the Viet Minh," Mueller said. "Can you bring them here?"

"No Viet Minh here," the proprietor repeated, but then he left the room.

Mueller waited. Other villagers came to the café and stood around, some drinking coffee, all watched him. He was surrounded. He sensed someone behind him, but he didn't turn, just waited. A blow against his head sent him forward onto the dirt floor. For several minutes he felt the rain of blows. Then he floated in brilliant light, drawn into a tunnel. He'd spent his life running away through dark tunnels. This time was no different.

When he woke, he was suspended in a tiger cage, its bamboo bars no more than five centimeters apart, coolies carrying it along a jungle trail.

The Stage is Set
Early Colonial executions such as this one in 1891
British Kowloon set the stage for future uprisings.

Coming Ashore
French Expeditionary troops wade shore from a landing
craft in operations against the Vietminh.

Vo Nguyen Giap and Ho Chi Minh
Giap who led the Vietminh to victory over the French at Dien Bien Phu,
with Ho Chi Minh who became president of North Vietnam.

On Patrol
French NCO communicates his units position
during an operation against the Vietminh.

Captured Viet Minh
Members of the French Foreign Legion capture a Vietminh fighter.

Bringing In Supplies

French P.O.W.'s
After a 55 day siege, French garrison at Dien Bien Phu surrenders.

Advancing in the Trenches
Vietminh await word to launch attacks against the
French stronghold at Dien Bien Phu.

CHAPTER 34

Tong, February 23, 1947
Dawn
A new start

As Mommyson approached her, Dawn knew it wasn't good. The old lady, as close to a mother as she'd ever known, sat next to her without speaking.

"You want me to leave here, don't you?" said Dawn.

"You haven't been right since Leah died, child. Get away and try to forget her."

"You think the same thing might happen to me."

"That sergeant always worried me. I should have done something about him. I should have sent Leah away. I don't want anything to happen to you."

"This is all the family I have," Dawn cried. Recently her crying came without warning, several times a day.

"Look at you," said Mommyson. She wiped Dawn's eyes. "Take this card. It's a private club in Ha Noi belonging to a man I knew a long time ago. He'll give you a job. There's more money in this kind of business for you there with the high-ranking officers and French diplomats. And not so many of the rough and tumble combat types we get here. A beautiful girl like you will have no trouble."

"Have I done something wrong?"

"No. Let's just say its time for you to have a new start. Perhaps you can pick up on Leah's dream.

"To live in France?"

"And why not? You're what a man wants. Just be careful to pick the right one."

"What about providing information?"

"Someone will contact you."

"Who will it be?"

"The less you know the better. Just in case."

Dawn returned to her room, lay on her bed, and cried. Her dream shattered with Leah gone, and now losing her home. She looked around at the things that gave her comfort: the old brass bed covered with a comforter and pillows; the red Victorian bureau with her hair brushes and curlers; the little jars of makeup, rouge, eyeliner, lipstick, face creams, shampoos, an eyebrow pencil or two, all beneath an aging mirror tilted forward that only gave her a view of the floor. It was all she ever had and she wouldn't have it any more. She wondered what she looked like with all the crying, but she didn't tip the mirror back to see.

She slid an old leather suitcase out from under the bed and threw it among the pillows. The brittle straps made a cracking sound as she opened them, releasing the smell of the old man's tobacco. She tried to remember the old man's face, his smile when he greeted her for that weekly rendezvous, which gave him so much pleasure. He had left her his personal things that he used to travel back and forth from France. He was too old, but he had treated her so well she'd never told him not to come back, even when she knew he would never take her with him because he loved his wife and three grown boys in France. Sometimes it amused him to say his sons would find her desirable. He called her his little luxury, the one thing he did for just himself. So many others since then, why did she remember him? She threw clothes into the unfolded suitcase, cleared the bureau top, and covered the bottles she packed with the last of her slips. Her weight was just enough to press the leather flaps on the suitcase together.

She recovered her savings, taped under a bureau drawer, and hid them in her blouse. Slumped on the bed, she waited, still not looking up, not looking into the mirror. At lunchtime the bartender knocked on her door. She had expected him earlier. He lifted her suitcase without asking, and she followed him to Mommyson's shiny and freshly waxed Citroën in the alley.

"She said take you to the bus stop," he said. "You be careful from there. Remember, in the end everyone sticks with their own kind. They won't worry over you. Don't be getting hurt."

"Thanks, Jimmy." She said it without looking at the bartender, afraid she'd cry. She got out where the waiting buses all said Ha Noi. The bartender handed her a ticket and money and smiled. The bus driver lifted the leather suitcase on to the bus roof as she climbed inside. When she looked out the window from the back, the car was gone.

If she had traveled before she didn't remember it. Perhaps it had been as a child when her mother left her at the brothel and moved on, afraid of her own child's skin color and hair. But Mommyson was her mother now, and she was sending her away.

After the French checkpoint at the edge of the village, the bus never slowed, the driver constantly using the horn. The bus left the dust swirl of an overturned tornado. Watching it through the back window, Dawn caught glimpses of human apparitions, gaunt souls who struggled to keep on their feet, refugees of a famine that land reform had brought to the countryside, dragging themselves toward the cities.

The woman seated next to her held a bag that kept moving on the seat between her legs. Finally the woman opened the bag a crack, letting a rooster stick its head into the light. The rooster was a fighting gamecock, its natural spurs removed, replaced with those of metal when needed for a fight.

"Didn't want someone stealing it," the woman said.

"I understand," Dawn said.

"With all the people starving, can't be too careful," the woman continued. "You understand, don't you?"

"Of course, I understand," Dawn said, but she had only heard rumors that thousands had starved. At the brothel, French francs kept them well supplied with food.

"At the next stop we can move up and take a seat in the middle," the woman said.

"I like this seat just fine," Dawn said, uncomfortable with the woman's tone of familiarity.

"If we hit a mine, it'll be safer away from the wheels."

"I hadn't thought of that."

"You can't be too careful. That's why I never take a morning bus. By now someone should have hit any mines. Viet Minh put them out every night. French patrols sweep the roads first thing in the morning, but they never find them all."

The scenery changed after an hour, the empty village streets thoroughfares for buses speeding through abandoned markets, past street cafes that once catered to bustling crowds, clusters of monochromatic structures coated with highway grime and left undisturbed. The bus never slowed. No one asked to get off. No one waited along the road, although Dawn doubted the driver would have even paused. So she and the woman with the rooster remained in their back seats, bouncing whenever the bus hit a pothole or rock.

At an intersection outside an abandoned town, villagers lay beside the road, their bodies decomposed. Here a small detail of men, mirages in the heat, heads and faces rag-covered against the smell, struggled to break the hard, dry, cracked soil with wooden shovels. A truck waited, a guard crouched in its shadow. The dust from the bus drifted over the burial detail and caused the men to pause to cover their faces, straightening from their digging.

Dawn pressed her face against the rear window, her knees up on the seat.

A half hour later the bus braked to a stop, throwing Dawn off the seat.

"Quick, hide your valuables," the woman said, slipping off a ring and hiding it between her legs.

Two Vietnamese soldiers in militia uniforms entered the bus. The younger of the two carried an old carbine slung over his shoulder, its stock wrapped together with fence wire. The second soldier, who wasn't armed, questioned the passengers, methodically working his way down the aisle. Watching them she thought she knew what kind of men they were: the older one hardened by the years, the other not yet that way, perhaps too afraid. As a child growing up in the brothel, she had seen their kind, listened to them barter, and seen what desire made of men. The men never understood their harm, never acknowledged what they must have seen in themselves, as if their money were dispensation enough. At the same time the men condemned the women. That was in all men. War brought it out. And Dawn had stood by and watched her best friend Leah fall into blind love with a terrible man, as if all it took was love to lift her from where she had fallen and restore her dignity.

Dawn felt the soldiers' stare. The older of the two reached her first.

"Let me see some identification," he demanded.

"I never had to have any where I live," Dawn said, trying to conceal her fear. "Now, by what authority do you question me?"

The soldier slapped her, the sound of it silencing those seated forward in the bus. Dawn felt blood trickle down her chin. She drew back, but didn't flinch, didn't take her eyes from the soldier's eyes. He hesitated at the challenge, and then lunged towards her. The woman next to Dawn caught him in mid-air, swinging with her open bag, the rooster flying with talons forward into the soldier's face. The soldier grabbed and choked it by the neck, at the same time struggling to release its talon's grip on him without further tearing his flesh. He held it aloft and away from him, twisting and twisting to break its neck, its wings flapping until all life was expelled. He threw the rooster to the floor. The soldier, now holding his face, turned toward the woman.

"You assaulted my daughter," the old woman said.

"You whores!" the soldier said.

"Yes, and for the Moroccans at their post outside Ha Noi. They're expecting us today." The woman, who to that moment had seemed no more than a street waif, spoke calmly.

The soldier hesitated, clearly aware of the Moroccans' reputation for revenge. "I'm taking this," he said, lifting the limp rooster from the floor. As he backed down the aisle, the younger soldier preceded him, waving his carbine so that those closest to the aisle shrunk down in their seats. Before the soldiers left the bus, they forced the driver to pay a toll to continue past their checkpoint.

Peering out the back window, Dawn watched the two soldiers, their hands waving in explanation to comrades who rested beside the road under a canvas tarp stretched over a bamboo frame. She caught the wildness in their eyes, the anger that followed their failure to procure little more than a rooster. The older soldier dropped his hand from his mutilated face to gesture a profanity at the bus. Dawn turned away.

"Thank you," she said to her companion. "You took a terrifying risk."

"Militia aren't much for soldiers."

"They weren't Viet Minh?"

"Oh, no, child. Viet Minh, you and I'd be dead."

"How did you know about the Moroccans?"

"I am from that post...one of their cleaning ladies."

"For a moment I thought of you as my mother."

"I wish I were. You showed a lot of spunk."

"Here, I at least owe you for the rooster." Dawn pulled the money from her blouse.

"No, dear, you keep your money. You'll need it more than me."

—⚏—

A half day later, after twelve more stops for road blocks and as many tolls, the bus reached where the road widened to a full two lanes. At the first French-manned fortification, Dawn was detained. She waved farewell to the woman who had saved her. When she thought to present the card of introduction, an officer was immediately summoned.

"This is where you stay?" The officer spoke in French, handing back the card.

"Of course it is." She answered in his language with a coyness in her tone.

"But you are not dressed for the place." She noted his confusion as he spoke to her again.

"I am not there yet," she said, her tone unchanged.

"I see." The officer wrote furiously on a paper, handing it to her. "This will prevent your further delay."

She snatched the paper from his hand, almost running, excited to be on her way. She found all manner of humanity funneling down the road and across the Doumer Bridge into Ha Noi. Even late in the afternoon farmers pushed, carried, and dragged the sparse crops of the countryside to the city markets, where the greatest profit waited.

At the edge of the city a great embankment held the river back, dirt piled on dirt, nothing more, then the toil of generations of laborers who lived at the water's edge, their work always an immediate and necessary activity for their survival.

In the outskirts the city appeared to be a great village, row after row of hovels crowded along every street with open ditches carrying off sewage. Beggars, hawkers, and streetwalkers beseeched all who passed by them. Dawn cut through a market, stopping to buy a banana, then continued on, occasionally asking directions to the address on the card. No one seemed to know the exact street. Dawn felt as if she traveled in a foreign land, her first time beyond the district where she'd been raised. Here the humanity grew on top of itself, pressed within the great dikes behind which they'd filled the lakes and swamps to make room for an exploding population.

Dawn heard a persistent horn, deeper than the Citroëns or even the buses. She glanced back to see nothing between her and a one-ton military truck. She stepped away as the bumper of the truck brushed her. French soldiers inside the cab shouted cat calls and soldiers seated in the rear of the truck cheered her. She waved. Vehicles and pedestrians closed in behind the truck. She continued in the same direction, knowing those French soldiers would have heard of the street on the card.

By dark the streets had emptied for the curfew. Despite warnings from those whispering to Dawn from inside the buildings, she continued to search the streets that sparkled with quaint gas lights. Her image reflected on a pavement that glistened with the fresh rain that had soaked her. A full moon cleared away the night's darkest shadows. An empty tram hurtled down the center of the street, throwing white sparks off the electric cable connected above it. Her feet hurt. She hadn't eaten all day except for the banana.

Finally, Dawn stopped two French soldiers on patrol, one sullen and silent, the other animated, giddy and always talking into the other's ear. She handed them her pass. What had the officer written? She couldn't read the French. It didn't matter. The soldier was satisfied. "You shouldn't be out here."

She handed him the card. "Do you know where this is?"

"Yes, of course." He handed the card across to the other soldier who examined it and handed it back without a word.

"Perhaps you can show me to the place?"

"We can do that." The soldiers shouldered their rifles. She walked between them. They marched her across the center of the Old French Quarter, past the empty markets, around a quiet lake to a section of three- and four-story buildings, their great shimmering walls, long windows and domes catching shadows cast by the tamarack trees that lined the boulevard. The soldiers pointed to a building with an elaborate facade where a doorman paced beneath the canopied entrance. She advanced while the soldiers waited in the street.

"Is this ....?" In French she repeated the address from the card, expecting to be wrong.

"It is," the bespectacled doorman addressed her coldly.

"Is Monsieur Henri Dalat here?" she asked.

"He is." The doorman blocked the door and didn't move to open it. "Who is asking?"

"My name is Dawn." She handed him the card given her by Mommyson.

"I will take this to him." He gestured to a bench just inside the door. "You sit there."

The soldiers still waited, arguing between themselves. When they looked her way, she waved her thanks to send them off. She entered the hallway and waited where the doorman directed, beside a great tall clock with fine wood inlay, its golden discus swinging from a pendulum, ticking constant as a metronome. The wait was over quickly. An elderly Frenchman with night cap, his handlebar mustache well waxed and groomed, advanced to greet her. If she hadn't known better, she might have taken him for an ancient king in his red flannel bathrobe and matching slippers. She felt him judge her in a glance.

"How, pray tell, do you know the woman who gave you this card?" he asked.

"I worked for her."

"And she once worked for me, mademoiselle." The word mademoiselle from a man of his imperial demeanor lifted her spirits, confirming what she sensed; that his judgment of her had been favorable. What a flattering language that made even the common seem royal. She tried to imagine Mommyson working in the place before her beauty faded. He continued to speak, "She had a way with the men. Eventually there was one in particular. She left with him. Did she have his child?"

"A child?"

"I guess not." He hesitated, examining her more closely without the slightest discretion in his glance. "It was a long time ago. Of course, by the time she left here she'd saved a great deal of money. I presume she used it wisely. She was very frugal and had a good business sense."

"Still does," Dawn laughed, feeling a common bond,

for each knew without speaking it that Mommyson had the dignity so many lacked and could not gain with wealth or position. Dawn sensed that was what the old Frenchman Henri Dalat had never forgotten about Mommyson. What he couldn't know was how Mommyson had repeatedly taught that same dignity to those she called her girls, teaching them to speak proper French, to walk with poise, to sit and eat with the manners of a princess. She had fought against the terrible status society assigned them, raised them from their poverty and fear, and given them hope.

Dawn realized he had been speaking to her.

"I'm sorry," she said. "I was thinking of Mommyson's kindness."

"Understandable. You must be tired. You will be shown to your room. You come with a fine recommendation. Tomorrow we'll discuss the terms of your employment. I'm sure you'll find everything more than satisfactory. "

The doorman walked ahead, her suitcase in hand, to a room on the second floor, a short climb up circular stairs and down a silent and dim hall lined with busts of European conquerors. The doorman worked the key, entered the room, and placed the suitcase on an open folding frame. No need to speak as the doorman left. The room sprang at her: a four-post bed covered with lace and silk, mahogany dressers glistening with polish, a vanity with an unwavering mirror, reflecting a clearer image of her than she'd ever seen. She kicked off her sandals and curled her toes in the carpet. A crystal chandelier set the room aglow. She flung herself onto the center of the bed, bounced on the mattress, then rolled to the edge. She jumped up and explored, opening doors to a walk-in closet and to a private bath with tub, toilet, sink, and bidet, clean towels neatly folded and piled on a rack over the tub. She danced in the center of the room, singing a Western tune.

The suitcase opened easier than it packed. She spread her cosmetics before her on the vanity and stored her clothes.

Later she heard voices in the hall, the heavy sound of a man's voice, his breathing, the lightness in a woman's response, and then laughter. A door slammed, and it was quiet again. She strained to hear talking from their room. Just quiet. She undressed and slipped between the sheets.

In the morning she made the bed so it looked as if it she hadn't used it. She stood at the window, glancing down into a courtyard. The home was once a family villa, behind it private grounds with flower gardens, a second building for the servants, a third the carriage house and stables, now a garage for cars. Surrounding the house were thick masonry walls with wire barriers strung along the top. Gardeners weeded and planted colorful patterns of flowers on the grounds. Dawn pulled a chair to the window and watched until they gathered up their tools and wheeled them into the garage. She waited patiently as the first rays of sun reflected off distant buildings, leaving the garden still in the shadows. Lights along the wall were turned off by a guard, who walked the perimeter of the wall.

At breakfast she met the girls living on her floor. They introduced her to men they called their dates. A bartender took her aside and explained what was expected from her. What the girls earned from entertaining club members they kept, Henri Dalat being content with the proceeds from club dues, the bar, and several gaming tables. Dawn would soon be in a position like Mommyson to go away and start her own business. But Mommyson had left because she was pregnant. Dawn found it hard to believe she was so careless.

CHAPTER 35

Tong, February 24, 1947
Lao
Recruited

Beneath the merchant's table, Lao lived the fantasy of Lac Long Quin, forgetting his friend Khong, and at nightfall he rushed to where the other beggar kids already surrounded the storyteller.

The storyteller grinned. "Good evening, Lao. I'm glad you could join us."

"Good evening, sir." Lao crouched with the other boys, startled and embarrassed at recognition, yet pleased to hear his name from so important a man.

"Tell me what you've seen," the storyteller said.

Lao told him him about the French lieutenant, the old merchant, and the troops he'd seen patrolling the streets.

"You get in good with the French, just like the old merchant suggested," the storyteller said, as he turned to the others to hear what they'd learned.

"About Lac...." Lao started to say. He had forgotten the name.

"Lac Long Quin." The storyteller smiled. "You want to be like him?"

"I didn't say that."

"No, but you seem a keen young man, the kind that would want to fight for his country just like Lac Long Quin."

"You got me figured wrong."

"I don't think so. I'm pretty good at judging men."

"Lac Long Quin wasn't real. Someone just made him up to make us all feel better."

"Oh, he was real all right and a patriot a long time ago." The storyteller squatted on the ground among the boys and crossed his arms. "We follow Ho Chi Minh who is much like him. You heard of him?"

"I heard the name."

The other boys nodded.

"Well, that's the name he's used recently, but he's been around a long time using different names. He was always hiding, a phantom they never caught and never will; seen here, seen there, sometimes two or three places at once."

"Lots of people are wanted by the French."

"None like him. He's studied the French ways and the great revolutions in the world. He traveled to France, and then to America, Britain, Russia, China. All that time he told anyone who'd listen that Viet Nam must have its freedom. You can understand why the French put a hefty reward on him."

"I'd have found him quick enough, if they paid me," Lao said sarcastically.

The storyteller ignored him. "Two years ago he spoke in Ba Dinh Square and declared our freedom."

"I saw him there," Lao interrupted. "I worked the crowd. He was a skinny old man."

The other boys laughed.

"Maybe you should think about what he said." The storyteller spoke without any tone of criticism in his voice.

"I didn't listen."

"Uncle Ho said our country was completely independent and free from colonialism for the first time in years. He

said a lot of patriotic Vietnamese died to achieve that freedom, and it was up to us to keep it free."

"I got enough trouble."

"We're talking about making things better for you."

"How are you going to do that?"

"First we rid ourselves of the French."

"I told you, I got no interest in that kind of thing."

"You're riding a downhill horse."

"I got no horse."

"It's a figure of speech. A downhill horse only takes
the easy way. Soon enough it's at the bottom and got nowhere
to go."

"I never seen a horse in Ha Noi. You got a wild imagination."

"We're just asking you to do what's best for you."

"Recruiting, that's what you're doing. You're not here
just to tell us stories. You want us fighting the French. Nothing doing. I've seen what a French soldier does to Vietnamese, he gets crossed."

"If you're squeamish, just leave."

"That's exactly what I'm figuring to do." Lao stepped
back. "Any you guys coming or has he found himself a bunch
of fools?"

Lao darted across the street and dropped into the
shadows of the nearest alley. Khong appeared beside him.

"Stay close, Khong," Lao said. "Watch out they don't
follow us."

Shadows off the buildings reduced his vision. He used
his feet as a cat might use its front paws, searching out any
hidden obstacles to his retreat. He stumbled into a cardboard
box and pointed his knife toward it. His eyes acclimated. A
form wavered in the shadows against the alley wall. Lao's
heart jumped against his chest. He crouched instinctively,
his grip tightening on his knife. He leaped forward in a run
that turned into a dead heat with the shadow that emerged,
threatening him with its knife. He felt the swipe of the blade
as it sliced his sleeve. He smelled nuoc maum on the strange
breath. His own knife thrust into the softness of flesh.

Lao rushed into a street lined with gold shops, resembling a series of prison cells, their iron-barred entrances in a lock down for the night. A slight glow of light from inside each suggested life. The street itself was spotless. Gas street lamps increased his exposure. Likely the area was patrolled by police, a constant threat his kind never escaped. The series of circular red welts, cigarette burns, up and down his legs, served as a reminder. He paused to look back again.

Ahead, he spotted three featureless shadows attending a windless fire at the edge of the street. A dog cautiously circled the fire, which hissed with sparks thrown up by dripping grease. One of the men extended a piece of mangy flesh on his knife. The live dog sniffed, then retreated, her neck hair bristled like a barber's brush, her tail curled inwardly beneath sagging breasts. She'd have puppies hidden somewhere nearby. The dog glanced backward before it leaped into a metal wheelbarrow cart propped against a lamppost.

"Go ahead, get," the man who had done the coaxing shouted, suddenly on his feet, throwing rocks that flew wide of the snarling dog. The three men kicked over the skewer above the fire, sending sparks in all directions, lighting up their silhouettes. Lao withdrew into the shadows. Crouched in a fetal position, he turned away and tried to sleep.

In the morning he looked over the ochre buildings and figured out from the rising sun the direction of the market. As he walked, he created excuses to tell the old merchant, depending if the table was gone or if it was still there.

Instead of greeting him, the merchant shook his fist, standing over the table, fruits spread out orderly. The first women into the market were lifting them to test and retest their weight. Lao tried to explain, but the old merchant kept waving him away as if Lao was an unwanted stray. When Lao started to go under the table, the old man struck him across the back with a board and struck him again as he retreated. Lao let out a howl. He stumbled against a woman and caught loose coins spilling from her purse before she clutched it to her chest. As he withdrew, dangling arms seized him by the neck, tightened on him, and caught his arms. The storyteller held him against a wall.

With his one arm free, Lao pulled out his knife. "You got a hand in this. You told that old man a pack of lies."

"You've told the pack of lies, son. Now it's time we had a talk." The storyteller wasn't alone, and one of them reached for Lao's knife. Lao slashed into the air.

"Now, son, don't make a mistake." The storyteller still held onto Lao and tightened his grip.

"What do you want of me?" Lao shouted.

"Come with us."

"I'm not going anywhere with you," Lao said. "Come on, Khong, let's get out of here."

"Who you speaking to?" the storyteller asked.

"My friend."

"There's no one there. You're too old to pretend."

"You have Lac Long Quin and all those stories about him and Ho Chi Minh."

"What I said was real."

"I never believed you. Khong says I shouldn't listen. He's never been wrong."

"Son, you're coming with us."

—⁂—

The storyteller later vanished, leaving Lao and several other young boys guarded by local Viet Minh militia. Officially they said he was "recruited," but they watched him closely. That first day they held him inside the city limits. In the middle of the day, during the hours set aside for rest, they relocated from one safe house to another. At dark they climbed the great dike, and descended onto a plain that stretched to the distant river, that still contracted within its banks. The homes that were built on stilts were already occupied by the seasonal farmers.

An hour of steady walking brought the small group to the river's edge near an iron bridge. French patrols marched back and forth on the superstructure. Their feet against the metal punctuated the night silence. The recruits crept under the bridge and down along the shore where they were met by men in loin clothes. Those men tied ropes around the boys' waists to prevent the current from sweeping them away. The boys clung to logs and drifted down river to the opposite shore, where a guide led them into the jungle. Heavily armed guards took control and marched them to a training camp.

Lao stayed away from the other boys, but some wanted to prove they were tough. He fought several boys and won, but he figured odds were against him in the long run, so he started hanging out with the other street kids from Ha Noi. Khong approved.

Everyone played games between the lectures and the drills, which filled most of the hours from the predawn bugle call until darkness. One of the sergeants taught them a game called soccer. Lao enjoyed the running. He hated the time after the day's training when they should have been sleeping but were forced to listen to political cadre telling them how they were all victims of the French imperialists. If they hadn't kidnapped him he thought he'd be in business supplying the French and living wealthy.

After the indoctrination, the cadre called upon all the boys to engage in what they called criticism and self-criticism. That was about ratting on your comrades and yourself. Lao made up stuff about himself just to keep them off his back. He told the political cadre that, with all he had to learn, he didn't have time to notice anything about the others. They told him that was a serious problem. He had a duty to protect the Communist Party. That was how they started in on him. Then they gave him books written by the party and discovered he couldn't read. First thing the next morning, they made him attend a school set up outside the barracks.

"I hate this," he said to Khong. "You want me to run away, don't you? I don't think we can get away, but you're the only one I trust, so I guess I'll try it."

In the jungle Lao quickly lost his way, and the next day they caught him. They paddled him like a school child. The next day he ran away again. When they caught him the second time they forced him to watch the execution of a soldier convicted of capitalist thinking. They made it clear to him that in the future running away would be viewed in the same way.

So why not become a hero of the revolution? Heroes of the revolution had their pictures displayed on a bulletin board outside the headquarters.

CHAPTER 36

Bac Ninh, August 17, 1947
Pasteur
A little joke

Lieutenant Pasteur wrote to his father: *It's hard to believe nine months have passed since the Viet Minh retreated to the countryside. The Viet Minh fought desperately to hold Ha Noi, but without the weapons or skilled soldiers their withdrawal was inevitable. I heard their commander, General Giap, has no military training, which may account for his willingness to use terror. By doing so, he hopes to prevent the Vietnamese giving us the information we need to mount full scale operations against his jungle bases. By now we've seen the worst of it. I am certain when we locate the enemy forces we will deal them a fatal blow. In the meantime we must practice patience, something you'd agree isn't my strong suit. Nor, I hope, is it that of our generals.*

The new posting outside the city suits me well. I have plenty of time to read and a ready supply of books brought into the camp over the last few months. The men are easier to control here with few bars for them to get drunk and no women to distract them. Under these circumstances they're not a bad lot. We drill every day,

*sometimes twice a day, and occasionally we patrol the surrounding
villages.*

*Please try to accept my decision to extend my service to stay
in Viet Nam. After all, it is what they trained me for, and now with
my experience I feel the army is getting its money's worth. I'd like to
see this war through to the end, which shouldn't be too much longer
since we control the cities. I don't think a posting to Africa or even
southern France would provide a suitable challenge. Here the shortage of officers ensures me the assignments I request.*

*If anything I've written in this letter has been blacked out by
the censor's pen, don't worry, none of it was foreboding. Most days
it's safer here than driving the streets of Paris.*

Your loving son,
Charles

Lieutenant Pasteur folded the letter into thirds, careful not to tear its thin tissue, and slipped it into an envelope
that he had previously addressed. A short letter but what
else could he say to his mother and father? What he never
mentioned were his continual thoughts about the first man
he killed, a funny looking little farmer running across a field
with a gimp leg. The carbine the farmer carried had caught in
the mud and thrown him forward on his face. Lieutenant Pasteur had never seen a face so puffy and red where the bullet
tore away the forehead and left a hole like a Hindu third eye.
Or was that a trick from his mind?

Nor had he written home to say he hadn't felt bad
when two of his men had died in an ambush. Or that they'd
taught him never to walk down a trail, but that day he hadn't
refused when the colonel gave the order. Because he followed
orders, it meant his men's deaths were something he'd never
have to explain, except to himself. Over days and weeks, the
killings itched at his consciousness like jungle rot.

He leaned back in the hammock and rolled onto his
back. In the light from the single kerosene lantern he checked
the mosquito netting for gaps. He tried to light a cigarette, but
the pack must have soaked up his sweat. He spit the soggy
tobacco from his teeth. A bell clanged. He leaped from his

hammock, and rolled into a nearby bunker, landing on his knees among the others.

One of the soldiers struck a match to read his watch. "The Viets are dependable."

"I wish they'd take a night off and let us get some sleep," another said.

"Shut up, I need to rest."

In the dark the red tips of cigarettes leaped around like manic fireflies. Lieutenant Pasteur listened to the shortened breaths of the others. Mortar rounds popped and fell on the parade field. Counter batteries fired back, shaking dirt off the sides and ceiling of the bunker.

"They are getting better," someone said. The bell clanged again.

"Time to go." They rushed to the perimeter trenches to protect the compound from ground attack. Everyone knew the drill. Moonlight made the night amber. Tracers bounced over the rice fields like ricocheting golf balls. Black stick-figures crossed the horizon. Lieutenant Pasteur set his rifle down, closed his eyes, then squinted and looked back at the horizon. The forms remained beyond the tracers. Someone shouted to cease fire: At that distance no point wasting the ammunition.

"Anyone heard from our squad out there?"

"Not yet."

No one spoke about the squad again.

Lieutenant Pasteur crawled past soldiers fighting over soccer standings they'd read in a month-old Paris newspaper. They'd still be arguing when he got back, amused by their own dull witted voices. Wasn't this enough sport for them, Pasteur wondered? He checked his platoon, going through the motions required of his rank.

More prattle rose from the trenches ahead. New laughter occurred every time the weasel-faced soldier spoke. Always a serious fellow in Lieutenant Pasteur's presence, the soldier entertained the platoon in a way that betrayed another nature.

"What's all the merriment about?" Lieutenant Pasteur

asked. The platoon went silent. The weasel-faced soldier slid off his feet and in among the others.

"Just a joke among the fellas," an unidentified soldier ventured.

"Come on, I'm sure I'd enjoy it," Lieutenant Pasteur said.

"I'm telling them about the women in the Delta," the weasel-faced soldier said. "Couple of real cuties. Found them hiding in a hut. Didn't have much fight left in them by the time we finished."

For an instant Lieutenant Pasteur hesitated in the face of the soldier's audacity. "What happened to them?"

"Spoils of war, sir." The weasel-faced soldier grinned.

"There'll be none of that here," Lieutenant Pasteur spoke, his voice steady and firm. He thought he knew the weasel-faced soldier well enough to tell when he was stretching the truth for the others, but this time he wasn't certain.

"And why not?"

"You need to ask?"

"It's different in the field, sir. Don't deny us a little pleasure."

"I'll shoot the first that tries it," Lieutenant Pasteur said. "Now you men get up and go back to your bunkers."

The soldiers climbed over the sandbags. Lieutenant Pasteur watched their faces closely as they passed him. Only a few could be trusted away from his immediate control. That was what he got with men so down on their luck they gladly accepted a life remote from the luxuries of civilization. No letting up or he'd lose control to the likes of the weasel-faced soldier. His father had called discipline and hard work the great pillars of Western civilization. Lieutenant Pasteur found himself smiling at those lectures.

The weasel-faced soldier remained behind.

"Forgotten something?" Pasteur demanded.

"No, sir," the weasel-faced soldier grinned broadly, his words fawning.

"Then catch up with the others."

"Thought you might want to hear what it was like

in the Delta. I can tell you how we kept the savages in line. Put good order to them, we did." The weasel-faced soldier plucked at his teeth with his bayonet. "We must do the same out here."

"I heard enough," the lieutenant said. The weasel-faced soldier meant to provoke him.

"Not interested in learning the noble methods of your cause?"

"Catch up with the others."

—m—

In the morning the squad sent out the night before straggled through the compound gate, drenched with red soil that oozed from their uniforms and left puddles as a trail wherever they paused. They huddled together, facing in all directions. They resembled a litter of newly born and still wet poodles.

"No one hurt?" Lieutenant Pasteur addressed Fisk, who led that squad since Haussmann's transfer.

"No one hurt, sir," Fisk whispered, "but a bit nasty out there last night. Could have used more counter-battery."

"You can speak up now." Lieutenant Pasteur said. "You're not on ambush."

"Thank you, sir." Fisk picked at his face where the mud began to dry. "Our radio fell into the water. No one noticed until the Viet Minh started flooding out of the jungle."

"When we didn't hear from you we presumed the worse."

"It wasn't good, sir."

"Did you count them?"

"We weren't in no position." Fisk spoke rapidly. "We buried ourselves in the mud. They walked right past us."

"Surely you can estimate."

"Hundreds. Maybe thousands."

"Impossible. They'd have overrun us. Your mind played tricks on you. Calm down and think."

"Maybe they're waiting for the right time. Maybe

they're waiting for orders." Fisk spoke quietly. "We'd wait for orders."

Lieutenant Pasteur ignored Fisk's answer and addressed the remainder of the squad, "Get your boots off so I can examine your feet. No one goes on sick call with emersion foot. Take out dry socks. Clean your equipment soon as I'm done with you."

"Sir, the men are awfully tired," Fisk said.

"They'll have plenty of time to rest," Lieutenant Pasteur said. Men of low status, his father called them, men who lacked the nature of gentlemen. As if they failed to appreciate the limitless opportunities for glory in war. The kind to watch for malingering, though it was a human tendency when boredom was the norm. And what about their human side, their feelings? No one told that story. Inconvenient in his father's world where they remarked only on the great battles and great leaders of the day.

The soldiers worked their bootlaces through eyelets until the boots fell free or were kicked off. As Lieutenant Pasteur approached, each soldier elevated both his feet for inspection. Not a blister or infection in the squad.

"Now go scrape the mud off." Lieutenant Pasteur stood and straightened his shoulders. "You look a mangy pack."

A soldier nicknamed the Peanut, the smallest soldier in the squad, suddenly bawled and leaped to his feet as he dropped his pants. A stream of blood ran from his groin and down his leg. A leach had gorged itself full and the blood continued to flow. The Peanut quickly struck a wooden match and put the flame to the leach's head until it let go. Lieutenant Pasteur managed not to join in the general laughter. "Pull those trousers up," was all he said.

"He's one of les petits jaunes," a soldier shouted out.

"Yes, like the little yellow men who love him," another soldier pointed.

"Think you left a leach hanging there," another called out.

The Peanut reflexively glanced down, and then sheepishly looked back to the lieutenant, as if expecting his support. More laugher followed.

"Guess you got caught by that one," Lieutenant Pasteur said.

The Peanut pouted as he pulled his trousers high on his waist.

Lieutenant Pasteur felt an instant of regret, and then laughed aloud. The soldiers continued to laugh at this welcome turn.

CHAPTER 37

Lang Son, October 7, 1947
Haussmann
A casualty left behind

"Ready to make a show of it, men?" the colonel shouted from the veranda. The entire battalion on the parade field at Lang Son let out a cheer. "This is the beginning of the end for Ho Chi Minh and his bandits. Now forward for France!"

Another cheer rose from the ranks as they began to march, passing by the colonel, eyes right in review. Around Haussmann men shuffled their feet, ready to step off as soon as those in front of them advanced. The eerie and slow marching song of the legion rose in a musical mist. "Here's the blood sausage, the blood sausage, the blood sausage/ For the Alsatians, the Swiss, and the Lorrainers/ There's none left for the Belgians 'cause they're shirkers." Mundane phrases sung with chilling effect. Haussmann felt his skin still tingling as he climbed into the back of a lorry.

"Where we heading Haussmann?" said one of the soldiers, already stretched out on the metal floor, leaning back on his pack and tightening the laces of his boots.

"Wish I knew. Times like this we need Mueller. He always knew."

"He was crazy," a voice shouted from up front in the cab.

"He had a mean streak in him from the beginning. It was bound to happen sooner or later."

"We're gonna miss him, things get worse," Haussmann said.

"You was always kissing up to him," the squad leader snapped.

"Maybe you'd listened to him a little more, you wouldn't be sitting there picking shrapnel out of your legs."

"F... you. Least I'd recognize my own daughter before I slept with her. More than you can say for your sergeant."

"Guess it shows how well you Frenchmen trained him." Haussmann had ignored the nasty rumors, figuring there was an element of jealousy in everything the others said. After all, the lieutenant had chosen Mueller as a platoon leader over the senior French sergeants. He added, "Still wish he was here with us."

"Yeah, I wish he was here, shouting at us, f... this, friggin that, telling us how beginning with his mama all women was whores. Ordering us around. Nothing like it."

Haussmann stared at the squad leader to see if he was being serious. "You still got a problem with Mueller?"

"I got a problem with pretending he was anything but a no good bastard." The squad leader plucked a piece of shrapnel from his leg and tossed it so that it struck Haussmann in the face.

"You start judging, won't be none of us left." Haussmann said.

"You Krauts stick together," the squad leader said. "How can you call yourself a preacher?"

"I never called myself a preacher. You did that. Your papists did worse things than me or Mueller."

"So where do you think he's at?" another French soldier asked as if to break the tension.

"No idea," Haussmann said.

"Probably heading back to Germany," the squad leader said.

"There's nothing for him there. Besides, they'd catch him if he tried to board a ship," Haussmann said.

"Bet he joined the Yellows. Krauts don't care who they work for as long as they get paid." The French soldier who spoke stood up as if to challenge Haussmann but returned to the bench as the lorry started to move forward.

Word was the battalion would capture General Giap along with Ho Chi Minh hidden in the northern jungles near Cao Bang. The first parachute assaults earlier in the day had found Ho Chi Minh's outgoing mail waiting for his signature.

Haussmann's battalion would sweep north to join the paratroopers. A third force traveled north by river. The Viets would be trapped within the pincers of the French army. It had been less than a year since Giap had defiantly ordered his soldiers to stand and fight in Ha Noi, less than a year since the French in street-to-street fighting had driven Giap's rag tag forces from the city into mountains eighty miles to the north.

The convoy edged forward along the road, cautious fearing ambushes and mines. The resistance was weak, and sporadic: a tree felled in the road; a trench dug across it. These inconveniences required the convoy to halt while Haussmann's squad, in one of the first trucks, dismounted and removed the tree, and filled the trench. Snipers soon added to the harassment, prompting the tanks to fire into the limestone cliffs.

"Chia, chi, chi...chia, chi, chi," a bird kept singing from inside the edge of the jungle as if it was following beside them, warning those ahead. Other birds joined in the singing. One of the soldiers shouted out the name of a different bird to identify each sound, claiming he'd been an ornithologist. Someone reminded him these weren't the same birds seen back in France.

When a mine exploded in the road, the squad leader ordered the soldiers out of the truck, then to move forward of the tanks to assess the damage to the road.

A bugle sounded from the wilderness.

"Ambush," shouted the squad leader, as he landed on his feet off the tailgate. That was his last word. A bullet caught him in the throat, and he toppled head first onto the road.

Enemy machine guns fired down from the limestone cliffs. Grenades, thrown from the embankments, fell like hot hail. Ahead, an armored car spun off the highway, its metal bumper striking trees. Soldiers were tossed in all directions. A burst of flame lashed away the canvas on a truck that followed, exposing the soldiers to gunfire from the woods. Troops leaped into ditches, hugging mounds of earth that provided little shelter. A tank exploded sending a plume of ignited fuel into the canopy.

A second tank roared forward in an attempt to push the burning wreckage off the road and clear an escape path for the column of soldiers. Small arms fire ricocheted off its turret. Its mighty gun roared repeatedly to suppress the retorts from the dense vegetation that surrounded them.

An awkward silence followed. Standing there, waiting beside a tank, Haussmann's fear-glazed eyes searched the endless jungle. A form rose from the ground, hoisted a rocket propelled grenade to its shoulder, and took aim. Frozen to the moment, Haussmann did not immediately respond to the danger. A tank turret swinging in his peripheral vision, fired at point blank range. The explosion turned human form into mist that sprayed across the jungle. Nothing of the man remained.

A bugle sounded again. It brought the mass of Viets pouring down on the column. A French officer shouted orders lost in the din, but his flailing arms made it clear he expected the legionaries to counter attack. Haussmann drew his bayonet from a sheath on his waist and locked it on his rifle. He rose to meet the fury. He fixed upon a single face, distorted by the frenzy of the moment, a single man he might have passed on a Ha Noi street, now turned to beast, the crazy man's eyes like a dragonfly's, taking up half his head. Haussmann aimed the rifle sight between the eyes and squeezed. The head flew back, split in pieces, a bloody hole in place of the nose and eyes there an instant before.

A dozen more Viets sprang from the earth, their fiery faces streaming down on him. He sat back and cradled his rifle, drawing on the closest figure, rifle balanced, elbows forced against the inside of his knees, cheek weld and rear sight posted, trigger squeezed, then repeated and repeated as they fell, a carnival game with metal figures, and at the end, life the prize. The sun burned and twisted in the sky. He felt his invincibility dissipating in the heat. Shuddering, he fell toward the earth, abandoned by his God.

Invisible men cried out from the jungle, beckoning him, taunting him in phrases of pigeon French. The wounded cried, seeking help. He waited, calculating the distance back to the nearest of the tanks that remained, a solitary outpost of steel that had withstood the rain of rockets from the trees. If he ran, he would be exposed. The will to live too strong in him, he decided against that martyrdom. Instinct alone remained to be called upon. No God protected him now.

At Haussmann's boarding school in Germany where he had learned to be a soldier in the Hitler Youth, his principal had chided him: Duty, Haussmann, what about duty to your comrades? Strange fleeting thought, now pushed aside by the crush of events. He crawled into the thick vegetation and closed off his entry point with palm branches to conceal his location.

Quiet and motionless in this hidden place, he watched the Viets methodically dispatch the wounded and search a charred chassis for ammunition and weapons. Coolies used machetes to kill the wounded legionnaires as they cried out for mercy in their many native languages.

Viet soldiers, responding to orders, moved into the woods and searched in every direction. A legionnaire rose from hiding to surrender, hands over his head. A Viet led him back to the road. An officer approached the legionnaire with a bayonet and stabbed him with a single impaling blow. The Viet officer placed his foot on the dead man's chest and yanked the bayonet from his ribs.

The searchers drew closer. Haussmann recognized the

steady rasping sound of a Viet with asthma. The soldier was straining to pull enough air into his lungs. As the muzzle of an ancient carbine pushed aside the palm leaves concealing Haussmann, a child's face stared at him, horrified, almost crying, then allowed the palms to drop back in place. The child walked away, his eyes averted from the man in the bushes. Nothing was said. Haussmann waited, anticipating the rush of Viet troops upon him. Instead the troops continued their search, their voices growing more distant.

Listening for the Viets, Haussmann heard the distant drone of the first French fighters to respond. The terrain, a combination of rolling hills topped with jagged limestone ridges and narrow river valleys, hid the planes from immediate view. The Viets, intent on stripping the dead of their clothes, seemed not to hear the approaching aircraft.

The Spitfire fighter-bombers, their pilots unquestionably briefed on what had happened, did not circle for reconnaissance but dove straight down and flew along the road as it rose and fell, winding along the valley. Their guns ripped a line through the ranks of Viets like razors cutting men in half, as survivors fled towards the woods. Bombs toppled from the wings, exploded among the metal skeletons of the smoldering vehicles.

For an instant a bomb caught in the limbs of a tree, unexploded. Another struck near it, detonating the first with devastating effect, killing an entire platoon of Viets as they fled toward the shelter of the jungle.

Their ordnance expended, the Spitfires disappeared. Coolies reemerged from the jungle and lifted their wounded and dead onto stretchers. They carried them back into the jungle, silently disappearing on trails concealed in the vegetation.

—⁓—

The first French tank that appeared fired blindly into the jungle. Soldiers walking beside it kept their rifles at the ready. The relief column edged past the carnage, hesitant to

touch the few wounded who had survived by playing dead
but who now cried for help. Medics were afraid of booby
traps, so the outstretched hands of the wounded were first
tied with rope. They were then dragged their body's length.
Only then did medics rush to treat them.

Haussmann watched, afraid to stand, afraid to cry out
lest he be shot. He waited, composing his words, his action,
trying to remember the daily password. The armed column
moved past. He thought of deserting, walking back to the post,
shooting himself. He struggled to the edge of the road, crawling to hide from those who might be watching. He waited.

A second column approached in the distance. By the
sound, Haussmann figured it was supply trucks. He stood
up with his hands over his head so that he was clearly pro-
filed against the clearing sky. A jeep headed the column. A
machine gun was mounted over the driver and a Vietnamese
gunner stood behind it, finger on the trigger. The jeep closed
in on him, the machine gun never wavering its aim straight
at his chest. A passenger, clearly in charge, pushed the gun
barrel away and smiled.

"You're a lucky bloke," the British legionnaire officer,
spoke casually. "Where's your unit?"

"You're looking at it, sir," Haussmann said.

"Nasty business here. Climb in behind me with the
Viet. We'll get you to the rest of your battalion. It must be up
ahead. Didn't they pass you?"

"I was too far off in the jungle."

"Too bad." The officer lit a cigarette. "After this, don't
suppose you're in any hurry to get back in the fighting."

"True enough," Haussmann conceded.

The Brit was an amiable sort and offered his canteen.
Haussmann enjoyed the taste of straight whiskey and shared
a smile with the Brit.

Now that he was near the head of a column again,
Haussmann felt secure enough to stretch back in the seat.
The jeep rode easily over the shallowest potholes, around the
deepest, the driver keeping in the freshest tire tracks in case a
mine had been missed by the units ahead of them.

Viewing just the hilltops and sky, Haussmann day-dreamed of his native Germany: days on leave; a blanket spread in a Berlin park, sun in his face; a local girl showing him the sights; a week's relief from the collapsing Eastern front. Then the Russians overrunning the city and his structured world replaced with chaos. Determined not to be captured by the communists, he had joined in the looting to take civilian clothes from an abandoned men's store. Dressed as a businessman, he had fled west. He had escaped to a series of displaced persons camps and finally used his boarding school French to enlist in the foreign legion. A taste of bitterness rose in his mouth as he imagined the stark reality of communism that now engulfed the town where his mother had moved during the war: Russian troops billeted in the house, his mother their maid, if not worse, just to keep wood in the stove, food on the table.

Too late now for his homeland, but here in Viet Nam there was hope. Hope but little else. Nothing of Germany's crisp morning frosts, the turn of seasons in the air, peaceful walks along the clean sidewalks of the cities. Here heat, filth, soaking rains for weeks on end. Malaria. The smells of rivers used as open sewers. Pickpockets, petty thieves, and prostitutes shadowing the crowded streets. Crafty businessmen, cheating, bargaining with lies. Inbred families, taking many wives, and excusing it as tradition. Were these bounyouls, as the French labeled them, worth saving from themselves?

Goddamn, Haussmann muttered, trying to figure out where he was, finally remembering the back of the jeep, and then figuring he'd been unconscious for several minutes. Sounds coming back, groans, then someone standing over him, "Are you all right?"

"Just dandy," he said. "What happened?"

"You hit a mine. You'll be all right."

"Nonsense." Haussmann floated off his chair in the back of the classroom. He stood erect and at attention, shivering in the cold winter classroom, facing the fierce stare of the headmaster, afraid to breath and then gasping for air. The headmaster scowled back and impatiently repeated, "Non sequitur."

Was he expected to answer? Or was it about something he said?

"Non sequitur..." he stuttered. "Latin. An inference or a conclusion which does not follow from the premise." His voice cracked as he answered, fighting to ignore his classmates' stares.

He woke suddenly, settled in his own excrement.

"We thought we'd lost you." A French medic continued to press his fingers against the side of Haussmann's throat. "Your pulse is steady now."

Blue heat off the jungle floor wavered across the vegetation. A patrol dropped off the hillside, the men's bandana-wrapped foreheads soaked, their brittle fingers curled through trigger guards, worn to silver. "Nothing out there."

Haussmann glanced at the stretchers next to him. The poncho-covered forms were motionless. He wondered if he was soon joining them but lacked the strength to raise his head to see the extent of his own injuries. He struggled to speak.

"Just lie quietly," the medic said, painlessly stabbing into a vein, taping the needle in place, before raising the IV bottle over Haussmann, securing it to a bamboo rod laced upright on the stretcher frame. Those around him formed a sea of bobbing heads, anxiety in their faces as they prepared to move the stretcher to the back of a truck, lifting him quickly to hands that slid him next to crates of ammunition and food supplies, tying the stretcher to the closest posts on the truck bed. The canvas overhead protected him from the start of a gentle pattering rain that reached him when the wind picked up and blew into the tail of the truck. Someone clattered up next to him and pulled the canvas shut, leaving him in the dark, then stumbled and cursed, struck a match that burned long enough to reach a seat beside the stretcher.

"Be right here with you all the way." Haussmann

recognized the medic's voice. His steady breaths smelled of wine. Haussmann tried to speak. As if the medic understood, he wiped Haussmann's lips with a cloth soaked with water. "Just you relax. Save your strength for getting better. Let me know if you need more morphine."

That accounted for no pain, certainly a relief considering the distraught expressions of those who had observed him. Why hadn't they explained his injuries to him?

The truck engine cranked, revved, faltered, caught and revived. He heard the distant rattling of the ammunition crates next to him but strangely didn't feel the motion of the truck and assumed it moved from the medic's shadow swaying. The pounding in Haussmann's head increased, drumming like a base drummer next to him. They waved and saluted, those standing along the street as the band passed playing the German national anthem. Men removed hats. The entire city turned out to cheer them, dressed in starched uniforms, strutting like little peacocks. The drumming increased. Louder. Louder. The drumming drove out everything. Then a pure blue silence. He glided along painlessly.

Suddenly he was staring up, the medic pounding his chest, the medic's foul breath, his lips against Haussmann's lips. Then his lungs exploded, air rushing in on him. His eyes blinked rapidly.

"Close one. Don't scare me like that again." The medic spoke urgently, climbing off Haussmann's chest, resuming his seat. Maybe I'm not going to make it, Haussmann thought.

Later, when they pulled to the side to let a convoy pass them, Haussmann overheard the medic talking with soldiers beside the vehicle: "He can't survive any more ride."

"Leave him at this outpost."

"There are no medical personnel."

"Doesn't matter."

They mean to leave me to die with a minimum of further suffering, he thought. So be it, I have always been in

God's hands. Just wish I'd spent more time with him, but it's not an easy thing when you're struggling to survive. The pain keeps you away, the mind wandering where it will.

He dragged on the cigarette the medic held to his lips. Smoke oozed from around the poncho tied around his chest. That's the worst of it, he thought.

"Slacking off, are we?"

Haussmann shifted his head toward the familiar voice. He spit out the cigarette. "What are you doing out here, lieutenant?"

"You think you have a corner on the glories of war?" Lieutenant Pasteur maintained a smile, all the time surveying Haussmann's wounds. "We've been brought forward to bail out your precious legionnaires."

"Guess we can use it. The little buggers don't seem too keen on conversion today."

"You got that right." The lieutenant bent down and removed the book from inside Haussmann's fatigue. "You still got this. You hang on to it."

Haussmann felt the pocked book cover. His fingers doodled in the sticky blood and loosed a shell fragment imbedded in the cover. He gulped in short breaths. "Looks like the book did me more good than you imagined."

"So it has." The lieutenant tightened the straps binding the poncho around Haussmann's chest. "You'll be back to Ha Noi before long."

"Thank you, sir."

"For what?"

"Lying."

The lieutenant wiped his eye glasses, then re-set them carefully on the bridge of his nose and stretched their thin wire frames behind his ears. "You are going to be all right," he said calmly. He withdrew his canteen from its holster on his hip and wet a handkerchief, which he applied to Haussmann's lips, "Wet your mouth, but do not swallow."

Before he put his canteen back in its place, the lieutenant sponged Haussmann's face.

"Is this the same lieutenant who marched us back and

forth, back and forth on the deck of the Beam, who drilled us even in the mid day sun like he was a mad Englishman?" Haussmann tried a smile. He felt his throat tightening.

"It was always for your own good."

"Sorry, sir. I wish I'd stayed with you, sir."

Lorries rushed north along the road in shrouds of dust. Overhead black vultures drifted south, circling on the thermal. The wafer sun bleached the green from the hills, the sky of its blue. The blood attracted the flies. Lieutenant Pasteur swished them away from Haussmann's face with his bush hat. He watched as more troops dismounted and searched the jungle. A burial detail hacked crosses from the brush and marked the site where they interred French soldiers. They dragged the dead Viet Minh into stacks set beside the road.

"You better catch up with your unit," Haussmann smiled and closed his eyes. "I'll be fine. The medic sees after me."

"You hold onto your faith, preacher." The lieutenant tipped his hat back onto his head.

CHAPTER 38

Bac Can, October 9, 1947
Hahn
Unexpected help

On the parade field a single platoon, all that was left of the cadet company, stood in formation, their rifles slung on their shoulders, barrels down. All shuddered in the rain like beasts tethered to the ground. Their faces were worn with the recent terror.

A slight murmur carried the platoon's sense of betrayal through the headquarters. Hahn watched them from his desk. A boy stood naked, wringing water and blood from his uniform. Several cadets cried as the coolies carried in the first of the dead on poles slung between them. Others averted their hollow eyes. The wounded soon arrived on stretchers, crying out to their comrades as they passed and wailing incoherently. The formation broke as cadets left the ranks to clutch their wounded companions' outstretched hands. None held back their tears. A Vietnamese priest whom Hahn had allowed in the camp said it was God's will. Only the intervention of the first sergeant prevented the cadets from attacking him.

The acting cadet platoon leader and the remaining

squad leaders reported to Hahn all at once. From what he ascertained from the babble, the cadet company had at first found the French easy targets as they moved in a column north along the road. A platoon had fired at the trucks. The few regulars who had accompanied the cadets destroyed the tanks with RPGs, after which the surviving Frenchmen ran into the woods. The cadets dragged them back onto the road, where coolies killed them with their machetes.

The cadets hadn't been afraid when they first heard enemy aircraft. Then the napalm bombs came, setting many of the cadets on fire. A French relief column counter attacked. Their tanks fired at the cadet company as it fled into the jungle. More cadets fell to shrapnel from the French supporting artillery.

For a moment Hahn felt a tinge of sorrow for the boys. Youthful enthusiasm wasn't enough. They hadn't been ready. From the first, he had questioned the operation, but kept it to himself. Party leaders weren't concerned over casualties, and they expected the same from him.

"Return to your barracks," Hahn said. He acknowledged them no further. They saluted and rushed away.

At the infirmary Hahn found the wounded being taken off the makeshift bamboo stretchers and placed on cots. A medic tried to subdue the worst bleeding. Blood covered the plank flooring. An orderly spread diesel fuel to prevent the staff from slipping. The post nurse, accustomed to the cat calls of the young cadets now drew respectful looks as she sponged the fevered faces and whispered words of encouragement. Walking among the wounded, Hahn reminded them of their heroic tradition. He ordered the dead removed and buried in a single, unmarked grave. The French must never know what casualties they inflicted. Although it was against orders, Hahn ordered a record kept of dead boys' names to inform their next of kin.

In another month most of those lost would have become fine officers and led ten times their number. Their value had been to the future of the cause. Now the embarrassment of their loss made his reassignment a near certainty.

At dusk Hahn ordered all lanterns extinguished in case French planes searched for the remnants of the cadet company. The medic and nurses continued their work. Their candles flickered all night.

The next day at dawn Hahn watched the first sergeant hobble toward the barracks, and tried to head him off. The first sergeant had grown up in the hills, living off the natural things he'd found, hunting with an old carbine. When the French set out to tame the natives, he'd joined the resistance and quickly become a legend. Hahn imagined the old sergeant had once navigated the jungle with the stealth of a tiger, using snares and punji stakes, setting mines where French patrols were most likely and the locals never farmed, learning French ways to improve on his killing them. Although the first sergeant couldn't read, watching others had taught him plenty. If he understood about colonialism, democracy, or communism, he never let on. It was enough that foreign control of his country wasn't right.

"You can let them sleep," Hahn said, returning the first sergeant's salute.

"You got to keep them going, sir," the first sergeant said, "otherwise the fear controls."

"The cadets are in shock," Hahn said. "You want to take them back into the jungle?"

"Not that yet," the first sergeant said, "but we can use the German deserter to drill them. That will keep them up and going."

"Don't know that I can trust him."

"You give the cadets ammunition, he won't try to run," the first sergeant said.

Hahn reached the barracks several steps ahead of the first sergeant. He marched down the center aisle striking each bunk with his pistol. At the end of the hall the cadet leader jumped to attention.

"Have the bugler sound reveille," Hahn ordered.

"Got no bugler alive," the cadet leader said.

"Get someone to blow it."

"Got no bugle." The cadet leader's cold black eyes challenged Hahn. "Look what you've done to us."

Hahn swung with his pistol angled so the blow crossed the cadet leader's face like a blade, throwing him back against his bunk. The cadet leader leaped forward but checked himself, feeling his cheek. A welt surged just beneath his eye.

"What's that for?"

"Impudence. You're a soldier. Act like one."

The cadet leader hesitated. "You never warned us about the planes."

"Your training wasn't complete," Hahn said. "If it hadn't been an emergency, you would never have been sent. We had to deal with an enemy incursion into our territory."

Hahn glanced at the other cadets, who had lifted their heads to listen. They climbed from their mats at the same time. They moved with uncertainty in the new reality. Their faces still appeared ashen as they drifted from the barracks across the drill field. They swarmed around the first sergeant as he posted the daily duty roster, as if to read their names affirmed they lived.

Hahn walked to where they kept the prisoners, tiger cages made from weathered bamboo tied with hemp and secured by locks the size of handbags hanging from the doors. Eight of the cages were empty. The last contained the German.

The caged man with stone eyes clenched the bamboo bars. A sadistic grin exposed bad teeth. If the heat and rain had affected him, it didn't show. "This the way you treat your guests?"

"You're a guest?"

"You think you could capture me, I wasn't willing?"

"I think you got something to hide, just like the rest of the legionaries," Hahn said. "What it is I can only guess at."

"I must have you plenty scared; you think all this is necessary." The German held out his wrists rattling the manacles and clicked the shackles around his ankles.

"Maybe so."

"This is no way to treat a man trying to be a friend."

"Maybe not."

"We both hate the French." .

"It's not the same when you don't have a cause."

"Frenchies have a cause. They're bringing a primitive nation into the twentieth century."

"You think that's right?"

"Never cared enough to think on it," Mueller said. "Just let me be a soldier, we'll get along fine."

"You understand we'll shoot you if you try to escape," Hahn said. He signaled the nearby guard to open the cell door and remove the manacles, and then walked away from the stench of the cages without looking back at the German. The German caught up to him and walked beside him. His stride had a natural militancy to it, shoulders back, head held high. Hahn headed straight for the supply tent.

"Find something for this man to wear," said Hahn. The clerk at the desk jumped to his feet and vanished into a nearby bunker and returned with a single set of black pajamas, the kind worn by local partisans.

"This will do for now," Hahn said. "Find some uniforms that fit him. And see if you can obtain a uniform like the one he's wearing. Dig up dead Frenchmen if necessary."

Hahn watched the German change into the black pajamas. But for the scars and the tattoos that impregnated his skin, he might have been the model for the statues in Western art books. With his torn uniform at his feet, Mueller buttoned the shirt half way up, leaving his chest exposed.

"Too tight," Mueller said.

"It will have to do," Hahn said. "We'll keep your old uniform in case we have to bury you in it."

By the time Hahn was ready to introduce the German to the cadets, the first sergeant had them formed in the center of the parade field. At the sight of Hahn, the recruits braced to attention without any further order from the first sergeant.

"This man will train you in close order drill," Hahn said. "Later, he'll teach you the French tactics. That will help you know what to expect from them in the future."

The first sergeant ordered the cadets to stand at ease. None of them moved.

"Someday you will understand why I am doing this," Hahn spoke directly to the group, his voice stern like a lecturing parent. The German stepped forward.

CHAPTER 39

Bac Can, October 15, 1947
Lao
A strange encounter

L ao's face burned as he lay on his bunk. He looked at the sun through a break in the palm leaf roof. Fix the hole before the next rain, he told himself. The rest of the platoon rocked in their hammocks like silk cocoons. Why were they confined to the barracks? At least today he hadn't been singled out for punishment as frequently happened over the seven months since his kidnapping by the Viet Minh. He twisted in the hammock and sprang to his feet without knowing where he was going.

"You didn't listen, comrade," the recruit next to him smugly whispered.

"Listen?" Lao hesitated. "Why is that, comrade?"

"The sergeant said we can't leave the hammocks."

Lao settled back into his hammock. "What kind of training is that?"

"Something's wrong with the officer training class."

"Are they back?"

"They're out on the parade field now," the recruit said. "Can you see them from there?"

"I only see a platoon."

"That's all there is left."

Only the previous day Lao had envied them as they marched into the jungle with real rifles and ammunition and new uniforms, to operate as regulars of the Viet Minh. Now they were bandaged, their skin cut and blistered, their clothing tattered rags. A cadre addressed the cadets, but his words didn't carry as far as the barracks. When the cadre finished, the tall cadet across from him exchanged words, and the cadet saluted. The platoon marched toward their barracks.

"You suppose they were scared?" the recruit said.

"Don't care," said Lao.

"You're still mad one of them called you a coolie?"

"He wished he hadn't."

"You sucker-punched him," the recruit said.

"Are you calling me chicken?" Lao was on his feet, leaning back against the hammock.

"No."

"Better not be." Lao pulled up his feet and started to rock in the hammock. "That bean pole outweighed me fifty pounds. Bet you never saw anything like the way he went down."

"You hit him in the voice box. That wasn't exactly fair."

"I didn't mean to. He shouldn't have been so tall."

"You almost killed him."

"Their precious little cadet was never so scared."

"Will they send us next?" the recruit said.

"I don't know." Lao swayed in his hammock and imagined what had never occurred to him before. He was fighting the French alone and crawling toward them with a string of grenades around his waist. The French must not have seen him for there was no gunfire, no sound of any kind. Then he felt the strings in his hammock vibrating. "What are you doing?"

"Look out there."

The cadets had formed on the parade field. The platoon drilled at the orders of a large man who spoke in strange, yet familiar accent. It was Mueller, killer of dear Leah in command.

"You know him?" the recruit said.

Lao shook his head.

"I thought the colonel was going to execute him."

"I wish he had," Lao said.

At dusk Lao waited in the barracks while the cadets ate. When the drill instructor ordered them to the outdoor kitchen, Lao hung back, afraid of being seen by Sergeant Mueller. He ate alone in the trampled grasses outside the mess area.

When Colonel Hahn appeared, a nervous titter swept across the area, and those who could not avoid him saluted politely. When he moved outside the mess area, Lao rose to his feet and dropped his bowl. "A word aside, sir."

"At ease, son," Colonel Hahn said.

"Sir, I know the German."

"You know the sergeant?" Colonel Hahn said.

"He's a murderer, sir."

"Killing is true of most soldiers in a war," Colonel Hahn said.

"Not like what he did, sir."

A night wind sparked the fires and illuminated the Colonel's stern expression. "Tell me what you know."

Lao rushed the story, at times almost panting as he spoke.

"Was Leah really your mother, son?" Colonel Hahn asked when Lao finished.

"She said someday she would be," Lao said.

"And the German was to have been your father?"

"I guess so, sir," Lao said.

"Let's keep this between us," Colonel Hahn said. "I'll see you're reassigned away from him. Not a word to anyone about this. I promise I'll take care of him."

CHAPTER 40

Outpost between Lang Son and Dong Khe,
October 16, 1947
Haussmann
A remote outpost

Four stout legionnaires carried Haussmann on the stretcher. His head twisted from side to side as he inspected the outpost nestled between hills in the only clearing for miles. Indefensible, Haussmann realized: just several rolls of barbed wire outside a berm covered with protruding bamboo stakes. A moat was now a residue of foul water. Inside the perimeter a half dozen fragile huts housed a platoon of native auxiliaries and their families. Two legionnaire advisers lived separately with their congaies, pretty Vietnamese prostitutes who dressed like French women. A sentry with a Bren gun manned the two story watch tower in the center of the compound.

On Haussmann's arrival the congaies partitioned the legionnaires' hut with tarps strung from ropes so that the advisors could enjoy the women with some privacy.

In the space the congaies provided, the medic left bandages and bottles for the IV and a medic's bag with a syringe and several vials. He kneeled beside Haussmann. "They will care for you here until a truck returning to Ha Noi comes this way. You'll get the best care in Ha Noi. I'll make sure they understand what's to be done for you until then."

The medic's eyes watered as he turned away. Haussmann heard the convoy moving down the road. The occasional murmur of the Vietnamese as they crossed the compound sounded very far away. What if he choked or started bleeding? The medic had always stayed at his side. Don't panic, nothing is going to happen, he told himself. There was nothing to be done but to wait. He tried to understand what the distant voices were saying. It was turning cold. Why didn't they come and give him a blanket? He tried to imagine convalescent leave in Sai Gon, or even better, on the sandy beach at Vung Tau with pretty French girls in the surf laughing, and then running back to a blanket beside him. They'd laugh at his accent, maybe a little afraid, but excited by the adventure of an affair with a German soldier.

At the end of the day a congaie came to the hut and sponged his face with water. She changed the bandages around his neck and on his chest. The rest of what she did he was unable to see. He thought she might have left until she placed a candle beside him. He tried calling to her, but the wound in his neck had swollen further, preventing his speaking.

"Blink three times if you want it left burning all night," she said in pigeon French. He blinked three times. She smiled and placed his Bible in his hands. Talk to me more, he begged with his eyes. She swept up an armful of bandages and disappeared behind the canvas.

At dusk the compound quieted. A bell sounded. The soldiers and their families went to eat at the meeting house. He heard pans emptied, light-hearted chatter, a child or two crying. The congaie brought Haussmann a bowl filled with steaming noodles and broth with mushrooms. Holding his head forward, she let him sip until he shook his head for her to stop. She disappeared as quickly as before.

After dark they maintained maximum security, with

sentries on the perimeter striking tin cans every quarter hour. Haussmann followed the banging sound around the perimeter each time. Aside from the constant croaking of frogs, there was no other noise until the advisers slipped into the beds with their congaies. Their silly banter indicated liberal intoxication. After several minutes of silence, they set to work with sex. Before that night Haussmann had believed sex the divine act of lovers. Now he heard undignified groans, pained squeals like pigs in a trough, snouts submerged, struggling to pull free. He imagined long entangled limbs, awkwardly struggling toward an accommodation. Haussmann suspected the congaies contrived their outcries. After gasps from the men, silence again.

The frogs outside increased their pitch. Haussmann floated in timeless waiting. His thoughts and emotions came and went without reason. Was he dreaming? He tried to imagine the land beyond the sounds of the frogs. Since wounded, he traveled in a narrow expanse of reality: things he'd never noticed, moments spread, hours lost, uncertainty of the value of what he'd learned, a feeling that everything repeated until something never imagined must occur. He felt no security from his Bible. He needed all his strength for clinging to life. He let the book fall to the floor.

Behind him something rustled. The new activity turned into the scampering feet. A rat climbed on his chest, its wild eyes glistening in the candlelight. The rat hesitated. Haussmann shook his head. The rat leaped onto the floor.

Now there was only silence. The frogs were no longer singing. He imagined he was permanently paralyzed. That was what no one ever actually told him, that he'd never walk, never run the beaches at Vung Tau.

An explosion in the middle of the compound sent shrapnel through the roof. An advisor tore the canvas down, as he threw bandoleers of ammunition over his shoulders.

"Take him into the bunker," the advisor shouted to the congaies. "We'll be on the perimeter."

The two congaies stood over Haussmann for an instant, staring down at him. Then they rushed through the door left open by the advisors, leaving him behind. Other mortar rounds exploded outside the perimeter. A machine gun fired into the post. Haussmann heard grenades exploding inside bunkers. Someone on the inside must have opened the gate. A hut burst into flame, lighting up the compound as if it were day. Haussmann watched other huts explode and burn. The firearms ceased. Only shadows struggled together, sometimes their curses carried to Haussmann above the roar of the expanding fires. The earth trembled when the ammunition bunker exploded.

A Viet Minh soldier paused in the doorway, and then swept through the room, overturning the soldiers' bunks, rummaging through their belongings until he noticed Haussmann on the stretcher. The Viet Minh wore nothing but a loin cloth, his skin covered with mud so only the white in his eyes stood out. His sweat glistened in the candlelight as he lifted a machete above his head. He stood over the stretcher.

Haussmann's heart beat rapidly, almost like a rabbit. If that was fear, he dismissed it, as he listened to the blade descending in a whisper of air.

CHAPTER 41

Ha Noi, October 16, 1947
Doctor Astray
Casualties

Casualties came in waves, or more accurately in seasons. Like so much in life, there were patterns, if you could only detect them. So when casualties increased, Doctor Astray assumed it was just the rain lifting that allowed men to resume their butchery of each other. No need to look beyond nature or to resort to pieties such as God's will. It was just another cycle.

If Doctor Astray had been a younger man, he thought he might have viewed the violence as a bumper crop of experience given to few surgeons before their rise to top floor Paris offices. At his age he felt tired. Time for a change, he decided and grew a beard.

The officers' wives at the hotel bar cooed that the beard's great swirls of white added to his already distinguished looks. He laughed. The wives didn't matter. Only his young nurse mattered, and she didn't notice the change. He sighed. Young attractive girls like her were out of reach unless he paid for them. He tugged at his beard constantly and nibbled at the hairs that hung over his top lip. Decades of smoking had yellowed his teeth and fingers. His beard added to the ferocity of the face that appeared in the mirror. Each morning he examined the wrinkles furrowed in his brow, the receded hair line concealed by a forward stroke of the comb, the age spots dotting his temple and almost completely covering his hands. He still had fine surgeon's hands, but for how long?

A sudden pain shot down his leg, interrupting his trance. He leaned back, shifting his weight and waited for the spasm to pass. He'd seen many ruptured discs on young artillery soldiers who constantly lifted shells, but he was certain his problems were genetic. He remembered how his father had stooped and limped in old age, always complaining of chronic pain. There was nothing to be done. Hours standing over patients at the operating table prevented a respite. The smell of an imported aftershave temporarily raised Doctor Astray's spirits as he dabbed it on his face. He stole one last glance in the mirror. What better face for his work, one that carried no false promise of a bright future.

—ɯ—

The guard stopped him at the front gate to the hospital.

"Identification, sir."

"You've seen me go through this gate for years," Doctor Astray said.

"I'm sorry sir, but they've ordered me to check all identifications. Some kind of security threat since Operation Lea began."

"I don't see why. Based on the casualties we've taking in, I'd say the Viet Minh has no need to come here. They're doing just fine along Route Four."

"Sorry, sir, got to check you."

Doctor Astray dug for his wallet. His only identification, an old driving license he'd had back in France, was stained with sweat. He tossed it toward the guard and watched him struggle to catch it, and stoop to pick it from the ground.

"Doesn't look much like you," the guard said, stretching to his full height.

"It isn't."

"Sir?"

"Just kidding. Back then I didn't have the beard."

"I see that." The guard spoke with a formal tone. He handed back the license. "You may enter now."

"Why thank you."

"Due respect, sir, you ought to get a new identification card."

Why bother, he thought as he entered the hospital. In another six months I won't look the same.

By the time he reached his office, the absurdity of the guard's demand hit him fully. Lately even the nurses had started to question him. Are you sure such a heavy dose is all right? Shouldn't you send the patient for an independent consultation with Doctor _____? What time should we give the patient his dose of _____? He threw his medical bag on the desk and barked for his young nurse to assist him on his rounds. No one responded. Then he heard footsteps running down the hall.

"Late." He heard his own voice echo off the walls.

"Sorry, sir, checking in on the patients," his young nurse said, straightening her blouse, raised no doubt by her bouncing breasts. At least he still noticed some things.

"You'll report here when you arrive. I'll tell you if you need to check on my patients without me."

"Yes, sir. I meant no harm."

"And I accept that, but it would be nice if someone around here listened to me."

"Sir, with so many new patients coming in every day, we're all just trying to help you keep up. You're a wonderful surgeon, but you can only do so much."

"You let me determine my limitations. I assure you I do know them."

He plunged into the ward to complete the rounds before they brought a fresh flood of casualties. The young nurse trailed him like a cowered pet, afraid to speak. She anticipated his needs with fresh bandages, scissors, and a stethoscope. In the midst of the foul and antiseptic smells, whiffs of her distracted him. He brushed against her when he could as he moved from patient to patient. To him there was really no age difference between them.

At each bed, he reviewed the charts of the night nurse, written with a steady hand. He probed healing wounds for infection. No matter what the circumstance, he tried to sound reassuring to his soldier patients. He took mental note of those with gangrene or jaundice for further treatment as time allowed.

Several beds had emptied in the night. He couldn't picture the faces that had disappeared, their beds already stripped and readied with fresh linen for new arrivals. The entire ward was cleaned, the patients covered in fresh sheets, bedpans emptied, floor mopped and still slippery with the antiseptic that covered much of the smell. The nurses and staff had labored all night and early into the morning to prepare the ward for his arrival, as if his importance demanded nothing less. Yet he felt no joy or pride in it, their effort so little deserved, his skills inadequate for his task. He should have just stayed a doctor to the wealthy and watched them and their children grow older with their minor aches and pains, the natural progression of life. Here in the ward naive young men suffered and died, their bodies broken for patriotic slogans they little understood and he could never explain. He drowned in the echoes of their voices, their faces a blur that unremittingly filled his memory. The wax gaze of the dead haunted and condemned him. Yet in his work, engulfed in his patients' endless needs, he found unexplained relief.

"Do you have a family in France?"

His thought interrupted, Doctor Astray felt the hot blush in his face. "What?"

"Do you have children? I'm sorry I never thought to ask before and I'm not sure what makes me think of it now." His young nurse, beside him all the time, tried to smile as she spoke.

"I never married."

"I have a fiancé," his young nurse said, seeming eager to say more.

"I see," he whispered.

"His letters seem so juvenile to me now."

"You are both still young."

"I don't feel young anymore."

"You must not think that way. This is just a phase in your life. You have a lot ahead of you."

"Do you really believe that?" She didn't wait for him to answer. "Were you ever in love?"

"I don't think so." He wanted to add, but do you count?

"Wouldn't you know?"

"Sometimes I look back and think differently about things that happened. I'm not sure what might have been. I guess I always had my work to love."

"There's someone here," she hesitated, "who reminds me...." All this time she was getting to a point her face was filling with tears.

"A young French soldier, I suppose." Doctor Astray tried to sound concerned as his young nurse guided him towards the back of the ward and into a separate room where the most desperate were isolated.

Ahead of him, she threw back mosquito netting at a bed, quickly pulled a sponge from a bucket on the floor, and gracefully leaned forward to tenderly sponge a young soldier. Blind with fever, the soldier reached toward her, his words incoherent as she clutched his hand. Feeling a flash of envy, Doctor Astray paused, and then stooped to observe the young soldier beneath the netting. The mind behind those desperate eyes still flickered with the hope of some glimpse of understanding of a grand design that had left him there as a victim. Doctor Astray quickly realized that infinite circumstances had combined to seal the young soldier's fate and crushed him with a random whim that no science could alter. For an instant the doctor wished there were a god to call upon. He checked the young soldier's pulse. "Have you ever spoken with him?"

"No. He hasn't been well enough." The young nurse paused. "Is he getting worse?"

"I think so."

His young nurse flinched at the words. "Promise me you won't give him that medicine. That you will try to save him."

Doctor Astray paused in his examination. "Bring me the sulfur powder."

His young nurse quickly handed him the can of powder. "Thank you, doctor. God bless you."

—⟋⟍—

Doctor Astray yearned to linger by the bed and console his young nurse, holding her as his own, but already the operating room nurses shouted for him from the corridor. He awkwardly dashed toward the small whitewashed operating room. Beside the metal table lay a stretcher with a bloody mass, nurses stripping off its clothes, their spotless surgical gowns quickly soaked in blood. Traumatic amputation at the knee, an arm filled with shrapnel, blood concealing other wounds. He checked the breathing and turned up an eyelid. Too often he'd wasted time on dead men.

The nurses dressed Doctor Astray in surgical robes as he scrubbed in a nearby basin. They tightened a mask across his face as he stepped to the operating table. He shook his head. Don't loosen the field tourniquet. He trimmed back burned skin impregnated with whatever the man had been standing next to at the time of the explosion. Oh yes, a land mine case. He used a hacksaw to cut a clean and even cross section above the shattered bone, and stretched the skin to cover it. He sutured with the skill of a valued seamstress, stitches as even as boot laces.

The nurse beside him read his mind fast enough to hand him each instrument as he needed it. She remained faceless to him behind her surgical mask. He only acknowledged her when he finished. Another nurse worked independently of him, delicately picking metal scrap from blood crusted pocks of skin. He paused to admire both women. Their eyes turned towards him. He blushed behind his mask. He was cheating on his young nurse.

"Doctor, we must continue," the nurse said.

"Of course we must," he heard himself say, waving for the orderlies.

The young French orderly and a Vietnamese trailing behind him, lifted the still mass from the operating table to a stretcher. The nurses threw water across the table and sponged the blood. Soldiers carried in another form. A glance beyond them revealed an endless line of wounded along the corridor walls. Floating weightlessly above the body, he no longer waited for nurses to strip away the cloth, but went straight to cutting and sewing exposed flesh.

CHAPTER 42

Quang Khe, November 1, 1947
Thi
Ashes

For weeks lethargy kept Thi in bed. She no longer worked the fields with Phan. She slept to escape, until the horror of dreams tore her from sleep. Searching the ashes for a keepsake of her family, what she found she hid; several buttons from her mother's only dress and her father's cigarette lighter given for service as the village chief. They became sacred relics. She continued to search, digging in the ash. One day she found a tooth with a gold filling she'd seen whenever her father smiled at her. She kept the tooth in her pocket. She wandered through the village waiting for her father. She sensed his spirit was displeased because she didn't work the fields with Phan. For the first time in weeks she drew water and bathed.

Finally, on a day the ground fog lifted into the trees at the edge of the jungle, her father came to her again. The wind blew slightly as her father's voice whispered in the mist. "Through you we'll never die. You carry us in your mind."

Though Thi never heard her father's voice again, she had discovered the means to understanding him. Every day for several hours she sat cross-legged at the edge of the jungle. She listened and watched for the subtle changes of the earth. Her inner voice guided her.

Occasionally Phan asked her how she felt, as if she had suffered from a cold. After an initial reluctance, he welcomed her new willingness to care for their son while he was in the fields. His devotion encouraged her to believe that they would remain in the village.

One day Phan complained, "It would be easier if a water buffalo had survived the French attack. There was no reason to kill them."

"Everything got out of hand," Thi said. "We pressed the French with too many demands. We should have waited. In time they would have left our country."

"The French are the ones killing anyone who speaks out."

"But we could stop the violence," Thi answered.

"Let them get out. Then we will stop," Phan said.

"Do you think Quang Khe was ever on a French map?"

"It must have been."

That night she slept with him. She listened to his heavy breathing and thought of her father, but once asleep she dreamed of Chuan De, the Buddha of compassion with a thousand arms and eleven heads, pure white with radiance, the warmth of infinite acts of charity. In her dream Chuan De drew a thousand swords. The soldiers from Viet Nam's armies—Vietnamese, Chinese, German, French—attacked her from all directions. Mandarins and Catholic priests mingled in their ranks. Viet Minh led the attack. Chuan De defended herself but never struck a mortal blow against the vast attacking armies, whose sheer numbers should have been overwhelming. As they hacked off her arms, Chuan De remained calm, her many eyes filled with tears of compassion. Her bloody stumps rejuvenated, and the severed arms, fallen to the ground, turned into other images of Chuan De. Her tears filled the sky, extinguishing the flames.

Thi woke covered in sweat. She remembered her father had once taken her to a pagoda in the oldest part of Ha Noi . On the center altar Chuan De held out her arms with a single eye in the palm of each hand. Her many heads stacked on each other and looked in all directions, seeking the way of good deeds. Her uppermost face smiled on those who came to worship. Her deep blue eyes were crystals.

Thi's father had fallen to his knees in prayer, rocking forward, his forehead to the floor repeatedly chanting "om mani padme hum." At the altar worshipers offered incense, the burning colors — red, green, deep magenta, blue — seeded deep in Thi's memory. She was young, yet her father had treated her as his companion and adviser. In private moments he confided in her that of all his children she held the most promise. He favored her, although his oldest son was to take his place. She alone shared his confidence on special occasions.

Her father had led her into a dark room where tiny black lacquered boxes lined the walls with the ashes of the dead.

"Someday you must bring me here," he had said. Now that was not possible.

CHAPTER 43

Chu Moi, November 14, 1947
Mueller
An attack

The French patrol crossed the open rice paddies, casually making a wide circle, staying in sight of the compound. The soldiers filed along dikes stretched like wires toward the jungle. They paused to question the farmers harvesting rice. They detained a farmer, tied his arms behind his back, and drew him along with a noose around his neck. As the patrol came closer Mueller could see the stubble that covered their chins and the sweat on their foreheads just below the berets. He heard their breathlessness. These soldiers were unworthy of the uniform. The French patrol's casualness left him feeling disdain toward his former comrades. Their flopping canteens rattled and flashes of sunlight reflecting off the bare metal betrayed their location. The soldiers bunched together at a tree fallen across the trail. He imagined giving orders to spread out and keep the interval. As they paraded past, Mueller concealed himself among the snarled roots of a banyan tree. He buried his nose in the sparse, drying grasses and pinched his nostrils to not sneeze. He felt invisible. As he waited an impulse to throw up his arms and walk into the open and warn the French patrol quickly passed. After all he had done for them, the French had branded him a criminal and placed a reward on his head.

His muscles tensed, ready to spring up like a wild beast and escape into the underbrush or to kill them if necessary. Over his shoulder he glimpsed Colonel Hahn ease the safety off his rifle and drop his chin to the stock. The bastard would shoot me in the back if I ran, Mueller thought.

Earlier that morning the colonel had ordered him to dress in a French uniform. At the time, Mueller showed no reaction to the name HAUSSMANN embroidered over the breast pocket. They had marched him to outside a French fortress with a single watchtower and surrounded by a moat.

As the French patrol disappeared in the hamlet beside the compound, Colonel Hahn gave the order to move up onto the road. Mueller stood beside a cart as the Viet Minh loaded it with their rifles and a legionnaire's bag. Then they ordered him to lie down in the cart and covered him with rice stalks.

Several Viet Minh soldiers who had dressed as farmers dragged the two-wheeled cart down the street. Mueller heard the colonel direct them and exchange greetings with local villagers as they headed toward the hamlet. The wooden wheels accentuated each and every pebble in the road, each indentation of earth. Mueller cursed. He estimated the distance traveled by the rotations of the wheels. Allowing for the times they stopped, they should have already been in the hamlet. He thought he heard the faint music of a French hand-cranked Victrola.

The cart men dropped the pulling handles, slamming Mueller's head against the front board. Awkwardly stretching out his legs, he stepped down.

"I can't get into that outpost. I'm AWOL, and they'll check my papers."

"You won't need to." Colonel Hahn gestured toward an earthen hut with thatched roof and several sheets of tin above the entrance. He handed Mueller the legionnaire's duffle bag. "Take it in there, open it, and hit this switch. You have three minutes to get out before it explodes."

Mueller smiled at the simplicity. The patrol's sanctuary from the heat, a primitive bar that provided cool drinks was without no guards. He crossed the street and ducked under the wood framed doorway. The room was windowless. The mud walls and mud floor added to the gloom. Legionnaires sat like apostles along a single table, listening to their sergeant. They cheered when he cursed and kicked the prisoner at his feet.

With no place to sit at any table in the room, Mueller lifted himself onto a bar stool, leaving the duffle bag at his feet. A fly buzzed at his ears. He swatted it away. A young legionnaire approached him. His face was poxed with red ant bites.

"What's in the bag?" the youth said.

"Traveling clothes."

"Are you on leave?"

"Something like that."

"No one comes out here on leave." The other legionnaires turned to watch.

"I said something like that. Don't stick your nose where it doesn't belong."

"Maybe you should see our lieutenant."

"He's here?" Mueller stared at the other soldiers.

"He's in the post down the road."

Muller slid off the stool, reached down into the open neck of the duffle bag and flipped the timer, at the same time taking out a pack of cigarettes. "Let's go see him."

Mueller walked past the tables toward the door, nodding to the boastful sergeant, who watched him suspiciously. Three minutes. The youth followed him, past the doorway and into the street.

The explosion threw pieces of the building over Mueller and the concussion knocked him to the ground. When he got up, he cursed that three minutes hadn't allowed enough time. The young soldier moaned and struggled to regain his feet. Mueller stepped beside him, seized the youth's pistol from its holster, and put it to the youth's head. It misfired twice. The youth now on his back bewildered, pleaded with his eyes. "Bungling fool," Mueller muttered. He drew the youth's knife from his web gear and sunk it into his chest. Mueller felt the knife break through the bone as the tension of the body relaxed. The empty gaze was mildly satisfying.

Another French soldier staggered from the hut. Mueller, quick upon him, stabbed him repeatedly in the neck. A French reaction team from the fortress was running down the road, half dressed, their rifles waving in all directions, their faces contorted in disbelief at a daylight attack. The Viet Minh rose from their concealment in the ditches and counter attacked to overrun the fortification. Mueller crouched behind an overturned table that had been thrown into the street by the explosion. Bullets scarred the ground around him and tore into the cart and table, but nothing struck him.

When the gunfire ended, villagers emerged from other huts and warmly greeted the Viet Minh. Children darted among the dead Frenchmen stripping their clothes and field gear. Several assisted the Viet Minh in loading the cart with the French weapons.

A naked Frenchman as white as cream burst from a hut. He stumbled, fell and rose, and ran again across an open field toward the jungle. Mueller waited for the eruption of gunfire.

"Don't you see him?" Mueller shouted. The Viet Minh had paused from loading captured weapons to watch the frantic man. "You're letting him escape."

"Escape?" the colonel smiled. "You think a Frenchman can survive out there?"

"What if he saw me?"

"Not that it's of consequence, but that knowledge won't travel." The soldiers around the colonel smiled.

"You're damn fools not killing him," Mueller spat.

"You have a knife. Go get him, if you want." The colonel resumed sorting through the weapons thrown into the cart. He removed an officer's pistol from its holster, and then exchanged it for his own.

Mueller spat again and settled back against the cart and watched the Viet Minh dismantle what remained of the fortifications before burning the French compound.

They took nothing from the villagers. The villagers were gathered around the cart and forced to listen to a lecture on the colonel's version of right and wrong.

When the Viet Minh patrol left, several village boys joined them.

CHAPTER 44

Quang Khe, November 17, 1947
Phan
A villager's life

The days of farming had become months, then almost a year. Phan felt his shoulders strengthening. The muscles in his legs had grown firm, the bottoms of his feet tender, his toes spread more noticeably without shoes to constrain them. Before dawn each day he headed across the village, so familiar now that he no longer noticed the shadows of the homes that had finally stopped smoldering. In the total darkness he walked the narrow jungle trail to the vast, open fields.

The still air contained the fragile smells of morning. The heat and humidity came later with the sun. At the edge of the clearing he leaned his back against a tree. He placed his conical hat beside him on the grass, and watched the first pale yearnings of the day appear between two hills. He listened to the throaty warblers, who had sensed dawn's coming even before a pink hue brightened the cloudless sky and the sparkling diamond stars dimmed. The sun bestowed a few perfect moments before its energy burned away the innocent beauty.

Phan replaced the wide brimmed hat on his head. The sun already consolidated moisture in a cloud covering that by mid-afternoon would explode in torrential rains. He rose, stepped off the dike, and slipped into the rice paddy. Mud oozed over his feet and he sunk to his knees in the water, aware of the difficulty of working alone to remove all the weeds that would otherwise choke the new rice. Each day was the same since his wife had fallen into her torpor. He bent to weed.

Maybe rebuilding on the foundation of Thi's family home had been a mistake, but that was what she'd wanted and in fact insisted, something she'd never done before. He took her new assertiveness as a sign everything was working out. The first week after returning to the village, she'd plowed the fields with him from dawn to dusk and at night they'd constructed a home by candlelight.

Then one night he had awakened and heard her whispering. He rolled over and saw her sitting on the edge of the bed talking to her father as if he were standing in a doorway. Phan never brought it up though it happened nightly in the weeks that followed. What would he say? He realized she'd been burying the hurt, struggling to sink that which floats. As she withdrew into herself, he worried she might never escape what had happened. At first he had crawled next to her on the wooden bench they'd constructed as a bed, but even if he caressed her, she remained motionless and stared into the rafters of bamboo and palm leaves. Her silence unnerved him. Her eyes fluttered and pierced other worlds. Those worlds stole her, leaving her motionless on their bed.

For weeks, she lay on a mat in the somber light of their home, not answering him. The rice he placed beside her went uneaten for days. Day after day, she didn't speak. She ignored Trang's cries. Phan carried the boy to the fields, afraid to leave him with her.

Then the last night, just when Phan was about to get into his hammock, Thi walked over and started talking to him as if nothing had happened. Her slender form folded into the shadows as she bent to rest against an areca palm tree that had withstood French artillery and towered over the hammock.

Thi's words floated into the chilling night air. "Things need to change. When our son grows up we can't make him marry who we... who you... want. We can't force him to work here farming or send him to the city just because we see fit. Let him decide what he wants, let him choose how to see things. It's not right that families...fathers really.... decide how their children are to live their lives."

"Or decide for their wives? Is that what's been bothering you?" Phan said. That was when he noticed Trang in his wife's arms.

"I listened to my father. You need to listen to him, too," Thi whispered bitterly.

Phan flinched. "I don't believe in ghosts."

"Our ancestors are not ghosts. They speak to their children. You don't hear them because you lived too long with the priests."

Phan slipped from his hammock and joined her crouched on the ground beneath the tree. With his thumbs he wiped the tears on her cheeks. Cupping his hands to hold her face, he lightly kissed her forehead. His eyes caught in hers, vacant eyes pronounced within dark shadows, staring back at him. He shuddered and pulled a blanket from the hammock and wrapped the three of them.

"You aren't well yet. Not yet, really. Let me take our child." He ventured his reach

Thi drew back, tightening her grip on Trang cradled in her arms. "I'll take care of our son."

—m—

Now, standing in the sludge, he was worried because he had agreed. Trang no longer lay placidly on a mat, but crawled swiftly, his back arched like a lizard. Or he stood wobbling, grasping the closest object for support, then raced to the next object, furniture or tree, grasping at anything that reached his newly discovered height. Was his wife ready to cope with him?

Phan resumed weeding from a ribbon at the spot he had left off the previous day. He tried to bury his thoughts in the mindless work, picking out the weeds, but it didn't work. Was Thi just being confrontational? She couldn't have it both ways: worshiping ancestors when it suited her but living as a modern free spirit at other times. Loyalty to the ancestors was only part of it. There was piety and fidelity, son to father, wife to husband, yet he hadn't said it, afraid of her delicacy. He had saved his argument for the time it mattered, the time when she opposed him.

He turned the plow towards muddy water but then sunk his hands into the mud to pull weeds by their roots, shake them clean in the water, and let them float away. He'd concede the land that had barely provided for the village would grow an abundance of food for three. They could live alone without depending on the winds of political favor blowing their way. They might try to draw their freedom from the earth, but escaping into the jungle hadn't worked before. Freedom in a vacuum lacked reality. There had to be something to be free from. And just escaping wasn't the same thing. He stumbled in the mud, but caught himself. Was this time different? He stared into the muddy water. The earth was now their sole provider.

To live alone was easy to say, but they needed more than rice. The fruits of the jungle were limited and seasonal. Their clothes were already little better than rags. They needed a rooster before the hens grew too old. There was a lot they needed to buy in the city, but for now it was better to keep the French believing the village no longer existed.

A black snake, not more than a foot in length, curled and gliding in an S shape, snapped like a whip across the water. It quickly disappeared in the deep grasses along the nearest dike. From a perch somewhere within the jungle, a falcon sailed toward the snake's parted trail. Outstretched talons struck the earth with a violent thump, and the falcon tumbled forward. Empty talons rose. The falcon, flapping rapidly, turned and climbed into the sky. Its parting shriek pierced the air as it disappeared beyond the trees.

A surreal form carved out of distant blackness made its way toward.

"I thought you'd want to see him," Thi said. She paused to stretch and placed Trang on his tiny feet. His hands clung to her arm, and then released her. He charged across the distance between them, son to father, and fell into the water that separated them. Trang struggled to the surface, sputtering out water as Phan reached over and pulled him to his feet. Trang remained sullen, an expression of betrayal etched on his face.

"There," Phan said.

Thi reached to embrace Phan. "I haven't been much of a mother or wife lately."

"You had a lot to deal with." Instantly, Phan wanted his words back. Thi's face reflected disappointment as her eyes drifted downward. He felt a flash of annoyance. What was she expecting him to say?

CHAPTER 45

Quang Khe, December 1, 1947
Thi
The river doesn't change

Thi spent the days at the jungle's edge watching Phan labor in the paddies and wondering if he too tried to forget. She struggled to ride within his mind, an uninvited passenger, seeing it all. He tossed next to her at night. His dreams must have haunted him, yet months in the fields did not take away his lust for writing, his imagined heroics, and his vision of becoming a leader in the cause of Vietnamese independence. It wasn't anything he said that told her. She read it in his face and what he left unsaid. Would he never understand the answer was right in front of him: a village away from the dangers of a society in anarchy? Were his dreams so important that he dreamed without practicality? She understood his attempt to forget those aspirations by working in the fields. Women used the same techniques, trapped by traditions, that relegated them to cook, mend clothes, and care for their child.

She stepped into the open where he would see her.

"Where's our son?" he shouted.

"There, against the tree," Thi pointed, annoyed by his question.

Phan forced the blade of the hoe into the mud so that it remained erect and rushed to Trang. He picked the child from the mud where he crawled and splashed in the water.

"I thought you were getting better," Phan said.

Better than what, Thi thought. Better at concealing my grief ? "I'm just fine," she said.

"Don't leave him alone again. Something can happen."

"I thought you'd be glad to see us. Here's water and some lunch." She offered a bowl with rice and a charred military canteen from a reed basket. He handled it awkwardly, his fingers collectively shaped like a lotus as he pressed the rice to his mouth. He gulped from the canteen.

"You are making progress," Thi said.

"An ox would do better."

"But we don't have an ox."

"There's nothing left out here."

"We have what we need."

"You think life's that simple," Phan said. "What about the world beyond here?"

"It's crazy right now," she said. His craving for excitement frightened her. What of his role as family provider, his duty to remain at home?

Trang howled, disturbed by the tone in his father's voice. Thi reached for the tiny outstretched hands, snatching the child from Phan. The child calmed, snuggled to her bosom, sucking his thumb.

When Thi glanced up, Phan had resumed hoeing the field. She knew she'd lost him, although she was uncertain exactly when or precisely how it had happened. Now there were only fragments of conversation between them and even the nights of his lust without any conversation at all were somehow lost.

The hoe struck harsh, rhythmic blows against hard, baked earth just below the surface of the watery slime pumped from an adjacent canal. Drops of water caught the sunlight, sparkled and danced, newly formed crystals released into the atmosphere. The entire field sparkled.

Thi studied the strong, rhythmic blows, the strong arms sweating and swinging behind them. She admired her husband's perseverance, his determination to complete work as interminable as the seasons. Why wasn't he satisfied with it?

She leaned against that one, solitary tree and waited for him to finish the day if never the task. She wished he'd reconcile himself with the land instead of trying to prove he was its master. For the first time she wondered if someone raised in Ha Noi could ever understand that nothing ever really changed. You stood in the river and the river went around you or it knocked you over and carried you off.

Her husband carried ideas of freedom in his head, ideas read from Western books, too different to be imposed on his adopted country. They were ideas without roots, and they'd be swept away just like the French, who now stood too deeply in the river. That was the trouble with a lot of those dreaming books that pretended their worlds were real, their solutions attainable, and her husband was consumed by the fever of those books.

Thi stretched her feet out over the dike, dangling her sandals above the silvery water, and then she let her sandals fall. Simple individual splashes, and then it was quiet. She pressed her bare feet down into the warm mud as it oozed between her toes until they were covered. Trang crawled to the edge of the dike next to her and watched with curiosity as she wiggled her toes above the surface. He stretched one hand to reach the toes, but the banking was far too high for him. He tottered like a tipping stool, losing his balance.

"You want to try, then go ahead and try," Thi said as Trang tumbled headlong down the banking, splashing and sputtering. Flailing little arms quickly righted him. He sat in the water, plump pink legs out in front and grabbed at her nearest toe. She withdrew the toe beneath the surface. He grabbed at another and, when it disappeared, looked straight back at Thi grinning.

"Smart," she said, satisfied with him.

She resumed watching her husband, knowing he was trying to hoe the entire field before nightfall. A demonic presence within goaded him toward unattainable goals. He continued to work as shadows stretched like claws far beyond the jungle. He worked into the night. Thi watched him grow frustrated. In his self-righteousness, he craved a perfection in himself that did not exist in anyone. She attributed it to the beliefs indoctrinated by the French priests. She never understood their strange god who sacrificed his own son for the benefit of mankind, a god who demanded strict loyalty and devotion to him before all else, including family. Now Phan couldn't escape that demon implanted within him, his loyalty misdirected by the foreigners and their false teachings. Thi realized she was being defeated. Tearful, she ran to the village with Trang on her hip.

Phan returned in the middle of the night. Thi rekindled the fire to reheat the rice. She grilled a strip of meat cut from a monkey killed several days before. Phan stood in the shadows against the wall. She heard his breathing in the slow even tempo of bellows from a forge. His smell overwhelmed the fragrance of the freshly cut palm she'd woven into the walls, overcame the smell of smoke intermingled with the savory scent of meat. As if it was the whisper of a ghost, his voice unfolded through the darkness. "You shouldn't wait up for me."

"It's what I want to do." She spoke gently.

"I'm afraid to stop." His face reflected the fire as he squatted next to it. He tore meat between his front teeth, and then spooned the rice. When he finished, he hung his shirt to dry.

"We could move back into the city," he said.

"I'm happy here," she said.

"In the city there are more people to look out for you if anything should happen to me." His words cascaded. "Pretty things to see... a lot more kinds of food."

"It isn't about me. I'm used to this," she said. "I'm used to you and being here."

"We haven't even heard whether the French conceded us freedom."

"That what you want? You want to go find out?" He nodded.

"Your obligations are here," she said, stretching out on the mat and turning her back toward him. He lay next to her but did not touch her. She listened to his breathing, heavy with exhaustion. Then for a short time it rained, a gentle rain that pattered on the roof and for a moment reassured her.

CHAPTER 46

Ha Noi, January 19, 1948
Pasteur
A night out

When housekeeping knocked on the door, Lieutenant Pasteur was asleep in the tub. He dreamed that generals briefed him in preparation for Lea, the military operation three months before. In his dream he argued that it wouldn't work, That traveling along the road in an armored column was too dangerous, exposing the soldiers to ambushes. To that argument, they pointed out his inexperience for where was he at Normandy or the Battle of the Bulge? He led them to lines of shallow graves outside the outpost and pointed out the names of his men who died in the operation. He pointed out the grave of Haussmann, found beheaded on the floor of an outpost hut. The briefing continued as if he were invisible. Then he realized the knocking sound wasn't in his dream. A Vietnamese woman knelt beside him at the edge of the bath tub. She shook him. He thought she said, "You okay, soldier?"

"Yes, okay," he said very slowly. "Thank you. I might

have drowned."

She watched him without expression.

"Khong biet Phap?" he said. "Phap...French."

"Khong biet Phap," she said.

She didn't speak French. "And I don't speak Vietnamese," he said. "Now what do we do?"

The woman reached into the water and retrieved a floating soap. She rubbed it across his chest and then into the water on his stomach. He smiled at her, and she smiled. Her blouse was wet, but she didn't seem to notice. Where her skin turned white along a line, beneath her clothes it was smoother. There the years of sun hadn't aged her. She kept washing him as if he were her child. Leaning back he rested his head on the cold curvature of the porcelain tub, lifted a foot to the faucets, and used his toes to run hot water to restore the warmth. Her breath smelled of Vietnamese coffee. He touched her silky, grey hair. She kept washing him. She let the soap pop to the surface and splashed water to rinse him. The water turned chocolate. He stood and stepped over the rim of the tub, holding on to steady himself on the tile floor. She dried him with a towel. She followed him to the bed. She was old, but it didn't matter. Afterward he gave her money, and she left. He felt relaxed, as if there wasn't a war and he was a child. He wrapped a towel around himself and sat at the desk beside his bed. He wrote:

January 19, 1948

Dear Mother and Father, Although we remained in our outpost for Christmas, I've just come to Ha Noi on leave. It is TET. This time last year I was on an operation and missed the celebration. Try to imagine one big party going on for a month. The Vietnamese holiday began last night, the first night of their new year. There was quite a parade with floats and life-size dragons running through the streets, then fireworks. The Vietnamese have decorated their homes and businesses far beyond anything I'd expected they could afford. Paper lanterns line the streets, and at night their magical glow creates a fantasy land. All the vendors stay open, so there is plenty to eat. It is quite exotic the way they serve it. I get my fill just from the samples they give out to coax me into their restaurants. They take great pride in hanging animal carcasses in front of their businesses for the passerby to examine: pigs, chickens, ducks, hung by their heels, the severed heads of cattle sticking out their tongues. My interpreter took me into a Chinese drugstore and showed me tiger's liver, rhino horn, snakes pickled and coiled whole in glass jars and a number of things I won't describe. Apparently these are used to restore your virility and ensure long life. We made a few jokes about their claims. Now with my interpreter off visiting his family, I have time to write. I will go out shortly just to enjoy the celebrations. It's hard to believe they'll carry on like this for an entire month. I guess we should think of it as their Christmas. It's January in the heat. No bundling up.

Mother, I did find a Catholic church with an old French priest to hear my confession so please don't worry about my soul.

This hotel is wonderful. Isn't their stationery magnificent? The illustration hardly does the place justice. I have my own private room, welcome after living in tight quarters with my unit. It's a wonder I could stay here on such short notice. I guess that many of the locals have returned to France, and there aren't a lot of tourists. Your letters express too much concern. The Paris newspapers must exaggerate the danger. Do not worry, Mother. I have a wonderful platoon, and they won't let anything happen to me.

Oh, I almost forgot. Colonel de Castries stays here. I saw him earlier today. The concierge, a wonderfully friendly fellow, has pointed out other celebrities. Their names escape me at the moment, but you would know them. Aren't you envious?

This will be my last leave for some time. If I'm slow to write, don't worry. The mail takes a long time getting back to our unit's compound when we're in the field.

Your loving son,
Charles

Lieutenant Pasteur folded the letter and placed it on the dresser to post the next day. After returning to soak in a fresh tub of water, foam from the bath soap rising to his chin, he dressed in a pressed uniform and slipped his pistol into a belt under his shirt, which he inspected in the mirror to make sure it didn't bulge.

The lobby was crowded with ex-patriots, military officers, newly arrived officials of the French government, and bell boys kowtowing to orders snapped by clerks at the front desk. In the center of the lobby laughter floated from the ladies surrounding Colonel de Castries as he spoke to his aides. The ladies' perfumes invited the attention of the young staff officers waiting expectantly in groups of four and five along the walls. Their carnal eyes searched through the crowded lobby, as if they were back in France. Lieutenant Pasteur bolted past them towards the door, pushing aside a bellboy's polite approach, and a waitress with a plate of fresh pastries, the golden delicacies still hot from the oven of an invisible kitchen. Free of the lobby, Lieutenant Pasteur backed against the hotel wall under the outside portico at the entrance and paused to adjust to the dimmed and inadequate street lighting. A colonel whom Pasteur didn't recognize emerged hunched in a uniform sagged with sweat, his handlebar mustache drooped in the humidity. A civilian car pulled up to the door. The Vietnamese driver rushed to open the rear door for the colonel. The colonel hesitated, glanced into the crowd that followed him and was being kept back by guards with rifles held like fence rails. Lieutenant Pasteur realized the colonel was staring through them at him.

"You there, lieutenant," the colonel pointed at him.

"Me, sir?" Lieutenant Pasteur's own voice surprised him.

"You can drive, can't you?"

"Yes," Lieutenant Pasteur hesitated. "Sir."

"Let him through," the colonel spoke to the guard blocking the way between them.

"Sir?" Lieutenant Pasteur stood at attention in front of the colonel.

"You drive this thing," the colonel said.

"But, colonel."

The chauffeur stepped away, and Lieutenant Pasteur took his place behind the wheel.

"Can't be too careful," the colonel said.

"It is TET, colonel. There's a truce each year."

"And more and more the truce gets broken."

"I hadn't heard."

"We keep it quiet, son. You young soldiers need a break from the tensions of war." The colonel turned in his seat. "You know the way to the ... club?"

"No, sir."

"I'll tell you where to go." The colonel directed him through an intersection crowded with bikes, each carrying two or three Vietnamese, some entire families out to celebrate the TET. "Use the horn. They'll move. If you hit one, don't stop."

The colonel insisted the windows be kept rolled up, despite the heat. "It prevents breathing that filthy, diseased air stinking of nuoc mam. They drown their food in that rotted fish sauce as if it might preserve what isn't fit to eat. At times I think this entire nation is embalmed in nuoc mam. And windows up prevents a grenade being tossed inside the car, sending us both back to France, wrapped and packaged and stuffed in a ship's hold, not exactly a first-class cabin ending to our tour. The savages got it in for us."

Their car edged forward in a sea of handlebars. At the colonel's insistence, Pasteur pressed into the crowd, sounding the horn and flicking the high beams on and off. At the intersections, he drove straight across into oncoming traffic. The car headlights caught hostile eyes in backward glances from bikes weaving to get out of the way.

"Pull over here," the colonel ordered outside an old French building.

At the curb, the colonel quickly exited. "I'll send a guard over. Give him the keys. Then come in and have yourself some fun. I'll get someone else to drive me back to the hotel."

"Thank you, sir," Lieutenant Pasteur said. He expected to be left with the car most of the night, but a sergeant quickly appeared to relieve him.

The palatial home had been converted into a private men's club for those with enough money or rank to be invited to join. The doorman waved Lieutenant Pasteur through a mahogany door to a ballroom where businessmen drank with senior French officers and lounged beneath the crystal chandeliers, around tables that appeared set for tea. A newly constructed mahogany bar extended the entire length of the room. Enormous red silk curtains hung from ceiling to floor, covering the windows facing the street, beside them cut flowers in a porcelain vase. Congais from the provinces, Thai and Chinese girls, fatherless outcasts, some fathered by Western soldiers by their looks, and poor girls sent from France, whirled among the older men, flirting, giggling as if they were debutantes at a school prom. The men smoked cigars and drank port, boasting casually of long past travels and adventures. Around them the stale cigar smoke battled women's perfumes and a sea of alcohol.

The colonel nodded his slightly balding head and winked as Pasteur crossed to the bar. Lieutenant Pasteur stood behind a stool and reached across and placed money on the counter.

"You drinking in here?" The bartender paused from cleaning glasses, his one good eye aimlessly wandering, the other just an empty socket.

"Ask the colonel, you got doubts," Lieutenant Pasteur said.

"What do you want?"

Lieutenant Pasteur named it and waited. The bartender muttered something, but got him the drink, taking all the money.

"What do you mean, doing that?" Lieutenant Pasteur said.

"You want to drink in here, it costs you." The bartender pointed around the room. "You don't see them complaining."

She was almost bronze, and taller than the other girls. She dressed in Western clothes, her shortened skirt exposing flawless legs. As a boy in Paris Lieutenant Pasteur had seen a few girls like her, out of his reach back then and there. She watched him but remained at the furthest end of the bar. Though other men approached her, she turned them away.

Was she waiting for him? She walked up along the bar, hesitated beside him, and said something in Vietnamese to the bartender. Her earring fell near her bare feet. Lieutenant Pasteur bent to retrieve it, but she was quicker and held the silver earring pinched between two fingers as she stood, her blouse low, breasts partially exposed. His eyes diverted, and then he saw her eyes smiling at him. He felt the flush in his cheeks, and in the awkward moment returned to the bar stool.

"You're with the colonel?" she asked.

"No."

"You came in with him," she said.

"I drove him here, that's all."

"I see." She stretched to seat herself on an adjacent stool. "Do you want me to stay with you?"

"Yes, but not here."

"Everything here is very expensive."

"What's that mean?"

She said a price.

"I see what you mean," Lieutenant Pasteur said, "but I'm not saving for my retirement."

"Of course you're not. You're younger than the rest of them in here." She smiled at him. "You must pay the bartender."

"Those clothes...."

"You prefer something more conservative?"

"For where we're going."

"I'll change. You arrange it with the bartender." As the girl disappeared through a door at the end of the bar, Lieutenant Pasteur signaled the bartender.

"It will cost you more to leave the club," the bartender said.

"Then it costs me more." Lieutenant Pasteur's voice had an edge to it. He hadn't wanted to be that way.

"You must pay in advance." The bartender repeated the sum. Lieutenant Pasteur pulled it from his pocket. The girl returned and waited beside him while he paid. She followed him into the street, distantly at first, not a word between them. She was wearing a beautiful long Western skirt.

It made it easier for him. The issue of the money was past him now.

The streets were deserted in accordance with the curfew, which Lieutenant Pasteur's rank allowed him to ignore. Although there were lanterns along the sidewalks, they didn't work in the wind that came up. The streets still glistened from a passing shower. In the dark only lingering smells betrayed the nature of the neighborhoods as they walked along the blocks. Most of the buildings glowed gently with light from within. The sounds of their soft murmuring voices barely reached the street.

"Where are we going?" the girl asked.

"The Metropolitan Hotel."

"That's a very nice place, but it's very expensive. They'll make it difficult if I'm with you. I know a better place."

"No. The Metropolitan Hotel. I'm staying there." He wouldn't let her discuss it further.

The soldier at the front door saluted them. Lieutenant Pasteur returned the salute. The old man who ran the elevator from on a stool asked the floor. He never looked directly up at them.

Inside the room Lieutenant Pasteur reached to turn on a small table lamp, but she prevented him, touching his hand. He sat on the bed. She stepped to the window, stood a moment to watch the street below, then pulled the curtains closed, leaving them both outlined in a dim yellow glow. She reached to her back and pulled the blouse over her head, let her skirt drop to the floor, and slipped off her remaining clothes. He admired her standing there motionless and golden in the subdued light. She crossed the room to him and loosened his clothing, touching his flesh. He shifted on the bed as she urged him, so that his clothes came off easily in her hands.

"What's your name?" he said.

"Dawn," she said, then put a finger up to his lips. Her breasts pressed against his chest, her stomach against his. He rolled her within his arms, holding her, tightly, desperately. She moved with him, and he felt her rushing through him.

When he could think again, he wondered if all there was to him was a series of senses, nothing to be mistaken for a soul. That would explain that moment when powerful desires allowed him to escape the agonies plaguing him in the field, that crush of painful emotions that unbalanced him, causing him to loose control. His good sense had left him. She was a security risk, an unknown, and yet he wanted to linger with her, the two of them alone, separated from the rest.

Later he heard a couple arguing in the street below them. He kept them out of his thoughts by watching the girl as she slept beside him, her breathing calm and even.

In the morning the sun struck Lieutenant Pasteur's face through a crack between the curtains and the window casing. A fan blew a gentle breeze across the bed. Dawn had drawn a sheet over them in the night. He slipped from under the sheet, pulled on his fatigue pants, and tightened the military belt around his waist. He opened the curtains.

Litter blew down the street. An occasional trishaw passed, splashing the night's rain onto the sidewalk. Homeless people slept in the doorways across the street. The room smelled of dampness and age. He opened the window to allow fresh morning air.

Dawn rolled over in the bed and pulled the sheet tight over her without waking. He watched her nestled in her own sable hair. That much he'd take with him forever.

He watched Dawn wake by degrees. She turned over so that her face was in the pillow, protected from the light. Later she turned over again and opened her eyes. She sat up and smiled at him.

"Was I the first?" she said.

"No."

"You are cute when you lie."

She climbed out of the bed and picked her clothes off the floor and went off to the bathroom. He savored the fleeting golden image. He listened to the water running in the tub and the splashing.

When she came back, she was dressed, hair wet and tied back. As a child, he had seen his mother that way. They walked together down the stairs and into the lobby. The clerk at the desk nodded a good morning. When they were seated at breakfast, they watched each other like children, not speaking but making silly faces. Their laughter carried through the dining room. The waiters averted their eyes. French wives seated together at a table in the corner turned from their food to glare across the room. Dawn smiled in their direction.

"Nothing ever bother you?" Lieutenant Pasteur asked.

"Not when I'm with you."

On the street they walked side by side trying to be serious and not touch each other. Across the street chauffeured cars were arriving at a French administrative building with a portico entrance that reminded Lieutenant Pasteur of an enormous Kremlin hat. Chauffeurs opened doors and tipped their caps to Frenchmen in suits. They walked past and turned in the direction of Hoan Kien Lake and its central park. In the early morning light a fog lifted off the water, the Turtle Pagoda appearing in the mist like a haunted castle half way to the further shore. A pile of paper canisters littered the park. Lieutenant Pasteur reached to examine one of them.

"From the fireworks last night," Dawn said. "We can watch them tonight."

"I see enough of that kind of thing," Lieutenant Pasteur said.

"I should have thought of that," she said. "Then the water puppet show?"

He nodded. They rested on the grass and watched the early morning reflections on the lake. Silhouettes began to march past them, backs to a morning sun, and the two speculated on where they meant to go. Some were easier than others, their clothes or possessions telling all there was to know about them. Others shrouded their purposes with ordinary appearance and empty arms. After an hour at the game, he asked her to talk about herself.

"There's nothing to tell," she said.

"Everyone has a story, he said. "And every life has its importance."

"Not in Viet Nam," she said.

He reached and held her hand as they watched each other in silence. Then without her asking, he told her about France, the cities with their museums and sidewalk cafes and how every apartment and home had its own kitchen and bathrooms inside the buildings, that women had closets as large as rooms that they filled with clothes and shoes. Walking down the streets of Paris was a fashion show, which everyone watched from sidewalk cafes sipping wine and eating pastries. He said she was as beautiful as any of the models he had seen on the Parisian streets. He wanted her to see it all once the war was over, and she blushed and said she had always wanted that.

She told him of Leah and the dreams they had shared, that Leah was to be married and go to France, but then she was murdered. The Surete suspected that it was her betrothed, a French soldier named Mueller, but she never believed it, although she understood he had deserted afterward. A guilty man might do that, but a man with a broken heart might do the same thing.

That was when he leaned over and kissed her. They held hands and circled the lake. She pointed out the theater for the puppet show. They walked across a wooden bridge to where a tower stood on an island in the lake. When they returned to the shore, he asked her to take him to a French café that he had heard was like those in Paris.

The café was still closed and the chairs stacked next to the front door.

"This is like Paris," he said, laughing as he spoke. "Where nothing is open in the morning, but the restaurants stay open late at night. Only here there is a curfew."

Lieutenant Pasteur pulled down chairs and placed them next to a table. He wiped the seats with his handkerchief. "We should sit down."

A French waiter from inside unlocked the iron doors. "I'm sorry sir, we're not open yet."

"We'd like some tea," Lieutenant Pasteur said.

The waiter turned to Dawn, "Mademoiselle, we are

closed." The waiter retreated back into the café.

"He thinks we are married, and you will make me understand," said Lieutenant Pasteur. "If we were married perhaps you would."

"You shouldn't joke with me that way," Dawn said, her face with a blush over it.

Later the waiter returned with two silver pots of tea and cups of fine French china and dainty napkins. He had dressed in a dinner jacket with a vest and a white towel over his arm. He was very polite, and they spoke to him of how it was back in France. He thought that he would go back there on holiday. In Paris he had been very poor and lived in a basement in a rundown neighborhood.

"Now I have servants and a Vietnamese wife to look out for me. We'll have children some day. I don't think I could ever leave," the waiter said. "How is the war going? I don't know what will happen to me if the Viet Minh drive the French army from the country."

Lieutenant Pasteur said, "I only know what I see. My platoon survives but it's becoming difficult."

The waiter wished them both well together and refused to let Lieutenant Pasteur pay for the tea.

The streets had become crowded by the time they left the café. As they walked beggar kids hung behind at their heels.

"Do you ever want kids?" Dawn asked

"Yes," he said, "I think it's a good thing, but often entered into too soon and much too casually by couples eager to please the church.

"I agree. I can see you would be a good father. Most men here only want children to carry on their name. Children should be respected in their own right and not just seen as an extension of their parents, to care for them and their ancestors. In Viet Nam it's worse for girls. Someday maybe it will change."

They laughed at their new seriousness until they reached the hotel.

THE
UNREQUITED

CHAPTER 47

Quang Khe, March 1, 1948
Phan
Visitors

F ar across the fields, two men emerged from the jungle, rifles slung over their shoulders. If they were seasoned troops, as Phan suspected, they wouldn't be alone. They started across the clearing, keeping five meters between themselves. Little doubt they were point men for at least a platoon waiting in the woods. Mid-field they dropped the rifles off their shoulders and aimed at him. Phan raised his hands and waved so they could see that he was not armed. Neither man acknowledged him. He squinted. They wore the latania leaf hats of the Viet Minh, faces grim and covered with sweat, uniforms soaked, bearing the newest Chinese rifles with web gear taped for silence, and a belt of grenadesover their frayed uniforms.

"Welcome to Quang Khe," Phan said, acting calmer than he felt.

"Where are the other villagers?" The first soldier shouted back at him. "Why aren't they in the fields?"

The other soldier waited several meters distant, his rifle pointed at Phan's chest.

"There are only three of us here. My wife and child are at home."

A look of confusion crossed the soldier's face, and then he sternly said, "Didn't you say this is the village of Quang Khe?"

"It is, but almost a year ago French soldiers murdered everyone. We came to visit relatives and found it as you'll see it."

"Where are you from? You don't sound like a farmer to me." The first soldier eyed Phan suspiciously.

"Ha Noi."

"Did you work with the French?"

"I was raised by French priests. But my wife has lived here all her life."

"Are the French coming back here?"

"Not likely," Phan said.

"You look Chinese to me."

"I grew up in Ha Noi." Phan didn't like the way the soldier rubbed the trigger of the rifle. He suspected these men were political cadre trained to indoctrinate peasants and to eliminate those they couldn't change, determining the difference quickly and efficiently.

"You're a city kid."

"I've been out here farming a year."

As Phan suspected, a platoon of soldiers emerged from the distant woods. Most had older rifles except for several with RPGs, which they carried on their shoulders. They crossed the open rice field, trampling tender sprouts, leaving trails behind them. Among those hardened, resigned faces, two stood out with feudal scars across their cheeks. All were tired and ready to rest, their stooped backs loaded down with packs. Phan led them to the village. Once across the field, the soldiers spread out across the village, kicking at the ashes, walking through the skeletons of doorways, probing into the darkness of the jungle that isolated the village. They searched the solitary hut and brought Thi and the child to Phan's side.

"Where are the other villagers?' the soldier demanded once again, his rifle off his shoulder.

"I told you, there are no others. Just the three of us," Phan said.

"You are hiding others."

"He's telling the truth. They wouldn't burn their own village." The soldier now speaking wore the pistol of an officer.

"What should I do with him?" The point man addressed the officer with respect.

"When it's time, we'll question them all. For now you help secure the perimeter."

The platoon cut bamboo at the edge of the clearing and built shelters with palm leaf roofs. They hung their hammocks. Working at one of the mounds of ash, an old soldier with brown-stained teeth, built a cooking fire for the platoon. There he hung an iron pot filled with edible leaves from the jungle with rice from the bags Phan had saved. He killed the chickens and added them.

The officer who directed the platoon wore wire-rimmed glasses. Phan imagined him as a teacher once, the type who dispatched swift discipline to his students. Now with that same self-assurance, he directed the construction of a military compound, ordering sharpened stakes and barriers placed around the clearing and a trench dug where the trail entered the village, a machine gun positioned behind it.

At twilight the officer called Phan and his family over and questioned them about their past and about the village. Phan held nothing back. At the first opportunity he mentioned his friendship with Hahn and said that he believed Hahn was a party member. At first this had no noticeable effect, but after the formal questioning, the young officer was almost apologetic. "You will be compensated for the chickens and rice we ate. Tomorrow we will discuss division of the land. There are many landless workers in the surrounding villages. Nevertheless even landlords are allowed to retain up to three mau for their family use."

"We are not landlords," Phan quickly interjected.

"That's clear enough, but what about your father-in-law?"

"He's deceased," Phan said.

"There's the question of your being Chinese," the officer paused, "and Catholic."

"I renounced the Catholicism," Phan said. "I can't change being Chinese so easily."

"True enough." The young officer did not smile.

The cooking fire died into embers twinkling like fireflies. A log was tossed on the fire to last the night. The soldiers huddled just beyond the light. Their voices murmured strange confessions of failure: a comrade left on the battlefield; a bourgeois thought; weakness in resisting the oppression of the colonialists; temptations from the luxury and idleness of the cities. The soldiers spoke using terms like dialectic and materialism, reeducation in the teachings of Marx and Lenin, land reform, and the necessary alliance of city proletariat and country peasants.

There was no discussion of individual liberty or free enterprise, or the sanctity of the family and their ancestors or mention of Voltaire, Locke, or Jefferson.

A solemn and deep voice rose above the rest, the tone throbbing like a primitive drum beat from an ancient age. The speaker was the old soldier, and in the flickering light of the fire his face reflected the history of his nation. The younger soldiers fell into a respectful silence and listened as he spoke. He began by reminding them that there was never a time when Viet Nam wasn't struggling to free itself from tyranny. He recalled great men and their legends as if they sat around this very fire. "Near here in Giong village they celebrate a mute child of only three, who answered the call of his emperor to fight invaders. The child ate and ate to gain strength quickly and grew into a giant who rode an iron horse and vanquished the enemy with a golden sword before finally disappearing in the clouds."

"Was that recently?" a young soldier teased. He drew a nervous laugh from the others.

"Go ahead, laugh," the old soldier said. The way he sat, his legs crossed, his hands folded, he might have been an ancient monk, if he didn't cradle a carbine. He spoke as if he looked directly into the past and understood how it connected with those who now listened. The young soldier pushed a log in the fire as he might poke a snake. It sparked and broke into flame, letting Phan see the terrible expression dancing over the old man's face. The old soldier resumed: "If you want to hear about these times, I will tell you. Several years ago Vo Nguyen Giap met with Ho Chi Minh and thirty others around a fire much like this in a mountain cave near the Chinese border. They started what has become our army of Viet Minh. At the time, General Giap had read Marx and Napoleon's writings on waging war. It was enough that he was selected to command the army. His determination to destroy the French had already been sealed by the killing of his wife. She had delayed fleeing her hometown because of their young son. The French Surete detained her at Hoa Lo prison. They hung her by the thumbs and let the weight of her broken ribs suffocate her. I remember when they brought him the word."

"You were there?" a soldier ventured.

"I was there," the old soldier answered without changing his tone.

"And were you there before that?"

"Yes, before that too."

"What was it like?"

"We were scared and in hiding. The French guillotined many."

The young soldier turned his back and pretended to be cleaning his rifle. The old soldier continued to speak.

"We were hunted as criminals. We who were born here! What would they say if we called them criminals for wanting to free their native France from the Germans? They would laugh at us no doubt, just as we scorn them." The old soldier seemed lost in his memories. "The National Party led us then, but they lacked leadership and proper training, and so they acted before we were ready. We only had scimitars, and a few of us had home-made bombs. It was the end for the National Party. Most of the leaders were caught. The bravest made their little patriotic speeches, but the guillotine didn't hear them. After that others tried to explain away what they

did with excuses and lies to save themselves. They didn't understand the niceties of French law in which an accomplice is
as guilty as those who actually killed a precious Frenchman.
There were more trials, more guillotines, and there was begging and pleading to live, a pathetic thing to watch. Those
men shamed the generations who had died trying to gain
Vietnamese freedom. Better a heritage washed with the blood
from the guillotine. It was so disgusting that I along with
many others who survived left the National Party and joined
the Viet Minh."

The fire of glowing embers popped and crackled. A log
fell, sending up a plume of smoke. A soldier coughed, cleared
his throat, and spit into the hottest coals, then lay back among
the others. Soldiers nestled together like children napping in
a school yard, their expressions caught in unguarded innocence. The old soldier lay on his side and slept against his
pack.

Only the officer remained awake. He wrote dispatches, then heated a seal on a stone next to the fire and pressed
the wax where each paper folded together. He placed the papers in a small French military pouch with a red star painted
over its original flower insignia, then taking it by the strap,
the officer woke a young soldier from among the men. The
boy slipped off his uniform and sandals and stood erect, his
body a thin brown overlay of skin covering lattice ribs, his
face aboriginal, from one of the tribes in the mountains, his
hair flung wild as if caught in an unseen ceaseless wind, his
eyes aflame with demonic pride.

The young soldier jogged across the clearing wearing
only the military pouch slung over his shoulder. In a moment
he had disappeared into the darkness. The officer returned to
his position next to the fire and curled himself in an opened
blanket roll.

—✗—

At the first light, Phan watched without moving from
his bedroll, not a prisoner, but not free to go, so said the of-

ficer when he had allowed Phan's wife and child to return to their hut. The first to rise among the soldiers prodded the fire with a stick until a single ember glowed. On this he threw the stubs from burned logs that bracketed the fire. Other soldiers gathered new wood.

The cook threw rice into a stew of the previous night's leftovers. The sentries on the perimeter were rotated to receive their portion of the stew. More rice was brought and added to the stew. Two weeks, three weeks at most before the soldiers would consume what would have been enough for Phan and his family until the next crop was harvested.

The aboriginal messenger returned with the saddlebag pouch over his shoulder slapping against his chest. He broke stride when he reached the officer, seated with his back against a tree, his legs peculiarly crossed as if double jointed. The officer opened the pouch, ignoring the boy gasping to recover his breath. A soldier threw the boy a canteen.

The officer sorted the letters. He broke the seals with a knife. He held each letter in sequence, his lips silently mouthing every word.

"Come here," the officer spoke to Phan. Stiff legged with night cramps, Phan limped to the officer.

"Appears they know you," the officer said. "You're to return to Ha Noi, same place as before. Someone will contact you there."

"When am I to leave?"

"Now, and don't come back here." The officer handed the letter to Phan. "Take your family with you."

CHAPTER 48

Ha Noi, March 4, 1948
Dawn
A visit

For two weeks Dawn didn't return to the club. Then she stayed in her room for two weeks, her meals brought to her, before Henri Dalat came to her door. She said she was in bed and unpresentable, but he used his key to enter the room.

"Your regular clients are asking for you," he said. "I couldn't continue to tell them you're not feeling well. They thought me a louse and insisted I call Doctor Astray. He only treats the French, so he's doing me a favor. Will he find something wrong?"

"You must not let him see me." She rose straight up in bed, with one hand holding her silk pajama top tight around her neck, her face turned to conceal recent tears.

"Ahh, a matter of the heart," Dalat laughed, then stopped. "You do look sick, child. Is it the young lieutenant?"

"I think so," she said.

"He hasn't come around?"

"He's gone back to his unit."

"They're not so far from here. You go see him."

"That's permitted?" she said.

"Of course, my dear."

Dawn sunk back into a bed of pillows. Later, Henri Dalat drove Dawn to a bus stop, took her through the checkpoint and paid the fare. Nothing was said between them, except his final "good luck." Aboard the bus, she felt out of place in her Western dress. Never mind, she told herself. My looks betray me no matter what I wear. She squeezed into the only remaining seat between two women. The women didn't speak to her. She looked out the windows to the passing countryside.

—⚬—

The bus halted abruptly, throwing Dawn against the seat in front. Two French soldiers appeared at the front of the bus, waved their pistols, and ordered everyone off. One soldier remained at the front, cursing and shoving them along. He struck several with the butt of his pistol. Dawn prepared herself, but when she reached the soldier, he smiled and winked.

In the street the crowd from the bus was ignored by the other soldier, who talked on a radio. Dawn could see the head of a soldier on the bus bobbing up and down the aisle, inspecting under every seat, and at times reaching up into the overhead. When he finished, he joined his companion at their jeep, his eyes roaming over the crowd. Dawn avoided his glance until he walked over to her.

"May I see your papers?" he asked.

"Yes, certainly," she answered in French, trying to keep her voice steady. She reached into her purse and handed the soldier a letter of safe conduct signed by a colonel of artillery, and forged by Henri Dalat. He held it up and inspected it.

"You will come with us," he said taking her firmly by the arm and leading her back to the jeep. The two soldiers argued a moment over what should happen to her. They ordered her into the back of the jeep with the soldier who had winked.

"You have seen my papers," Dawn pleaded.

"Everyone has forged papers out here."

The jeep left a trail of dust behind them on the road.

"We are searching for French deserters using Vietnamese transportation and also for military contraband," the soldier next to her said.

"You can't think I am a deserter. Certainly I'm not contraband," she said, trying to get the soldier to laugh.

"What is your purpose out here?" The soldier asked, pressing against her.

"I am going to see my fiancé," she said.

"And who is that?"

"Lieutenant Pasteur at ..." She said his name and the camp with great confidence. "He is a platoon leader with the 9th Infantry."

The soldier hesitated. "Who is his commander?"

She said his name and rank.

"His first sergeant's name?"

Again she answered his question.

"Does he know you're coming?" the soldier asked her.

"Yes, he's expecting me," she lied. The soldier slid away from her on the seat.

"You are very fortunate. We are from his unit. You must tell him how we helped you to find him." He said it as an order. She replied a simple yes.

The jeep continued its careless rush as if it could fly over mines. The driver leaned on the horn to warn those ahead.

A water buffalo accosted them in the middle of road, its tiny young master standing in a ditch. The driver stepped from the jeep. The water buffalo wrinkled its nose, raised its head, and turned from side to side as if near sighted, standing its ground despite waving arms and shouts from the soldier. The water buffalo charged. The soldier fired his pistol into its snout, but the buffalo's advance continued. Another shot between the eyes. The water buffalo stood in place, legs locked, bracing itself. A third shot brought it to the ground. The young boy glared at the soldiers as they drove around the dead animal.

"That was probably the only water buffalo his family owned," Dawn said weakly from the back seat.

"The boy should have kept the beast out of the road."

Other than roadside monuments numbering the kilometers, the landscape was indistinguishable, a monotony of fields overgrown with weeds. The road beneath turned into a blur, the jeep dodging the deepest pot holes, hitting others, down the road like a skipping stone, careening off each contact with the ground. Dawn gripped the seat in front, airborne and thrown from side to side.

"Last few kilometers are the worst. It's where the bastards mine the most," the soldier beside her shouted over the rush of air, his exuberance unrestrained. The base camp of the 9th Infantry appeared as a monochromic gash on the earth from which it had been built.

The two sergeants continued to display an inexplicable enthusiasm. They entered the compound on the fly, received a hail of recognition from a sentry, and clamored from the jeep. Dawn followed behind them, trying to smooth her clothes.

Artillery barrels protruded over circular enclosures of sandbags piled to the height of the shirtless men who readied the guns. The smells of gun oils, sweat, and powder blanketed the area. Dawn heard a single voice giving commands. Working like men possessed, the artillerymen responded without a single demur. Then as if they meant to shun the instrument they caressed, they stepped away with cupped hands over their ears, all save one who shouted, "Fire in the hole" and yanked at a lanyard. An artillery piece barked, spewing flame from its barrel. Each gun around the compound fired in sequence until all rested silent in a shroud of smoke.

The soldiers led her through a series of concrete mounds to an entrance into a bunker. An officer emerged, his face camouflaged in shadings of blacks and browns, his uniform of tiger stripes wrapped with a webbing of grenades and belts of ammunition. A bush hat identically patterned with his fatigues concealed his eyes beneath the brim.

"Dawn," he said, "what are you doing here?"

She blushed, for it was her lieutenant.

"What are you doing here?" he repeated without warmth in his voice.

"To see you," she whispered. "What has happened to you?"

"I lead an ambush patrol tonight."

"Are you mad at me for coming here?" She began to cry.

"Of course not," he replied and reached out to wipe a tear away but then held himself in check. "It's just that it comes as a surprise."

He lifted her tiny suitcase and started down inside the bunker. An underground sump hole from which no air escaped, the bunker stunk of sweat and tobacco and wines and cooked meats. The lieutenant spoke to shadowy spirits shifting restlessly on their bunks, "This is Dawn. She'll stay in my bunk tonight."

There was no response. He threw her suitcase on an empty bunk, which she assumed was where he slept. The artillery above them shook the earth, a faint rumbling where they stood.

"Why are they firing?" Dawn asked.

"It is called harassment and interdiction."

"What is that?"

"They have no particular target, only chance."

They climbed the narrow stairs to the surface as the artillery ceased firing the second volley. The lieutenant's platoon was waiting just outside the entrance. Camouflaged as remarkably as the lieutenant, African and white were indistinguishable in their ghoulish appearances. They circled around a map thrown down in their midst. Some wore necklaces of ears, others strange talismans and crosses that Dawn imagined used in religious rites. They hunched under the weight of packs lashed with socks and shirts hung to dry. Patches of skulls and cross bones decorated their sleeves.

"My sergeant does the briefing. The others can't read a map." He laughed in a manner seeming only for himself. "Stay in the bunker. The sergeant will see you're fed. We'll return in the morning. Then I'll have time to spend with you."

The lieutenant fell in among the soldiers as they peeled off from their circle. They silently headed toward the gate. The sergeant who remained behind acknowledged Dawn with a touch to the brim of his kepi.

Later Dawn opened the lieutenant's footlocker. If the lieutenant had someone else, she found no sign of it among his things. She slept on his bed among the remaining officers. She listened to them snoring and tossing in their sleep. She wondered if the lieutenant thought of her on ambush patrol.

She woke in an empty bunker. A bugle outside completed reveille. She listened to military orders being shouted and the scuffle of feet marching together in formation across the compound. When the lieutenant's patrol returned, she remained in the bed. Later the lieutenant appeared at the foot of the bunk, his face cleaned of the camouflage creams.

"We can be alone now," he said. She heard him climb the stairs and slip a paddle lock into its clasp. When he returned, they embraced, and she felt his warmth and was reassured.

They lived as man and wife for a week, sometimes strolling the compound but more often remaining alone together in the bunker. Nights she waited for him, trying to picture the life he promised her back in France. Each day that life felt more real as he talked about his country, his family, and his childhood.

One day she told him she had never lived outside the city. What it was like fighting in the jungle?

"Most of the time we are fighting to cut through the underbrush, taking turns and trading off using the machete," he said. "Fatigues are quickly soaked with sweat. Insects attack: red ants from the trees, leeches in the water, and always the mosquitoes. When we run short of water we fill the canteens from any ditch, accepting the taste of rotting vegetation to quench our thirst. We drink diseases so there are high casualties from fevers, dysentery, and malaria. Boredom and fatigue soon make us careless. Someone steps on a mine or falls into a punji pit. At night we sleep in hammocks, hanging and swinging alone with our personal nightmares, often burning with fever. The next day we stumble into an ambush, thinking it's a dream until the feel of blood fills our boots, draining our thoughts. For many, death is welcomed. After a while those who survive go through the motions of living, waiting their turn."

He ended in a monotone. Then he told her there were dignitaries coming to inspect the compound, and he'd have to send her back to Ha Noi. He promised to see her on his next leave. He drove her to a village where she caught a bus.

CHAPTER 49

Ha Noi, March 13, 1954
Father Custeau
An old friend

Each time Father Custeau coughed into his handkerchief the blood increased. There had been earlier signs that he failed to acknowledge: fewer visits to his parishioners; excuses for refusing invitations; diminished energy. He understood what the cough meant. He had observed the inevitable end many times before, received the call for last rites, often too late to bless the living soul. At times the parishioners he visited had suffered beyond his expectations, their agony lasting for years; at other times their end was swift and terrible. There had to be a Maker to explain it, and Father Custeau accepted that God's will be done.

Now that he was bed-ridden, the other priests insisted they call Doctor Astray. Father Custeau had avoided his old friend for weeks, knowing what the doctor would find in his examination. He had used the doctor's persistent blasphemies against God as his excuse. The doctor had always claimed man was just a complicated machine that doctors would one day turn on and off to replace its broken parts. Machine indeed. That didn't explain the soul and spirit of man. A series of electrical signals? Nonsense. He smiled as he remembered the hours of debate.

Now he heard pounding at the door, tenacious in the way it reverberated in the hall. Then scuffling of bare feet, sliding locks, distant voices. "What is it you want?"

"Father Custeau," the familiar voice demanded.

"He is indisposed."

Through the entryway and down the Spartan corridors, determined feet. Father Custeau lacked the strength to intercede. He settled back onto his pillow and waited.

The doctor burst into the room.

"Doctor Astray. I thought you'd gone back to France," Father Custeau said. Better a little lie, so easily forgiven, than to hurt the doctor's feelings.

"That's why you didn't send for me?" Doctor Astray's intensity diminished. "You didn't get my note?"

"I've been laid up. Perhaps my staff misplaced it."

"Let's look at you." Doctor Astray dropped his bag and sitting on the bed, rested his hand across Father Custeau's forehead. Spotting the handkerchief Father Custeau had tried to hide in his clenched fist, Doctor Astray pressed against the priest's thumb until his hand involuntarily opened. He examined the fresh blood that saturated the white linen and took Father Custeau's pulse.

"Don't tell me what I already know," Father Custeau said.

"Like the old days," Doctor Astray said. "This is the real reason you didn't send for me."

"And what would you have done?"

"Still placing all your faith in God?"

"That's my currency."

"Preaching to heathens always did sustain you."

"I like to think I've helped the Vietnamese."

"They really only want our medicines."

"The church gives them hope." Father Custeau fought the impulse to cough, not wanting the doctor to have the satisfaction of watching him vomit more blood into his handkerchief. "But enough of this. What secrets have you overheard in that old hotel of gossips?"

"Are the secrets of the confessional not enough?" Doctor Astray smiled. "Well, then perhaps the genius of the generals will prove more to your liking. I overheard them at the bar. General Navarre has ordered the continued defense of Dien Bien Phu. Thinks he'll draw the Viet Minh into a fight. He says it protects Laos and deprives the enemy of rice."

"You don't think his plan will work?" Father Custeau tried not to show interest for the doctor didn't seem to understand the significance of what he said.

"Oh, it will work." Doctor Astray's face had taken on a look of disgust as he listened to the priest's chest. "All these plans work to give our eager young surgeons plenty of practice."

"Will you go to Dien Bien Phu?"

"I'll leave that place to the military doctors. I've see enough wounded soldiers in my day. They'll make use of the civilian hospitals quick enough if things don't go well."

"And what would you have us do about the Vietnamese?" Father Custeau thought a change in subject best now he knew the doctor would remain safely away from Dien Bien Phu.

"Why not leave them alone and let our young men go back to France and grow old telling stories of exotic adventures."

"And the communist problem?"

"Let the Vietnamese make their own mistakes."

"Do they have a choice with the communists?"

"Perhaps not."

The response annoyed Father Custeau, the doctor conceding so quickly, treating him like an invalid, as if the debate would weaken him. "Of course I'm right, doctor. You worry about men's bodies. Their souls are mine."

"Agreed." Doctor Astray laughed robustly. He turned to Charlemagne as he drew an envelope of pills from his old medical bag. "Three times a day. Stick them in his food so he won't argue with you."

When Doctor Astray left, Father Custeau waved Charlemagne to his bedside. "Throw those pills away. And bring me a map. Find out the number of troops going to Dien Bien Phu. Their units. How many are native troops. How many Catholic. How we can reach them. If they stay there, they'll need a priest."

"Which of the priests will you send?"

"If it's what I think, I have only one in mind." Father Custeau smiled at the anxiety in Charlemagne's face. "And yes, you may accompany me."

CHAPTER 50

Ha Noi, March 13, 1954
Doctor Astray
Preparations

"Metropole Hotel," Astray said, settling into the trishaw. The driver bowed his head and began to peddle without rising off his seat. A bike chassis to the rear replaced the handles once in front to pull rickshaws. The limits of modernization, Astray chuckled to himself. How did they peddle the trishaws by themselves? Someday I must dissect one of these small, marvelously strong creatures.

Astray seized the coolie's fan folded on the seat next to him, a filthy piece of bamboo reeds primitively tied. As they peddled the empty streets, he fanned until his arm tired. Only mad dogs and Englishmen came out in the heat, and in Viet Nam you could add Frenchmen. The buildings so like his dear France, were so orderly and planned but foolishly built on filled swamps and lakes. The buildings were a triumph for the empire rivaling the finest in Paris but surrounded by disease.

Why hadn't he remained in France? There was no kidding himself; it was a matter of being practical. After the war, when the old patrons of society returned to Paris they brought the collective memory of his past, his decades' of indiscretion as a medical parvenu from the University of _____, a third rate school at best. According to their gossip, he inveigled his way into the highest society, only to be exposed by Lady _____, her daughter allegedly his victim. The truth didn't matter when it came to a one-time village boy, who was easily seduced in his middle age, then pledged to perform an abortion at the young girl's insistence. He was willing to do the honorable thing and marry, but she viewed it as a fling, and not the only time, judging by her medical condition. Such were the ways of fine French society. On a foolish whim he had once returned to France, but among the elite, memories never faded. He had come back to Viet Nam and re-established his practice. Fortunately they never received the Parisian gossip about him or chose not to hear it and a shortage of Western doctors combined with the casualties of the guerilla fighting, ensured enough work.

At the time he thought great medical challenges were still ahead of him: diseases not known in Europe; fungus and viruses from the jungles; undiscovered strains of coli bacteria; dysentery, cholera, tuberculosis and malaria, of course; together with fevers, chills, strange malignancies; infections, even from the smallest scratches, not to mention those caused by booby traps and mines. Also he would see the steady flow of surgical amputations of fingers, hands, arms, feet, and legs. Surgical saw and forceps became his surgeon's tools, little changed since the Middle Ages.

He was presented with a medical cornucopia not seen by most doctors in a lifetime. He tried thinking practically, how to make this bounty lucrative, to relieve his constant and nagging feeling of poverty. Middle....no, old aged, and without a bank account or an inheritance for the time when he could no longer make house calls.

Now he obsessed over the war's effect on his patient base. Fomenters, secreting themselves among the French population, already reduced the number of colonials with their stories of horror. The prosperous clientele vanished before the doctor's eyes. Those fleeing the countryside often stayed at the hotel for a day or two before their departure, great attractions to the parlor gossips who bled them of rumors and tales as efficiently as early Christian doctors bled their patients of real blood. Doctor Astray, the only real doctor, watched with consternation, as French families rushed to depart, abandoning plantations they'd maintained for decades, even in the face of Japanese occupation. Invasive and malignant fear left no doubt that the Viet Minh covered the countryside like maggots in an open wound.

As the trishaw passed along the streets, the doctor watched the crowd for any sign of the growing impertinence. He searched for landmarks as reassurance that the coolie who peddled the trishaw lacked a devious purpose. He remembered the old man had failed to smile when he'd been selected outside the church compound. He peered through the crack between canopy and seat back but could only see the coolie's legs pumping vigorously. Those calves. Yes, a dissection was called for, first opportunity.

An abrupt stop threw him forward in the seat. At the hotel Doctor Astray glanced back into the eyes of the trishaw driver, who waited for his passenger to disembark. Yes, inscrutable, the doctor thought. Who was it first wrote those words to describe the Asians? This very driver might be planning a bombing for the coming night. Astray tipped the man generously, acknowledging his repeated bows. The hotel loomed over him like some great, white-walled fortress, its vastness broken by row after row of windows, their black shutters sealed to repel the afternoon sun. A last bastion of French civilization, the hotel was where westerners sought sanctuary with their peers.

Three doormen greeted the doctor. One held the door while the other two stood at attention in their little red uniforms with brimless caps. He swept past them without a smile to acknowledge them. Ridiculous how they fawn over us, he thought. What arrogance we French still display to hire three when one would do, so little value do we see in them. And to dress them in those foolish uniforms, making them look like

the organ grinder's monkeys seen on the street corners back
in Paris.

He hesitated in the lobby, glancing toward the bar,
ready to greet any acquaintance, accept any invitation to linger for a drink. He discretely inspected the women, a European or two, the plain wives of high officials and of little interest
to him. Much more interesting were the congais of the officers
and the Eurasian girls, serene and demure products of decades
of lust. Several were dressed in aoi dais that flowed to the
floor. The rest wore the latest Paris fashion. These were truly
beauties, the finest of Ha Noi, women completely dependent
on their comeliness and charm to keep them off the streets and
out of the common brothels that satisfied the enlisted men.
There were too few women in a city where men already out-
numbered women three to one, where the war added a new
desperation to a man's natural sex drives. Someday he would
get around to writing an article for French medical journals:
the war zone soldiers' increased psychic drive to procreate.

Inside the bar there was always a multitude of the
colony's protectors. Early in the war the bar filled with the
ordinary officers of the French army, drinking white wine
with a drop of liqueur, but now more and more officers wore
Beret Rouge, the glorious mantle of the foreign legion. One of
the commanding officers, Christian Marie de Castries, was in
residence with his wife. They were often seen although quite
unapproachable.

The journalists were another matter. These writers
weren't ordinary drinkers. They were always buying Doctor
Astray chasers. They hoped that because he treated casualties
at the nearby hospital, he would be first to hear of the latest military encounters and confide in them long before the
formal briefings of the military staff. Often Graham Greene
stayed at the hotel and hung out in the bar but seemed more
interested in friendships with colonials and foreign legion officers than with a doctor of medicine. There had been a parade of French actors and actresses too, though Doctor Astray
couldn't remember a single name. Why should he? Imposters
all, without a single shred of themselves, their personalities

lifted entirely from their roles on stage or on a primitive movie screen. Living charades, really.

Doctor Astray's presence again went without notice. He started to climb the stairs. Rooming on the third floor had been a mistake for he was afraid of the lift, especially in the heat, when closing the elevator door cut off the air and any possibility of escape if something went wrong. The stairs meant pouring sweat. Still he had wanted to be away from the street noises. The view of the dome of the municipal theater was magnificent from his room in the back of the hotel. Although the room was expensive, in this time of trouble with all the European civilian doctors fleeing to France, his fees for private patients dramatically increased. Being able to take private patients was one of the terms of his return. In his later years he was becoming a practical man, thinking of the future, when one of the diseases he treated daily could shackle him with its debilitating effects. Such was the real fate of most men in a war, not the glorious wounds they preferred to imagine.

On his side of the building the maid had already reopened the wooden shutters where in the early morning he could watch sunrise. As he entered the room, he turned the fan to its highest setting and watched it shudder and gain speed. He felt a sense of relief. He noted the mahogany floor had been polished by the maid, his few clothes neatly folded, his bed made and turned down for the night with fresh flowers set on the bureau. Only the scattered papers on his desk remained untouched. Careful not to slip on the glistening floor, Astray lifted his medical bag to the desk he called his office, dropped it in the center of the disorganization, and fell into the rattan chair.

Later, he pulled a ragged map from the middle drawer and spread it across his desk. Why had Father Custeau reacted to a passing remark about Dien Bien Phu? He searched over the map until he found the village nestled in the contour lines of mountains, astride a trail to Laos. Tiny Dien Bien Phu. He ran his finger back along the roads to gauge its distance from Ha Noi. The future jumped from the crumpled sheet.

What madness possessed the generals? Over two hundred kilometers from anything strategic. Impossible to properly re-supply or reinforce. They were contemptible in their arrogance. The pompous fools only looked to increase their fame. And the work from their stupidity will fall to me. He beat his fist against the desk.

After his rage subsided, he pulled a folded blanket from the bed and wrapped himself to his chin, turning slightly to one side in the chair. In that position he slept sitting up at the desk.

In the morning the sun struck his face through the shutters he'd never closed, slash marks across a grimaced expression as he tried to raise himself from the chair on his stiffened legs. He rocked forward and almost fell onto the map, catching himself as he banged against a drawer. The empty room surprised him, for in the night he had dreamed of himself with his young nurse. Five years with her at the hospital, her soldier languishing in terminal care, there for her and her alone. Yet nothing changed. The bright light had startled him. Now he teetered over the map, staring down through the wire-rimmed glasses he never removed. This time he studied the map without the anger. The terrain was inhospitable but that might work to the benefit of the French Army. A small airfield made re-supply by air possible. The Viet Minh would have to carry all their supplies overland, and that would limit their use of heavy weapons. He started feeling more generous towards the French generals. Give them their due. They too played at God. Now he knew to prepare the hospital for new casualties.

CHAPTER 51

Ha Noi, March 14, 1954
Thi
Rumors

It was as if they'd never left Ha Noi. Phan expected her to shop for food twice a day and care for their son. She was never free to read or to write or to think for herself. He took those things for granted for himself but never realized she too might value them. He expected her to wait on him just like before. Ranting in a diatribe against the French, he refused to discuss the political situation with her. He ignored her feelings and her claim on their mutual destiny. Not that he was cruel. She knew he thought of her as an ideal woman who wasn't supposed to express her thoughts or emotions and certainly never in the company of men. When she did express herself, she knew he felt her female irrationality overcame reason. What nonsense. She threw down the broom she was using to clear the last dust balls on the floor. Trang looked up from his wooden ship models then continued to play.

She lay on the mat next to her son and forced herself to breath deeply. She quickly fell asleep and dreamed she had remained with her father in their village. There he died, and she demanded his place among the elders. Together the women from her village joined with women from village after village to guide the country toward peace. French women did the same, demanding their sons be returned to them in France. In her dream the women accomplished what men had failed to do for centuries. All it had taken was a transfer of power to them. It had been that simple, for the forces of life had always belonged to women, emanating from their wombs. Women sustained the life force, but out of fear men had kept them from their right. Never before was a dream so clear and simple.

Afterward she tried to imagine what made her dream that way. Now afraid that the dream sprung from an evil force, she stopped thinking about it and listened to the men in the stairway gambling and quarreling.

At dinner she ladled a bowl of pho and watched Phan eat like a wild animal come upon a carcass. When he finished, he went to the mat and stretched out. She followed him.

"Why don't we ever really talk?" she said.

"About our son?" he said.

"About what we're going to do. About the fighting."

"Don't let it worry you. It's late. I need to get some sleep. I'll be getting up early. There's a lot going on." He rolled onto his side and drew a blanket up to cover himself.

In the dark next to him, Thi realized she could never change the way he thought. Though their son resembled his father, she planted her seeds of hope in him. He must become a man of greater understanding than his father.

She lay quietly, listening to men coming back, their voices loud with drink. Several wives started yelling at them. One of the men started cursing, saying his wife forced him to the streets for what he needed. Why were they wasting their breath on the likes of them? Men like that never listened.

When she woke, Phan was shaking her, telling her she'd overslept. She rose off the mat, not speaking to him, but watching to see their son's reaction. The child was playing with toys he'd made for himself and didn't seem to notice his parents. She lifted the iron kettle that contained the previous day's chicken, its fat a solid block of grease at the bottom. She carried it to the alleyway where a cooking fire still smoldered. She turned a rusted faucet and water spurted into the kettle, its brown hue hardly noticeable in the swirl of bones. She strained to lift the kettle directly onto the coals.

Soon the kettle boiled and the water spurted off the top, hissing in the fire. It was hypnotic like ocean tides, or sunsets, or her son's even breathing as he slept through the night. Several women approached with a basket full of rats they'd trapped during night. Once gutted and skewered, they held the rats over the fire away from the stray dogs that circled them. Stoop-shouldered hawkers shuffled through the alleyway, carrying fresh produce in dual baskets balanced like the scales of justice on poles.

The stew pot burned Thi's leg when she lifted it, but she managed to walk it to their cubicle. Her husband watched her as she filled their bowls. Trang left his toys to join them on the mat. He sipped directly from a bowl, blowing to cool it.

"Look at his manners. You see what's happening to him staying here?" Thi said.

"Where would you have us go? They've promised me an assignment." Phan waited for her reaction.

She stared at him.

"I'm meeting with them again today," Phan said.

"And what about a real place to live?"

"We just get by on our allowance from the party."

"You call that your freedom?"

"You're always complaining." Phan spat a bone off his tongue and rose to leave. "Can't you at least get the bones out of the stew?"

"It's the only nourishment in the stew, unless you want to start trapping rats like the others who are forced to live here."

Phan placed his bowl back on the mat and squared his hat to his head as Thi had seen French soldiers do. He paused, about to speak, but then just walked away.

She started crying, keeping her back to her son. Better to have stayed in the countryside. She'd known it all along, but Phan never listened to her. She'd heard the gossip that he wasn't sharing. It could only mean one thing: he was going to Dien Bien Phu. He was only keeping it from her to make it easier on himself.

CHAPTER 52

Son La, March 16, 1954
Lao
On the march

The platoon needed the break from marching. Lao dropped his pack, stretched his legs, and felt himself floating without the weight. Then he stumbled off his feet and rested his head against his pack. Five years in the infantry had taught him all the little tricks. He stared coldly at the others, their names familiar as his own. They were his family now, although not the family he had imagined for himself. Khong had disappeared years ago. His heart still ached for Leah. He had loved her. She had given him a moment of childhood, but now that too was only a memory. In the platoon everyone was dependent on the other for everything, including the little humanity the war had not wrung from them. There was no choice. There was no one else.

An officer shouted to resume the march. Lao fought with the weight of his pack, lifting it from the ground as he struggled to pull the straps over his shoulders, then bounced on his toes so the pack rode high up on his back, comfortable for an instant.

The mountain trails from the northern border region were heavily traveled now, but the coolies carrying supplies scrambled to the side and let the platoon pass. They marched during the day. They marched at night. No one said where they were going, but they were heading south with Chinese advisers. At times Lao slept as he marched. Then he would dream of food, until he stumbled into the soldier in front of him. He no longer remembered the number of days since leaving base camp. The rain soaked him, and mud clung to his feet. Climbing hills, he fell forward, then fell down backward on his pack. When rain ended the sun above the canopy changed the watery jungle floor to choking steam that turned cold at night and chilled him whenever the column halted.

Soldiers fell off the trail, delirious, vomiting, coughing, gagging. Some dropped dead marching. Occasionally the platoon passed a small medical station, its few bunks occupied by near corpses, but most of the sick collapsed along the trails.

Dry rice sustained Lao between camps. At them he gulped a bowl of stew. A bribe brought a piece of meat. The pain and stiffness quickly disappeared in the foggy hallucinations that overcame him. The shadows took on life. Imaginary enemies lurked at every turn in the trail. Someone was screaming. He recognized his own voice. His sergeant struck him, told him to get hold of himself. A thousand shadows, ten thousand shadows, he no longer comprehended their numbers. In the night Lao marched among them. What drew them towards the south? No explanations, just the order to continue.

One night they were allowed to sleep in a cave. The next morning after each soldier received a steaming bowl of pho, a political officer lectured them on how Ho Chi Minh had always provided for them. No one laughed. They chanted Ho Chi Minh muon nam. Under his breath Lao kept repeating his own name and tried to remember and hold onto his own dreams.

As the trail width expanded, the traffic increased. All day Lao's platoon climbed and then descended, climbed and descended, until the muffled sound of artillery reached his ears and French planes flew overhead. The apprehension always present in infantryman heightened. Wild speculations spread, but all those speculations included a common name, Dien Bien Phu.

That night when the units in front of them failed to move for several hours, Lao's platoon slung their hammocks. They were not disturbed until daybreak. Although the sun never actually pierced the canopy, Lao felt its presence. The jungle glittered with predawn dew. Lao remained in his hammock, massaging his sore feet and sleeping fitfully. A rumor spread down the line that a battle raged at Dien Bien Phu, less than thirty kilometers up the road. The rumor erased Lao's fatigue. Here now was the moment for greatness he had imagined all his life. For five years he had dutifully fought in a series of battles that left him feeling like no more than one in a swarm of ants. Now he understood it had been preparation for this moment. Those years of suffering anonymity were about to end. He was prepared. He pictured himself penetrating an enemy fortification, fighting bunker to bunker, and in a final great moment of triumph, raising the flag over the fallen French fortification as an entire company surrendered to him. A grateful nation created a new legend that carried his name, Lao, Liberator of the People.

When his sergeant came around, Lao questioned how could anything so major as a battle be so quiet. The sergeant said that the ferocity of the fighting in the previous days had sapped both sides and that when it was time for the fighting to resume they would be sent forward to gain a great victory for Uncle Ho. The young soldier in the next hammock let out a whistle.

"You afraid?" another young soldier said.

Lao kicked the tree between their hammocks without giving an answer.

"Don't think about it," the sergeant said, and continued down the line of hammocks.

"You talked him out of here," Lao snarled.

"What's the matter with you?" the young soldier said.

"We don't know much more than before he came over

to speak us," Lao said. "Maybe he'd have told us something important if he thought we had any common sense."

"You calling me stupid?" the young soldier said, sitting up in his hammock.

"Sounds about right," Lao said getting ready, making sure his feet were free to drop to the ground.

The young soldier didn't move any further. "Anyway, it's enough to know we're going forward."

"I'd kinda like to know more about something might kill me," Lao said.

The command to move forward came midmorning. Light-headed with the euphoria of their high-minded purpose, the platoon moved easily along the widening trail. At times they burst into patriotic songs. Lao's mind filled with apocalyptical journeys in which few survived. He tripped over a root, producing a ripple of laughter. He blushed and swore at those around him Everything around him seemed indifferent to his fate. His spirit fell as he reflected on the unfairness of it all. He couldn't recall when something had gone right for him. Circumstance favored others. Now his only desire was to wrest vengeance from the battle being thrust upon him.

In clearings just off the trail, soldiers reassembled artillery pieces under their officers' directions, the strained silence occasionally broken by the strike of metal against metal. The air was heavy with the smell of gun oil from newly unpacked weapons. Ammunition carried from the south for months was massed in bunkers under huge camouflage nets. As coolies cleared new sections of jungle, they were careful to leave enough canopy to prevent French air surveillance.

Ahead of the platoon, coolies dragged assembled artillery toward the bunkers Lao imagined just behind the crest of a hill. Beside the artillery pieces, men threw themselves into thrashing at the jungle to make room for the enormous guns to pass. The platoon was forced to pause.

"Dien Bien Phu is just over the crest," a messenger from the front of the company whispered as he passed on his way to the platoon leader to bring him forward to confer with the captain.

"It's too quiet," a Nung soldier resting beside Lao replied to anyone who listened. Typical of his Chinese tribe he was tall and thin and spoke as if he alone understood the military tactics because the unit had Chinese advisers.

"They wouldn't bring artillery this far forward," an old veteran said.

All those around him agreed.

"Wouldn't the messenger know?" Lao said. He was met with icy glares.

A soldier went on his knees and raised his hands in prayer or meditation. The old veteran struck him. The veteran held his rifle aloft, caressing its barrel, then shaking it in the soldier's face, "We are Viet Minh soldiers. The battlefield is our temple, the rifle the instrument of our salvation. It's all we need. You make sure to remember that."

The soldier stood and replaced his pack, glancing about for anyone who might join him in rebuking the veteran. The platoon remained quiet on the jungle floor. The soldier settled by himself against a tree.

"Where's Colonel Hahn?" Lao ventured.

"The commanders are never around when we attack," the old soldier said. His words brought renewed silence.

The peak of the hill was indistinguishable until the artillery vanished over it. Then only coolies stood at the crest where the gun had been a moment before. They clung along a rope with heels dug in, as they struggled to hold against the great gun's weight. When the coolies disappeared, the platoon pressed forward. At the summit the soldiers bunched together, astonished by the vista that stretched before them through a plunging canopy. Far below a treeless plain stretched to a river. On the other side of it an airfield ran the length of a great valley. Fragmented aircraft smoldered on the runway. The surrounding hills were covered with French fortifications, a series of trenches and bunkers interlocked and protected by wire fences.

The platoon melted into the edges of the jungle, where they lounged. Lao alone remained standing at the peak. He tried to absorb the significance of what spread before him. He strained to distinguish details lost in a first quick observation. On several of the fortified hills the land outside the trenches appeared pocked by artillery and mortars. What remained of uniforms and the men who wore them was scattered over the wire fences and rutted terrain. The outlines of several solitary trees endured as gnarled skeletons. He imagined jungle might have once covered much of that land.

An enemy patrol wound its way across a no mans land. An occasional mortar round landed near them, throwing off a puff of dust. Each time the enemy patrol paused, and then continued toward the outline of trenches being dug by Viet Minh coolies in a steady advance toward the French positions.

Lao picked his way among soldiers, stepping over outstretched men when necessary, until he reached his squad.

"Find out anything?" the young soldier said.

"Nothing." Lao stood in the midst of the platoon.

"Before he left I heard the lieutenant say General Giap has taken personal command," the Nung said.

"Bad for us if he has," the old veteran said.

"General Giap is a great strategist," the Nung said.

"Maybe so," the old veteran said.

"Something you're not telling us?" Lao asked.

"Bringing so many infantry here means he'll use human wave attacks," the old veteran said.

"Did seem like a lot of dead outside the French perimeter," Lao said, trying to sound casual.

"You think they'll use us like that?" the young soldier said. His eyes widened as he spoke.

"Likely as not," the old veteran said. Lao noticed the man was chewing betel nut very rapidly.

"See all the Chinese advisers around here. We got nothing to worry about," the Nung soldier said.

"Guess we can rely on that." The old veteran laughed, settling back against his pack and chewing.

So the old veteran reckoned this was going to be a slaughter, Lao thought, slumping off his feet among the others. Before, his platoon had used guerilla tactics, sometimes with other units, sometimes alone, striking with surprise at French weakness, then retreating into the jungle before the enemy could respond. Always with only a few casualties. Here thousands of meters separated the enemy perimeter from the jungle. The enemy was fortified in trenches and bunkers, prepared and waiting. Even if the coolies dug trenches to the edge of the perimeter, without surprise they would have to climb from their trenches in the face of enemy fire, then cut the wire and cross the minefields to reach the enemy's trenches and bunkers. What Lao had observed surrounding the enemy fortifications were the dead young soldiers from other platoons. The battlefield he had inspected now narrowed into a single simple concept of survival: them or us.

The lieutenant climbed the hill, his face red without his being out of breath. The platoon sergeant jumped to his feet and bolted forward to meet him on the trail. After what seemed like an hour to Lao, but was only minutes, the sergeant returned to the platoon.

"On your feet," the sergeant barked.

CHAPTER 53

To Lang, March 17, 1954
Phan
A forward observer

The first days Phan and his guides walked trails high on the hills parallel to the roads to Dien Bien Phu. At night they peered down on lights from watchtowers the French called postes kilometrique, strung out like streetlights along the roads. Periodically they witnessed a night attack on one of those watchtowers: First a tremendous explosion, then the crackle of small arms and the French supporting artillery, then usually but not always a blaze like a Roman candle. At times several attacks were coordinated, forcing the French to choose which tower they'd support while the others were overrun. Phan found this part of the war exciting to study from a distance.

At first Phan and his two escorts traveled alone, but soon they caught up with small groups of soldiers and then columns with hundreds, all traveling in the same direction. When they were intermingled with coolies carrying supplies, Phan realized there was to be a large scale operation. Dressed in somber grey or the black of village peasants, many bare to the waist, the coolies moved in endless lines carrying the supplies for war. Wearing conical grass hats against the piercing sun and pelting rains that penetrated the jungle, few coolies had shoes, most just sandals, but as they went on, bare feet became more common. Nothing protected them from the attack of jungle ants, mosquitoes, and flies. Exhaustion and disease felled them: dysentery, malaria, beri beri, typhoid, and jungle fever. They suffered injuries from falling, blisters and cuts, infected feet and hands.

The coolies were treated at aid stations along the trails, but because most stations lacked the necessary medicines, the toll in lives was exacerbated. A slight injury often proved fatal, life and death determined by the stamina and luck of the individuals. Graveyards were peppered along the way. Thirty thousand at first, the number of coolies swelled to double that number and the fever of patriotism spread through the provinces. Word had traveled fast; a great battle was brewing that would determine their national independence at a place called Dien Bien Phu.

A spider web of trails funneled troops and the heavy weapons to breach the French defenses. The coolies carried artillery broken down into pieces with ammunition, and mortars and a mixture of weapons: Russian, Czech, Chinese, French, British, German, and American. Weapons captured, purchased, or given, together with food and clothing, hammocks, and tools; all carried in packs and in baskets on poles, and sacks on bicycles, and in carts. Sometimes donkeys and small horses aided the men.

As engineers widened trails, hundreds of Chinese trucks, together with trucks captured from the French and American trucks taken by the Chinese in Korea joined the laborers. The wheels churned mud to the coolies' knees and slowed their advance. Still a truck did the work of a hundred porters.

The trails they followed climbed the sides of the limestone mountains, winding to the top and over, dropping as steeply as they climbed to follow another valley and then to the next mountain. Sometimes high strung rope bridges brought them across, swinging to the cadence of wind and feet. The trails were camouflaged to avoid French interdiction from the air, bridges across rivers concealed by placing them below the water level. Teams of laborers from nearby villages repaired the damage from air attacks, filled the ruts left by passing trucks and those from the steady pounding of a thousand individual feet.

At night the jungle howled with wildlife. There were terrifying stories of tigers carrying off coolies, though the bite of deadly snakes seeking warmth was more common. Sometimes the coolies constructed bamboo huts off the trail. Just as often they slept in the open, slumped over the loads they carried. Political cadres at way stations urged them on with nightly lectures on the glory of the revolution.

From the north came the sound of chanting, a choir like no other, the words imploring patriotic fervor. As the sound drew near, the coolies put down their burdens and moved aside. A phalange of tan uniformed soldiers blitzed down the trail. Rifles on their shoulders bristled like porcupine quills. The pith helmets cocked forward on their heads partially concealed their resolute expressions. The nervous energy of men determined to prevail drove their cadence. They were a generation chosen to be severed from their families, to be expended for the freedom of their nation. A spontaneous cheer rose from the coolies. The battalion snaked past, equipment taped to enforce noise discipline, their helmets covered with local foliage to blend them into their surroundings, the mud churning under their sandaled feet. In the dim light beneath the canopy a quick glance left Phan the impression of hunchbacks with their packs swollen by supplies and ammunition and hammocks for the night.

They disappeared down the trail as quickly as they'd come. The somber work of dragging the artillery resumed. At the gesture of the soldiers who accompanied him, Phan followed them, scrambling around the barrel of a 105 artillery piece set across the trail. At least a dozen coolies tried to hoist it over a fallen tree. He stopped to note the end of the barrel was jammed with a red checkered rag, protecting it from the filth that covered everything. The coolies were ingenious, lifting the barrel on a stretcher of bamboo, handing it across the massive tree. A rope secured it, preventing loss if it fell from their grip.

Phan scurried to catch his guides, two young boys amused at his trouble keeping up with them. Their calloused feet betrayed them: Like their fathers and the generations before, they had only known the way to the edge of their village clearing before the war. Now they were intent on enjoying a man's adventure. They fondled their French carbines as they walked, laughed and prated about their days in training so recently past.

The older of the two droned on about his secret visits to a village just outside the training camp, how a girl who cleaned their uniforms had taken a liking to him and invited him one night to quarter in her house. He bragged he rode her like a bull, her all the time screaming he was the first, not to hurt her and later demanding money to have it taken care of so there wasn't any harm come from his little foray. "Don't it beat all," he exclaimed, "that not a week later my peeing burned like hot peppers."

"That, what it's like?" the younger soldier asked him.

"Medic gave me something, said stay away from her."

"That's not how I want it to be," the younger soldier complained, his face filled with childish anguish.

"You're a little boy."

"If you waited it would have been better."

"You think we have a long life to wait for it?" The older of the two refused to talk further, sulking as he concentrated on the trail.

Phan continued on behind them, feeling like an intruder. They were children and unaware of the consequences of the game they played. Country boys were the the best kind, he'd heard Hahn once explain, and he was right. Later, if they survived, there would be time for them to learn the meaning of their freedom.

They dropped to a river, where the water came strong off the hillsides and funneled through a gorge. Phan drank from his cupped palms, throwing the cold water over his face. Careful not to stir the bottom, he filled his canteens and secured them to his pack. Strung from side to side, a rope steadied the the river crossing, as more than once each of the three slipped from their feet on a bottom sanded smooth by the rapids. Bursting from the icy water, they shook like dogs. The work of pulling themselves up the cliff by the exposed tree roots quickly warmed them. The two young soldiers scrambled ahead in a race. Phan cursed as the dislodged rocks bounced off his pack. Off to the sides coolies rested like corpses in the trees, some tied by rope to prevent their falling to the valley bottom in their sleep. None stirred.

At the summit the trail snaked off across a ridge and descended without offering a panorama beyond the jungle foliage. The young soldiers captured a squirrel with a snare, cut it into strips, and spread the strips on edible leaves, sharing their feast with Phan. Shortly afterward his stomach turned hard as a fist, doubling him over with pain, forcing him to crawl. The boys hung the hammocks to allow him time to recover.

During the night the coolies continued to pass them along the trail. They moved in total darkness. At dawn the two young soldiers, commenting on Phan's ashen appearance, divided the contents of his pack between themselves. They urged him to continue, promising they'd soon reach the medical platoon that traveled with their battalion.

The cramping in Phan's stomach continued throughout the day. He found it strange the way the young soldiers worried over him. He reconsidered his harsh judgment of them.

They passed the artillery barrel again. He recognized the red checkered rag. They skirted several open areas that appeared recently clear cut of trees, a no man's land of death with still unburied corpses stacked at the edge.

"What caused this?" Phan inquired of a group of coolies collapsed beside the trail.

"French artillery from Dien Bien Phu," the stoutest coolie answered. He seemed to be deciding whether it was safe to speak further, watching the expressions of the others. "It was meant to destroy our artillery."

"And did they succeed?" Phan said.

"Not a single one. The artillery is forward from here in caves," the coolie whispered proudly, as if sharing an intimacy. They were behind the crown of the hill, and where the artillery should have been located. What was going on? On the forward slope the guns would be subjected to direct fire from the French. The coolie explained General Giap had perfected the use of caves. By concealing their entrances and only rolling the artillery out to fire, the Viet Minh were effective and secure. They expected to quickly destroy the French runways and French artillery that was so arrogantly open to view in the valley below. The unanticipated often succeeded. The young soldiers made inquiry of their battalion and were directed forward to a clearing.

Great nets half the size of soccer fields were slung between the trees. Covered with vegetation and raised high over head, they blocked off the sky. Several of the nets were being lowered and wilted vegetation replaced with new. Beside the path that led forward, Black T'ai warriors from the local area huddled, their turban-covered faces animated in loud conversation as they waited to guide units to their positions. Soldiers reassembled arriving artillery and mortars, that were quickly sent forward.

The two young soldiers signaled Phan forward to where they stood. There Phan had his first view of the French in the valley, their hedgehog of compounds positioned around a metal runway built from P.S.P. A soldier positioned on an outcrop with a scope rattled off the stronghold names as known from captured documents: Dominique, Elaine, Claudine, Hugette, Anne-Maire, Gabriella, and Beatrice. Phan thought it strange the French used women's names in such a primitive and desolate place. Each French position had bunkers half into the ground with no attempt at camouflage. The headquarters bunkers were clearly marked by bristles of antennas, and they were tied by communications trenches to the others. Artillery was set in circular pits, ammunition stacked nearby and often unprotected, the empty shell casings thrown aside. Rows of barbed wire strung on iron posts surrounded the perimeters, tangle foot wire stretched between and beneath them. In several compounds, tanks lodged behind waist high rows of sandbags. Equipment previously dropped by parachute into the open fields between the compounds lay in disarray.

A deserted village nearby, once no doubt beautiful and quaint and alone in the valley, was being torn apart for the wood. A French patrol crossed the open plains headed toward the distant jungle. Inside the compounds, new bunkers were under construction, new trenches being dug to connect them.

Sporadically a mortar round landed on the runway. A puff of dust exploded. It was met with return fire from the French artillery blindly sent into the surrounding hills. The proud French presented themselves to draw General Giap from the jungle. They were isolated from the Red River Delta and their cities, dependent on re-supply by air, their runways in the open and exposed. Phan now understood the means and method of French defeat. This was what was so important, that Hahn wanted him to see and report for posterity. And for them, their moment, their dream from the days at the orphanage, had arrived.

The rains that followed the lifting of the morning fog formed heavy mists that winds played into ghostly shapes the locals believed were their ancestral spirits haunting the valley. Phan watched French soldiers throw off their shirts and wade to their waists in a river that snaked through the fortifications. The soldiers filled old petrol cans with water, and then trekked back toward their compounds.

The soldier sitting next to Phan mapped out the fortifications on a schoolboy's chalkboard and marked the trails the French soldiers used to avoid their own mines. Phan leaned over to admire the man's drafting skills and the soldier smiled at him.

A sudden strange growling floated off the hills. An aircraft lumbered overhead just above the tree line, parting the mist like a great fish as it rapidly descended into the valley. The soldier next to Phan was standing, firing his carbine at it and loudly announcing, "American C-119."

Gunfire crackled from the rest of the hillside. The great plane landed on the airfield, reversing its engines, lurching to a halt. Frenchmen raced from its belly, pulling bags and boxes and throwing them to the side, scrambling for the nearest bunkers. An ambulance crossed the P.S.P dispatching its wounded into the plane. Plumes of grey smoke from Viet Minh artillery dappled the runway. The French fired their artillery off into the jungle. The plane wheeled around and thundered into the mist followed by trails of anti-aircraft fire.

"We'll get them ... eventually." The soldier lowered his carbine, setting it carefully next to him. He squatted and resumed watching, neatly adding to his diagram very accurate lines for the footpaths.

CHAPTER 54

Dien Bien Phu, March 20, 1954
Mueller
Understanding the French

In the valley the French fortifications were exposed as if in a rampage someone had kicked off the top of ant hills. Mueller knew the French had trapped themselves. They had built the trap and caught themselves in it as quickly as circumstance and General Giap allowed. To imagine that those so easily conquered by Germans on their own home soil might successfully defend such a distant post was preposterous, the madness of French élan.

Mueller foresaw the certainty of his retribution against the Frenchmen who had driven him into the jungle and stolen his dog, an enemy who hunted him from camp to camp, seeking him among the Viet Minh who gave him shelter. They had placed a reward on his head. Their bombing had recently fractured one of his legs, and their warrant on him kept him from seeking proper medical attention. Now he suffered an unexplained paralysis in his arms that came and went with a loss of equilibrium and a lack of sensation in his legs. Damn the French, he thought, I owe them nothing.

Ever since he had helped them destroy the French out-post, the Viet Minh had kept him confined inside their camp and limited him to training new recruits. They only trans-ferred him to Dien Bien Phu to identify the armor and artil-lery used in the defenses and to evaluate the French capabili-ties. But what did he know? How could he judge the strength of foolish men's hearts, or their will to persevere? He would give Colonel Hahn the information he wanted, but sometimes a single squad held battalions at bay, and sometimes divisions retreated before the probe of a single platoon. Chaos ruled the battlefield and in its glory the difference in men was to be found. That much he understood. And that nothing made sense until it was too late. Later the arm chair generals and historians who hide in the rear made it all fit their pet theories and conceit.

The Viet Minh mapmaker who had squatted next to him stood and disappeared into the jungle. As Mueller's head continued to spin from the height, he caught sight of binoculars left to weigh down a map left open on the ground. He drank from his canteen again and again. Then he reached down and took the binoculars and lifted them to his face. He searched the valley, careful to systematically scan all within the wire enclosures as he attempted to discover even one familiar and hated face. Blurry Frenchmen labored without shirts, digging trenches and filling sandbags and reinforcing the bunkers, their features remaining obscured. Occasionally a French sol-dier stood and stretched, and then he'd pause to stare toward the mountains, his eyes seeming to meet Mueller's through the glass. Mueller quickly shifted to study another group. The years of isolation in Viet Minh camps had confirmed his per-ception of the French as a weak race, a colonial power grown afraid, no longer with the will for power. Now he watched them working frantically to bury themselves from view as if that could protect them from destruction.

A Viet Minh artillery piece discharged from some-where behind him. The round whistled overhead and explod-ed harmlessly on the French airfield like a rock thrown into a pond. Although the artillery missed a specific target, the blast sent the Frenchmen scurrying to their bunkers. He watched as Frenchmen scrambled to their artillery and fired into the mountains, the muffled retorts echoing back and forth across the valley. In that instant Mueller had a vision of the future and smirked.

A single propeller aircraft emerged from hiding in a sandbagged hanger and taxied down the field, pursued by explosions of Viet Minh artillery. Quickly aloft, the plane circled the mountains that surrounded the French camp. Rifles shot in the plane's direction sounded like popcorn. The plane continued to circle, directing an impotent French retribution. Mueller laughed. The Viet Minh artillery struck a certain group of Frenchmen outside their trenches, drawing a cheer from the mountain. In the binoculars Mueller watched medics drag away the wounded and the killed. They disappeared just in time, narrowly escaping another artillery shell.

"Are you finished watching?" The voice of the map maker interrupted Mueller.

"I've seen enough," Mueller said, lowering the binoculars, his head still spinning. "There's not much worth seeing."

"But you can see it all from here," the mapmaker said. "It's as fine a show as seen performed by great orchestras at the French Opera Building in Ha Noi."

"You're stupid to think so," Mueller said. He caught himself thinking French and Vietnamese alike were fools. One of them had to lose. Which one didn't concern him. He drank from his canteen as he felt the mapmaker study him. "You got nothing better to do?"

"May I have my binoculars back?"

Mueller slapped the the binoculars against the mapmaker's chest. Only then he noticed Colonel Hahn standing to one side "Well, colonel, you seen enough too?"

"You stole alcohol from our medical supplies," the colonel said, "and now you're drunk."

"You accusing me?" Mueller felt a flash of rage at being addressed like a child. His face flushed and his neck stiffened. "You have no proof."

"Not yet, but only alcohol is missing," Colonel Hahn said. "My men would never take it."

"Then I suggest you carry on with your investigation."

"War is just a game to you."

"You'd be a fool to see it differently."

"We've got a cause that you will never understand."

Mueller gulped from the canteen.

"Let me see that." Colonel Hahn put the canteen to his nose. "You put the alcohol in the juice."

"You're guessing," Mueller said. "Drink some if you suspect me."

The colonel emptied the canteen on Mueller's feet.

For an instant Mueller had the strange feeling his mother watched him. "Damn you," he shouted.

"What?"

"The French will slaughter your soldiers," Mueller said. "You've earned your right to die." He watched the colonel closely, all the time imagining his mother.

"You need help," the colonel finally said. He reached toward Mueller.

"Never touch me." Mueller sprang forward at the colonel's throat. He heard only his mother's voice as he tightened his grasp around the rubbery neck. Then he felt the the repetitive blows.

When Mueller woke, the colonel and the mapmaker and several soldiers he had never seen before stood over him.

"We're only trying to help you," the colonel said.

"I know what you're doing to me." Mueller struggled against the ropes that bound his hands behind him. The soldiers yanked him to his feet.

"When you're sober we'll untie you," the colonel said. The soldiers tied him.

"I'll remember you," Mueller roared, straining at the ropes. The men who had bound him drew cautiously away. Mueller laughed at their timidity. Did they think the colonel protected them? Their simplemindedness blinded them. Let the valley devour them. He'd avoid their fate.

The artillery sounds seemed a distant dream. His head ached as he tried to implant the images of the faces who had humiliated him. The ringing in his ears ceased. He tested the ropes. They held. Nothing focused. He screamed defiantly for his canteen, for something more to drink, his mouth parched by the heat. "Damn your yellow race," he shouted. "I know you're there," he kept repeating. "I know you're there. Answer me."

Now he listened, time to catch his breath. The jungle matched his breathing, its rhythm a constant flow of wind blowing through the top of the triple canopy. He waited his release, certain that in the attack he'd survive them all. When he closed his eyes, the earth whirled around him, so he lay back with his eyes open and scrutinized the forest trees. The intermingled limbs swayed in rhythm. The sun persisted in glimpses above the canopy, reaching into the jungle at every opportunity, drawing moisture toward it out of the fetid ground. In the shadows the soldiers whispered, and Colonel Hahn assured them the value of their sacrifice. A mass of soldiers built around him. The bitter smell of their sweat betrayed anxiety as they prepared to overrun the French fortifications. Near Mueller soldiers crouched around a fire. Their helmets and backs were covered with fresh cut bramble. They had the deportment of campaign veterans.

But Mueller wondered who among them would soon walk into the valley between life and death. Who would watch his own body depart and not chase after it? Mueller fought against his bonds. His wrists bled and that blood felt cold and foreign running down his hands. Around him soldiers struggled to their feet, ready to march against Dien Bien Phu.

CHAPTER 55

Dien Bien Phu, March 25, 1954
Hahn
Sending out the troops

The tiny lanterns captured the glow in the six faces as they anticipated Colonel Hahn's every word. Inspecting each in turn, he stared into their eyes, searching for any sign of fear, but youth gave them fearlessness and adventure kept them keen. If they knew that death awaited them, it didn't diminish their fervor. Hahn checked their gear for readiness. The bags around their waists were bloated with grenades, their pins straightened and half pulled, the satchel charges wrapped in canvas with straps slung across their chests. He smiled at this special little unit that had just completed training as commandos. Once aimless street urchins, now each had a purpose, a sense of importance, and dedication to the cause. What fine simplicity in youth. When taken individually, they were insignificant, but now their numbers would bring victory. Since his transfer from the training camp to a field battalion, Hahn had prepared these young soldiers for this moment.

Hahn understood these sappers, the mirrors of his youth, forsaken children, abandoned and unloved. No, not so harsh. In a country where death came suddenly, the loss of loving parents wasn't uncommon. Part of the pain in being alone was never knowing why and the impossibility of finding the answers. Here they had one future, one purpose. Now Hahn acted in loco parentis. He repeated the term to the sappers, during his lectures. They understood they were his family. He taught them duty to the party. They trusted him and accepted what he taught them. He sentenced them to martyrdom because the party asked it. Was their trust a gift that he betrayed? Was their youth something they were entitled to keep? Sometimes he questioned his own belief that this was a better thing for them, a brief but glorious moment that most men never enjoyed. Perhaps all great causes made "expendable" too easy to say, but to create a better world, the party sometimes had to destroy those who believed in it.

"You will make us proud of you," Hahn said, then cut his comments short, afraid his voice would crack and betray the hopelessness he felt for them. They returned his salute.

This night a cloud-covered sky blessed the boys who advanced through the trench past those digging and carrying dirt in baskets to the rear. The trench still ended far from the river and the French fortifications. At the end of the trench the boys climbed a ladder and crawled into the open fields toward the river.

A sliver of moon broke through the clouds providing the light by which Hahn glimpsed the youthful sappers as they reached the river bank. They shed their uniforms down to skin tight shorts or nakedness, their smooth hairless bodies glistening white. The six slid down the bank together into the deepest part of the river, those with grenades and satchel charges carrying them over their heads. Several paused to playfully splash each other.

After they crossed the river, each boy coated himself with mud dredged in fistfuls from the shoreline. The squad looked like an aboriginal tribe having risen from the earth as they disappeared into the darkness of mine fields and wire entanglements.

Hahn slid back into the trench. He held his head in his

hands, pressing his fingers against his eyelids, his thumbs in his ears.

"Are you all right sir?" said one of the coolies digging near Hahn's feet.

"Yes," he whispered. "I just need a minute."

Hahn heard the baskets slap in one palm, then the next and the next as the coolies passed along the red clay. When the earth embankment collapsed near him, Hahn fell against a coolie, the man's breath in his face, as the two stood in mud. The other coolies froze, passing the baskets ceased.

Hahn braced against the wall of dirt and wrested himself from the mud. "Don't worry about me." He squeezed past the line of laborers and as he quickened his pace he pushed startled coolies out of the way, distancing himself from the river and his sappers, as he imagined them crawling across the no-man's land, crawling towards the French bunkers to a point never reached before. Every night Hahn's sappers got closer.

And what small part in this was his? They did what he ordered. If some ever returned what would they say to him? Why was he chosen to survive this way? Now he retreated from the front, his breath in gasps, guided by the trench walls. He stumbled over startled workers, in a darkness filled with outstretched arms. A flare a hundred meters overhead reflected off the water at Hahn's feet. His heart fell at the sound of the explosions.

"All down," shouted a distant and unattached voice. Around Hahn shadows flattened and merged in a human mass. An arm yanked him to the ground. His sweaty face in mire, he felt the earth tremble beneath the blows from French mortars. His sappers had been spotted by the French. The heavier quake from the French artillery walked across the fields and trenches, raining mud on his slouching back, his neck, his arms wrapped around his head. In the silence that followed, Hahn imagined he heard the distant wails of his sappers. The coolies who surrounded him were outlined in the unnatural blue sunset of the fading flares. As the last flare expired, the baskets passed by him as if he was no longer there.

Hahn waited against the trench wall. He ran his hands across his uniform, brushing away clods of earth, and his right hand fell to his side to check for his holstered pistol. He fingered the trigger guard. A sudden rush of basket laden coolies dislodged him, forcing him into their movement towards the rear. He cowered among them unnoticed and moved along until they turned down a side trench. With a new bitterness, he convinced himself he was not the one who sent the sappers to their deaths. No, it was the French who were resolved to occupy his country.

With his remaining strength, Hahn climbed from the trench and dropped to the ground. He lay face down and tried to rest, but when he closed his eyes all the earth around him seemed to move. He felt as if he were falling into an abyss. He turned onto his back and watched billowing clouds choke off that last slice of moonlight, too late to save his sappers. Then he lifted himself to his feet, brushed off his uniform, straightening the pleats, and started towards the base camp.

—⁕—

As Hahn moved across the early-morning grayness, a patrol of his men, laughing at some untoward joke, appeared out of the mist. They saluted him as they continued towards their guard duty outposts, their laughter carrying back into the camp. His first sergeant greeted him just inside the perimeter and followed him into the headquarters bunker. Hahn sat at his desk and reviewed the orders for the next day. Still no order from General Giap for a general attack by Hahn's battalion. Still time to probe the enemy and discover the weaknesses of its defenses. But time was running out.

"Where are the assignments for tomorrow night's sappers?" Hahn demanded of his first sergeant.

The first sergeant handed him a single sheet of paper. After a moment, Hahn handed the sheet back. "Double their number. Last night the sappers were discovered, but they almost penetrated the enemy perimeter."

"Do you think that wise, sir? We've lost almost fifty men."

Hahn leaned forward, his forearms pressed against the desk's teakwood finish. He felt the wood's coolness and stability against his skin. "We do as we're told."

CHAPTER 56

Dien Bien Phu, March 26, 1954
Father Custeau
In a Godless place

Father Custeau glimpsed the fire of dawn through a small window across the C-47 cargo plane. He bowed his head. Holy Mother, protect us. His single barking cough, tense and guttural, echoed off the cargo hull. Thirty forms bent forward in their seats along the fuselage as the crew chief strutted down the center aisle. "Buckle up, ladies. Prepare for landing. Store your gear beneath you."

The plane descended, its propellers feathered. Another C-47 flew in front, full lights on and at a higher altitude, as if to parachute men and supplies. It was a decoy to draw the anti-aircraft fire, and it wasn't working. Black smoke from artillery bursts surrounded Father Custeau's plane, which shuddered, then rocked side to side during the sudden drop in altitude. The pilot steadied the descent, rolling the plane in a turn pointed toward the runway at Dien Bien Phu. Endless green hills sparkled with the flash of anti-aircraft guns. An engine burst into flame. One last gasp of power from the remaining engine leveled the plane just before the wheels bounced on metal runway.

"Stand up, ladies, grab your gear, this is where you're getting off."

The plane taxied to a stop between two destroyed C-47s. The tail opened. "Run, ladies. Run to the right until you're in the bunkers."

Two crewmen pushed against supply pallets centered in the plane. Young men in camouflaged uniforms, staggering under the weight of their packs, lumbered toward the opening, a yawning mouth of light. Father Custeau, standing by the open cargo door, blessed them as they passed. He waited for the last of them before making his way off the plane. The pain deepened in his legs. He hobbled across the cargo hatch, Charlemagne holding his arm.

The cool metal revetments gave way to ones of searing heat as the ungodly scarlet sun burned away the crachin fog surrounding them.

"What is God's will for me in this place?" Father Custeau said under his breath. The heat parched his throat. He stopped to administer last rites to a young boy, struck seconds before, his throat pierced with metal torn from the runway by a mortar shell. The boy blessed him in turn and seemed to fall asleep. Charlemagne pressed Father Custeau to leave as he glanced back to appraise the abandoned plane. Mechanics worked furiously at a damaged wing, the engine already in parts on the ground. Artillery fell randomly like great hail stones on the runway's PSP, the artillery not yet adjusted by the enemy in the hills.

"This is an evil place," Father Custeau said. Charlemagne nodded.

They reached the edge of the wire strung around the outpost at the beginnings of a cemetery, wooden crosses lined up in rows erected in fresh earth. With that effort abandoned, bulldozers had dug larger and more practical pits, still open and left to fill. The dead were wrapped in ponchos and waited on pallets to be interred. All the earth looked overturned from the fury of artillery and exploded mines.

Father Custeau recognized the devil's work. Murder lay at every turn, as the men struggled to survive. He paraphrased God's words: Thou shalt not die until I choose to have it so. Divine will worked in strange ways, as if God and devil played out some great game of chess, men mere pawns to them. At times it had even occurred to Father Custeau that it made sense only if no such thing as God existed and that circumstances alone precipitated what happened. A life of penance had suppressed the thought, but now the idea troubled him again.

A soldier covered in mud rose from the earth and pulled Father Custeau after him into a trench. "You'll get yourself and your partner killed walking around out there."

"What's your name son?" Father Custeau asked.

"Malpass, sir."

"Well bless you, Malpass."

Father Custeau inquired when the soldier had last taken mass. When he did not receive a response, Father Custeau said he'd return to give a mass as soon as circumstances allowed. The soldier nodded and provided a guide to escort him to the headquarters.

At first the trench paralleled the hill's contour and was level, frequently interrupted with firing ports in which pairs of soldiers crouched on platforms a step above the mud. All the soldiers were coated a single brown color. Only their blinking eyes distinguished them from their surroundings. These men remained expressionless when Father Custeau passed. He accepted that it was a forsaken place in which none called upon God their father. At times the mud rose above his knees. His feet felt like weights increasingly encumbered by each step. He tried holding up his robe as he'd seen French brides do before a wedding. He hacked up phlegm and blood, spitting it into the mire.

They crowded past a soldier probing the mud with an iron rod like a blind man with a stick.

The guide explained, "The Viet Minh dig tunnels and trenches trying to get inside the perimeter for a ground attack. If we get lucky, we find their tunnels first and explode them."

A spindle-legged skimming bird pecked at clots beneath the water surface, working its bill like tweezers. Father Custeau was almost on top of it before it whistled an alarm, and then with fluttering bursts flew up over the berm and out of sight.

A sudden turn in the trench brought them up against a mound reinforced with animal bones and salvaged revetments from an ancient fortification. A human skull adorned the entrance, a hole through which a man could pass only by crawling on hands and knees. A totem carved from a red wood supported a crosspiece strung with ears, a blasphemy to Christendom. Father Custeau reached to tear it down. The guide held him back. "Father, this is their custom."

"This sacrilege must cease," Father Custeau said.

"Perhaps a word to our commander later, sir. But for now leave it be. These men are not like you and me."

The voices that carried from within the entrance were at a low pitch and in a foreign tongue, and when Father Custeau entered he thought them Africans or Arabs, the layers of caked mud on their skin making a determination difficult. A foul stench emanated from a kettle centered over their fire. Smoke layered the room and slowly rose toward an opening at the bunker peak. The blackened soldiers surrounded the kettle, their uniforms removed, their chests glistening with sweat. They dipped their tin canteen cups in a steaming brew that stained their lips blood red. Father Custeau quickly withdrew and stumbled forward as Charlemagne grasped his arm and pulled him toward a ladder.

The trench appeared to dead end over a wall that inclined up the hill. Against this last natural edifice the ladder, so heavily used that the wood rungs were covered with a muddy gruel, was worn like the cow stairs found in French barns. The guide easily bounded up those steps. Father Custeau struggled to climb what was not vertical or horizontal and so required both his hands. At the top of the ladder two burned planes and another hill compound was encircled in wire.

"That is Beatrice," said the guide.

"Beatrice is the symbol of divine love," said Father Custeau.

"Sorry, sir, but the strongholds are named for General de Castries' mistresses." The guide responded to his quizzical expression. "We call them his ladies."

"I prefer to think of them as saints."

"Perhaps I'm misinformed." The guide smiled broadly. As he spoke there was a crackle sounding like distant thunder, then an explosion of dirt on the hill near Beatrice. A second explosion followed just below the first.

"Artillery," the guide said, his countenance unchanged. "They'll soon have our range. They haven't learned to bracket or it would already be too late."

The three scampered into the trench ahead, Father Custeau assisted by Charlemagne. A round struck close to where only seconds before they had rested. Mud broke loose from the walls and covered them. When they reached the crest of the hill, the trenches were covered with logs supporting mounds of earth. Within that labyrinth, the bunkers were connected by a series of covered trenches. There was no light except that cast from clouded lanterns hung from beams. Here the march of feet had created a watery mash, and the unventilated air burned the throat. The guide refused to proceed without further direction from some higher military authority.

Father Custeau and Charlemagne continued alone wandering through bunkers. In some men ate and in others slept. Some bunkers were administrative offices in the underground military city. In each section at least one bunker was designated with a red cross for medical treatment. The wounded could be heard as they underwent surgery. A number of bunkers served for storage since anything above ground was subjected to enemy artillery, snipers, and the increasingly frequent waves of Viet Minh sappers.

As the two wandered, they continued to hear the muffled sounds of artillery and men arguing and shouting profanities. Father Custeau frequently stopped to pray for the souls of those trapped in the maze.

CHAPTER 57

Dien Bien Phu, March 27, 1954
Pasteur
A glimpse into reality

Lieutenant Pasteur estimated the enemy strength had grown by a battalion within the last day with the addition of six hundred Viet Minh regulars weighted down with packs and weapons. His platoon remained in enemy territory to get an actual count. Only then would the French high command believe what Lieutenant Pasteur already knew, that the communists meant to overrun Dien Bien Phu. Still, Lieutenant Pasteur feared the generals would deny it. The generals were deaf to reality, hearing only what they wanted, unable to accept that men in the lower ranks understood the situation more accurately than they.

As he thought of facing the Viet Minh, commanded by the cunning General Giap, Lieutenant Pasteur's pulse quickened, his face reddened, his heart echoed off the hard earth beneath him. At times he thought that if he survived, he'd never feel as totally alive again. He'd wind up back in Paris lecturing students or like his father in the diplomatic corps until he died in bed of old age.

Hidden just off the trail, the platoon rested among mangled trees destroyed by random artillery bursts. Fragments of wood were entangled with chunks of earth and with the leaves and vines that had once climbed toward the light above the canopy. The vines now hindered every step, a noisy impediment to their movement.

Pasteur counted his grenades. If the platoon was discovered by the Viet Minh, he doubted there were enough grenades, and to use rifles would risk betraying their exact position. Stay alert, he repeated to himself. Insertion had been the easy part. The challenge was to get everyone out alive. The platoon depended on him. In turn they guarded him when he slept, their vigilance unwavering. Now each man mattered and must do his part, a change from the days of the barracks.

Covered in tiger camouflage, bush hats down over their foreheads, bandanas covering their necks, they hunched in their hidden position. Their hands and faces were painted with the dull greens and blacks of war theater makeup. He'd tried to get the platoon to chew betel nut to blacken their teeth, but they had refused, "We're not old women."

"Then keep your mouths shut in the jungle," he'd said, smiling for an instant.

Now he daydreamed about Dawn while waiting for some new sign of the enemy. She had become his one weakness, a real presence in the dark. At times he thought he felt her breath on him and once he'd caught himself about to speak her name aloud.

Dusk was the hardest time. Images seen clearly during the day took on new shapes that had to be memorized for recognition in the dark. Even the most experienced soldiers might fire at a tree or bush that appeared to move in the dark. Then they had to move, because the noise compromised their position. This time there could be no shooting, no mistakes.

All eighteen soldiers slept in a clump. Lieutenant Pasteur ordered those on watch to wake him if they heard movement on the trail. A careless engagement, a shot fired, even a whisper, would endanger them all. The enemy could smell Western soaps, so no one had bathed for weeks. He tried to sleep. His instincts fought that desire. He waited. He listened. Rustling sounds. Of the wind? A flurry of activity and an animal's snarl. The returning silence gave him time to imagine. What happened to time? In the total blackness no way to tell. Silence. Waiting. Listening.

A distant light flickered through the trees. Another light slowly floated toward them down the trail. Lanterns. Lieutenant Pasteur touched those who might have been asleep but said nothing. The black forms returned his touch to say they understood. The first sounds reached them, equipment striking equipment and then the sandaled feet, their muffled treading within reach. He counted feet crossing in front of him. Numbers started to blur as the endless centipede of an army wound past. He dropped a single piece of leaf near his chin each time a hundred soldiers passed. He would count those leaves in the morning. The hand-held lanterns were close and bright as street lights. The Viet Minh soldiers marched without caution but maintained their silence. A passing soldier spit into the bushes over Lieutenant Pasteur's head. The spit dribbled down over the leaves onto him. He didn't move. He wouldn't be the one to betray his platoon. Please don't let them see me, he thought, regulating his breath, clinging to the earth.

He heard the distant engine of an airplane. The enemy column halted and extinguished their lanterns. He knew the plane would come overhead. Please don't let it see them, he prayed, although he knew it didn't help. He had stopped going to the priests, although he kept lying about it in his letters home to his mother. There was no point upsetting her. He couldn't imagine getting home alive. Maimed would be even worse. Did a soldier ever tell his family what he had seen happen to his men or what they did to the enemy?

The airplane circled overhead. Lieutenant Pasteur kept repeating the prayer. As the airplane descended, Viet Minh artillery pounded the runway at Dien Bien Phu. The plane must have been trying to land. The Viet Minh were relighting their lanterns. In the light he saw the worn sandal of a man, his hairless leg below a green uniform. The man was motionless. A tiny red ant made its way over the sandal and up the leg. Then it disappeared under the green cloth. Don't bite him now, Lieutenant Pasteur thought. The foot shifted and moved forward. Lieutenant Pasteur resumed dropping the leaves until the last man passed.

In the twilight half sleep he saw trees with strange hands on massive arms shaking ferns and leaves in shapes like none found in Europe swaying high in the canopy. A tree frog croaked close to his face.

What would he say to a father who still believed the Indochinese colonies depended on the French aristocracy, that what the Vietnamese needed was French protection from the foreign designs of British and Chinese? That all that didn't matter? That he, their child of innocence and charm, had irretrievably changed and now fought on a strange planet far from France? That now he knew each part of the earth had its own individual reality, and no words could transmit the truths between them? That what he'd come for wasn't possible, any attempt at heroics doomed and that all that remained possible was a macabre form of martyrdom?

Lieutenant Pasteur woke to the salt taste of a soldier's hand across his mouth, quickly exceeded by a smell of rotted garlic. The exotic birds singing in the canopy foretold the dawn.

CHAPTER 58

Ha Noi March 29, 1954
Doctor Astray
Casualties

Early morning sunlight streamed through the curtains and across the dining room. Doctor Astray lingered over breakfast, admiring the linen covered tables and polished silver tureens. Steam rose from each tureen. Well-dressed French officials opened and closed the tureens for inspection and filled their plates. The buffet provided a delightful combination of fine French pastries, eggs cooked in all manners, bacon, hams, a curry of chicken, rice fried or steamed, and Vietnamese pho. A separate table was dedicated to multi-colored breakfast juices; orange, cocoanut, pineapple, grapefruit, mango, and tomato, all in pitchers chilled with ice. French waiters stood in place. A French chef cooked behind a grill where fry pans sizzled with individual requests. Vietnamese kitchen help scurried to clear tables and keep every tureen filled.

In the hall a military orderly removed his rain coat and placed it on a chair before approaching the maitre d' hotel. The maitre d'hotel pointed in the direction of a table of officers and French ladies. Doctor Astray recognized the orderly as an acquaintance from the bar and stood to intercept him.

"What news?" Doctor Astray whispered as he approached the orderly.

"No doubt some relief for you doctor. No further casualties can be evacuated from Dien Bien Phu." The orderly paused to make certain no one overheard him. "The airfield there has been destroyed. Dien Bien Phu is cut off."

"I see," Doctor Astray said.

The orderly continued to a table in the corner, where he saluted a general officer. Doctor Astray didn't recognize the officer, although the general was seated next to Madam de Castries and several other finely dressed women. In due course the general paused in his conversation with the ladies, nodded, and proceeded to read the dispatch. The other officers signaled the waiters away. The general bent and whispered to Madam de Castries.

"Oh my poor husband," Madam de Castries exclaimed, clearly wanting to be overheard by the entire room. "Why did they force that place upon him?" Such was arrogance of power. As if the disaster of Dien Bien Phu meant only her husband's loss of face and, in turn, her humiliation.

The posturing and recriminations began. General de Castries only followed orders. Indeed, wasn't that enough? A loyal and faithful soldier of France captured by the Germans in the World War. Escaped. Dashing, aristocratic man. Cavalry, of course. Posted first to Vietnam in 1946. A sterling reputation now at risk. This was something different. Rumors already surrounded him. That the strongholds at Dien Bien Phu were named after his mistresses. That he remained in the command bunker, paralyzed with fear, afraid to check his troops.

The doctor had once seen General de Castries in the lobby, surrounded by his aides, a strutting peacock with his cane, wearing the red cap of the North African cavalry, petite silk scarf around his neck. Perhaps the arrogance of French generals came from the time of Napoleon. Had they forgotten how often their allies came to their aid, how rapidly the French army fell to the Germans? Even now they were sustained by American military equipment and financial aid. It was rumored French diplomats were pleading for direct United States military intervention.

Doctor Astray watched those at the breakfast table reacting with confusion. The general rose. The other officers at the table snapped to attention. For an instant the general tenderly held madam's hand, then he saluted, and left the dining room, the other officers following in his wake. As the general swept past Doctor Astray, he saluted as if to acknowledge the general adulation due him by the people in the room. The doctor remained motionless until he attacked the pastries. So where's my self control, he thought. When he'd had his fill, he started toward his room.

In the lobby Doctor Astray found himself in the midst of the officers. Several were waving their arms. He caught the word treason.

"What is it?" he asked, startled by his own boldness. He stood squarely in front of the concierge's desk where the officer who had shouted "treason" centered his gaze. A local French newspaper was spread across the desk: AIRFIELD CLOSED BY VIET MINH: FRENCH ARMY FACING DEFEAT AT DIEN BIEN PHU.

"What, no censors?" the doctor exclaimed.

The vocal officer interpreted the remark as condemnation of the headline's author, although the doctor hadn't meant anything except to indicate his cynical surprise. "Yes, how did such a headline escape them?" said the officer.

Before the officer uttered another word the general reappeared in the lobby. The unbroken starch in his uniform indicated he'd already been up to his room and changed for the inevitable newspaper interviews. In the silence he advanced directly to the desk, read the headline, then crumpled the paper in his fist and threw it to the floor. "Find the swine who wrote this," he said.

"Is it true?" Doctor Astray asked.

"What do you think, my friend?" the general said.

"How am I to know?" said Doctor Astray.

"Ahh, there you have it," the general said, glancing at

his staff. "The headline isn't believed by our patriotic citizen here... issue an immediate denial."

"Then it's not true?" There was relief in the lieutenant's voice.

"Of course it's true. It's just not a good time to admit it."

"But, general," the lieutenant began to speak.

"My poor boy, what you fail to see is the advantage of confusion. Make the most of it. A plausible denial can be as good as the actual truth on your side. The population that chooses to believe us will only increase their loyalty, rushing to our defense. Those who sympathize with our enemies will begin to question what they've heard. After all why wouldn't we admit to the simple facts? I'm telling you, let history quibble over the truth later. We have a war to win."

Doctor Astray returned to his room, drew his medical bag down off the shelf, then readied himself to return to the hospital. At least now the steady flow of wounded soldiers would in fact stop for a while. He would concentrate on his paying civilian patients. He paused at the sink, ran a comb through his hair, and studied himself at the mirror as if facing a stranger. That damn grey hair. Hard to deny, that an old man faced him. He was falling apart. Medically, he understood the process. What had happened to the years? He still thought of himself as a teenager, at most in his late twenties, yet that had been decades ago. And he once again remembered: a promising surgeon to the prominent, and the slip of the knife that ended it. No use, the bitterness of the years. It was wasted time. Precious time and now very late. He scrubbed his hands vigorously, raising a lather, studying the extended veins, the age spots that would not now or ever wash away. Disheartening. Yes, he'd walked vigorously again today. That thought alone rejuvenated him.

In the dim hallway he was vaguely aware of the Vietnamese maids who always politely acknowledged him. At the top of the stairs he peered down through the chandelier, into the lobby, a habit since his childhood when he'd peered through the balusters watching unobserved, listening to his parents talk. Now the lobby was empty. He hurried down the stairs, through the lobby, and into the street.

Several young boys started to beg from him, but the doorman chased them away. Trishaw drivers waved to him from across the street, now kept away for security reasons, each beckoning and pointing to their empty seat. He shook his head, determined to exercise by walking to the hospital. Can't let the Viet Minh win by isolating him.

"Riding sir?" the doorman inquired. "I'll get you someone who can be trusted."

I bet you will, Doctor Astray thought, and one who knows how to pay a bribe. That's how it works here, though a bit more complicated now with all the enemy infiltration. "No, thank you."

In the street traffic flowed easily, the bikes a steady hum. He walked slowly and patiently across the street, allowing traffic time to go around him. It was mostly young women on bicycles, faces behind scarves. Very few young men traveled openly any more with both the government and Viet Minh using strong armed methods to recruit them. On the sidewalk the doctor walked rapidly for personal security but primarily to exercise.

There had been incidents: a gang of local youths had beaten an unarmed soldier. An explosion in the bar of a local hotel. A military jeep blocked in traffic and its occupants shot. A prostitute and her French lover stabbed as they slept in her room. Censorship was imposed to quell the anxiety that caused the waves of migration back to France. That was why the newspaper headline about Dien Bien Phu was so surprising.

Off the main street through a single width alley, turning down another, quickly, quickly, he reminded himself, his pace already dropping. He was not yet half way. He turned away from an alley where cardboard boxes completely blocked the passage. Only the day before a street gang had blocked it, taking up residence.

The hospital might have been any other administrative building, shuttered windows facing the street. The French soldier standing guard at the door was reassuring in these times. At the edge of the hospital grounds Doctor Astray hesitated to straighten his tie and slip into the white suit jacket which he had carried draped over his medical bag. As usual, his shirt was completely soaked with sweat from the walk. At least the jacket concealed much of it. He nodded politely to the soldier at the door. "Good morning, sergeant."

"Good morning, herr doctor," said the soldier, whose own age kept him safely at the rear.

Doctor Astray still tried to time his arrival for after the patients had been fed, their bed sheets changed, and everything left in a clean and orderly fashion. He slipped past the nurses station unnoticed and quickly closed the door to his consulting room. The night nurse's notes were already carefully placed in the center of his desk. Nothing noteworthy except the unfounded optimism over several patients with abdominal wounds. He didn't recognize the handwriting or the signature from the words he read. A new night nurse no doubt. He thought the words spontaneous, if not impulsive with boldness in the letters, as if challenging him to cure the patients and prove her right. But there was no way to cauterize the internal wounds. He could only treat the outward infection, all the time knowing that inside the body cavity poison spread. Thinking that controlling the pink inflammation of the skin cured the patient raised false hopes. Frequently a healthy appearing patient with internal wounds suddenly developed a fever and died. Nothing in the notes raised his hopes that any of the patients were recovering from their wounds. Maybe the nurse knew that. He paused. Time to make the rounds.

The nurses' station was busy.

"What time will the first flights from Dien Bien Phu arrive today, doctor?"

"Don't you nurses read the papers?" asked Doctor Astray.

"We're here at six, doctor. It's a busy time of day."

"Yes, I see that," Doctor Astray said. "The runway at Dien Bien Phu has been cut off by the Viet Minh. No more flights for now."

His young nurse watched him and waited.

"Well, come along, we'll check the patients we have here."

"Yes, doctor."

Today he hardly noticed the fresh antiseptic smell in the common room where beds lined the walls. He attended one of the internal wounds first in order to test the accuracy of the new nurse's notes.

"Do you think you could find me another coffee?" he said to his nurse as she followed him from the corridor.

"I will try, doctor."

He pulled a chair up to the new boy, the last for a while, and sat down. He had seen the likes of the boy around the city before the battle, the pride of France, high spirited and boisterous boys, singing late at night in Ha Noi streets, and then seen them bare-chested in line for inoculations, finally marching in formation making their way to the airport, naive boys still. Even if they'd seen combat before, he imagined it was nothing to compare to Dien Bien Phu.

All the young soldiers flown in from Dien Bien Phu were weakened long before receiving their wounds, emaciated from months of living under siege. They'd told him he had to be at Dien Bien Phu to really imagine it, but they were wrong. He had seen pictures of the victims of the holocaust recovering in France.

The night nurse had been right about the boy's appearance. His skin had pinked. His eyes opened in response to hearing his name. That was the extent for the hope. Terror lodged deep in the hollowed sockets of the eyes. Deepening despair. War had turned the boy's hair grey. Or was that a trick of the lighting, the shades? He placed his hand on the boy's forehead. No fever. Not yet anyway. Doctor Astray looked away. Bedpan, night stand, on it a letter. He glanced to see if the boy was watching him. He recognized the handwriting as that of the new night nurse. He fumbled awkwardly with the pages as he read the dictated words. The boy understood his condition. It was all there underneath the more obvious meaning of the words he'd written home. Telling them gently, the hopelessness not apparent until the letter concluded. Nothing he said, just the otherworldly nature of the words. A child trapped in a deadly game, he innocently explained it was too late. Doctor Astray dropped the letter back on the table. The boy didn't respond when he spoke his name again. Now the doctor walked to the medicine cabinet, where he quickly found the medicine. He carefully poured the dark liquid into a tablespoon, returning the bottle with the skull and bones to its inconspicuous corner in the cabinet. When the liquid touched the young soldier's parched lips, he immediately swallowed.

Doctor Astray concealed the spoon and sat back and waited for his young nurse to return with coffee. He stared across at the doorway to his office where for years she stood each morning, coffee cup in hand, a friendly word to greet him, almost translucent with the golden morning sun to her back. What grew between them went unsaid. Perhaps it existed only for him. Never mind; what mattered was the sense of existence only their relationship gave him. Whenever she confided in him, he wanted to turn and tell her how he felt, but the fear that he would loose her held him back. Instead he had always nodded as if he listened to what she said. She had told him when her lover back in France had found someone else after three years of separation. During those years she had always had an excuse not to return to see him even on her annual leave. And did her lover ever know of the young soldier in the coma? Of course not. How do you tell someone you are already living with them through another and that you have created their substitute from the chaos of your heart? The young soldier in the terminal care ward remained the doctor's secret with her, and he kept that secret alive despite his promise never to allow a patient to suffer beyond the time of hope.

He watched the soldier resting next to him, his breathing slowing and deepening. The inescapable left him with a feeling of desperation.

The young nurse extended her hand with the coffee.

"We should visit with your young soldier next," Doctor Astray said, gently touching her arm.

"I'd like that," she said, glancing at the soldier who was now smiling in his sleep. "Your patient seems better."

"Yes," said Doctor Astray. "I think he will be." He rose from the chair and held the steaming coffee away from himself as he walked to the terminal care ward.

The young nurse stepped ahead of him when they reached the room. She immediately removed the leather straps that held her soldier in bed and leaned him forward into her arms. His head flopped side to side until she cupped her hand around the back of the shaved head like she might steady a newborn. Doctor Astray placed his stethoscope against ribs ready to pierce the soldier's parchment skin. The heat beat strong and steady as it reflected through the outside window. He inspected the scar stretched tight over a distended stomach bloated with its own poisons. Then he closed the hospital robe. The examination complete, he leaned back and watched his young nurse caress the soldier's expressionless face. He drew a deep breath.

"He's in an unalterable coma." Doctor Astray hesitated, and continued. "I think we should let him go now."

"You can't just let him die." His nurse drew rigid, immobilized with panic. "Not while there's still hope."

"There never was hope," Doctor Astray said.

"What about the cases who come out of a coma after years and years. You can't ignore them. They're documented in all the medical journals."

"Those are statistical anomalies discovered by Christian clergy to justify their doctrines toward life."

"He's all I have left," she pleaded.

"I know," said Doctor Astray, his voice a whisper. "I can't help it. It's not my fault."

"But if you kill him it will be."

"I won't do that," he conceded. So she loved a ghost.

Maybe that was what she needed, the safest thing with only commitment and no response. It fit being a nurse and always giving but with no real relationship to be faced. Maybe that was what was wrong with him too, why he practiced medicine. Just that now it didn't feel right. Watching her hold the dying soldier made him want to live in ways he'd never experienced or even considered possible. A combination of lusts seeded the emotions he felt watching her in the sun that cast its radiance across her, outlined with her soldier deep in her arms. He felt the glow of sun reach his face, and with the heat, wave on wave of an inexplicable joy rippled through him.

CHAPTER 59

Dien Bien Phu, March 29, 1954
Lao
Comrades

The platoon was squeezed together within a vast army that filled the entire clearing beneath the canopy. A rumor spread that General Giap was about to address the troops. A soldier shouted for silence, and those around him repeated the command.

"Bo doi of the Iron Division, today you will deliver a great victory for our cause," a political officer shouted, then paused as if waiting to hear himself confirmed. "Today you must take the hill the French call Dominique. The future of our nation is yours to make."

"Fine for him to say," the old veteran muttered loud enough for everyone in the platoon to hear.

"Will we live to see that future?" the young soldier asked ignoring the old veteran.

"We are the future," said Lao. Any doubts he might have had vanished. The Viet Minh numbers were so great that no French force could resist them for long. In such numbers he knew he was inconsequential, yet he felt a surge in pride.

"Your future dies here," the old veteran said.

A bugle sounded.

"Forward...forward." In a messianic trance the political officer pointed across the valley towards Dominique. Lao glanced at those surrounding him, waiting for something to happen. Then somewhere near them the forward movement of the mass began with the sound of shuffling feet. Dust quickly engulfed the platoon to their knees like it was a dreary fog. Ahead of them soldiers cascaded down the hill, soldiers collided, fell, bounced over each other, back on their feet, catapulted by their destiny or some force beyond their power. As the forward motion of the troops created room, Lao's platoon advanced in the rear of the melee.

"We're going to miss it all," the young soldier said.

"We got to stay back with the platoon," Lao said.

"You boys don't worry; there will be enough killing to satisfy every one of you." The old veteran clenched his teeth and checked the clips of ammunition in his rifle and on his belt as he marched.

At the foot of the hill the troops dispersed into the open, led forward by their officers. Enemy artillery began to randomly explode in their midst. Still the mass surged forward with the first troops quickly entering the slit trenches ahead, trenches no wider then a man but deep enough for that man to remain erect without exposing himself to rifle fire.

Three times in a month Lao's platoon had been brought forward but never this far. Still waiting in the open, he crouched with his companions as if such a precaution protected them from the random killing of the enemy artillery. Hunched like livestock in a rainstorm, they waited their turn to advance into the trenches.

Lao cursed the days he'd wished to test his courage in combat. He cursed the propaganda that replaced his instincts. He renewed his pledge, made when the Viet Minh first forced him to join the army, to escape and return to the streets of Ha Noi. Why had he allowed Colonel Hahn's lectures to influence him to volunteer for a line unit?

A shell fell on a platoon to the left. The screams were

quickly drowned out by more explosions. The young soldier tried to crawl beneath the old veteran who remained on his knees, leaning forward on his rifle, watching the distant French perimeter.

"Get up," the old veteran shouted, striking at the youth.

The enemy artillery struck another platoon to the right as if bracketing for a final round directly on Lao and his comrades. Earth, metal, fragments of equipment and flesh, fell among the men of the platoon. A series of soldiers' oaths burst from Lao's mouth as if such curses could create a zone of safety.

"For a young kid you got a salty tongue," the old veteran laughed. "You boys wanted a taste of this. Now it's not to your liking?"

"They can't leave us out here," Lao said.

"That so," the old veteran replied. "If we see any generals out here, I'll tell them what you said."

"They must have planned this attack for after dark," Lao said. "Only it's not dark, it's just late in the day."

"Night, day, day time, you'll see ... it's all the same on the battlefield." The old veteran remained motionless like a mantis. The artillery explosions drifted further away, annihilating several platoons as it shifted. The order to advance was finally issued. Lao felt out of place as if in a field of dead contortionists. Clouds darkened the sky prematurely. Lao almost prayed for rain, thinking it would dampen the spirit for fighting. He clung to the slightest hope that a terrible battle wasn't at hand, for he understood who paid the price for such delights of the generals. Never before had he felt that his life held so little value.

A flare exploded in the sky, adding little light, but changing the hue of all that Lao surveyed.

As he marched next to Lao the old veteran stood erect with only a slight tilt forward as if leaning into a volley of bullets. "You think this is terrible? There are places on this earth where the forces of destiny continually collide with each other in conflagration. This is one of them. When you live near those places, you can't escape. That's just the way it is."

"I only want to get to the trench," Lao said anxious to avoid conversation. Now he was running with the others. He flinched at every pop of the artillery. Only a short distance to go yet his dread continued to build.

As Lao stumbled forward into the narrow passage all he perceived was the back of the soldier in front. He experienced no sense of time or distance. Dark shadows spilled into the trench. Illumination rounds from enemy artillery burst in starlight clusters. Lao collapsed in the mud until the advance resumed.

Lao's platoon emerged from the trench into a tangle of wire and craters. The first waves of soldiers had thrown reed mats over what remained of the enemy fences. Mines had exploded under the mats when previous platoons dashed across them. The dead lay amid the destruction produced by artillery and machine guns. The mangled bodies provided a bridge over no man's land. Clusters of flares exploded and drifted from the sky, creating a continual alternation of light and darkness. Lao paused in disbelief. Those behind him pressed him forward.

"Hold on, boy, keep your senses about you," the old veteran said as Lao stumbled among corpses. In the general pandemonium Lao welcomed the familiar voice. Friendly artillery from the hills exploded directly in front of them. They advanced behind its shield.

"Forward ... forward." Lao heard shouted in French somewhere in front of him. The Frenchmen quickly intermingled with Lao's platoon, striking into them with their bayonets.

Lao was screaming without any sound coming from his lips. Chaos stretched across the enemy compound. He felt as if a rubber band had snapped, throwing him forward, free of his body, free of the battle sounds that terrified him. As if he watched from outside, he witnessed the young soldier's arm torn away. Again something jarred him. His ears were ringing with nothing in focus, ghostly shapes floating around him. For an instant he discerned Khong rising in the midst of the smoky battlefield. Then everything disappeared.

CHAPTER 60

Dien Bien Phu, May 7, 1954
The Pilot
Alone in glory

The French pilot flew alone. The rest of the squadron required maintenance. He climbed higher and higher through the clouds into blue sky where only the sun reached him, first warming his back, then against his cheek, and then directly into his face causing him to squint as he approached Dien Bien Phu. For an instant he thought, how can colorless space be so damn beautiful, but then he caught himself. The Sorbonne-trained pilot his comrades called a pretty boy with his jet black hair, his long thin fingers meant for a piano keyboard now wrapped tightly about the stick that gave him altitude, wanted to throw open the Hellcat's cockpit, let the air flow through that jet black hair, and raise himself like Icarus into the sun. Instead, with one eye on the fuel gauge, he circled and waited for a break in the clouds.

Flying from an aircraft carrier in the Gulf of Tonkin stretched the limits of his fuel; he had only minutes to complete the mission. Static filled his ears. The radio didn't work, seldom did. He found his way alone, flying low along the now familiar valleys within range of small arms, relying on his sudden approach and departure to protect him. In the cockpit he smelled fuel. He checked the wings. Nothing was wrong. He tightened the gyre.

Then like everything in his life, nature obliged him, lifting the clouds in sudden gusts of wind. The clouds wisped through the valley like frightened ghosts exposing the horror of what they had covered from his observation. Even from such height the carnage was apparent, the once orderly French fortifications cratered, the peaceful village obliterated. The earliest sun still failed to penetrate the dark trenches and bunkers of the enemy as artillery began its random search for victims.

The pilot searched the ridge lines for the camouflaged positions he knew were hidden in the hills. Then he peered down into the valley. Something was different. He felt the thrill of a hunter finding his prey, enemy movement in freshly dug trenches just outside the French positions. As he watched, Viet Minh soldiers rose together, leaving the trenches and the rats and lice behind, their cheers carrying them into no man's land. The pilot studied them. From his great height, their formation looked like a sidewinder snake crossing open ground on the African desert. He would destroy them without guilt for they were just toy soldiers on a child's bedroom floor back in France. He waited for them to reach the point where they couldn't return to the safety of the trenches. Descending through the last lingering clouds, his speed increasing, he fired the machineguns set on both wings beyond the propeller. Tracers waving up and down along the line of wavering men cut the line into pieces.

When close enough to see individual helmets on the advancing men, he pulled back on the stick and the plane lurched upward. He released the bombs and they twisted and tumbled toward the diminishing earth behind him. The plane screamed toward the open sky. Only when he reached a height where small arms fire couldn't hit the plane did he turn in the cockpit to look back. The bombs splashed like eggs, some of their yolks rising toward him. Then came the thudding sounds he always heard seconds after the explosions.

"... didn't stop them." The radio crackled with life. He realized he hadn't been listening. "Say again," he responded.

"They haven't stopped. Come back again." The radio voice was too high pitched, too filled with fear.

"Relax, boy. I'll get them," he answered calmly, his voice concealing his disdain. The Viet Minh troops were attacking at the center of the camp again as if to spite him. There were more explosions, now close to him but below. Anti-aircraft fire flashed from the hills. Nothing reached him. Nothing could. He soared without sound, defying them with a graceful sweep around the valley, dropping in altitude as he prepared to dive like a falcon on the kill. His hand tightened on the machinegun trigger. He aimed the Hellcat at the broken line of troops that still tried to cross the French defense berm, pushed on the stick to aim and shift into the heaviest concentration of enemy troops. The plane failed to respond, didn't change altitude. He glanced from the target to inspect the fuselage and wings.

A chip in the wing. Nothing serious. It must have been there before. That smell of gas. He should have paid more attention to it. He pulled back on the stick. Nothing responded. He felt the shudder, terrible vibrations. Still he held the plane in line long enough to release the two remaining bombs. A sharp slapping sound. Black smoke belched from an engine. He felt the increased gravity as the plane nosed down against his pull. He slid the cockpit canopy backwards to leap free. The wind tore him safely away from the plunging plane. The rip cord released. He snapped erect, floating free, hearing the rush of air, and the occasional snap of small arms fire aimed at him. Below him Viet Minh forces continued to attack one of the remaining redoubts. Artillery shells fired from indiscernible positions exploded in random puffs of smoke. He drifted aimlessly over the attacking troops, unobserved by them. The immediate grip of fear left him. Now sound began to reach him. The wind carried him toward another redoubt, this one not under attack for the moment. His rate of descent seemed to increase. He focused on the tangle of wire coming up toward him, trying to shift his feet to avoid it. Too late. It caught him throwing him forward onto his face in red mud. He pulled at the harness to release the parachute as it continued billowing in the wind, now a target ripped by gun fire from a distant sniper. He cut the harness free and the parachute continued across the open terrain, rippling like paper in the breeze. The wire tore through his fatigues. He drew his pistol.

"Quickly, quickly," a grinning French face confronted him, rising out of the mud. "You're in no man's land."

The French paratrooper signaled for the pilot to follow. The pilot attempted to stand and at the same time crouch. He fell back into the wire. At first he thought the wire held him. A sharp pain radiated up his left leg. He realized his leg was either sprained or broken.

"Grab hold of me," the paratrooper said.

"You're covered in mud," the pilot protested.

The paratrooper let out a loud guffaw. "And look at you. Not exactly a tar baby, but close."

The two men laughed. Bullets hit near them spitting up mud.

"They're getting our range," the paratrooper said, hurrying to carry the pilot along as if he was weightless. Sure-footed, careful not to step on mines, touch a trip flare. They reached another fence entanglement. The paratrooper slid on his back to get beneath strands of wire, then pulled the pilot through by his collar, then carried him again. He slipped and struggled in the slop of earth that reached above his calves that weighted him, dried into chaps.

"I can walk now," the pilot volunteered.

"You'll only slow us down."

A gully just inside the wire was completely filled with bodies. The maggots and the stench indicated the soldiers had been killed days before. Beside the trench a pit with severed limbs and other medical waste covered with lime.

"We're almost there," the paratrooper said, dropping down into one of the communication trenches.

The wounded filled the connecting trenches, funneled

toward an opening at the hospital bunker. The flies that covered them brought no response, their remaining strength directed at the effort to survive. Coolies stacked bodies on the roof of the bunker. The paratrooper pushed through the column of wounded toward the front of the line. The mud beneath his feet yielded the corpses of those who had died waiting their turn at the operating table.

"Where do you think you're going?" a guard at the entry to the bunker demanded.

"This man's a pilot, an officer," the paratrooper said, as if that fact brought French victory closer.

The guard hesitated, and then stepped back.

Inside the light of lanterns filtered through stagnant air illuminating the ghostly presence of the wounded on stretches everywhere. Coolies lifted them one by one to operating tables in the center of a huddle. Medical personnel hunched over those, methodically cutting away uniforms and boots, washing away the mud from wounds. In their midst a French doctor directed the flow of patients, evaluating each, determining which to treat and those to quietly place against the wall to die. Shirtless, his back and chest covered with black hair, his head shaved clean. He towered over the Vietnamese and stood a head above the French nurse who followed him as he crossed the room to another area and another operating table where he went immediately to work.

"That is Major Grauwin," the paratrooper said, following the pilot's glance. "You insist on seeing him and no one else. He is the best."

"Thank you," the pilot said, realizing the paratrooper meant to leave him. A sudden friend lost. No real need to thank him.

The doctor was like a general at his work, doing what was necessary without any show of emotion. His hands, bearlike claws, worked a surgeon's saw across a soldier's mangled leg. The man was held down by several medics, gagged so that his screams were muffled. Blood oozed and an artery squirted into the doctor's face. The nurse wiped the blood and perspiration away from his eyes with a cloth. He never broke off the steady sawing. Then he stretched blood-pinked skin over the stump and sutured it, dropped the severed leg into a bucket beside the table. Though he never spoke, the pilot imagined the word "next" on his lips as he stepped back.

The nurse carried a bowl of fresh water bubbling with surgical soap, placed it on the table as the coolies slid the man without a leg back on a stretcher. The doctor cupped his hands, rotating them together in the bowl and shook them dry. Another soldier was already being prepared, his arm drawn out for an intravenous. His chest was wrapped with a poncho. "All right, remove it," the doctor ordered.

The pilot turned away. He left the bunker, limping through the trenches toward the line of soldiers who waited at the perimeter for the next assault. "What has brought us to this hell?" he asked. No one answered.

CHAPTER 61

Dien Bien Phu, May 7, 1954
Phan
Reporting on reality

Viet Minh soldiers scurried into the trenches, heads down, shoulders hunched, quick as feral cats, and Phan was swept along. Shoulder to shoulder the soldiers leaned against the walls, their rifles between them, bayonets fixed, helmets and backs covered with fresh vegetation. Phan watched the first battalion to be sent disappear over the top. Only a sense of their ghostly presence remained hovering in the air. The din of fighting muffled the sound of coolies frantically shoveling to repair where trenches collapsed.

When the coolies retreated from the trenches, Phan knew that the time for the next wave of the attack was near. The obstinacy of French generals created this inevitability. He cursed those enemy generals who chose a code of honor and their pride over an expeditious surrender.

Standing behind the soldiers in the trench and looking down the line, Phan couldn't see a single face. Just as well, he thought, noticing his stomach cramping, his heart pounding wildly against his chest. Nothing sharpened the senses like the smell of cordite. Why had he asked to follow in the attack? He wanted to collapse into the mud and disappear into the earth until it was over, never again to hold a pen in his sweaty palms and write how brave men killed each other.

His rubber sandals kept sinking deeper into the mud until he continually shifted his weight back and forth and lifted out his heels. He was thinking about the mud when the whispered order came down the line. The soldiers elbowed up over the berm and silently disappeared into the pocked landscape, each now in his own world of fear. Or were some men different, truly brave, and not just putting on the expected bravado?

Phan vomited the poison from his fear into the ditch. He crawled from the trench to follow the battalion, and scrambled to hide in the first deep artillery hole he reached. The fear drained his strength and left him without the use of his legs. He looked down on those legs in horror. They were still there. He pressed his hands against them, massaged them, pleading with them to move him forward.

In front of him French voices quarreled, too distant to be understood. Likely they questioned their eyes, tricked to believe the jungle crept toward them. A sliver of moonlight broke through the clouds, giving the land an eerie cast. The French bunkers stood out against the horizon, close enough for Phan to see their bristling radio antennas. He rolled onto his back, following where he saw other men crawling, his feet pushing him under barbed wire strung in fences, constantly afraid he'd hit those invisible wires that triggered warning flares. At that moment staring up at the sky made him think about the way he rested on his back next to Thi and they never said anything, though he always felt her warmth and felt very alive. Looking up into the sky. Into the stars. Just the two. As if together they touched something out there.

A flare popped. Damn, he cursed, knowing the flare exposed them all, and ended what he felt, perhaps forever. The French shouted. The Viet Minh ahead of him rose to their feet, desperately cutting at the wires. A single rifle fired green tracers into the bunkers ahead of them. The tracers ricocheted away. Other soldiers fired their rifles, most wildly into the air. Tracers arched overhead like shooting stars reversed and torn from the heavens. Still no return fire from the French. Were they preserving ammunition? Those around him ran, an ocean of men surging forward across imaginary beaches. Running to reach the bunkers before the enemy responded, as if it was possible to survive. They ran with their desperate hope driving them like a wind at their backs. As Phan sprinted his lungs felt like exploding bellows. His head throbbed thoughtlessly, the fear driving him to keep within the soldiers' ranks, as an animal kept to the pack as if the formation protected it.

He never saw the plane dive from the sky or the men near him who fell with gaping bloody wounds. The concussion had thrown him to the ground. All moved slowly around him. Sounds faded and disappeared. His legs failed him though he saw no blood, felt no pain. The universe opened, and he walked into its timelessness. Afterward he said he must have fainted, but at the time nothing disappeared from his vision. To the contrary, he had seen everything very clearly: cold and crisp and sharp, without his senses interfering. A strange well-being had overcome his other emotions. He felt as if he was laughing until everything came rushing back toward him. Then he stood and fell again.

The Viet Minh artillery barrage that cleared a path through the mine fields had unearthed a cemetery inside the last perimeter of the French defense, raising the dead from their shallow graves to meet the advance. A body reclined beside Phan, his clothing rotted away, a rancid hand reaching out, fingers open as if grasping the sky. Hair still clung to his skull like a cheap wig, otherwise only bone remained as a face without expression, crushed and bleached in red from the soil in which it rested.

The falling moon turned red as the sun rose on the horizon, burning away the clouds. Viet artillery shells screamed overhead and exploded on the nearby bunkers. Stalin's organs fired rockets in volleys from stacks of tubes on the back of trucks in the distant mountains.

"Tien lien, tien lien," a trumpet sounded. "Forward

now" the shout, and those Viet troops still alive rose in a human wave, screaming over the chatter of a solitary machine-
gun cutting through their ranks. The forward elements threw
themselves onto the remaining concertina wire that stretched
like broken tumbleweed around the French bunkers. Those
that followed ran across their comrades' backs and toward
the compound firing blindly into the flame and smoke remnant from the artillery barrages. Legionnaires' fixed bayonets
appeared in the smog between the bunkers and in the trenches that connected them.

Then, as if by mutual consent, the fighting ceased.
The surviving Frenchmen surrendered their weapons without raising their hands. After months under siege, they were
skeletons. Their captors, little more than children's size in
comparison, marched them away. Three Viet Minh soldiers
climbed to the top of the command bunker and raised the Viet
flag. A few surviving Viet soldiers nearby cheered, but the
wailing of the wounded soon drowned them out.

That was how the battle for Dien Bien Phu ended. At
least that was how Phan would remember it, over and over
again, carrying it with him as a dream, telling it, writing it for
others, but never totally recapturing the horror and the joy in
it.

CHAPTER 62

Dien Bien Phu, May 7, 1954
Phan
Impressions

The sun remained after the fighting ended. The sky tarpaulin over the battlefield turned cobalt blue. Phan crawled on top of a bunker overlooking the valley and took out a notebook and pencil to write.

May 7, 1954

Impressions of the aftermath:

The barbed wire that crossed and re-crossed the open fields, once rigidly strung and staked, has now been severed. Bangalore torpedoes and the weight of our fallen comrades destroyed it. The dead remain draped in the wire, their bodies fragmented, spread like red confetti, lifeless mimes. Quiet replaces the tumult. And across the quiet the wounded rise as phantom wolves and their wailing shatters the stillness of the valley.

A tank smolders in the distance. A nearby French defensive position with its bunker walls now collapsed still burns like a Roman candle. A blackened skull, its skin removed by flame, is lifted from the fire on the bayonet of a passing soldier; whether he means to lay it to rest or as a memento is not clear.

Before the last attack the French had stacked their dead in rubber bags for transit. A mortar shell ruptured several bags. The corpses are exposed. We watch them as they watch us with indifference, as if there is nothing left to question.

By standing on the headquarters bunker, the runway can be plainly seen, burned out aircraft scattered along its length. The river meandering through the valley is motionless, its flow halted by a bottleneck of corpses that create a lake. The distant mountain from where our artillery fired appears undisturbed in its green richness.

In the French trenches nearest the river the bodies are bloated and float in deep water because they failed to make provision for the rain. Higher up the hill corpses stand mired to their waists in mud, their torsos cast into the slope like clay figures. Already maggots eat away their features. Near the summit a single dead soldier accents the approach like a ship's bowsprit carefully set in place. He is perched atop a metal fencepost which he meant to climb across. His intestines, left behind him in a trail when he kept running, are interwoven in the wire. A look of madness is frozen on his face.

The bunkers collapsed under repeated battering by the heavy artillery the French generals glibly predicted could never reach Dien Bien Phu. The collapsed bunkers leave craters, foreboding what lies underneath.

Just in front of this position, enough rations and ammunition in no man's land for several battalions, fallen among mines where it can't be safely retrieved. Everywhere discarded weapons; rifles, Tommy guns, pistols and grenades, ammunition scattered, artillery shells unexploded, casings shattered among unidentified debris.

The French hospital bunker remains intact, its roof covered with the bodies of those who could not be saved by the doctors. A lime pit at the entrance is filled with arms and legs. Blood blackens the decomposing flesh, feeding armies of flies and maggots, a scene that tests every survivor's spirit.

Wounded Frenchmen on their way to the operating

rooms lie along the walls in the covered trenches. Some soldiers died where they waited. French medics with lanterns and stretchers pick their way through the trenches, seeking those who might still be saved. They are ordered out by Viet Minh soldiers, forced to join prisoners being grouped and marched away. Still there has been no formal surrender, no white flags. The French, who simply stopped fighting, laid down their personal weapons or destroyed them, spiked the remaining artillery and waited. There is no resistance, little said.

There is a universal pause as when a marathon race has finished, a contemplation and a re-ordering of each soldier's mental state to accommodate the new realities, absorb what has passed. The soldiers' stares lack focus. Shock has eviscerated their nervous systems. Commands go unheard. A soldier is weeping, not a coward's crying, but the sobs of a man unable to believe he has survived.

I've written these words contemporaneously. Yet words fail to convey this terrible thing. Was it necessary? Couldn't we have out-waited them in a prolonged siege? Or was this loss of life really about the negotiations beginning in Geneva, and a political statement? Is this the victory we wanted and needed to end the war?

Will I ever find the words to preserve these terrible moments and give them meaning? Can my words serve as a warning?

Phan chewed the nub of the pencil. A Viet Minh political commissar swaggered towards the bunker. His uniform was clean. Considering the circumstances it was impeccable. Rows of colorfully interwoven medals above his pocket flashed in the sunlight. He held himself erect, motionless, his eyes demanding answers. The men standing behind him looked down at their feet.

"May I help you sir?" Phan said, annoyed at the intrusion on his writing.

"You can't loiter here soldier. Get back to your duty," the commissar said.

"This is my duty." Phan paused, resting his pencil in

the fold of his notebook. "I'm a reporter."

"Let me see your orders," the commissar said.

"I have no written orders, sir." Phan said. "Colonel Hahn sent me."

"Let me see what you've written." The commissar snatched the notebook. When he finished reading, he stuffed the notebook into his fatigues.

"What are you doing, sir?"

"This is sedition," the commissar muttered, patting his uniform where the notebook securely rested, a bulge beneath his ribbons.

"There is no sedition in the truth," Phan said.

"We'll see. For now you stay with me. I can use another soldier as a guard."

"But I'm a reporter."

"It doesn't matter. Everyone is needed." The commissar stood frozen in place like Giap himself when he reviewed the troops. He surveyed all that lay before him. Phan remained at his side, hesitant to speak further.

Nearby French prisoners were huddling together. Several of the guards squatted beside a stack of artillery-fragmented wood they had gathered and were trying to ignite. The smoke encapsulated them. They swatted at it as if it were a hive of bees. Others stirred a putrid-looking gruel as they waited patiently for the fire to spark.

A young captain from the Vietnamese General Staff hurried past and entered the French command bunker with a platoon of men. He emerged within moments walking with a tall Frenchman, pale and grave, his uniform fresh, a rainbow of ribbons across his chest. General de Castries, soldiers whispered. Behind him his staff, faces of unyielding stone, unchanging in their lassitude as they disappeared into the new formations of prisoners.

To assert his authority over those who crossed no man's land long before him, the commissar shouted for the troops to stop and listen. The soldiers paused and listened sullenly as the commissar sprayed venomous propaganda against the captives. This man who would lead arrived too late. He ordered the prisoners divided, separating the officers and leaving the wounded alongside the developing column and reluctantly they complied.

The assemblage of enemy soldiers resembled a multicultural jamboree, the pasty skinned Frenchmen intermingled with besotted chocolate Africans and yellowed Asiatics. Many wore uniforms tattered to rags as if they had stood in a typhoon. Those from artillery units wore khaki shorts. Their gaunt bodies revealed every rib and bone. Their stone eyes displayed their illimitable exhaustion. The commissar ordered them all further separated by race and nationality, and then he turned his attention to Phan.

"You stay and keep guard over these. We'll deal with your treason later" The commissar waved the notebook in the direction of the French prisoners splayed beyond his feet, and he bent down, swept a rifle from the dirt, and thrust it into Phan's arms. The commissar worked his way along the vaguely formed column of prisoners as if he were a merchant overseeing the rearranging of shelved goods, here and there stopping to give an order.

After several hours the prisoners stirred like animals waking from a nightmare's slumber, the first of them turning and tossing among the others, their eyes searching without direction or ascertainable purpose, gesturing to the guards for water and food. A young officer had been left in charge by the commissar. He appeared disconcerted, speaking in stumbling French to stem a steadily growing restlessness among the prisoners. He offered his canteen. Awkwardly and at first reluctantly, French soldiers seized it and swallowed. Watching as he stood guard, Phan realized the young officer empathized with the pain those men felt in their defeat. And he understood that what they had in common was more: In a way it was desperation they were all fighting. They were trapped in a world in which there was little compensation for honor. Not for lack of courage had they fallen. A common purpose was prescribed to them by those whose judgment they had trusted more than their own, and it had led to their ruin.

"What are you doing?" the commissar demanded, returned from his walk down the column.

"We have no rations for these men," the young officer said. "Still they must be given water."

"Let them retrieve their own food and water."

"Retrieve their own from where, sir?"

"Those crates with the parachutes still attached." He pointed.

"That's no man's land, sir. The place is mined."

"So we'll use the prisoners."

The commissar sorted through the French prisoners, selecting those few still capable of resistance. "Send them, lieutenant," he said, pointing to those he selected.

By the time they left, the sun had disappeared and was replaced by a crescent orange moon. In the jaundice light the French soldiers edged into the minefield, their Vietnamese guards trailing far behind. Phan watched them from atop the bunker. They walked on bodies where they could and where they couldn't they got on their knees and probed with pocket knives, groping in the dim light. They continued deeper into no man's land. Their outlines moved across the stark horizon, blackening and without wind, without sound or smell or signal to the senses. What was happening was left to imagination. Phan felt a shiver run through him, and a strange sense of relief for himself, as he recalled the previous night. As the fate of the men play out before him, he idly bit at his fingernails.

An explosion, another. The smell of cordite sprayed against Phan's face. At that instant the thought of the commissar's heartlessness flashed through Phan's mind. This is all too much, he thought, to so suddenly condemn these men. Yet it removed them from the sufferings that lay ahead for the prisoners of Dien Bien Phu. That must have been the consensus for there was no outcry over this needless renting of life. Or was it just indifference born from exhaustion? There was no rush to help or even a crowd of the curious. Almost as if the blast ratified those who survived and cleared an obstruction to giving them life.

At that moment Phan realized his indifference, as a

slide into depression started. Giving up was what the political officers called it, as if something was wrong with men
who felt hopeless in war. As if in some way not fit for society
among other men.

A French soldier started singing the French Interna-
tionale. His tin voice haunted the valley, and trailed off into
the silence.

In the nighttime fighting continued on Isabelle, a
strong point more than two miles to the south. The sounds
carried up the valley, faint and limited to small arms. Around
midnight a messenger brought word to the commissar that
an attempted breakout by the French had failed, and Isabelle
had been taken.

In the morning, the Viet Minh officers from along the
column showed great deference as they reported to the commissar, apparently a man of great importance. Phan overheard him say they must control over seven thousand French
prisoners, perhaps as many as ten thousand ... French, Algerians, Moroccans, Vietnamese, Germans, Italians, Spanish,
and Eastern Europeans ... and there was a five-hundred-mile
trek ahead of them. Several officers pleaded that the prisoners were all weakened from the two-month siege, and many
wounded too severely to walk. The commissar coldly replied
the march was to begin as soon as they were grouped as he
had previously ordered. He directed the interrogation of all
the French officers.

Many of the seriously wounded had died in the night.
The commissar ordered details from the prisoners to bury
them and others to continue recovering the dead from the
battlefield. Cemeteries were created for the French and the
Viet Minh on separate hills. The commissar gave orders with
cold efficiency. At every opportunity he berated the Frenchmen for their arrogant imperialist affectations. He singled out
the Algerians for special propaganda to plant the seeds for
future rebellion. Special scorn was directed to a small con-
tingent identified as air force pilots. The commissar required
the pilots to dig up the mass grave of villagers killed by misdirected air strikes and re-bury them individually in marked

graves next to their ancestors. Prisoners were selected and paraded past a Russian camera crew. The last moments of the battle were restaged and the North Africans used as extras when the French paratroopers refused.

—⚶—

After several days a French doctor named Huard arrived by helicopter to negotiate safe release and passage for the wounded. Although the commissar was informed of the negotiations he did not participate in them, clearly frustrated and eager to begin the march, yet still restrained by orders from the general staff. The food supply diminished each day.

The Viet Minh generals demanded a guarantee from the French that Highway 41 not be bombed so their own wounded could move freely back to bases in the north. The French at first refused, afraid of an enemy re-deployment against their weakened forces. Doctor Huard's helicopter was allowed to carry a few wounded back to Ha Noi, taking word of the horrors faced by those left at Dien Bien Phu. The French military relented in their position. The work of re-opening the runway began. The commissar received orders to begin marching the prisoner groups north, the nearly eight thousand men, intermingled with the Viet Minh infantry and artillery in case the French attacked with fighter planes.

In the middle of ordering a group of paratroops to their feet, the commissar suddenly asked, "Do you think this will end the war?"

"Seems likely," Phan replied all the time watching those paratroopers nearest him, checking them for weapons or any sign of trouble as they grudgingly began to walk.

"You see the brilliance in our general's plan?" The commissar had taken out the old notebook and tapped it against one knee as he raised his boot atop a discarded ammunition crate.

"I see it now," Phan said.

"You must never question your superiors, even when you don't understand their reasons."

"Like they're gods," Phan said.

"Yes, like gods." The commissar grinned broadly. "We communists must have our gods."

A Soviet truck plunged down the hill in front of them, sliding sideways in the mud, stopping when its wheels struck a dead mule in a rutted track. Its cargo of French officers, with their hands bound behind them, toppled off their feet.

"What have our godly generals to say about food?" Phan said, emboldened by the commissar's tone.

"There is enough rice." The commissar was no longer smiling.

Phan studied the commissar's eyes. "Not for French appetites."

"They must learn to eat like Vietnamese. We've survived."

"They're not Vietnamese, and their condition is already weakened by the fighting."

"Some of them will survive," the commissar said, his eyes now unblinking.

Phan stepped back. An entire grouping of the French paratroopers passed them. There were many wounded among them, and their companions supported them. The few walking freely stopped to drag the dead mule off the roadway, and pushed the truck until it started to climb slowly toward the hill across the valley ahead of them. Several officers in the back of the truck regained their feet and shouted encouragement to their men. After giving orders on how the rest of the prisoners were to follow, the commissar started after the paratroopers with a platoon of guards. Phan walked beside him. It started to rain, which made the mud like grease. They all fell repeatedly, laughing at first but then becoming grim. They walked past Viet Minh trenches dug near the French lines and into an area where a division of Viet Minh infantry was camped. These were the lucky ones, Phan thought, brought up to the trenches but never sent into the fighting. Certainly they were different from the retreating column. They waved and cheered from their positions sprawled along the hillside, as if the prisoners were paraded in review for their amusement.

After the valley there were no more troops to cheer them and the trails grew more treacherous because of the rain. Just the effort to continue overwhelmed many of the paratroopers. As they lagged, they intermingled with the guards and units of Viet Minh infantry, themselves exhausted from the battle to overrun the strongholds at Dien Bien Phu.

At the rise of the hill where the trail entered the jungle, a paratrooper was collapsed in the bushes. The commissar went over to him and kicked at his back. The man turned slowly sideways toward the commissar.

"You can't do that," the man said in a thickly accented French.

"What did that prisoner say?" the commissar demanded.

"He said you hurt him," Phan said.

"He can't stay there. He must continue marching." The commissar drew his pistol and waved it.

"What is the matter with him?" said the paratrooper. He was covered with mud so that Phan could not see how severely he was wounded but noticed the sling around an arm.

"He is a devoted communist," Phan said.

"I, too, am a communist," said the paratrooper. Phan did not respond. "In my native Yugoslavia I am a party member. The legion is only out of economic necessity."

"I am not a communist," said Phan.

"There you have it."

"What did he say?" said the commissar.

"He understands. Just give him a minute."

"A minute is all he gets."

"You intend to shoot him?"

"If it is necessary."

"And just because he doesn't walk?"

"We can't allow a breakdown of our discipline."

"I don't think that's what he means to do."

"Meant or not, that's the effect."

Phan turned to the paratrooper and said in French, "He's trigger happy. He isn't a frontline soldier like you. You must try to walk or he means to shoot you."

"Bugger him," the paratrooper said, but at once grasped branches and pulled himself onto the road.

"There, you see," said the commissar, replacing his pistol.

"Yes, I see," said Phan.

"You must watch them more carefully in the jungle," the commissar said conspiratorially.

"You think these men are capable of escaping?" Phan said mocking the seriousness of the commissar.

"Just be careful about them," the commissar replied.

The column crept forward. The jungle smelled fresh after the putrid battlefield. The rain continued, washing through the canopy but its force was broken. They continued past coolies resting in shelters alongside the trail, waiting for instructions on where to redirect the supplies they carried. After months of walking with their heavy burdens, they seemed reluctant to believe that the fighting for Dien Bien Phu was finished. Desperate in appearance, these nomadic creatures in loin rags, left with no protection and little modesty, were overseen by Viet Minh officers who withheld the slightest recognition of their common humanity.

At dusk all the staggering soldiers halted collectively. They fell together where they stood, guards and prisoners inert and intermingled, resting against each other like tossed pillows. At rest yet without relief from mosquitoes, flies, and red ants that spread their diseases as they continued descending in unrelenting attacks. The swarms concentrated around coagulations of blood on the wounded who were unable to defend themselves. Phan watched an enormous luna moth, its crescent wings patterned to appear as eyes, flickered between fallen soldiers, as if to watch and judge them.

At night the jungle formed impenetrable walls that trapped them in a lightless tunnel. Around him Phan felt the collective will to live decrease with each moment. For some the life process had condensed from decades to months, to weeks, days, moments to time meaningless at the end, alienated and alone.

Next day word reached those who survived the night that there had been a general abdication of the countryside by the remaining French forces around Ha Noi. Thereafter the march was without caution and in the open. The messenger also brought orders from Colonel Hahn that Phan was to rejoin him. The commissar reluctantly acceded to the colonel's order.

CHAPTER 63

Ha Noi, May 8, 1947
Doctor Astray
Reality

At the time the headline DIEN BIEN PHU FALLS INTO ENEMY HANDS had left a hollow in Doctor Astray's stomach. It had been almost unthinkable, an army of primitives defeating a modern army. Changing times. He had folded the paper and replaced it on the hotel counter with a sigh, knowing at least the killing had ended. There hadn't been any wounded brought to the hospital since the airfield at Dien Bien Phu was closed. Now those poor buggers would be brought out of that terrible place. Just hope it's not too late for them, Doctor Astray thought.

Two weeks passed before it was settled. The surviving French troops were marching out, the most seriously wounded returned by air. The Viet Minh had demanded and received immunity from air attack. Now they removed their troops with the French prisoners from Dien Bien Phu. Poor Doctor Grauwin. Due to rotate home, he'd volunteered to relieve another doctor taken ill at Dien Bien Phu. He had remained there, a prisoner of the negotiations, and now cared for all those too severely wounded to travel, French and Vietnamese alike. Until recently the air drops of medical supplies had been cut off. For safety reasons the Viet Minh had said, but Doctor Astray suspected it was to add pressure on the French diplomats to settle things. There ought to be a Hippocratic oath in the political codes of war.

What had the young soldiers who'd soon fill the hospital beds thought when they'd enlisted? That their country needed them? That they fought for the freedom of France? That was often what they said at first. But the doctor could remember that in his youth he too sought adventure, an opportunity to prove himself, or at least a chance to test his capabilities. By the time the boys reached his hospital they had lost all those dreams. Reality had no room for such foolishness. The brave ones were resigned. The others cried out for their mothers, or raged against some imagined, or more often real, betrayal. Their rage was acceptable. It often fueled a faster recovery.

Doctor Astray knew his days in Viet Nam were ending. The French at home had no appetite for defeats like this, not the casualties, not the need for the new troops. The mercenaries and volunteers were depleted. Though the Americans would provide funding, they would not send their soldiers. What firestorm would ignite when the wounded returned to France with tales of the horror? It was over.

What future would be left for him? When the communists governed they would institute land reform, which meant denunciations, show trials. Those with wealth, those with any trust in Western medicine, would flee the country. The masses of Vietnamese believed in herbs and needles, the quackery of Chinese medicine. Besides they had no money. So even if doctors were allowed to stay, he couldn't live practicing medicine. So it was back to Paris? He dreaded even the thought of French women with their complaints. Oh, doctor, can't you fix the wrinkles in my face? Can you see how my skin has fallen? And there were the elderly unwilling to accept their inevitable aging. The hours with his colleagues discussing their vacations to southern France, their children's education, their wives gone shopping. And can we expect you for cocktails tonight? No? Oh, you really must come. The hospital director will be there. You know how disappointed he'd be not to see you.

When Doctor Astray reached the hospital, he fell into his routine, reading the scribbled notes from the night before. Since that boy with the abdominal wound had died, the night nurse's bold lettering had turned into meek, unintelligible scrawls. He had tried to imagine her, a nurse he'd never seen, as she came in to find her fine young hero gone, carried off to the sullen field of wood crosses at the edge of Han Noi, in his place clean white sheets stacked on the newly made bed. At the time had the nurse wept, burying her head in the pillow where the boy's head had rested? A romantic possibility but not likely. More likely resignation, then acceptance to replace the indignation and anger, the sudden urge to strike out buried in work's routine.

Doctor Astray stared into the common room where the majority of wounded had been cared for when the airport at Dien Bien Phu was still open. Now all but a few beds were neatly made up with sheets requisitioned from the local French hotels. The high command anticipated a flood of badly wounded.

The orderly passed him.

"Where is my nurse? She's late." Doctor Astray shouted.

"I'm sorry, doctor."

"Find her now."

"I guess you haven't heard. She was driving our jeep and didn't see a trench the Viet Minh dug across the road. The jeep flipped. They said she must have died instantly for it broke her neck."

The words drummed around inside Doctor Astray's head. His heart pounded as if about to rupture. His skin flushed, and then turned cold. He closed his eyes to re-awaken, certain there had been a mistake. What he had heard violated all that was right. If he kept moving, perhaps it would change. He limped along the corridor to the terminal care room. Viet Nam had already trapped him, cut him off from his past, and now in an instant the future he imagined for her had disappeared. There at the doorway he paused.

A nurse from surgery walked down the corridor and into the room. "Doctor?"

"Have you seen my nurse?" As if he didn't know the answer.

"Not yet this morning, but I just got in myself. If I see her, I'll tell her you're looking for her." The nurse walked over to a soldier and took his pulse.

Doctor Astray moved toward his young nurse's young soldier, half expecting to see her holding him in her arms. The soldier was alone now; his nurse was dead. She had become another dream. Doctor Astray felt very old, very isolated, but no one in Viet Nam grew very old, at least not any one French. The war killed them or they returned to France long before they needed modern hospitals to keep them alive. And who was he kidding? No one except soldiers came to him if they were seriously ill. His whole life he'd kidded himself.

He found the medicine in its place in the back of the cabinet but no spoon. He went to the young nurse's soldier, rested the soldier's head on his arm, and placed the bottle to his lips. Then he continued sitting next to the soldier, watching him with the bottle nestled in his hands.

CHAPTER 64

Dien Bien Phu, May 18, 1954
Father Custeau
Faith

The first day the French prisoners marched out of Dien Bien Phu, Father Custeau struggled to keep pace with Charlemagne. The several hundred Frenchmen in his group started early, their column lightly guarded but followed by an infantry battalion of Viet Minh. The prisoners in the lead marched rapidly in step to military tunes. They were soon spread out along two or more kilometers; even the strongest of them had been weakened by the fifty-seven day siege and found it difficult to keep pace.

The procession slowly crossed mountains, not exactly the French Alps but hard enough for an old man to climb. They passed small villages and markets flooded with Thais. Some of the Thai women wore intricately patterned cloth skull caps and some great red pillow hats that balanced precariously on their heads. Since they had no money, the French soldiers were ignored.

Stragglers were abandoned beside the road. More than once the old priest fell over a heap of naked flesh, the

boots and uniform removed. The wounded fortunate enough
to have comrades were carried, though they frequently stumbled and occasionally dropped those who died in their arms.
At mountain streams they paused and drank the cool, disease-
laden water muddied by their feet. Unhealed wounds were
reopened and cleaned, bandages soaked and softened, then
reapplied. There was no meal at noon. Instead they climbed
another mountain.

Rice was served at dusk. The Vietnamese prepared it
over an open fire in a strange sort of gruel that made it easy
to eat with fingers. At least it's hot, Father Custeau thought,
for he suffered from the cold when the sun fell below the horizon. After the evening meal, the prisoners were forced to
their feet by guards, who prodded with bayonets any Frenchman who tried to ignore the commands. Some said they were
fed so little because the P.O.W. camps were more than eight
hundred kilometers away and that the rice they carried was
all they'd have to eat on the march. Others claimed that there
was no destination, that they were being marched in circles
until they all died.

As twilight spread, the prisoners crossed a valley into
another jungle, where the road narrowed to a trail under a triple canopy. When the order was given to halt in the dark, the
prisoners fell where they stood. Some who had fallen asleep
marching continued to march, stumbling forward over those
still on the road, which brought a chorus of curses.

Rains that followed them up the valley drove through
their tattered clothes feeling like spears. Men too thin from
hunger died from hypothermia, the effect of the cold rain.
Charlemagne rested against Father Custeau, picking at the
caked mud that filled the folds of his clothing.

"Look at these robes," Father Custeau said. "They are
weighted with muck, soaked by every stream, and torn by
every snag we pass. We can't continue this way."

The words no sooner spoken by him, Charlemagne
disappeared in the dark from the direction they had come.
Shortly, he returned with two pairs of pants and boots. He
cut away their robes at the waist with a knife he borrowed

from a French soldier who was using it to pick his teeth. "Try these."

Father Custeau, too weak to protest at this degradation of his faith and barely able to stand, dressed in the half uniform, pulling on the tight pants. The boots fit better on his swollen feet than the ankle high shoes he'd worn for years. He slept curled together with Charlemagne.

The morning meal was the same gruel as the night before. They ladled it cold from buckets. Father Custeau fed his rice to a tall soldier with ribs protruding through white parchment skin. The man might have once measured over six feet tall but only managed to raise himself to the height of a waist. As he was finishing the rice, a young can-bo, who'd railed against the despotism of the French at night, stopped to watch this man being fed like a child.

"He must have more to eat," Father Custeau demanded.

"He eats what we eat," the can-bo said.

—ɯ—

That day the priest witnessed men eating human flesh with vegetation torn from surrounding vines. The weakest vomited it along the way. More wounded fell behind. Those without hope dropped from sight, enveloped by the jungle.

On that day Father Custeau sensed his fate. His body suddenly burned with a fever that alternated with chills. When his temperature subsided, his clothes were cold and wet. Charlemagne comforted him with what the priest discerned as feigned concern, his manner betraying the distance between the living and the dead.

Father Custeau stumbled forward as Viet Minh troops passed by him. Hallucinating, he fell in among the dark savages he'd seen his first day in Dien Bien Phu, their amulets jangling in resonance with their shuffling feet. The black men uttered a quiet chant with words from a remote language. His ears ringing, his lips parched and cracked, Father Custeau pitched forward, uncertain where and when he fell. He choked, pushing away a canteen. A shirtless black savage bent over him. Although every rib on the black man showed, Father Custeau could see that the man had once had great strength.

"What are you doing?" Father Custeau demanded.

"I'm giving you a drink."

"You speak French."

"Of course I do. We're all French here ... all soldiers in this together."

"African?"

"Yes, we're from there." The black man corked the canteen and slung it on its strap over his shoulder. "You have a name?"

"Father Custeau."

"Father Custeau," The black man paused to think. "Are you a priest?"

"Yes. What is your name?"

"Rumi."

"Not a Christian name."

"No, but I respect your faith."

—⚉—

Father Custeau tried to raise himself. The black man lifted him until Father Custeau was sitting erect and leaned him against a tree. The priest saw that besides his own shirt, he'd been wrapped in a larger sergeant's shirt. They'd halted on the side of a barren hill, its trees long ago removed for firewood. From where Father Custeau rested, he could see into the valley below.

"How long have I been unconscious?" Father Custeau asked.

"Three days."

"And you carried me all that time?"

"We took turns."

Father Custeau glanced at the other men who paid him no attention. He suspected the black man named Rumi had carried him all that time.

"Are any of these other men of Christian faith?"

"No. We are a brotherhood of soldiers, not men of your faith."

"It doesn't matter, does it?" The priest conceded to himself as much as to the man beside him.

"It doesn't."

"When I started to hallucinate there was another man of God with me."

"We found you alone beside the trail."

"I see."

"We must continue to move." The black man reached beneath the priest and lifted him as he might a child.

The priest touched a talisman of great white teeth on a leather cord dangling around the black man's neck. "What happened to the ears you people wore around your necks?"

"We burned them just before the compound was over-run. They only brought us bad luck."

"Then why did you keep them at all?"

"It was what our white French officers wanted and not our inclination. Their way for us to demonstrate how hard we fought for them and prove our loyalty. That is what we had to offer them in repayment for our freedom and transport from our native land where we were slaves."

"Why are you doing this?" the priest asked. A grasp of God's intended path still eluded him.

"Doing what?"

"Carrying me. You should save your strength if you hope to survive."

"I haven't thought about it like that," the black man said. He did not slow his pace or speak further. He walked with such a graceful stride that it was as if he were some wild jaguar.

Father Custeau felt neither stride nor distance in the black man's gait. He could not vanquish the sensation of his own weightlessness, which reason forbade him to accept as reality.

Father Custeau heard a whispering, incoherent voice he recognized as his own, but it seemed distant from him. He heard a terrible thump that persisted as he dreamed. When he woke he realized that it was his heart struggling to beat.

He asked the black man if he believed in any God, and the man said no, that he only believed in the past and that it should be worshiped, for all that they were came out of it, and it was all they could expect. That was when the priest understood that desperate men did not turn to God but to themselves, some with inner strength, some with only their weakness. Circumstance alone saved some, took others, with no favor or distinction of merit or sin.

"Leave me beside the road," said a voice from within the priest.

"The guards would shoot you. They think it a kindness."

"Will you see to it I'm buried?"

"I will do that."

CHAPTER 65

Tuan Giao, May 21, 1954
Phan
Aftermath: Communist ways

A pony weighted with mortar rounds strapped across its back blocked the trail ahead. When Phan tried to squeeze past, the pony lost its footing and fell off the trail. Its hind legs caught in a tree over the abyss. Its head dangling in space, the pony brayed with terror. Soldiers wrestled to save it, but nothing worked. The terrified pony fought them. The soldiers abandoned their efforts and used bayonets to carve off the flesh within reach. Phan stumbled toward a thick forest, where darkness hung in day. A smell of burning wood started him thinking that there were camps he'd pass in which Hahn might be waiting. He asked for the headquarters location, but the soldiers around him were suspicious and wouldn't answer. Having no orders or rank to demand an answer, he searched each camp along the way.

The mountains rolled and rolled as waves in an endless sea. Phan felt drained of life, as he stumbled past another file of soldiers in which defeated and conquerors intermingled. He caught up to a battalion that marched to the northeast through gorges and over the same trails cut into the white limestone cliffs he'd marched over before. Nature ate at each soldier's strength. The little rice that remained was now rationed equally among the French and Viet Minh. When the column paused, men foraged into the jungle, tearing plants out by the roots and killing any wild life ill-fated enough to be seen. They marched with an instinctive knowledge they must continue or rot in the jungle.

Phan overtook Hahn's battalion forty kilometers from Dien Bien Phu.

There was little time and less conversation before Hahn set off along a path that followed the ridgeline of the mountain. Only when the path divided did Hahn hesitate. The soldiers ahead climbed with their hands gripping rocks, pulling themselves toward a fog-shrouded peak.

"We'll go down from here alone." Hahn pointed to a steep drop off on the other path where vegetation partially concealed a passage.

Phan felt a sudden quickening in his pulse. "What's down there?"

"You'll see soon enough."

The two traveled rapidly, dropping into a valley with a village nestled in the first clearing. At the far end of the village a crowd had formed, soldiers behind them in a rough military formation. Their whispers carried the tension. From the rear where Hahn insisted they stand, the backs of villagers partially obscured a peasant seated on a chair and tied to a stake. An old man, his face raw and swollen, he lacked the strength to raise his head. The villagers kept their distance, silently watching the old man and three empty chairs facing him.

"You brought me here to see this?" Phan said.

"You wait," Hahn said.

Soldiers emerged from a village hut with the political commissar who had retained Phan's notes. What was Hahn doing? Did he know about the commissar?

The commissar in his impeccable uniform went straight to the empty chair where he sat square and erect. Once he was comfortably seated, two officers took their places beside him. He crossed his legs and balanced a clipboard on his knee. Armed soldiers gathered behind the three. The commissar ordered the peasant to look at him but there was no reaction. A soldier at the edge of the crowd came forward and slapped the peasant's face. The peasant squinted in the direction of the soldier but didn't seem to see him.

"Over here," the commissar said.

"What is it?" The peasant turned like a blinded animal. The strength in his voice contradicted his bloody face and bruised arms and legs.

"These are very serious charges." The commissar appeared to be reading from a document on the clip board.

"Charges of what? I've committed no crimes."

"Your crimes are against the Vietnamese people." The commissar raised his hand in a fist.

"But I have committed no crimes," the peasant repeated, motionless, his eyes in a cold stare.

"You still deny committing crimes against the people?"

"I deny it." Nothing in the inflection of the peasant's voice changed. He remained motionless despite the rising pitch of the commissar's voice.

"Do you deny you own the largest tract of land in town?"

"No, I don't deny that. But my family has lived here for generations. My ancestors started with only a single mau of land and labored in the fields for decades before they saved enough to buy more land. I only have what they worked for and the very little I have been able to add."

"Do you deny you charged your fellow villagers rent to farm a portion of your land?"

"I rented it to them for their sake, not my own. I charged them less than a fair amount. Half what the French charged. When the party asked us to reduce rents, I complied."

"The villagers were starving at the time. You never gave them food."

"How could I? My own family was starving along with

everyone else. My youngest child died from malnutrition."

"Is that your only defense?"

"What more do you want me to say?'

"Confess you are a lackey of the French, that you have committed crimes. It will go easier for you if you do."

"You have no evidence."

The commissar pointed towards the crowd, "Bring the woman."

A soldier came forward dragging a woman, her hair snarled and matted, she biting at the soldier, pulling at her hair and screaming. "Rape ... murder ..."

The villagers, three dozen strong, let out a collective sigh. The soldier continued dragging the woman until she was at the peasant's feet. Like a rabid animal attacking what was nearest, she turned from the soldier to leap upon the peasant, biting him in the arm. The soldier pulled the woman away, she howling, "him ... him."

"Certainly she's not your evidence," the peasant said, trying to appear calm. His arm was now bleeding from the bite. "She's mad. Everyone here knows it. We've tried to care for her, but she runs into the jungle."

"It is you who are on trial here. You should take this matter more seriously. We deal with reactionaries very severely."

The peasant did not reply. He rested his head against the post and closed his eyes.

"So you refuse to answer further?"

"I refuse to participate in a mockery." The peasant's voice was barely audible.

"She accuses you. I have the charges here, her name signed to them. There are others." The commissar stood as if he intended to address the crowd, but his words were for the peasant. "You think you have friends here to speak in your defense?"

A soldier, taking the commissar's pause as a signal, shouted, "Death to the landlord."

When the crowd did not respond, the soldier repeated it louder, "Death to the landlord."

There was no response.

"Perhaps there are other reactionaries in this village," the commissar said, his voice heightened in its pitch. "We will soon deal with them in the people's court."

Another long pause.

Then the crowd chanted "Death to the landlord." They repeated it and repeated it until the commissar was satisfied. He signaled them to stop.

"That woman was insane," Phan whispered.

"She serves his purpose," said Hahn.

"What purpose? The man has committed no crime."

"Do you think the landless worked for our great victory without promises being made? Where do you think we'll find the land to give them? Statistics make that man a running dog of the reactionaries. The party works through the commissar. I wanted you to see it, to understand how he works. He was trained in China. He's the soul of the revolution. Watch him. You must admire his efficiency. He'll deal with you in the same way. I won't be able to stop him." Hahn nodded in the direction of the trial, "Watch him."

By then the commissar had huddled with the other two men, both leaning toward him. When they returned to sitting erect in their chairs, the commissar spoke with added solemnity, "You are found to be an enemy of the people. You have shown no regret. Therefore we have no alternative but to condemn you to death."

"Wasn't that what you always intended?" The peasant showed no other reaction. Phan wanted to cheer him.

The three-man tribunal walked to the edge of the crowd.

A single rock sailed from somewhere in the crowd, striking the peasant in the abdomen. He turned his blinded eyes upon the crowd. His sad contempt provoked a rain of stones. By the time they finished, the peasant's eyes were no longer distinguishable from the rest of his pulpy face. A single guard walked forward and cut the peasant's throat, then went behind him and cut the ropes that held him, kicking him forward off the chair and wiped his knife clean on the peasant's torn shirt.

The commissar spoke, "The property of the criminal landlord ... (Phan didn't catch his name in all the excitement) is ordered seized for the people. Tomorrow his land will be divided among you. His personal property will be divided now."

The crowd rushed to the hut from which the commissar had earlier emerged.

"Let's go," Hahn said, turning his back to the crowd and moving rapidly toward the jungle. At the edge of the jungle they turned and watched.

Soldiers hacked at the peasant's head with bayonets until it broke loose from the body. They lifted it on a pole, parading it like a flag to the dead man's house as the last of his possessions were being carried off. The dead man's lips were open in an attempted last word. His wife and children were brought out, dragged past him and led away by soldiers.

"Where are they taking them?" Phan demanded.

"To a re-education camp just south of here."

"At least they won't be killed."

"Perhaps." Hahn's tone sent a chill through Phan.

"That's why you brought me here? You could have just warned me."

"You are stubborn. The commissar is a dangerous man. I thought you ought to see it for yourself. And there's something you didn't tell me." Hahn stared straight into Phan's eyes.

"My notes," Phan said.

"Yes, your notes," Hahn said. "I know what they say. They're treasonous. You are in grave danger."

CHAPTER 66

Lanessan Military Hospital
Ha Noi, July 1, 1954
Pasteur
Coma

She stood over him shrouded in white, blending into the white surroundings. Her face was the color of cream and without a blemish, her sad blue eyes too intense. Her angelic expression frightened him.

"Where am I now?" Lieutenant Pasteur asked.

"You've heard of Lanessan Military Hospital?"

"I'm afraid I haven't." He was thinking slowly as he tried to focus on the girl. "Who are you?"

"I'm a night nurse." She was reassuring in her white uniform with a white scarf over her hair. He was beginning to understand her despite the whirling inside his head.

"Why am I here?"

"They brought you in a coma. You've been very sick."

"I see." But he didn't. He tried to recall the last things he knew and place them in order. There were the other officers who like him had survived Dien Bien Phu. They had marched for days or weeks, separated from their men. The Viet Minh drove them like cattle toward a mountain camp beyond the reach of the French forces. At night they slept on the ground, and every morning fewer of them stood to march again. That was all he remembered.

He felt her touch him. She was holding his hand and slowly caressing it. Her lips were quivering. She fought to hold back tears.

"There's something you're not telling me. What's really wrong with me?" He spoke with difficulty. His own voice sounded strange to him.

"It's not you. I'm sorry." Her voice comforted him. "You've reminded me of someone."

Could he believe her? He held up his arm and looked at his wrist. Every bone was visible. The flesh was wrinkled and the veins exposed and covered with punctures. He felt his face. It was hard, like teeth, and angular. "Do you have a mirror?"

"No, not now, not yet," she said.

He tried to sit up but failed. He was strapped into the bed with the other arm tied against a bed rail and punctured with a needle from a tube connected to a blood-colored bottle above his head. "Is all this necessary?"

"You'll be out of here before you know it," she promised. "We will only need a short period of observation after this."

"No rushing back to the field, I suppose."

"There's no danger of that." He could see she was trying to reassure him.

"I'm that bad?" He asked.

"My dear." She caressed his forehead. "But how could you know? The war is over. Everyone is going back to France."

Was it possible? Dien Bien Phu had been a disaster, but just a single battle. The war had taken bad turns before. And with the Americans worried about the communists, there would be plenty of support in the future. There would be no stopping the Americans. But if what the nurse said was true?

A soldier in an army at peace was no better than a civilian bureaucrat like his father. He'd thought about it all before. A world without adventure was what he had tried to avoid. Or had the army been an easy escape from facing adult realities? He tried to figure what it meant but felt lightheaded.

—ɯ—

When Lieutenant Pasteur regained consciousness a doctor with tobacco-stained fingers was pulling open his eyes. The old doctor's breath smelled of cognac, his face dripping with sweat. The doctor was still only a captain which meant he was incompetent. The night nurse waited behind him with a clipboard full of records. She was taking notes. She was beautiful, even with the inconvenient uniform that covered everything.

"Pay attention here," the doctor said. "She says you can speak. Let me hear you speak."

The doctor probed inside Pasteur's mouth without waiting, thumped on his chest. Listening through the stethoscope, he seemed to be counting. "You will get plenty of medals for this. That is what happens when the generals make a mistake. Also, girls like this nurse will want you. They cannot resist a uniform. You are a very fortunate boy."

The doctor removed the needle from the lieutenant's arm. He removed the straps. "Now that you're out of the coma you won't need this. The side rails should keep you in bed when you're asleep. You will want more freedom soon enough."

The doctor turned his back and read what the nurse had written, and then added notes of his own before signing the sheet. Then he left the room.

Lieutenant Pasteur spoke to the nurse in a whisper. "He shouldn't have said those things about you."

"Why does it matter, if it's true?" The nurse lifted his head and straightened his pillow, holding him in her arm until gently lowering him again. She had the clean smell of the

426

hospital, but with a perfume over it that made it all exciting. "Don't worry; he's not your doctor. Your doctor is Doctor Astray. He's a civilian and only here days. I think you'll like him much better."

"You have a name?" Lieutenant Pasteur wasn't thinking about the doctors.

"Jacqueline Bennett."

"Not French sounding."

"Half French, half British."

"How did you get here?"

"I volunteered."

"Your French is very good."

"My French half is speaking. I grew up in Paris with my mother. My father lived in London."

"Funny, I went to school outside London."

"That's nice." She sat down in a chair next to his bed.

She was watching him again and reached over and held his hand. He didn't mind. He wanted her near him even if all the time she seemed to be thinking of someone else.

In the morning the sun broke into the room around the curtain. The nurse went out of the room and returned with a pan filled with water. She sponged his face. The warmth of the water relaxed him. She sponged his arms and then his chest. He must have tightened for she smiled at him. "You must relax. I bathe you like this every morning. Now you are awake you will have to help me with your clothes."

When she finished, she called to another nurse in the hall to go over his chart. He watched her every movement, imaging much of her.

"Are you going?" he asked very excitedly.

"Yes, this isn't my shift. I will be back tonight." She was abrupt.

"What was your soldier's name?" he asked.

"You have no right to ask." She turned away.

He thought about her all day. He must have slept and been dreaming for when he awoke a tray of food was on the table beside his bed. He rang the bell. Another nurse came to his bedside. She was what a military nurse should be, very stern, her face without expression. She fed him in an officious manner. It wasn't the same as he imagined it would be with Jacqueline. Still it was wonderful to be eating. Someone had opened the curtains though it was dark out. He could see a small streetlight burning below, a trishaw beside it with a driver asleep in the seat.

"Isn't Jacqueline here tonight?" Lieutenant Pasteur asked.

"She is here."

"Ask her to come see me."

"I will ask her."

He didn't see Jacqueline that night, but after that she was at his bedside every night. The stomach cramps that came with eating disappeared after several days. His weight improved by several pounds from the ninety they said he weighed when they brought him into the hospital. Sometimes Jacqueline cried, but he never again asked whose ghost she was carrying around. He thought a lot about her during the days, anticipating their nights together. As they spoke about their childhoods, he realized she was a lot older. She told him about the first time she had seen Nazis in Paris, what they did to her family, and her hatred toward them, which had made her a fine partisan. She said now she was doing penance for placing bombs and the other kinds of killing she did in the war.

"What you did wasn't wrong," he said. "The Nazis had to be eliminated."

"But I did it out of hatred," she said.

He figured she needed the kind of doctor who worked on other people's minds to figure out their own.

After Lieutenant Pasteur had eaten meals for a week, Doctor Astray visited less than daily. "I don't know if what's happening between you and Nurse Bennett is good for either of you," the doctor said.

"She said something to you?"

"No, I sense it from her patient's notes." There was no confrontation in the doctor's voice. He was as gentle as she'd said, an old man with a warmth that contrasted with the anguish surrounding him every day in the hospital. "You must be gentle with her. She's suffered too much already."

"Doctor ..."

"No, don't protest. I know how you young men behave."

When Jacqueline came on duty, she immediately read the charts and doctor's notes. She rested the clipboard on the bed and wiped the corners of her eyes.

"What did he say?" Lieutenant Pasteur asked.

"He's sending you to the officers' quarters tonight after dinner. You're strong enough to be sent home on a convalescent ship where they can monitor you."

"I see."

"Is that all you can say?" Jacqueline asked.

"I think he was worried about us."

"What did you say to him?"

"Nothing. He read your notes, that's all."

"I didn't betray us," Jacqueline responded.

"What is there to betray?" he asked and immediately regretted it for it denied their relationship. She was walking out of the room. "Where are you going?"

"You will need clothes. Or do you want to walk around the streets in a hospital gown that opens in the back?"

She returned with civilian clothes. She said they were the only ones she found. Although they fit around his waist and chest, they only reached to his mid-arms and mid-calves. They laughed together, and she took him down the hall and into a small bathroom for the nurses and showed him what he looked like in a mirror.

"What a scarecrow," he cried out, trying to joke at the sudden shock he felt.

"They can find you something better at the officers' barracks," she said, giving him the directions.

"Will I see you again?" he asked.

"Are you sure you want to?"

"I'm sure."

"When my shift is over. You get a good night's sleep. You know I'm best in the early morning." She was smiling, and he felt good walking out, waving back at her standing in their window. The trishaw driver understood French and didn't need the directions. Lieutenant Pasteur huddled in the center of the seat under the trishaw awning trying to avoid the persistent mist that filled the night air. He was remembering the nights standing in trenches waiting for the sound of the incoming artillery, watching the flares drifting earthward weighted by rain. Rain and more rain, muffling the war with its indifference to suffering.

The barracks were like a civilian hotel except for the twelve-foot masonry walls and wire around them. The guard at the gate smiled but didn't comment as he reviewed the orders. There were officers moving out, joking among themselves, and others lying quietly on bunks, some asleep, others playing cards. The medical discharges, like him, were obvious by their physical deficits.

A sergeant at the desk glanced over the orders and brought out a stack of uniforms, several sets of boots, and told him to keep the ones that fit him best and leave the others. He handed Lieutenant Pasteur a set of metal captain's bars and said to pin them on the collars until others were embroidered.

"That's the wrong rank," Lieutenant Pasteur said.

"You haven't heard? You were promoted because of your service at Dien Bien Phu." Then without looking up from the paperwork, "Here's your bunk number. Shower's down the hall."

"What about issuing a pistol?"

"You won't need it. The fighting is over. We're all going home, tail between our legs, but I think you'll find even that will feel good. "

Immediately Lieutenant Pasteur stretched out on his assigned bunk. His boots hung over the edge and did not soil the sheets. Though it had been a short trip from the hospital to the barracks, he was exhausted.

He woke in the dark barracks with light from a lantern coming down the center. He remembered where he was and jumped up to find the officers' club and a drink.

The boisterous club smelled of cigarettes. A tiny Vietnamese woman negotiated her way through the crowd. He
tried to order a drink. She kept saying, "Repeat please, repeat please." A colonel standing next to him drew on a cigarette and blew the smoke in his direction. Lieutenant Pasteur
turned and walked back to the barracks room. When he tried
to sleep he dreamed of all those men he had left behind. When
he woke, Jacqueline was seated on the bunk next to him.

"How long have you been watching me?" he asked.

"Not long." Her smile invited him to overcome his exhaustion and his reluctance to get out of bed. "Now don't you
brood," she said. He knew her well enough to understand
she spoke to herself and that no response was required. "You
were brooding weren't you?"

"I was asleep," he said.

"Of course you were, darling," she said. "Can't you tell
what someone's thinking when they are asleep?"

"I never tried. I doubt it."

"But then you were never a night nurse were you?"

She was jovial, almost giddy in the way she was speaking, and he said so.

"I'm sorry, darling. It's just my way of coping. I lose all
you boys one way or another. Last night one of the abdominals died."

"Did he have a name?"

"Let's not be morbid, darling. Today we'll have the day
together before you leave. You want me to help you dress?"

"That might be fun, but I think I can manage."

She waited on the bunk watching him dress. When they
reached the street, she signaled a trishaw. Her apartment was
several blocks away. She paid the driver and pushed back her
iron gate like an accordion. Lieutenant Pasteur drew it closed
from the inside, and she locked it.

"We could have walked," Lieutenant Pasteur said.

"We need to save your strength."

"You live here alone?"

"Sometimes."

"Don't be cute."

"Don't worry about me," she said. Her home was a single room, at one end a kitchen sink and stove, a roll-a-way with dresser, desk and lamp. He sat on the roll-a-way already made up as a bed and watched her stretch to reach glasses off an upper shelf beside her dresser. The calves of her legs, their shape with the muscles worked, excited him.

"Where did you get this," he asked, inspecting a bottle of wine she handed him to open. He tried to ease the cork avoiding the pop that sent it bulleting into the ceiling. It didn't work. The cork ricocheted across the room. She laughed.

"When you're one of the few French girls left in the city, you have friends in high places," she said, offering the glasses for him to pour. It was different between them out of the hospital. He kept their glasses filled, thinking it might help. The wine quickly set his head spinning, a question of his weight and involuntary abstinence during his hospital stay. He slid back on the bed.

"How long have you known Dawn?" She was watching him closely, leaning against the sink.

He felt his face redden. He had not thought about her. "Did I cry out her name in my sleep?"

"Don't be silly, darling. That only happens in books. She came one night to the hospital looking for you. At the time you were still in a coma. She was so distraught I didn't have the heart to hurt her. I sent her away without telling her you were my patient."

"Was she all right?"

"A little pregnant."

"Because of me?"

"Because of no protection. That's the price we women pay for giving you boys a little extra pleasure."

"Don't get clinical. Was it because of me?"

"She didn't say, but a woman in her circumstances usually looks up the father."

Lieutenant Pasteur's head was really swimming. He started drinking directly from the bottle. Soon he was drowning, his senses occasionally bobbing to the surface, then submerging, mingling with thoughts of Dawn, then his family back in France. They'd never accept her. He felt trapped and lost. His platoon was lost, faces floating in the sea. He felt the breath, the touch on his clothes.

"What are you doing?"

"Undressing you." The voice was strange and distant. "You must forget her you know. You must go home."

—⁂—

Twilight. Jacqueline next to him, slipping on a blouse.

"I guess I tied one on," he said.

"You did. Do you feel better now?"

"A terrible head."

"Your nurse will get you something for it."

He watched her white blouse, her bare legs like silver pillars in the light, as she walked to the sink.

"Things caught up with me," he said.

"Last night you were lonely." Jacqueline sat next to him, handing him a glass. "I was lonely too. That's all there ever was between us. It's the same between you and the Vietnamese girl. You'll be better once you're back to France."

"I don't think I'm going."

"You must. There's nothing left for any of us here. It was a great adventure while it lasted, but we never belonged here." She ran her fingers through his hair, studying his face. "You have no choice. You can't take the girl back with you, if that's what you're thinking. Her future and her fate are here."

When Jacqueline left, he heard horns and bells and hawkers shouting in the street outside. He rested on his back watching the light from the window slowly disappear until it was completely black. He felt for his clothes. Something about the darkness always calmed him.

CHAPTER 67

Ha Noi, July 21, 1954
Pasteur
Invisibility

"Your orders are here, sir. You have a morning flight to Sai Gon and a ship back to France." The sergeant at the night desk wore a Cheshire cat smile. His white beard hid a weak chin, but he was otherwise a man of solid proportion.

"Is there something else?"

"No, sir. A jeep will be here for you at six." His grin continued to blossom.

"But there is something else." Pasteur watched the sergeant's face.

"No, sir."

Alone in the barracks, Pasteur found his assigned bed without turning on the lights. He walked in the shadows, listening, his senses keen. Night was the best time. He wasn't being watched. On ambush he'd felt the same way, more a part of the earth. In the day he felt like one of Kafka's insect struggling to survive in a world not of his making. His coma had been blackness. It had been a long painful journey, the road back a terrible mystery, but he had suffered through it and survived. It was nearly a final escape. Jacqueline had been mistaken. The hospital had only kept him alive, not saved him. Someone came up behind him, and he whirled around.

"I was here this morning, again this afternoon. The sergeant promised me you'd be back." Dawn held out flowers. "I brought you these."

"How did you get in here?" he demanded.

"I was clever," she smiled. "I asked for you at the gate. They laughed at me but said you were here. A guard called me a little Viet Minh whore and sent me away. It was all right because I knew you were alive. I found a truck carrying cleaning ladies. They let me hide among them. Once inside the compound no one questioned me."

"You shouldn't be here," Pasteur said. He studied her profile. He scrutinized her closely. Her face was pale, her ao dai tight around her waist.

"What kind of a uniform are you wearing?" she asked.

"It's the uniform they give you to go home. They wear them in France."

"I see." Her countenance changed.

"Do you need a doctor?" he asked.

"No." She held herself stiffly as if the slightest movement would shatter her.

"I have to leave for Sai Gon tomorrow," he hesitated. "I can't take you with me."

"I understand." She remained motionless. Tears began glistening down her cheeks. When she moved it was to whirl on her toes, run down the aisle and from the room. He heard her light feet disappearing down the hallway.

Then he was on his feet. He raced down the hall, past the sergeant at the desk, past the guard, and into the street. A long way from him several Vietnamese women, back to him, crossed through traffic and into an alley. He watched them until they were out of sight.

"Why did you let her in here?" he demanded as he walked past the sergeant's desk.

"No one came in here tonight except you, sir." The sergeant grinned.

"You're a goddamned liar," Pasteur said.

"Excuse me, sir?"

"You're a goddamned liar," Pasteur repeated. "These people aren't invisible."

"That's what it's all been about, now isn't it, sir?"

CHAPTER 68

Ha Noi, August 16, 1954
Phan
A refugee

Fourteen days after leaving Hahn, Phan crossed the Doumer Bridge and entered Ha Noi. He was dressed as a peasant. He had traveled at night to avoid both Viet Minh and French military checkpoints. In the mayhem following the truce, friend and enemy intermingled in the streets. French troops in their barracks, the Viet Minh not yet arrived, the streets of Ha Noi belonged to those who seized them. The dogs of change rampaged through the city in a general panic. Storefronts remained shuttered, markets closed. The sun never rose, and the torrential rains played devil to the streets, filling them with water and overflowing the sewers until the two were indistinguishable. Small bands of Vietnamese deserters from the French ranks fulfilled their unrequited passions, storming residences inadequately secured. Common looters followed them.

Only when the French quarter itself was threatened did the governor general in charge of all Ton Kin order troops from their quarters, imposing martial law with a dusk-to-dawn curfew. After several summary executions, the looters vanished from the streets.

A famine spread and disease reaped the weakened with a plenitude of dead. Necessity finally broke the boycott of commerce, merchant and customer alike reluctantly emerging to barter for scarce produce and goods. Water was boiled and sold as a valuable commodity.

Viet Minh cadres dressed as city workers circulated among the populace creating lists for retribution, the settling of old scores against quislings of the French. French flags were lowered and replaced with red stars. Large posters of Ho Chi Minh, Lenin, and Mao Tse Dung covered empty walls and billboards that had advertised the products of renounced capitalism. Priests sought out their parishioners to warn of the coming wave of godlessness, promising ships waited in Hai Phong to carry refugees south to Sai Gon.

Phan understood what he witnessed. Men followed causes. Just as water never left the riverbed unless outside forces intervened, so causes seldom changed. Change required chaos, displacement to make room for the new. He had to take his family south and hope for a change before the election that would unify the country. By the time he reached his family, he had decided to flee by boat from Hai Phong Harbor.

"Quick, pack," he barked as soon as he reached the family cubicle.

"Pack," Thi repeated, glancing up at him from on the floor. Then she resumed construction of paper buildings with their son.

"Daddy." Their son leaped to his feet and headed toward Phan. Then, seeing his father's expression, he stopped.

"We must get to Hai Phong. They'll take us from there to Sai Gon."

Thi remained motionless, distress apparent on her face.

"You're annoyed with me?" Phan said.

"Annoyed? Oh, certainly not that. You've just come back, and this is how you greet us. Angered, enraged, exasperated perhaps, but certainly not annoyed. It is such an equivocating word."

"What's the matter with you? Didn't you hear me? We've just got time to escape. The communists will come here to question me. They think I'm a traitor, a Catholic, a Chinese. Can't you understand the danger?"

"Pack was all you said," Thi replied.

Phan paused. "Now you understand?"

"No, I don't understand."

"We can't live here," he said. "We can't be always afraid, always in hiding, not able to write or to speak freely, not able to do as I want."

"As you want," she said. "That's it."

"I went to your village and tried farming. It didn't work out."

"You went because you needed a place to hide," she said. "If you'd stayed out of politics, we'd still be safe there."

"What brings this on?" he said.

"You have," she said but she began to pack.

"Are you all right?" Phan tried to touch her but she shrugged him off.

"Nothing changes," she said. "You will have your freedom."

"We can talk about this later," he said. He pushed clothes into his military pack and wondered if carrying it would raise questions.

"No," she said coldly. "We won't talk about it later. You've got your way."

—ɯ—

Old men, children clinging to their mothers' pants, infants to their breasts clogged the road from Ha Noi to Hai Phong. They carried their possessions in ragged bags and woven baskets, pushed them in two-wheeled carts, carried them on their heads. Families tried to keep together. Phan, like the other men, protected his family as best he could. The refugees advanced as one, silent except for the muffled tread of bleeding feet.

A strange little man in a priest's frock crossed himself and uttered prayers for safe travel. Phan immediately detected his disguise; a spy sent to cause panic. False prophets everywhere up and down the line protested to the heavens, wailing over the coming apocalypse.

By day's end they reached a tent city beside the road, constructed by French forces using coolies. It was set on the only high ground outside Hai Phong. Twelve rows of tents, twelve tents deep, one hundred twenty refugees per tent, a work of French military precision.

Rumors spread that the white powder, something called DDT, sprayed on everyone entering the compound, caused impotency, blindness, and worse.

The chocolate Cua Cam River flowed past Hai Phong. A monsoon mist concealed it. Several smokestacks, the primitive beginnings of the industrial age, added their pollution to the gloom. Along the shoreline the banks were coated with the silt from distant mountains in a yearly ritual of renewal. Great floating wharfs along a mile of docks were tautly tied to plank walkways running to the shore. Under the weight of refugees, the wharf rafts barely rose above the surface of the river.

Refugees quickly filled each French landing craft when they tethered alongside the wharfs. The refugees stood packed together in the holds, blind to where the boats carried them. Phan was crushed against his wife and child. Trang remained calm, resigned to endure what his parents had decided was best.

"Cast off," a French officer shouted from the conning in the stern. Thick ropes were cast from bollards on the ship's bow and stern. A ferocious bark from the engines vibrated the entire metal hull on which the refugees stood. It threw the boat forward, causing panic. As the landing craft motored toward the waiting American ships, it rolled in the swells, and tossed in choppy waves created in the wake of another landing craft returning to the docks. Many refugees lost their footing but were held up by the press of the crowd. Those who fell were lifted and held on their feet by those around them. The salty water crashed over the bow as the landing craft pitched.

Among the refugees were a group of orphans, their earlobes sliced by the Viet Minh to mark them as Catholic, and never to be trusted. The orphans held each other hand in hand, as directed by a young French priest. Their nervous laughter at each dip added to the overall apprehension.

The American freighter dwarfed the landing craft. Built to transport trucks and tanks for amphibious landings, it was now to transport a human cargo. American sailors lowered stairs to the landing craft.

"Now we'll find freedom." Phan said.

"And a home?" Thi asked.

" I'm certain of it," Phan said, staring up at the American ship looming over them.

—ɯ—

A VIET NAM CHRONOLOGY

2879 BC	According to a legend predating written history, the Vietnamese kingdoms of Van Lang and Au Lac separated from China under rulers descended from the founders of China.
258 BC	Kingdom of Au Lac created in north and east mountains of North Viet Nam.
208 BC	Nam Viet, which included Au Lac, the Red River Delta, and territory south to present-day Da Nang created by Chinese General Trieu Da.
111 BC	China conquered Nam Viet and reincorporated it into the Chinese empire as a military territory. This period lasted the "thousand years" Ho Chi Minh referred to in justifying some cooperation with the French after the Second World War to avoid Chinese occupation. It was also a period in which the Vietnamese absorbed much of Chinese culture including Buddhism, Confucianism, ancestor worship, and a bureaucracy based on mandarin education and hierarchy.
39 AD	Trung sisters led a rebellion and established an independent kingdom.
42 AD	Chinese re-conquered Nam Viet. To avoid capture the Trung sisters committed suicide by drowning.
248 AD	Trieu An, the "young virgin warrior," headed a brief rebellion against the Chinese, which ended in defeat and her suicide. She became known as the Vietnamese Joan of Arc.
543 AD	Ly Bon, a Vietnamese noble, staged a revolt and a year later named himself emperor. Using guerilla tactics he prevailed until 546 AD when he was defeated and beheaded by the Chinese.
931 AD	Chinese expelled from Viet Nam.
938 AD	General Ngo Quyen defeated the Chinese in their attempt to reconquer Viet Nam at the battle of Bach Dang, a naval battle fought near Hai Phong. Chinese defeat was followed by a series of Vietnamese dynasties.
1044 AD	A series of wars with the Chams to the south resulted in 1471 in the victory of the Vietnamese and their annexation of the

lands to their south.

1257 AD	Mongols began invasion efforts which reached their height in 1284 when they were repelled.
1407 AD	China under the Ming emperors successfully invaded Viet Nam.
1418 AD	Le Loi began rebellion against Chinese with a guerilla army. Successful in 1428, Le Loi became emperor and initiated a series of land reforms.
1550	First Portuguese Dominican missionaries arrived at Ha Tien, Viet Nam.
1615	First Jesuit mission sent to Viet Nam.
1620	Viet Nam divided by a wall at the River Gianh slightly above the 17th parallel. The North was controlled by the Trinh family, and the South was controlled by the Nguyen family.
1624	French Jesuit Alexandre de Rhodes sent to Cua Han (Da Nang), Viet Nam. He wrote the Vietnamese Cathechismus and became known as the founder of Vietnamese Christianity, increasing French influence and trade in the country.
1765	Pigneau de Behaine sent to Viet Nam and later named to head the French missions.
1773	Tay Son brothers began a rebellion in the South. By 1786 they controlled both North and South Viet Nam. Their movement was nationalist and anti-Chinese in tone.
1788	Chinese attempted to occupy Viet Nam but failed.
1802	Nguyen Anh, heir to the Nguyen throne, defeated last of the Tay Son forces with Pigneau's guidance and united Viet Nam. As emperor Nguyen Anh took the name Gia Long and moved the capital to Hue.
1861	French seized Sai Gon and by 1867 occupied all the south as the French colony Cochin China.
1883	French seized the citadel in Ha Noi. The French divided Viet Nam into the north (Tonkin) and central (Annam) protectorates and a colony in the south (Cochin China).
1885	Emperor Ham Nghi fled Hue and the Scholars Revolt started.

Ham Nghi captured in 1888 and revolt ended in 1897.

1905	Phan Chu Trinh resigned from the mandarin bureaucracy and in 1907 opened a Free School in Ha Noi for modern education of Vietnamese, but the school was closed in 1908 by the French and Trinh arrested.
1907	Phan Boi Chau, trained as a mandarin, used Japan as a base to lead a failed plot to poison French officers and seize control of Ha Noi.
1927	Anti-colonial Vietnamese Nationalist Party formed. An uprising on February 9, 1930, led to execution or imprisonment of most of its leaders.
1930	The Vietnamese Communist Party was formed. Within six months it changed its name to the Indochinese Communist Party (ICP) with Nguyen Ai Quoc (Ho Chi Minh) at its head. The first Red Soviet was in Nghe An province.
1939	Government in France fell at the start of World War II.
1940	The Japanese occupied portions of Viet Nam.
1941	In May, Vietnam Independence League (Viet Minh) formed a united front of Nationalists led by the Communists. July 29 the Vichy France and Japan negotiated a joint defense agreement.
1944	In August the Vichy government was replaced by the French Republic. December 22 the Viet Nam Peoples' Army was formed by Giap with armed propaganda teams.
1945	March 9 the Japanese seized control of Viet Nam. March 11 Emperor Bao Dai declared independence and was given nominal control of Viet Nam by the Japanese. August 15 the Japanese laid down their arms. August 17 de Gaulle announced a new high commission for Indochina under French rule. August 19 the Viet Minh seize control in Ha Noi. August 25 Bao Dai abdicated in favor of the Viet Minh. September 2 Ho Chi Minh addressed a crowd in Ha Noi and gave a Declaration of Independence for the Vietnamese nation.
1946	November 22 the French give warning to Vietnamese to leave their quarters in Hai Phong and then shelled the area

as a warning against resistance.
December 19 the Viet Minh massacred the French in Ha Noi.

1947   October 7 Operation Lea was initiated by the French to de-
            stroy Viet Minh strongholds north of Ha Noi.

1953   November 20 the first three French parachute battalions as-
            saulted Dien Bien Phu and occupied it.

1954   March 13 the Viet Minh start their final attack on Dien Bien
            Phu.
            May 7 Dien Bien Phu falls to the Viet Minh.
            July 20 a cease fire is signed at the Geneva Conference.
            August 1 the armistice worked out at Geneva takes effect.

PHOTO CREDITS

Cover:

Cover photo of two soldiers's faces; Associated Press.

Cover photo of sole marine; Associated Press.

Back cover photo of Vietnam mountain in color; Clipart.com

Inside pages:

Preface photo of sole marine; Associated Press.

Page 217: The Stage is Set; AFP/Getty Images.

Coming Ashore; Associated Press.

Page 218: Vo Nguyen Giap and Ho Chi Minh; Associated Press.

Page 219: On Patrol; Associated Press.

Captured Vietminh; Associated Press.

Page220: Bringing In Supplies; AFP/Getty Images.

French P.O.W.'s; Associated Press.

Page 221: Advancing in the Trenches; AFP/Getty Images.

189 NON-FICTION BOOKS ON VIETNAM

Adams, Sam	*An Intelligence Memoir* *War of Numbers*	Steerforth Press, 1994
Ainley, Henry	*In Order to Die*	Burke Publishing, 1955
Amnesty International	*Vietnam, Renovation, the Law and Human Rights in the 1980's*	February, 1990
Andrews, William R.	*The Village War: Vietnamese Communist Revolutionary Activities In Dinh Tuong Province, 1960-1964*	University of Missouri, 1973
Aparvary, Leslie	*A Legionnaire's Journey*	Detselig Enterprises, 1989
Appy, Christian	*Working-Class War*	University of North Carolina Press, 1993
Asprey, Robert B.	*War in the Shadows,* *The Guerrilla in History vol.1, 2*	Doubleday, 1975
Augustin, Andreas	*Sofitel Metropole Hanoi*	Famous Hotels, 1998
Bergman, Arlene Eisen	*Women of Viet Nam*	Peoples Press, revised 1975
Billings-Yun, Melanie	*Decision Against War:* *Eisenhower and Dien Bien Phu*	Columbia, 1988
Bloodworth, David	*An Eye for the Dragon* *Southeast Asia Observed: 1954-1970*	Farrar, Straus, and Giroux 1970
Bodard, Lucien	*The Quicksand War*	Faber and Faber, 1963
Borton, Lady	*After Sorrow*	Kodanshu Ameria, 1995
Bouscaren, Anthony T.	*The Last of the Mandarins,* *Diem of Vietman*	Duquesne University, 1965
Boudarel, Georges and Ky, Nguyen Van	*Hanoi, City of the Rising Dragon*	Rowan and Littlefield, 2002 (***** history of Hanoi with rare incites and information on Viet Nam)
Bradley, Mark Philip	*Imagining Vietnam and America* *The Making of Postcolonial Vietnam, 1919-1950*	University of North Carolina, 2000
Brennan, Matthew, Editor	*Headhunters*	Presidio, 1987
Broyles, William, Jr.	*Brothers in Arms*	Univerity of Texas Press, 1986
Butler, David	*The Fall of Saigon*	Simon & Schuster, 1985
Buttinger, Joseph	*A Dragon Defiant*	Praeger Publishing, 1972
	The Smaller Dragon *A Political History of Vietnam*	Praeger Publishing, 1958
	Vietnam: A Political History	Praeger Publishing, 1968
Canh, Nguyen Van	*Vietnam under Communism 1975-1982*	Hoover Institution, 1983

Chanoff, David	Portrait of the Enemy	Random House, 1986
Chaliand, Gerard	The Peasants of North Vietnam	Penguin Books, 1969
Chanda, Nayan	Brother Enemy, The War After the War	Harcourt, Brace, 1986 (A history of Indochina since the fall of Saigon)
Chi, Hoang Van	From Colonialism to Communism	Praeger, 1964 (dark side of communism
Chau, Phan Boi	Overturned Chariot	University of Hawaii, 1997
Chi, Hoang Van	From Colonialism to Communism	Pall Mall Press, 1964 (2 copies)
Chong, Denise	The Girl in the Picture	Viking, 1999
Cooper, Nicola	France in Indochina Colonial Encounters	Berg, Oxford, 2001
Currey, Cecil B.	Victory at Any Cost: The Genius of Viet Nam's Gen. Vo Nguyen Giap	Brassey's, 1997 (2)
Cutler, Thomas J.	Brown Water, Black Berets	U.S. Naval Institute, 1998
Davidson, Lt. Gen. Phillip	Vietnam at War The History 1946-1975	Presidio, 1988
Debonis, Steven	Children of the Enemy	McFarland, 1995 (oral histories of Vietnamese Amerasians and their mothers)
Devanter, Lynda Van	Home before Morning	Warner Books, 1983 (American nurse in Vietnam)
Diem, Bui	In the Jaws of History	Houghton Mifflin, 1987 (former South Viet Nam Ambassador to the United States)
Do, Kiem	Counterpart	Naval Institute Press, 1998 (South Viet Nam naval officer's story
Doan Van Toai	The Vietnamese Gulag	Simon & Schuster, 1986
	"Vietnam" A Portrait of Its People at War	St. Martins Press, 1986
Dommen, Arthur J.	The Indochinese Experience Of the French and the Americans	Indiana University Press, 2001 (**** political history)
Dooley, Thomas	Deliver Us From Evil	Ambassador Books, 1956, 1959
Dorgeles, Roland	On the Mandarin Road	The Century Company, 1926
Du, Nguyen	The Tale of Kieu	Yale University, 1983
Duiker, Willaim J.	Ho Chi Minh	Hyperion, 2000 (***** best for Ho's life
Ebert, James R.	A Life in a Year, The American Infantryman in Vietnam, 1965-1972	Presidio, 1993
Egendorf, Arthur	Healing from the War	Houghton Mifflin, 1985
Elliott, Duong Van Mai	The Sacred Willow: Four Generations in the Life of a Vietnamese Family	Oxford Univ., 1999 (****family life of well-to-do Vietnamese family.)

Fall, Bernard B.	*The Two Vietnams: A Political and Military Analysis*	Praeger, 1963
	Vietnam Witness 1953-66	Praeger, 1966
	Last Reflections on a War	Doubleday and Company, 1964
	The Siege of Dien Bien Phu Hell in a Very Small Place	Da Capo Press, 1966
	Street without Joy	Telegraph Press, 1961
Fenn, Charles	*Ho Chi Minh*	Studio Vist London, 1973
Fitzgerald, Frances	*Fire in the Lake*	Little, Brown , 1972
Forbes, John and	*Riverine Force*	Bantam
Williams, Robert	*The Vietnam War*	
Fromkin, David, James	*Foreign Affairs*	Council on Foreign Relations
Chace, John Wheeler	*Vietnam: The Retrospect*	Spring 1985
Gardner, Lloyd C.	*Approaching Vietnam: From*	W.W. Norton, 1989
	WWII through Dienbienphu	
Giap, Vo Nguyen	*Unforgettable Days*	Gioi Publishers, 1994
	Dien Bien Phu	Foreign Languages Publishing House, Hanoi, 1964
	Big Victory, Great Task	Praeger, 1968
Gheddo, Piero	*The Cross and the Bo-Tree*	Sheed and Ward, 1970 (Catholics and Buddhists in Vietnam
Gibson, James William	*The Perfect War: Technowar in Vietnam*	Atlantic Monthly Press 1986
Goodman, Allen E.	*Politics in War: The Bases of Political Community in South Vietnam*	Harvard, 1973
Grant, Zalin	*Facing the Phoenix: The CIA and the Political Defeat Of the United States in Vietnam*	W. W. Norton, 1991
Grauwin, Paul	*Doctor at Dienbienphu*	John Day Company, 1955
Guan, Ang Cheng	*Vietnamese Communists' Relations With China and the Second Indochina Conflict, 1956-1962*	McFarland, 1997
Hackworth, David H.	*About Face*	Simon & Schuster, 1989 (2 copies)
	Hazardous Duty	Morrow
Hahn, Tich Nhat	*A Taste of Earth And Other Legends of Vietnam*	Parallex Press, 1993
	Vietnam, Lotus in a Sea of Fire	Hill and Wang, 1967
Hammer, Ellen J.	*A Death in November America in Vietnam, 1963*	Dutton, 1987
	The Struggle for Indochina	Stanford University Press, 1954

Harrington, Anthony	*A Guide to the War in Viet Nam*	Panther Publishing, 1966
Harrison, James Pinckney	*The Endless War, Vietnam's Struggle for Independence*	McGraw Hill, 1982
Hart, Adrian Liddell	*Strange Company*	Weidenfeld and Nicolson,1953
Hayslip, Le Ly	*When Heaven and Earth Changed Places*	Doubleday, 1989 (***** excellent story of individual hardship in war)
Heberle, Mark A.	*A Trauma Artist, Tim O'Brien and the Fiction of Vietnam*	University of Iowa, 2001
Hendin, Herbert and Ann Pollinger Haas	*Wounds of War: The Psychological Aftermath of Combat in Vietnam*	Basic Books, 1984
Herrington, Stuart A.	*Silence Was a Weapon The Vietnam War in the Villages*	Presidio Press, 1982
Hess, Martha	*Then the Americans Came*	Rutgers, 1993
Hickey, Gerald Cannon	*Village in Vietnam*	Yale, 1964
Holman, Valerie	*France at War in the Twentieth Century*	Berghahn Books, 2000
Hoa, Nguyen Dinh	*From the City Inside the Red River*	McFarland, 1999
Huchthausen, Peter A. & Lung, Nguyen Thi	*Echoes of the Mekong*	Nautical and Aviation Publishing Company, 1996 (with autographed books)
Huynh, Jade Ngoc Quang	*South Wind Changing*	Greystone, 1994
Hubbard, Edward L.	*Escape from the Box*	Praxis, 1994
Jamieson, Neil L.	*Understanding Vietnam*	University of California, 1995
Jordan, Kenneth N., Sr.	*Heroes of Our Time*	Schiffer Publishing, 1994 (Medal of Honor, Vietnam)
Just, Ward	*To What End*	Public Affairs, 1968,1999
Karnow, Stanley	*Vietnam, A History*	Viking Press, 1983
Keegan, John	*Dien Bien Phu*	Ballantine
Kinnard, Douglas	*The War Managers: American Generals Reflect on Vietnam*	Da Capo Press, 1997
Koburger, Charles W., Jr.	*The French Navy in Indochina Riverine and Coastal Forces 45-54*	Praeger Publishing, 1997
	Naval Expeditions The French Return to Indochina, 1945-1946	Praeger Publishing, 1997
Krall, Yung	*A Thousand Tears Falling*	Longstreet Press, 1995 (Vietnamese family story)
Lacouture, Jean and Dan Cragg	*Ho Chi Minh*	Random House, 1968
Lam, Truong Buu	*Colonialism Experienced Vietnamese Writings on Colonialism, 1900-1931*	University of Michigan Press, 2000

Lamb, David	*Vietnam Now A Reporter Returns*	Public Affairs, 2002
Langguth, A.J.	*Our Vietnam Nuoc Viet Ta*	Simon and Schuster, 2000 (the war 1954-1975)
Lanning, Michael Lee	*Inside the VC and the NVA*	Ballantine Books, 1992
Larsen, Wendy Wilder	*Shallow Graves*	Random House, 1986
Laurence, John	*The Cat from Hue*	Public Affairs, 2002
Long, George W. Roberts, J. Baylor	*Indochina Faces the Dragon*	National Geographic, September, 1952
Long, Ngo Vinh	*Before the Revolution The Vietnamese Peasants Under the French*	Columbia, 1973
Long William	*Hanoi, Biography of a City*	UNSW Press
Luce, Don and Sommer, John	*Viet Nam: The Unheard Voices*	Cornell, 1969
Luong, Hy V.	*Revolution in the Village Tradition and Transformation in North Vietnam,1925-1988*	University of Hawaii, 1992
Macdonald, Peter	*Giap, The Victor in Vietnam*	W. W. Norton, 1993
Maclear, Michael	*The Ten Thousand Day War Vietnam: 1945-1975*	Eyre Methuen, Ltd., 1981.
Mai, Nguyen Thi Tuyet	*The Rubber Tree*	McFarland and Company, 1994
Mallin, Jay	*Terror in Viet Nam*	D. Van Nostrand Company, 1966
Mangold, Tom John Penycate	*The Tunnels of Cu Chi*	Random House, 1985
Mann, Robert	*A Grand Delusion*	Basic Books, 2001
Marr, David G.	*Vietnamese Tradition on Trial*	University of California, 1981
	Vietnam 1945: The Quest for Power	University of California, 1995
McAlister, John T., Jr.	*Viet Nam, The Origins of the Revolution*	Knopf, 1969
McLeave, Hugh	*The Damned Die Hard The Colorful, True Story of the French Foreign Legion*	Saturday Review Press, 1973
Metzner, Edward P. Huynh Van Chinh Tran Van Phuc Le Nguyen Binh	*Reeducation in Postwar Vietnam Personal Postscripts to Peace*	Texas A&M University Press, 2001
Minh, Ho Chi	*Ho Chi Minh on Revolution Selected Writings, 1920-66*	Praeger, 1967
Moise, Edwin	*Land Reform in China and North Vietnam*	Chapel Hill, 1983
Moore, W. Robert	*Strife-torn Indochina*	National Geographic, October, 1950,

Newman, Bernard	*Report on Indochina*	Praeger, 1954
Nguyen, Cuong Tu	*Zen in Medieval Vietnam*	University of Hawaii, 1997
Nordell, John R., Jr.	The Undetected Enemy French and American Miscalculations at Dien Bien Phu, 1953	Texas A&M University, 1995
O'Neil, Robert J.	*General Giap*	Praeger, 1969
Patti, Archimedes L.A.	Why Viet Nam? Prelude to America's Albatross	University of California Press, 1980
Phan, Peter C.	Mission and Catechesis: Alexandre de Rhodes & Inculturation In Seventeenth-Century Vietnam	Orbis Books, 1998
Pickerell, James	Vietnam in the Mud	Bobbs-Merrill, 1966
Pike, Douglas	PAVN: People's Army of Vietnam	Presidio Press, 1986
	History of Vietnamese Communism 1925-1976	Hoover Institute, 1978
	War, Peace, and the Viet Cong	MIT, 1969
	Viet Cong	MIT, 1966
	The Viet-Cong Strategy of Terror	Saigon, 1970
Plaster, John L.	SOG	Simon & Schuster, 1997
Poncins, Gontran de	From a Chinese City In the Heart of Peacetime Vietnam	Trackless Sands Press, 1957
Porch, Douglas	The French Foreign Legion	Harper Collins, 1991
Pratt, John Clark	Vietnam Voices: Perspectives on the War Years 1941-1975	University of Georgia, 1984
Prados, John	The Sky Would Fall Operation Vulture, The Secret U.S. Bombing Mission to Vietnam, 1954	Dial Press, 1983
Prados, John and Ray Stubbe	Valley of Decision, The Seige of Khe Sanh	Houghton Mifflin,1991
Pribbenow, Merle L. (Translator)	Victory in Vietnam The Official History of the People's Army of Vietnam, 1954-1975	University Press of Kansas, 2002 (*****from NVN side)
Race, Jeffrey	War Comes to Long An:	University of California, 1972
	Revolutionary Conflict in a Vietnamese Province	
Riesen, Rene	Jungle Mission	Thomas Y. Crowell Company, 1957 (French officer in Viet Nam)
Roy, Jules	The Battle of Dien Bien Phu	Harper and Row, 1965
Salisbury, Harrison E.	Behind the Lines-Hanoi December23-January 7	Harper and Row, 1967
Samuels, Gertrude	Passage to Freedom in Viet Nam	The National Geographic Magazine, June, 1955, p.858
Schliesinger, Joachim	Hill Tribes of Vietnam, Vol and ,2	White Lotus, 1997,1998

Scholl-Latour, Peter	Death in the Rice Fields An Eyewitness Account of Vietnam's Three Wars 1945-1979	St. Martin's, 1979 (2 copies)
Scruggs, Jan C. and Joel L. Swerdlow	To Heal a Nation The Vietnam Veterans Memorial	Harper & Row, 1985
Sevier, Elisabeth	War without A Front The Memoirs of a French Army Nurse in Vietnam	Wesley Publishing, 1997
Shay, Jonathan	Achilles in Vietnam Combat Trauma and the Undoing of Character	Atheneum, 1994
	Odysseus in America Combat Trauma and the Trials of Homecoming	Scribner, 2002
Sheehan, Neil	A Bright Shining Lie John Paul Vann and America in Vietnam	Random House, 1988
Sheehan, Susan	Ten Vietnamese	Alfred Knopf, 1967
Sidel, Mark	Old Hanoi	Oxford University Press, 1998
Simonnet, Christian	Theophane Venard	Ignatius Press, 1988
Simpson, Howard R.	Dien Bien Phu	Brassey's Inc., 1994 (***** favorite DBP book)
	Tiger in the Barbed Wire An American in Vietnam, 1952-1991	Kodansha America, 1992
Sorley, Lewis	*A Better War*	Harcourt Brace, 1999
Stanton, Shelby L.	*Green Berets at War*	Presidio, 1985, 1990
Stevenson, Monika and William	*Kiss the Boys Goodbye*	Dutton, 1990
Summers, Harry G., Jr.	*On Strategy, A Critical Analysis*	Presidio Press, 1982
Tai, Hue-Tam Ho	*Radicalism and the Origins of the Vietnamese Revolution*	Harvard University,1992
	Millenarianism and Peasant Politics in Vietnam	Harvard, 1983
Tan, Nguyen Phut	*A Modern History of Viet Nam 1802-1954*	Nha sach Khai-tri, 1964
Tang, Truong Nhu	*Vietcong Memoir*	HBJ, 1985
Tanham, George T.	*Communist Revolutionary The Vietminh in Indochina*	Praeger, 1961
Templer, Robert	*Shadows and Wind*	Penguin Books, 1999
Terry, Wallace	*Bloods, An Oral History of the Vietnam War by Black Veterans*	Random House, 1984
Thanh, Nguyen Long	*The Path of a Cao-Dai Disciple*	Tay-Ninh, 1970

Thomas, Liz	*Dust of Life* *Children of the Saigon Streets*	Redwood Burn, 1977
	The Outline of Caodaism	Tay-Ninh, 1972
Tin, Bui	*Following Ho Chi Minh*	University of Hawaii, 1995
	From Enemy to Friend *A North Vietnamese Perspective on* *the War*	Naval Institute Press, 2002
Turner, Karen Gottschang	*Even Women Must Fight*	John Wiley and Sons, 1998
United States Department of the Army	*U.S. Army Area Handbook* *for Vietnam No. 550-40*	Department of the Army, 1962
United States	*Weapons and Equipment Recognition* *Guide Southeast Asia*	Department of the Army, 1969
United States U.S. Senate	*The U.S. Government and the Viet-* *nam War (1945-1961)*	Committee on Foreign Relations, 1984
United States	*Leader's Guide for Operations in* *Southeast Asia*	Department of the Army, 1966
	Advisor Handbook for Counterin- *surgency*	Department of the Army, 1965
	Hamlet Evaluation System	Department of the Army, June 69
Vien, Nguyen Khac	*Vietnam, A Long History*	Gioi Publishers, 1999
Viet, Dang Van	Highway 4: The Border Campaign (1947-1950)	Foreign Language Publishing House, Hanoi, 1990
Veith, George J.	Code Name Bright Light The Untold Story of U.S. POW Rescue Efforts during the Vietnam War	The Free Press, 1998
Werner, Jayne Susan	*Peasant Politics and Religious Sec-* *tarianism: Peasant and Priest In the* *Cao Dai in Viet Nam*	Yale University, 1981
Williams, Michael C.	*Vietnam at the Crossroads*	Royal Institute, 1992
Woodside, Alexander Barton	*Vietnam and the Chinese Model*	Harvard, 1988
Yaeger, Jack A.	*The Vietnamese Novel in French* *A Literary Response to Colonialism*	University Press of New England, 1987
Zinoman, Peter	*The Colonial Bastille, A History of* *Imprisonment in Vietnam 1862-1940*	University of California Press

Printed in the United States
115666LV00003B/2/A